STEADFAST

Steadfast

By Michelle Hauck

Birth of Saints Trilogy
Grudging
Faithful
Steadfast

Kindar's Cure

STEADFAST

Birth of Saints Book Three

MICHELLE HAUCK

HARPER
VOYAGER
IMPULSE

An Imprint of HarperCollins Publishers

STEADFAST. Copyright © 2017 by Michelle Hauck. All rights reserved. Printed in the United States of America. No part of this book may be used or reproduced in any manner whatsoever without written permission except in the case of brief quotations embodied in critical articles and reviews. For information, address HarperCollins Publishers, 195 Broadway, New York, NY 10007.

Digital Edition DECEMBER 2017 ISBN: 978-0-06-244720-3

Print Edition ISBN: 978-0-06-244721-0

Cover design by Amy Halperin
Cover images: © Pali Rao/E+/Getty Images (knight); © Shutterstock (background)

Harper Voyager and the Harper Voyager logo are trademarks of HarperCollins Publishers in the United States of America and other countries.

HarperCollins is a registered trademark of HarperCollins Publishers in the United States of America and other countries.

FIRST EDITION

17 18 19 20 21   OPM   10 9 8 7 6 5 4 3 2 1

For my biggest fans:
my dad and stepdad,
both gone too soon.

Fifteen Years Ago

Santabe had long ceased to marvel at the way the stones of the small room had been cut so square and matched together so perfectly. She had never been in a place built of anything but wood until entering the Great Palace of Dal this morning with her mother and aunts, and she hadn't expected to stay more than the few minutes it took to read her augury.

The priest who put her in this bare room of naught but stone after her reading had instructed she remain on her knees and ruminate on her fate until fetched. She'd dutifully remained on her knees, but, after what seemed like hours of suffering, had allowed herself to lean backward on her toes. Her lower limbs went numb and dead, but she spared her knees the same agony.

"Obey," had been the last word spoken by her mother before she stepped into line for the augury to be cast.

"Obey in measure," had been the wiser advice from her favorite aunt.

The latch on the door—the only piece of wood

in the room—clicked, and Santabe shot up onto her knees so quickly, she lost her balance and toppled onto her side.

"Is this how you show your respects to Dal?" an angry voice demanded. "Lying at your ease?"

Santabe ducked her head to avoid the strap aimed for her temple, and the blow landed on her bent neck with a snap. Pain radiated down her back. She struggled to surge upright, but her numb legs failed her, sending her crashing to the stone again. The strap hit her hip on its second strike. She sobbed.

"Forbear," a new voice said. "I have seen this before. The body failed; that doesn't mean the heart yielded."

The younger priest in his plain white robe—similar to the one Santabe wore—drew back, taking his leather strap with him.

A man with white hair so thin his bald pate shone through in spots limped forward. His priest's robe was of white silk—sheer and fine—and it clung to every lump of his portly form. He leaned upon a cane of a white material like bone tipped with gold. "You know who I am?" he asked.

The cane crafted from the horn of the einhorn—the same material used to create Diviners, the slim weapons in the shape of a short staff most priests carried—told her the answer. Only one man was entrusted with such a priceless treasure—at over three cubits in length and over a tenth of a cubit in diameter, the horn of his cane could have made a half dozen Diviners.

Santabe swallowed hard to dislodge the lump in her throat. "Master Jemkinbu," she said dutifully, finally taking in the gold earrings in the shape of the sun in each of his ears, proclaiming him of the highest priesthood.

So very few priests earned two earrings. Jemkinbu and a few others she could count on one hand. She knew why Jemkinbu had earned his second: his skill with einhorn. The Master had been carving Diviners from horn since he was an acolyte. His skill was legendary. It was said he could produce the most Diviners from every piece of einhorn. He could see combinations and patterns no other priest could discern, as if Dal entered his dreams and guided his hand. With Diviners classified as the most important and rarest instruments of Dal, his skill was valued more than kingship.

Though a Diviner couldn't kill until it was soaked in sacrificial blood, nothing of the horns was wasted. Even the tiny slivers of einhorn were sold to the very rich to place in the mouths of the recently dead, to ease their passing to the next life.

Her eyes leaked tears as Santabe grabbed for support from a belt she no longer wore. Chosen of Dal wore no bindings on their bodies. All her clothes would have been burned. When the augury landed favorably at her feet, she hadn't even been allowed a final good-bye with her mother before being whisked away to this room. Now, her legs throbbed in such agony as blood returned that she could barely think.

The lesser priest deposited a stool on the floor and before he left, Santabe noticed that, unlike an Enforcer, who sought blasphemy among the populace, this priest was likely a clerk of some kind, and thus not important enough to wear a Diviner, let alone an earring. He departed, closing the door behind him.

Master Jemkinbu sat, the hem of his robe lifting to show a fine network of ropey veins about his ankles. "Do you know why you are here?"

Santabe gasped, forming her hands into fists so as not to clutch at her burning feet and shins. Master Jemkinbu leaned his cane against his knee and waited.

She stared at the cane, seeking inspiration.

Men braved the wilds to the far north to live at the fishing village on the edge of the sea to hunt for einhorn, despite the fact that every few years, Kolifell village was wiped out by famine, disease, wolves, or the arrows of the tiny tree-loving natives who occupied that land. To find a horn was to add your name to the list of those honored by Dal and ensure your passage into the next life—no one would take money for such treasure.

Through the swirl of pain, she put aside such random thoughts and fought back to earlier today in bits and flashes. The blue of the sky as she'd walked with her family to the Great Palace of Dal. The long line of others who'd celebrated their eleventh naming day of this life along with her and stood before the greatest altar of Dal. The priest casting the contents of bags of feathers, herbs, and pieces of bones on the stone at each child's feet. How the auguries had all looked the same to her as each child before her was dismissed. How at her turn a single piece of bone had landed on her left foot.

She looked up at Jemkinbu. "Because the augury touched me, Honored One." Right after that moment, she'd been stripped of her old clothing and redressed in front of an entire room of watching clerics of Dal. A shame she still felt in her soul.

"Very good, child. And do you know our main mission?"

"To ensure the light of Dal is instilled in every heart, fills every mind, flows from every tongue, and to root out any who fail Him with blasphemy," she recited from rote memory. The unbearable tingling in her feet and legs eased enough that she could clamber ungracefully to her knees.

Swifter than she could have believed, the cane cracked across her shoulder. She cried out before she could stop herself.

"Incomplete. That is our mission to the Children of Dal. What about our mission to Dal?"

She grit her teeth and said, "To stand ready when His eyes turn to this world again. To accept the joy of His presence unto ourselves. To provide the blood of the unworthy to Him?" She tacked on the last in case the Master was expecting it. All knew blood drew Dal's attention. Despite doing her best, she flinched, expecting another blow. But he just sat quietly, the cane resting in his hand.

"Yes. That is correct, child. Every twenty-five hundred years, Dal's immaculate eye rests upon this world again, and He purges us of the Glorious ones fit to travel to the next life . . . and also purges us of the Disgraced, sending them to the prior world with blood and pain. We stand in readiness of His coming, to ensure He finds the best of us. But there are deeper mysteries than this that you will learn as priestess to Dal.

"The mysteries of Diviners—white and red. Our hidden precepts that go deeper than what is shared with the Children of Dal. Why we keep Dal to ourselves and spare the world. Secrets that are told only to initiates. You are very favored, child."

She pondered his words dutifully, but had never seen a red Diviner—though the stories told that they returned life even as the white rods stole it—but right now her shoulder burned, as did the spot on her neck and hip. She couldn't care for talk of mysteries with this pain. Her mother had struck her but rarely since her ninth year in this life, and now Santabe feared this was just the beginning of the trial of her new life.

If Master Jemkinbu could see her lack of interest, he said nothing, only leaning the priceless cane against his knee again. "This is a favored day for you, child. Today, you take your vows to Dal. Are you ready?"

Santabe's eyes darted, finding no help. The deepest wish of her heart had always been to be a merchant like her mother. Her memory conjured up the wind in her hair as she rode on a wagon full of goods to the next city. Her joy of seeing someplace new and different. The feel of a bag of gemstones well earned by honest toil. Joining a fight to push off bandits determined to steal their goods.

All of that was lost to her now and replaced with blocks of stone and walls.

Yet if she said no, her life in this world would end, her blood would fuel new Diviners, and she'd return to the prior world to try again.

Master Jemkinbu traced a line in the stone with the gold tip of the cane. "Your teachers say you were an average student at best—nothing to recommend you to serve Dal. But I disagree. I see now why He called you: You are stubborn. No other acolyte has kept me waiting this long. Stubbornness is a virtue much needed in weeding out the blasphemous from the Children of Dal's ranks by the Enforcers. Perhaps your calling is there. But I warn you—my patience will only last so long. Your answer?"

To take the vows was to become one of the ruling class of the Children of Dal. To have power well beyond what a merchant could manage in a lifetime.

She would judge others, including her family. She could judge everyone. While delving deeper into Dal's mysteries did not tempt her, the image of an Enforcer did. She would lose the freedom of the road.

But she would gain so much more.

"I'm ready."

CHAPTER 1

Claire stood surrounded by the bodies of Northern soldiers she'd killed with her magic and next to the body of her grandmother, murdered by the hand of one of those same soldiers. The rage and anger that sustained her moments ago drained away. No longer did she feel the power to wield a Death Song, which killed without a touch. But she had no doubt that should another Northerner appear, the desire to stop the soldier's heart with her voice would rekindle. For now, disbelief at her own use of the magic beat at her, keeping even grief at bay.

Dimly, Claire noticed the villagers snatching their belongings as the fight with the Northerners ended. They moved in cringing silence—women, children, even the hunters all too eager to avoid catching her eye as they took their supplies and slunk away from the dangerous *witch*, leaving her with the dead. Did they think her magic would slip loose and harm them, after they'd tended to Jorga's arrow wound? Did it not matter that she had *saved* them? Could they believe she was that sort of monster?

Yet, she had no kinship or blood connection to ask them to stay, and no way to make them less afraid.

Distrusted. Feared by these simple villagers, the same as she'd been by Ramiro's people.

She was alone again. No Ramiro to stand at her side as a friend and refuse to shun her. No prickly grandmother to give her gruff lessons in magic. Only a fifteen-year-old uncle who might as well have been an infant for all the support he could give. It was she who would have to support Errol as he sobbed over Jorga's body.

Without knowing why she did it, Claire held her hands in front of her, unable to make out much detail in the darkness. The gloom kept her from seeing the dirt under her fingernails from their travels through the swamp or the new calluses from having helped maneuver Jorga's stretcher. They'd succeeded in saving Jorga's life yesterday, only for it to be snatched away today. All she could tell by the dim firelight was that her hands held steady, refusing to shake. A wonder considering Jorga was dead because of her— because she hadn't acted until it was too late. Afraid of her own magic.

Her fault.

Now the tears came. The guilt, the loneliness, the horror—

She jumped as Errol grabbed at her arm. "Help Momma," he demanded.

"I can't. It's too late. She's dead. I was too slow." Claire reached for his hand—strange as he was, the boy was her responsibility now, her only kin—but he pulled on her. Confused, she resisted. He only tugged harder, drawing Claire away from Jorga and to the pile of supplies Ramiro had left near her horse. Supplies the villagers had been too frightened to steal—frightened of her.

"Help Momma," Errol insisted, bending to roll a saddle bag at her. His eyes focused on her shoulder, demanding, hopeful.

"I don't understand. She's dead."

He pulled at the leather straps holding the bag shut and upended it, giving it a flick to send the contents spilling across the ground. "Help Momma!" The red Diviner lay in the midst of shirts and coils of rope. A slender staff about as thick as a man's thumb and the length of a forearm. "Hurry!" Errol said, pointing to the weapon.

Claire's stomach revolted and she stepped back. By the Song! What was she to do with that? It was a Northern weapon for killing, usually carried by their priests and found by Ramiro.

Her uncle was at her side in an instant, seizing her arm again and dragging her down, closer to the weapon. Errol was bigger, stronger, for all his child-like mind. Trying to pull away got her nowhere.

"Help Momma!" For the first time since they met, his eyes landed squarely on hers—not over her shoulder, not directed at her torso or chin, but making contact. They expressed utter confidence and belief in her ability to help.

This killing device could help her grandmother?

Errol nodded as if he saw into her mind. The muddled blue of his eyes was the same color as Claire's mother's had been.

She didn't understand—and she didn't understand how Errol was so confident—but by the Song, she had to try. She closed her eyes and held her breath and reached out, taking the deadly weapon gingerly in her hand. She stood slowly—the terrible thing stretched out from her body as if distance could keep something bad from occurring.

Nothing happened.

Errol danced ahead of her, back to Jorga, watching her expectantly. Reluctantly, she followed as he pointed to Jorga's prone body. "Help Momma now. Hurry." His gestures made it plain what he expected her to do.

Claire gathered her courage and touched the blood-red stick to her grandmother's cooling flesh. The moment of contact felt like a lightning bolt went off in her hand. Electric shock traveled up her arm and down her legs. Her hair stood on end, lifting from her head. Her fingers, instead of loosening, clamped tighter on the Diviner, beyond her control. She screamed at the pain curling her muscles and cooking her flesh.

The red color drained from the staff, running down the length as if it was alive, and into Jorga. For a heartbeat, her grandmother's flesh turned equally red. Then her body jolted, bouncing from the ground as if blasted. A stench of burning hair and spent lightning filled the air.

It ended. The Diviner rolled from her nerveless fingers. No more a frightening red, it had returned to its normal yellowish old-bone color. Sickened by what she'd witnessed, Claire collapsed onto ground still wet with Jorga's blood. Pain ran up and down her body in spasms, reluctant to let her go and leaving her body numb and unable to respond, paralyzed but tingling with a sense of life returning. Claire sobbed, partly in relief, partly in agony.

Never again.

The experience had almost killed her. She wasn't touching a Diviner again.

But then a gasp sounded inches away. Jorga opened her eyes, found Claire, and scowled. "Why are we lying in a puddle of blood? Who died?"

"*You,*" Claire said in astonishment.

CHAPTER 2

Ramiro patted his clothing as he dropped from Sancha, sending puffs of dust flying. Sand and grit coated him from hair to toes, along with the mare, as the summer rains had still failed to materialize. Each breath of wind sent swirls into the air, and they'd encountered several true sandstorms on their way to Aveston that had forced them to take shelter until the winds died. Ramiro twisted his neck to work out kinks from the long ride. Two of the three springs he could locate around Aveston had been dry, one not even muddy any longer. He felt as withered and thin as the curled leaves hanging from the olive trees around them.

Sancha shook, sending more dust into the air, except where the foamy sweat coating on her flanks and chest kept the dirt anchored. Her eyes looked at him dully. He might have pushed the pace too hard over the last twenty-four hours, but the emptiness around Colina Hermosa had been enough of a goad. All he found there were the remnants of a camp and the echoes of his voice. By the saints, not a soul remained around the burnt ruins of his home city, and that's when his indecision hit.

Should he venture toward Crueses or Aveston to find his father? Where did he go to turn himself over to the authorities for his desertion? The cities were in the opposite direction from one another. The figure from his dream had been no help in making a choice. There'd been no hint at all where to start his quest to stop the Northern god Dal from killing every living creature on the earth. Crueses seemed the more likely place to head to find his father and his fellow soldiers, but Aveston was the closer option. In the end, he took the way fellow soldier Alvito would have suggested and flipped a coin. It was as good a reason as any—until he saw the smoke rising ahead of them as he got closer to Aveston.

He'd circled Sancha around to the opposite side of the city from the smoke and approached through the olive groves, avoiding the roads as he'd done the whole journey. The dark stain in the sky hadn't looked big enough to proclaim the death of a *ciudad-estado* the size of Aveston, but it stank of human flesh, enough to choke him for hours, though God knew he'd encountered worse in the last days.

"Rest and wait here for me, girl." Sancha nuzzled his shoulder as he stroked her jaw and then down her neck. He leaned against her for a brief moment, afraid of seeing another shell of a city when he left the trees and finding that Aveston had joined Colina Hermosa and Zapata in death.

Whether that was true or not, he still needed to use caution. Like his armor, Sancha's dapple-gray coloring would give him away as a soldier of Colina Hermosa to anyone with half a brain, making it only common sense to leave both as he scouted. He wore his breastplate under a cloak, but the rest of his armor remained on his horse. He'd rather not be seen by Northerners at all, but if he was, he wanted to be underestimated.

Ramiro gave the mare one last pat and headed through the trees in a crouch. Going forward alone might be common sense, but that didn't make him like leaving his horse any better.

Nothing he'd done in the last sevenday had been happy or by choice, with the exception of befriending Claire.

And with that thought, he touched his breastplate over his heart—the spot where an ache had appeared when he left Claire behind in the swamp. Ever since they'd been apart, a niggling little patch of emptiness had dug its way inside him and taken up residence with the raw wound that was his brother Salvador's death.

He pushed that twisted pain aside less easily than the olive branch he bent out of the way to kneel at the edge of the orchard. To his relief the city remained whole, but he didn't have to guess at who held Aveston now. Yellow-and-black uniforms congregated in a sprawling camp outside Aveston's wide open gates, taking up much of the plain before the city. If there had been a battle here, his side had lost. The Northerners held Aveston. And something more.

The smoke rose, not from the *ciudad-estado*, but from the empty field surrounding Aveston. A huge pile of blackened and charred shapes had been fired and now burned itself out slowly.

Bodies.

But whether from a battle or civilians inside the city, Ramiro couldn't venture a guess. One thing he didn't have to guess: Whoever the dead were, his people were treated with absolute disrespect. Not allowed a burial as Santiago taught, and so not allowed to reach the afterlife. Treated like so much meat.

Barbarians.

His hand curled around his sword hilt as he stood.

"This is our land, invaders," he said quietly to himself. They'd sweat on it, died on it, been buried in it for centuries. Loved every inch of soil as kin. "You can't have it. I swear it by Santiago and all the saints. I won't let you!"

Several moments of deep, slow breathing gradually crushed the fury in his chest, enabling rational thought again. To rush forward to avenge a wrong he couldn't fix was suicide. He had to focus on the mission assigned to him and wait for the time of vengeance to come.

No one had heard or noticed him. Life went on as if he didn't exist. But his vow burned in his chest, partially filling the hole that was his pain and loss, a reminder that he'd see the promise through.

So many things to do: bring a warning to his people of Dal, hand himself over for leaving without permission, rid the land of Northerners. Each goal conflicted or overlapped with the next. He didn't want to think about them now, though, so he refocused on the scene before him.

A steady stream of civilians with the same brown skin and hair as himself emerged from the gate, moving unmolested down the east road in carts or wagons or afoot. All loaded with provisions and possessions. Not a single Northern soldier slowed the tide from the gates or attempted to stop the egress.

Were his eyes blinded by dirt? He blinked and checked again, but the scene remained the same. The Northerners let the people of Aveston leave freely. Was this some kind of twisted kindness?

Impossible—no such impulse beat in the breast of their foes.

Yet he saw what he saw. And more, such as Northern soldiers entering and leaving the city as well— those coming out wobbled much more than those going inside. *Drunk*, he noted incredulously. The refugees gave the soldiers a wide berth, but they didn't look scared of being attacked.

A woman's scream came from the sprawling army camp and quickly shut off. Ramiro's hackles rose. Apparently not everyone was allowed to flee.

A quick study of the Northern camp showed no sentries and little organization. Half of the tents sagged, their ropes not secured tightly. Instead of being placed in neat rows, the canvas structures were scattered haphazardly. A Northern soldier lay on his back at the perimeter, either dead, drunk, or asleep. Crates and tins lay scattered outside a supply wagon as if thrown. Most damning of all, no white-robed Northern priests moved about the camp. This disordered mess was not what he remembered of the Northern army camp when it lay in siege outside of Colina Hermosa. Then, they had been focused and structured.

This anarchy was more than the loss of their priests, then—if their absence even meant their loss. More than the death of a commanding officer. Commanding officers and civilian control could and would be replaced without a loss of discipline. No, something more was happening here. This change implied the soldiers knew Dal had returned, killing and shredding humans into lumps of confetti, and that knowledge had taken the heart from the Northerners.

Here, at last, could be a stroke of luck. Perhaps they didn't have to fight Dal *and* the Northerners. Perhaps the Northerners had lost their spirit.

The refugees at the gates scattered in all directions, capturing his attention once more. They moved to escape a large party in white emerging from the city. The priests. *So not lost,* he thought with consternation, *but holed up inside Aveston.* Twenty-five or thirty of the devils. People dropped dead as the Northern priests wielded their white weapon sticks called Diviners to clear a path, touching men, women, or children indiscriminately, all just to make room so they wouldn't have to slow. Ramiro's vision blurred and his hands tightened into fists again, but he held himself motionless.

In the center of the group, more priests carried stacks of the killing rods in their arms like they cradled babies. The priests turned away from the flow of refugees as they exited the gates and marched through the Northern camp, still easily spotted among the tents by their hurry and the directness of their path. They took a straight line toward the smoldering pile of bodies. Ramiro watched as they held out their Diviners and marched around the far side of the pyre, hidden by the smoke. They came back into sight by the count of twenty, now carrying weapons turned from the yellowish-white of bone to the crimson of blood—exactly like the Diviner he and Claire had been lugging in his saddlebags—

The one that had turned red after Dal had slaughtered near it.

The priests obviously manipulated their weapons from one color to the other on purpose and not by accident. But why? What did the change to red signify?

As he looked closer, Ramiro took note that one in three of the Diviners remained white. Not all had changed color. A priest pointed to a group of the white ones and shook her head. Five or six of them spoke together, their motions indicating disappointment. Again, people scattered as the priests swept into the city and vanished beyond the gates, taking death with them.

Ramiro waited around a little longer, but no more priests emerged and the scene remained the same, with only the addition of a scuffle between two Northern soldiers over a bottle of liquor—quickly broken up before blood could be shed—and another group of soldiers looting the cart of a refugee, while the civilians stood dully and let them take what they wanted. There would be no fresh answers here.

When he returned to Sancha, he threaded his fingers through her mane as he puzzled about what he had seen. The Northern army might have lost heart, but they still had overwhelming numbers and it didn't seem the priests had given up. Questions remained on how they'd taken the city, who were the dead—and did his father know? As *alcalde* of their people, Julian would want all the information Ramiro could discover. He'd also need to know about the priests' behavior and who might be in charge of the army.

So where were the Northern equivalents of captains and *alcaldes*?

Rather than head to Crueses, Ramiro should try to scout a bit more, accept the risk of being caught, and see if he could learn anything else or merely confirm his suspicions.

Fortunately, he had just the place to start.

A click of his tongue brought Sancha around to walk with him through the trees until they got a sufficient distance from Aveston, then they cut over to the road to intercept the stream of refugees. The people looked at him with exhausted faces and closed-off expressions, shoulders hunched and backs bent, already beaten down by whatever they had suffered. He knew the look all too well—it was the same his own people had worn after the burning of Colina Hermosa.

Would it be worse to see your homes and family taken by the enemy for their own use or to helplessly watch them consumed in fire?

He stood all the straighter to compensate for their misery, refusing to give in to his own. At least Colina Hermosa had beaten off the Northerners for a time, thanks to Claire's magic. He had that small victory to warm him, even as their downtrodden faces looked to sap it from him.

"I need information," Ramiro called to the packed road.

"Damn your *needs*," a man said.

Ignoring him, Ramiro pressed on. "Was there a battle? How did your city fall?"

An old woman on a wagon pulled her shawl higher, and spat. "With barely a whimper." She flapped her reins at her mules as if urging them away from Ramiro.

A thin man with a bundle on his back at the verge of the road said, "There was a battle. We lost every man of our *pelotónes*. Every gate guard. *Alcalde* Martin had no choice but to open the gates when the second army arrived." His face twisted. "They took my wife. My daughters." He stopped, gaze turned inward, a look of loss and heartbreak taking over. A single tear slid down his cheek, then he walked away, vanishing into the pack of escaping people.

"A *caballo de guerra*." A man with arms like a blacksmith's set down his handcart loaded with small children to point at Sancha. The children jostled each other for the best view, and Sancha pranced her feet and lifted her head high under their silent scrutiny. "Colina Hermosa was here," the man offered. "Outside the gates, I mean—fighting. I saw their troops in green and gray, their gray horses, from atop the walls. We were winning. Winning. Before it all went wrong."

"Winning?" Ramiro urged, drawing closer. "Our people fought together?"

"Aye. And Suseph. We pincered the Northerners between us when our men came sweeping out. Then they all started . . . dying. Us and them. Not a man left. At first, it seemed a necessary price to pay for our freedom . . . until the second army of *them* arrived."

"Dying? What do you mean?"

"I mean ripped apart. Nothing there. The wounds just appeared." The man touched head, heart, liver, and spleen. "I went to see the bodies before the second army arrived. The saints turned their back on us that day."

"Dal," Ramiro said, the word like a curse on his tongue. He'd guessed as much from the actions of the Northern priests. But the man must be mistaken about one thing: How could the soldiers of Colina Hermosa be here? "You're sure you saw green-and-gray uniforms? How many troops dead? How many *pelotónes*?"

"Thousands. I know not the details." A woman came and put her hand on his back, and the man took up the handcart full of children again, moving off.

"The Northerners let you leave the city?" Ramiro called after them.

"They seem to care not if we stay or go," the man shouted. "We decided it was safer to go." And then they were swallowed up into the crowd.

"Many of *them* deserted," a girl in a carriage said. A bruise stood out on her cheek, a purpling mark on her dark skin. "The barbarians. They put down their weapons and ran away after looking at the bodies.

The rest are animals. Animals! Animals! *Animals!*" She screamed the word over and over. Her mother shushed her and her cries eventually shut off.

Ramiro stood, letting the people jostle around him. Dread rose in him, stifling his tongue. It seemed the warning he brought of Dal's viciousness was unneeded here. As he'd assumed, the people of Aveston had already discovered the way the demon god killed.

It bothered him, though, the news about Colina Hermosa's army. Were they right? Was his *pelotón* here and Dal had butchered them? His mind raced and his limbs felt weak. How could they stop Dal without soldiers? It couldn't be true.

Yet the evidence was all around. The burning bodies. The streams of refugees. It was almost too much to bear, and he feared each massacre made Dal a little stronger, until the dark god would be able to strike at night and through city walls. There had already been one such butchery at Aveston.

How many more until Dal couldn't be slowed?

A wiry little man, with a beard cut close and scraggly enough to show flesh through the hair, stumbled into him. "You look lost, brother," he said with a knowing look.

Something was pressed into Ramiro's hand.

"Those seeking like minds and the will to fight go here." The man moved off as swiftly as he'd appeared.

A scout, Ramiro realized too late. He managed

the presence of mind to take Sancha into the trees before investigating the slip of paper, but only just. In cramped and hurried writing, it read,

north fork
Santiago monastery

He didn't hesitate as he urged Sancha forward.

CHAPTER 3

The words on the note from the scout were no great mystery or cypher to decode for Ramiro. North branch could only be where the road between Aveston and Colina Hermosa split. One section headed north before veering west again for Aveston and rejoining the other road. That north branch ended at the same destination, just after following a more roundabout path.

He'd passed the monastery dedicated to Santiago often enough. Its wrought-iron gates stood alongside the road—a place for weary pilgrims or travelers to stop for a night of hospitality with only a minimal donation to the monks. It was the only lead he had, and if there was someone there who could either help him find his people or were continuing to fight, it was worth investigating before turning to Crueses.

Sancha took him there in a few hours. Like the rest of his journey through his people's lands, most of the places Ramiro passed had been torched. Only a scattering had been left standing, as if the Northern army had randomly decided to spare the structures. Those still erect had been robbed of anything worth burning and any metal. Farms, orchards, craftholds, or homes, it seemed to matter not. Ramiro could pick out no pattern to the destruction. Foodstuff was burned as often as spared.

The north branch itself remained deserted—no one willingly took the longer route to anywhere in this time of trouble. The eerie quiet sent the same chills up his back he'd suffered around Colina Hermosa. Even birds had no heart to sing nor lizards and small animals to rustle in the sand, as through sensing the death waiting to pounce.

When they arrived at their destination, the gates of the monastery had been ripped from their posts, leaving torn places where the hinges had resided, but the scattered buildings still stood.

Whistles came from the usually carefully tended pecan trees along the roadside—the monks' pride and joy—and Ramiro looked up to discover boys hidden among the leaves. The first sign of life he'd seen since parting from the stream of refugees. An early warning system of some kind, though the lack of sentries at the missing gates made him hesitate. But Sancha swished lazily at flies, showing no worry, and the boys were as brown of skin as himself, so this was obviously no Northern trick.

The monastery buildings, covered in rich, creamy stucco, looked almost untouched. Just the metal bars and ornamental scrollwork had been stolen from doors and windows. He followed the short ride to the courtyard, where a boy came trotting to take his reins. A most familiar-looking boy, known yet never met. Ramiro had seen his type thousands of times, one of the many hangers-on with the *pelotónes*. The small army of helpers acted as squires and grooms. They came and went—some stuck around long enough to join a *pelotón* themselves when they were grown, and others took jobs in the stables. Ramiro had once been such a boy himself, not so long ago, doing whatever work needed doing in exchange for a little training with weapons or horses, tagging on his brother Salvador's heels.

"Sir," the boy said eagerly, his open face beaming with worship. "You survived."

He handed over a water skin, and Ramiro drank quickly. "Hi-ya. And the rest of the *pelotónes*?" A tiny hope remained in Ramiro's breast that his fellow soldiers were out on a mission, but the emptiness of the courtyard put dread in him. They wouldn't take every available man. Someone would be here as a guard if this were truly a sort of headquarters.

The boy hung his head. Ramiro managed to give the boy's shoulder a squeeze. These children had only survived by being out of Dal's range with the baggage train and supplies—much as Bromisto had been spared in the swamp because he stayed with the horses. "All of them?"

"Aye, sir. From our unit and all the others, except Captain Gonzalo and his men. They're with the civilians at Suseph, I heard."

Ramiro put on a brave face for the boy, but after the last weeks, this disastrous news only made him incredibly weary. He was wrung out and swept clean of any tears left to shed that their resistance was a few boys and a monastery with no monks. Heartbreak should be beating in his chest for the loss of so many friends and brother soldiers—all he felt was beaten. Ramiro almost couldn't bring himself to ask, "Then who is here?"

"A priest and some injured, and the lady of course. She came last night. Go inside, sir. They'll be happy to see you. I'll take good care of your horse. The stables are empty . . . enough." The hitch in the boy's words ended with him dabbing at his eyes, and then sobbing, thin shoulders shaking through his shirt.

Of course. Dal spared nothing. His brother soldiers' horses would be a target as well. All the *caballos de guerra* were dead. Sancha might be one of the few remaining in the world.

Ramiro glanced upward at the burning sky. *How can this be allowed to happen?* Soldiers expected to die for their charges, but not all at the same time. Not against an enemy that wouldn't face them in the field of battle. So many brave men dead. So many innocents threatened. It wasn't right. Wasn't fair.

And what help did they get in return? What kind of god did nothing but send some impractical dreams?

However tempting, ranting and shouting useless curses would solve nothing, and there was the boy to console. He handed over the water skin.

"Sancha. Her name is Sancha. It'll be all right, son. You've done well. They'd be proud of you and the others." The boy nodded blindly at the empty words and stumbled off to the stables with Sancha. The mare let her nose hang over the child's shoulder. Sancha would be the kid's best comfort now.

In a daze, Ramiro went through the open doors into the shaded interior. Light spots on the floor showed where rugs had been removed from the tiles and wooden furniture taken by the Northerners to fuel their campfires. His boots struck hollowly, sending up the sort of empty echoes that came from abandoned places. The study to his left was dark, the shutters closed, except where they'd been pried from the walls. Only empty bookshelves remained—fastened to the walls and finished with stucco.

All the shutters had been removed in the communal dining room, letting in bars of sunlight from the thin arrow-slit windows. The monastery had been built with defense from bandits and others in mind, but there were also some levels of comfort here—or had been. Expensive wooden paneling had been pulled free, leaving unfinished walls. Upholstered furniture was slashed and paintings treated the same way. A depiction of Santiago sleeping under his miraculous tree was almost unrecognizable due to slits in the canvas. The bottom half of the wooden frame had been taken in haste, and Ramiro wondered for a moment, why not the whole thing? Other icons of saints were thrown in a corner. The smell suggesting they'd been turned into a privy and urinated upon.

Bile burned in Ramiro's throat. He touched mind, heart, liver, and spleen as Santiago taught, but felt no relief. No matter how impossible he thought it, his enemy continued to find ways to bring fresh waves of hate from his heart.

He walked from one empty room to the next, sickened at the destruction. He considered calling out, but hadn't the heart to break the stillness. This had been a wild goose chase. He would take the boys with him to Crueses or Suseph to find Captain Gonzalo. It would slow him down, but he couldn't leave them here to go on playing resistance. They'd go as soon as he'd been through the whole building.

He paused. Was that a woman's voice, distant and muffled?

The sound led him to the long corridor of monks' cells, where the brothers would have slept. Doors hung open to reveal more emptiness, but the sounds grew into discernible words:

"Santiago, please don't take him. God, not yet. We need him. I need him. Leave him to me, I beg of you."

The teary pleading came from a room halfway down the corridor and wrung at Ramiro. He slowed, unwilling to intrude on such grief. One of the wounded soldiers must lie within.

"A wife needs her husband's arm in times such as these. All my life I honored you, Santiago. Intercede for me now. Now and forever."

Ramiro gasped. "Mother?" He tore to the door, then caught at the wall to hold himself up.

Julian lay on a narrow bed, his eyes closed and his skin waxen. His body covered by a thin sheet. His mother sat on the only other piece of furniture—a three-legged stool—with her head against Julian's chest and her hands tightened on the sheet. A bowl of water, bandages, and a scattering of herbs sat on a wooden tray on the pounded-dirt floor.

"Mother."

Beatriz looked up, revealing reddened eyes and wet cheeks. Her dark hair straggled from its normal neat dressing to hang about her face and shoulders. She always dressed more conservative than other matrons, in layers of stiff black fabric and lace, favoring an old-fashioned mantilla with yet more lace to hold up her hair and give her an extra foot of height. But now her finery was dusty and disheveled, something he never thought possible with his mother.

"Ramiro? Am I dreaming? You're here." She rushed

around the bed and into his arms, clinging like a child.

"What happened?" he stammered. He was used to his mother's normally cold hands, but now they were icy.

"Oh, my son. The battle," she said between sobs. "A horse fell on him."

"But he'll be well. He'll heal." There had been such accidents before—broken legs, crushed ribs—it was a slow process, but the men most always recovered.

Beatriz shook her head. "The healer says . . . says his organs are . . . crushed. His spine, too. Father Telo has given the last rites. They don't know how he survived the journey from the battlefield, but they had to get him away from the Northerners. They say there is no hope. It might be hours or days."

Ramiro felt like a tree repeatedly stuck by the axe until the last fell blow rived it from its roots and sent it crashing to the ground. Loss after loss had beaten against him—his brother, his home, his friends, his place in the military, Claire.

Now the final strike came to destroy him.

Beatriz hurried around the bed to clasp at Julian's limp hand.

"No," he said weakly. "They're wrong. He'll get better."

She brushed back Julian's graying hair and stroked his beard. "I pray and I pray, but so far God hasn't answered. But He brought you."

"I came as fast as I could." Ramiro couldn't move. If only he'd known, he would have found some way to get here faster. Done more. Stayed instead of going to the swamp with Claire.

All the way here, he'd fretted about how he'd be received by his fellow soldiers after deserting them. How his father would meet him after disobeying his command to let Claire go alone. Would they turn their backs on him? Disavow him? Arrest and punish him? All the time knowing no matter what punishment his commanding officers saw fit, Julian would also be there and would forgive. His fears like the petty worries of an anxious child meant nothing now in the face of reality.

All taken away.

He had seen too much death lately for denial to persist. His father had the same shrunken look as his friend Gomez when the sergeant had dying.

"He did as I asked," Beatriz said. "Your father stayed away from the fighting. He was on a hilltop—safe."

"No one is safe anymore." Bitterness burned Ramiro's tongue. He'd come back in faith that the burden of stopping Dal could be laid on his father before he surrendered himself to justice. That Julian, more than anyone else, would know what to do. That the help cited in his dream must be the wily *Alcalde*.

Dust.

All dust. Like Colina Hermosa. Like Salvador.

Like his dreams of stopping Dal.

Like his family.

He dropped into a squat, hands pressed against his face. Impulses flashed through him. To run. To flee. To curl up and hide. To smash and pound something into oblivion. To drink until he forgot. To knock himself senseless. All were thoughts he grasped and let slip away as unsuited to a man.

"Ramiro?"

His mother needed him.

More. He needed this time to say good-bye.

He circled the bed and squeezed his mother's shoulder, as he had the boy outside—an equally futile gesture, but the contact steadied him as nothing else could. With his other hand, he gripped his father's limp one, noting the slash marks on Julian's face and arms from the Northern demon god, Dal. Cuts already closed and scabbed over, healing on the outside while the man failed from within.

"How are you here, Mother? Were you at the battle?"

She looked away from Julian long enough to give him a thin smile. "Goodness no. Father Telo sent for me at Suseph. I shook off my guards and got here last night. Oh Ramiro, I'm sorry for your friends. You heard what happened?"

He gave a stiff nod, unable to talk about it. More than losing military brothers, they'd lost anyone trained to fight. That knowledge hung over them like a second deathbed in the room.

They waited in silence, listening to Julian's breaths grow shallower and slower as the sun crept lower in the sky. Ramiro brushed away flies and sought desperately for what he wished to say, but fear shut his mouth. To say good-bye was to make it real.

And how Julian must be fighting death. His father never surrendered easily. Julian would hate this: to die without stopping the Northerners. To not finish the task he'd set for himself of saving their people. To give up was never his father's way, even if it meant clinging to pain.

Ramiro choked back tears. Tears would keep him from hearing the ragged breaths that now came so few and far between, but he would not give in.

"No," Beatriz said suddenly, choking on the syllable. "Julian, you cannot leave me. God, you can't have him."

As she broke into sobs, Father Telo bustled into the small room. The dark-skinned priest in his dark robes seemed as burly and as hale as ever, though his expression was grim. He brought a wet cloth in his remaining hand, as the other had been taken by the Northerners not long ago. He nodded to Ramiro in greeting like a veteran comrade, and Ramiro supposed in a way they were—Father Telo had given them the first information about Dal that Claire had put in her Song.

The Song that had summoned the real Dal to begin his killing.

Father Telo laid the cloth over Julian's forehead. "The Lord has a plan for us all. Would that we could see it, my children. But never forget that our Lord will be there to welcome us all." He put his hand on Julian's chest. "May you see your Lord face to face. Standing in His presence forever, may you see with joyful eyes Truth revealed in all its fullness. Holy Santiago, obtain for this man the grace of perfect sorrow, sincere contrition, the pardon and remission of our sins. Welcome him to his new home. I would there had been time for me to know him better. His soul was as wise as his mind and his heart as big as your heavens."

Beatriz collapsed against the bed. "Good-bye, my love. Now and forever." She went still, and Ramiro prayed she'd fainted as that would be some relief to her terrible pain. Let her not witness the end.

Tears spilled from Ramiro's eyes. He grabbed blindly at Father Telo's hand atop Julian and clung to his father's leg with his other. His father's chest did not rise. "I love you, Father. Go without worry. We will save our people. That I swear."

Dimly, he was aware of another entering the room. A round shape stood next to him and lent her strength by joining her hand to his so that three of them now touched Julian's chest as one. "Cousin. I'm so sorry," Teresa said. "Would that he be spared."

Ramiro closed his eyes against the crushing weight

pulling him down. Beatriz stirred and began sobbing. He clung to his grip on Telo and Teresa's touch on him and looked deep into his heart, saying the words that came. "I wish him not to suffer anymore."

Their joined hands rose and sank as Julian's chest rose and fell.

"Look!" Teresa said. "Cousin! Lady *Alcalde*! Look!"

Ramiro's eyes flew open. Beatriz had sat up. The wizened, sunken shell of his father's body was changed. His flesh had filled out again. A normal rosy color touched Julian's cheeks. His chest rose in normal breaths with no more rasping and wheezing. Without opening his eyes, Julian raised a hand and brushed off the cloth across his forehead, the way a sleeping man will brush at a fly.

"Blessed are we. A miracle," Beatriz breathed.

CHAPTER 4

Claire treaded carefully toward camp, holding her shirt up to cradle a pile of blueberries in the fabric. A redwing blackbird trilled from a group of reeds to greet the morning before taking wing at Claire's approach. Her sharp eyes picked up a suspicious patch of ground, and she edged around the small area of quicksand. Too many hidden death traps lay around the berry bushes. Almost as if the Great Goddess made the reward of food also a test of awareness.

Claire smiled and gave a skip. She was more than equal to that challenge, at least. As well as the trial of foraging for their food—even if she had to do it all on her own. After the night the Northerner soldiers attacked the tiny swamp village, the villagers had rightly or wrongly blamed the deaths caused by the Northerners on the witches. Even the healers had gone, forcing

Claire to forage for food to feed them and for herbs to encourage Jorga's strength. Having her grandmother back helped her forget the villagers' fear of her—at least most of the time. The fright in their eyes still hurt. She supposed she should be grateful that the villagers had been too afraid to turn on them. Several of them had witnessed her killing the Northern soldiers with nothing but a Song and had no doubt thought twice. The Great Goddess knew she thought about it a *lot*. Because until that night, she hadn't known Women of the Song could kill with magic.

Finding out she could stop hearts still left her queasy and uncomfortable in her own skin. She tried hard not to think about it.

She tiptoed into camp—glanced at the sleeping Jorga and Errol—and transferred the blueberries to a large sycamore leaf. The water from the skin bag was flat and smelled of animal hide, but tasted wonderful as it slid down her dry throat. She fed a few small sticks to the fire to get it going again, waited until the flames blazed high, then added bigger pieces of wood. The heat drove her away to sit beside Errol and Jorga. Her uncle even slept curled in a ball like a child. Oh, he did as she told him and watched her with large eyes, preferring not to speak, but he was otherwise small help in making sure they survived. He might be able to see into the future, but he was little use in the day-to-day.

The number of things yet to do today overwhelmed her. She must take the horse to clean water and find it safe grazing. Ramiro had informed her that, unlike goats, horses couldn't be trusted not to eat poisons or gorge themselves sick, and she fretted about losing their only transportation to the point of making *herself* sick. She should dig more cattail roots to soak, then grate, for a nasty-tasting bread since they had no meat. Water needed to be boiled. They were low on dry wood. Jorga must be forced to walk or the old woman would never regain her strength. And worst of all, the longer they lingered here, the more impatient she felt about doing nothing.

Claire looked down to find Jorga watching with sharp blue eyes. "Soon, granddaughter."

Claire blinked. Was Jorga reading her mind now? Had the Diviner of the Northerners done more than bring Jorga back from the dead? Had it given her new abilities? "What?"

"The Women of the Song meet soon. You must leave me and go warn them."

"Oh," Claire said with relief. "You'll be ready to go with me in a few days. We can wait."

"No, you can't. This is more important than one old woman."

Three nights ago, Jorga had been dead. One touch of the blood-colored weapon had closed death wounds, reknit flesh, and brought Jorga back to life as if the injuries had never existed—but left the old woman weaker than a newborn goat. For two days,

Jorga hadn't woken. When she finally did, her limbs shook like she had palsy, unable to support her weight. The shaking had gradually subsided, but the strength was slow to return. Jorga refused to quit her blankets, except for necessity.

Claire simply couldn't leave her grandmother in such a state—not even to warn her people about Dal's killing. And truthfully, she didn't want to go alone to the annual meeting of the reclusive Women of the Song. Why would they listen to *her* about allying with the desert people? The Women of the Song had no love for men. They'd likely say the men got what they deserved and turn their backs.

"I'll think on that," Claire said. Despite her sense of urgency, she couldn't bring herself to move on the issue. "If I can gather enough food for you while I'm gone. And maybe get you a shelter from the rain." In truth, she didn't want to think about leaving Jorga alone at all, but the old woman was stubborn when she got something in her head. Claire picked up a stick from the kindling pile and drew lines in the soggy ground, keeping her eyes down. Eventually, though, she had to say something.

"Grandmother, I thought our magic worked on minds and not bodies. That it was illusion and manipulation."

Jorga grunted impatiently. "Who said otherwise, girl? That's what I taught you because that's how it works."

"But when you were . . . dead, I used a Song that killed. That isn't supposed to happen. You used the magic to convince Ramiro to harm himself, but you didn't shut down his heart or keep his lungs from breathing. That's controlling the body."

Jorga sat up slowly, shaking out her hands and mumbling about death being healed but her rheumatism remaining just the same. "Girl, listen well, because I'm only going to say this once: that *was* of the mind. It's not something we talk about, but deep in the mind, where we don't know it exists, is a part of our brain that keeps hearts beating and air in our bodies. You're kin of mine—you have the power to reach deep and influence places a person can't control on their own."

Claire dragged her stick in a circle and then a square, thinking. The explanation made sense she supposed, but didn't alleviate her worry. "I wanted to hurt them because they hurt you. I wanted them dead. But . . . but now I feel . . . dirty. Guilty, I guess. I wanted to use my magic to protect us, but maybe I was wrong." She hid her face behind a hand. She'd even left the Northerners' bodies lying at their old campsite. It had been too much work to gather wood to give them a proper burning at the time, so they'd gone to a fresh camp, and she'd left the dead for animals. Since then she couldn't bring herself to return and repair her cruelty. That was wrong on her part.

"Humph," Jorga said. "I think you did as you

should. Those men deserved death. Attacking old women, and children—because you're still a child, no matter your age—and I suppose those desert people who helped us didn't deserve swords in the night either," Jorga added reluctantly. "But there is a way."

Claire dropped her stick and uncovered her eyes. "What do you mean?"

"A way not to kill with that Death Song you used. It won't be easy. You have to cut it off at the right time—render the person unconscious, but don't kill them. It's a matter of timing and practice."

"Practice?" Claire said so loudly that Errol sat up. "How does one practice stopping a heart? On who?"

"Then don't practice. You'll just have to figure out how to finesse the length of the Death Song as you use it more. Too little and you'll make them woozy. That's dangerous, child. Better aim to kill and if you miss, it's accidental. Or don't use it at all. Have them kill themselves instead. I can teach you that Song."

"No," Claire said quickly. Jorga and that Song had Ramiro attempting to thrust a knife in his own eye. If Claire hadn't held on to his arm and stopped Ramiro, he'd be dead. Jorga hadn't even been acting in self-defense. Her prejudice against men had filled her with hate. She'd strike without knowing if a man meant her harm or not. "I'll never use that Song."

"Be not so quick to judge me." Jorga's mouth pinched in a scowl. "Who called an evil god into this world to destroy?"

Claire jumped to her feet. "That was to protect lives. I had no idea it would call a *real* god." She scooped up the pot—"I'll fetch more water"—and stormed off, leaving Errol with his mouth hanging open. He worshipped Jorga too much.

Sometimes, she saw exactly why Ramiro *didn't* like her grandmother.

Her head whirled with everything she'd learned and the guilt of it all. She set the pot to fill in the stream of flowing water—the reason she'd chosen this camping spot—and rested on her heels to think. She'd pledged not to be afraid to use the magic anymore. Yet, relying on Songs that only distracted the Northerners, like the Hornet Tune, was too risky. She didn't want to die because she wouldn't harm others. That meant sticking with the Song that caused death. She put her fingers in the stream and let the water tumble across her hands.

Perhaps, Jorga had given her a way out. She'd just have to manipulate the Death Song to stop short of killing. Then she could be safe and avoid more blood on her hands.

Of course, she'd also said that'd take time and patience. Easier said than done.

Panic squeezed in her chest.

To fight it, she built an image of Ramiro in her mind's eye. The way he looked when he turned his head over his shoulder to tease her: one dark eyebrow lifted and a smile on his lips, head tilted, and the set of his back firm.

The world seemed better when he was with her. She hadn't been alone, obviously, but she hadn't *felt* alone with him, either. The way she still did even when speaking to Jorga or Errol.

With a start, she noted the pot overflowed. Her mother would say sulking wasted time, and she'd be right. Claire withdrew the container from the stream and moved to a group of cattails, using her short knife to dig the roots out of the mud and liberally splashing her clothing in the process. She'd get Errol to pound the roots while she took the horse to water. She could clean up while it drank.

She staggered to the camp, having underestimated the difficulties of carrying a bunch of slimy roots and the full pot of water, to find Errol crouched over the fire with Bromisto, one fair haired and one nut brown. The boys had their heads together as the smaller Bromisto sharpened a stick with a notched old knife. Two skinned and cleaned rabbits already hung over the flames and the odor of cooking meat made Claire's mouth water.

"Let me try," Errol demanded.

"Next time." Bromisto gave the older and taller boy a shove with his shoulder and kept working. "You'll cut yourself."

"Will not." Errol shoved back and then laughed.

"Don't make me come over there," Jorga said. The woman had left her blankets for the first time under her own power in three days and stood leaning against a tree. The boys whispered and snickered together, obviously making fun of the only adult. "Pay attention to what you're doing," Jorga snapped.

Claire dropped several roots. Bromisto was here, out of nowhere, after being sent away? Her uncle was smiling and talking? Jorga was on her feet? A pang swelled in Claire's chest and suddenly tears welled in her eyes, without knowing why, until the answer hit her. It was all so . . . so normal . . . where nothing had been normal in a very long time. They had moved in fear for so long—even now she should be worrying about the smoke drawing down Northerners to kill them or that Bromisto would indeed cut himself and the blood would bring Dal. But she didn't want to speak about that. Didn't want to break this moment of ordinary, like a ray of brilliant sunshine through a thunderstorm.

It renewed her and gave her fresh strength. Her indecision and hesitation evaporated.

"Witch girl!" Bromisto called out happily. "I brought you some breakfast. Why are you standing over there? Come help. Cooking is women's work."

The boy didn't flinch from her. Claire dabbed at the tears with a muddy sleeve, covering up their traces, so she could glare in mock anger at his tiny chauvinist ways. From a grown man, the words would be insulting. From him, they were only comical. "Very funny, Trickster. After we eat, we're starting after the Women of the Song." Time to face the task before her. They might not get far today, but they'd make as many miles as they could until Jorga got too tired to continue. "All of us. You're welcome to come with us, Bromisto—there's plenty of women's work for you. Because all work is women's work and that includes hunting and fighting. My grandmother and I will teach you manners yet—after all, I taught Ramiro."

Bromisto grinned up at her. "You can try." He jostled Errol again and the two laughed.

"Start this water boiling," Claire said. "I have something to fetch before we eat and pack up." She left the pot and the roots and darted to her blankets to snatch a concealed shirt—one of Ramiro's that helped her sleep—then traversed the treacherous terrain to their old campsite. The smell of rotting flesh hit her before the mud and stick shelters appeared. She clamped Ramiro's shirt over her nose and mouth to keep from gagging, drawing in the safe odor of him that lingered in the material.

Quick glances at the ground let her avoid stepping on the dead bodies as she hurried to their former lean-to. Animals had scattered parts of the dead everywhere.

Next to the bunch of bloodied blankets where Jorga had been stabbed lay a slender white rod as long as Claire's arm. After using it to heal Jorga, she had left the weapon with the abandoned blankets as something else too foul for future use. She stared at the Diviner long and hard, mosquitoes whining in her ears.

What are you waiting for, silly head? It's not going to bite you.

Probably.

The white Diviners killed with a single touch.

She threw Ramiro's shirt at the evil thing and scooped both up before she could dwell on her actions, turning and scrambling in a mad run to her family. She'd give the Diviner to the Women of the Song and let them deal with how to use it. Maybe this proof of the Northerners would even help them believe her warnings. One could hope.

CHAPTER 5

Beatriz threw herself across Julian. *"Mi amor."*

"Let's give them a minute alone," Teresa said.

Ramiro nodded and followed the priest and Teresa into the corridor, closing the door to the monk cell after him. His mother's whisper and father's deeper rumbles were audible through the planks behind him. And like a boy caught stealing pies from the cooling shelf, their open affection still made him want to look away and be more then glad to heed Teresa and go into the hall.

Already his father had sat up in bed, talking animatedly, and would have been off the mattress and on his feet if Teresa and Beatriz hadn't insisted he wait an hour or so to be sure of no relapse.

"Julian is alive."

The words came from his own head and from the priest's mouth. Father Telo crossed the hallway to put his back against the wall and slide down to the floor. In an odd contrast, his lips beamed in a wide smile, while tears ran down his dark cheeks. He grasped the stump of his arm close to his chest.

"My father is alive, cousin!" Ramiro caught Teresa in a rib-squeezing hug, catching her so off guard she barely squeezed back before he released her.

"Aye. I was there," Teresa said, her plump cheeks almost choking her eyes with her smiles.

"The Lord sees us," Telo said amidst the tears, a combination of delight and awe in his voice.

"I kind of thought that was your thing." Ramiro joined the priest, sliding down the wall as well to sit in a jumble on the floor. He gripped the medallion of San Martin, patron of soldiers, hanging from his neck. Joy bubbled in his chest, and he held back a laugh that was half hysteria. "You know, to have no doubts."

"There's a difference between knowing and, well, *knowing*, cousin." Teresa had crossed her arms across her chest. Her figure was less round than the last time Ramiro had seen her, but it was still her most prominent feature. In opposition to societal trends, she wore trousers and peasant clothing, keeping her hair mannishly short. Ramiro couldn't have cared less—the sight of her warmed him.

"The last miracles were witnessed over three hundred and fifty years ago," she continued. "It's been a rather long time."

"Aye." Ramiro trusted a scholar from the university to have the dates correct. As a specialist in other cultures, Teresa had been part of his first mission to the witches of the swamp, the women he now knew to call the Women of the Song. He had saved Teresa's life from quicksand and she had kept him sane when Salvador died, making them *sangre* kin—or kin by ties other than blood. "It was . . . incredible to see. It kind of knocks a person off their feet."

"He is with us, my friends," Telo said, suddenly grabbing Ramiro by the shoulder and shaking him. "*He* is with us!" The priest put his arms across his knees and leaned forward to bury his face in them. Sobs shook him.

Ramiro thought of the ghostly figure from his dreams who wore his brother's face and sometimes gave him insight into what to do next—the figure he didn't want to speculate about. "I get that impression, too." This time the hysteria leaked free in the form of shaky chuckles.

Had they just seen a holy miracle? The priest seemed sure enough of it.

Mirth settled as dark thoughts intruded. Why had the dreams picked him as a witness? Ramiro felt more like a betrayer than a hero—deserter from his military brothers, abandoner of Claire, the one responsible for bringing Dal among them to kill thousands, perhaps millions. He should be shunned, not rewarded. He *would* be shunned when people found out the truth.

Ramiro touched mind and heart, his fingers glancing off his breastplate. The first time he wore his full armor, Julian had helped clothe him in the shining metal. Dead and now alive. This was a moment to celebrate; doubts could wait. "We just saw a . . . I don't know what that was. I could use a drink."

"There's ale in the kitchen," Teresa offered. "No stronger spirits, sorry. I already looked."

"Practical as always, cousin. You're a woman after my own heart." The words reminded him he should act with the same sense of responsibility. "Maybe we should check on the other injured. See if they got better, too."

"There are no other wounded here. All the other survivors of Dal's attack went to Aveston, as it was closer. We brought *Alcalde* Julian to the monastery because we thought he shouldn't fall into the hands of the Northerners. Some scouts and the grooms survived and helped us get him here, then one of them took the news to Suseph and to fetch the Lady *Alcalde*."

"It was a scout that directed me to the monastery." A scout and maybe some nudging from a higher source. Ramiro felt a little shaky at the idea that he'd been directed here to witness a marvel. He looked at his companions with fresh eyes. Which one of them had been the conduit for that power? Because it had not been him. Then something else struck him.

"Wait—what did you call my mother? Lady *Alcalde*?" He had heard Telo use the same words inside the cell with Julian.

"A little title I invented as there is no precedent." Again, a wide smile crossed Teresa's face, as if chasing away her troubles. "Your mother was elected *alcalde* for Colina Hermosa *and* Suseph."

Ramiro shook his head. "There is no Colina Hermosa and my father is *alcalde*."

"*Was*. He was deposed by a vote of no confidence of the councilmen and refused to seek reelection. And don't count Colina Hermosa out yet. The spirit survives. I have the whole story from your mother. The women came out and voted in great numbers— something not seen for two hundred and eighteen years, when a *concejal* suggested their voting power be removed. Lady Alvarado won in a landslide. Isn't it wonderful! It deserves to be recorded in the histories." Teresa's face fell. "Except all the histories are burnt with the city—and the university."

"I'm sorry, cousin." The reminder of Colina Hermosa's fall canceled out some of the pride he felt in his mother, but Ramiro still felt the need to celebrate— and forget. "But why am I not surprised? That sounds like my mother's sort of work. Good for her. Now . . . where did you say that ale was?"

"A barrel in the kitchen. Bring me a cup—and

maybe one for the priest, too. I've never seen him like this. Left at the end of the hall and then straight on."

Ramiro levered to his feet and found doing so took almost more energy than he had left. The events of the morning had stunned him. Joy drained almost as much as grief. His mother their new *alcalde*. His father dying and then somehow alive. His brother soldiers dead and likely burned in that pyre he'd seen in front of Aveston. A mix of terrible and fantastic news.

He took a right at the end of the corridor, passing into a more modernly designed and less feudal addition to the monastery, and stood blinking absently in a ruined chapel, where the Northerners had broken the stained-glass windows and overturned the stone lectern. A single square of glass remained intact in a window, showing a glowing halo in reds and golds above where the head of a saint should have been.

Ramiro realized his mistake and backtracked, finding the monks' kitchen behind a closed door. The glass over the two windows was intact, as well as everything else in the room, including a large table in front of the great stone fireplace. Either the Northerners had missed this room or they had preserved it for some reason. A handful of scouts greeted him from the table without bothering to get up. He gave them a two-fingered salute and crossed to the keg in the corner. A few flies buzzed around him. Wooden mugs sat atop the barrel, and he didn't bother checking if they were clean before putting one under the spout. The foam clung to his lips as he drank.

He'd put the mug under for a refill when something stung his arm. "Ow." A reflex slap smashed a horsefly as big as a coin. Its eyes were an odd red. Shouts came from behind him, and he turned to find the scouts slapping at other flies—the insects suddenly interested in nothing but biting. The room darkened. Another huge horsefly came for his face, and Ramiro waved his mug at the pest.

"Look at that!"

Ramiro spun. The windows were covered with thousands of crawling flies, buzzing to get into the room and blotting out the sunshine. Tiny impacts made loud by their numbers pinged against the door to the outside. Ramiro's feet backed to a corner without a command from his brain. The scouts shuffled around him.

"Saints." He'd never seen anything like the flies' numbers—or determination. If the glass hadn't been in the windows—"Saints!"

There was no glass in the windows of the room containing his parents.

He sprinted for the hall, picking up speed in the long, open space and careening through the monastery into the older section, drawing his sword as he went. Teresa and Father Telo were on their feet when he arrived. They swatted at the air as screams came through the walls. Ramiro pushed past them to throw open the door to the cell. Beatriz and Julian flailed under an assault. Flies covered every surface, descending on Ramiro in a biting cloud. He felt stings on his arms and legs, right through his clothing. They dinged off his breastplate and tore at his neck, crawling in his beard. Waving his sword might have hit a few, but thousands more moved at him.

He threw down his sword to slap at his body. Each strike killed dozens of the big insects . . . and did nothing to stop the attack. Dozens of tiny bites burned and stung already. Single, they would have done little than draw a bit of blood and create a welt. In the thousands, they ate him by inches.

He stumbled forward, brushing horseflies from his face. His heart thudded. Beatriz's cries of pain rang in his ears. The mattress lay discarded on the floor as though attempted to be used as a shield but found to be too flimsy. Beatriz and Julian had wound sheets around their bodies but the creatures bit right through the thin material. Ramiro could barely protect himself, let alone his flailing mother. And still more flies sailed through the unblocked window.

A horsefly stung his eyelid, and he beat at it with a cry of rage and frustration. The insects sought flesh with an evil-minded obsession. Beatriz stumbled from the bed, beating at herself, and knocking cups and bundles of herbs from a tray on the floor in her haste.

Ramiro dived for the ground and scooped up the wooden tray with the intention of putting it across part of the window. A vain idea. He swung the platter as he went like a fan and where the surface struck flies, the insects fell dead by the hundreds.

"The tray!" Teresa screamed from the doorway as she did her own macabre dance. "Keep swinging it!"

Every puff of air from the tray—the very ordinary and normal tray reacting in a most unordinary way—sent more horseflies tumbling to the dirt floor to lie broken and crushed. Ramiro hurried to his mother and fanned the platter around her. Insects fell in a rain of black bodies to cover the ground whether touched by the tray or air fanned from it. The wooden surface grew warm under his fingers. He used both hands to sweep the tray in great arcs. Flies stopped entering through the window and instead exited in droves. He slapped at a last sting on his wrist as the room went silent, except for wheezing breaths and a few struggling flies with the same unnatural red eyes, buzzing weakly on their backs.

"What the hell!" Ramiro panted, holding the tray in a death grip. "What the *hell!*" His skin roiled with revulsion. Beatriz scrubbed at her face, spreading blood from welts. Julian straightened slowly from where he tried to gather the mattress from the floor. All of them stared at the tray and then slowly raised their eyes to look at Ramiro.

Ramiro held the tray at arm's length, though it

looked perfectly ordinary, unchanged except for smears of fly. Just some thin and cheap boards glued together with a simple border tacked around it and a brown varnish applied unevenly. The hair rose on the back of his neck.

"What was that?" Julian demanded.

Telo staggered in the door, crushing horseflies under his sandals. "The Lord isn't the only power watching. It seems miracles draw unwelcome attention."

Ramiro glanced at the empty window and the sunlight streaming inside. "Dal. He works by daylight, but he couldn't strike at us inside—yet. Buildings give some sort of protection."

"So he found another way," Teresa finished.

"If this Dal cannot work by night or inside, then we leave as soon as it is dark," Julian announced. "Maybe it knows our location only and not our identities. Moving might hide us from it."

"Sancha," Ramiro said, panic rising again. "I have to check on her and the boys."

"Don't go outside," Beatriz called, but he was already out the thin slit of a window and running to the stable.

He didn't know if barns counted as walls, but he'd damn well find out. The eyes crawling across his back might have been Dal or his imagination as he reached the stable without incident. Boys sitting on piles of hay and cleaning tack looked up at his hurried entrance. Saddle straps fell into the straw as they took in the blood on his face and neck and the way he clutched a dinner tray to his chest like a shield.

"You need your saddle, sir?" asked the boy he'd met earlier, uncertainty in his voice.

"No. Not yet."

A dozen or more horses of chestnut or deep brown regarded him over their stall doors. No whites showed around their eyes. Sancha nodded her dapple-gray head, perfectly calm and unharmed.

"No flies in here?" he asked the boys.

"Flies, sir? There's always flies. No more than usual."

Embarrassment crept over him. He must look a lunatic, bleeding from dozens of bites and all frantic. He tucked the tray under his arm, wondering if it was a kitchen tool again or still something more. "Carry on then. We're leaving tonight, so you might get ready. Oh, and stay inside unless you absolutely must go out. Consider that an order, soldiers. Don't even stick your head outside."

"Yes, sir." Concern turned to pride on their young faces. They might not understand, but they'd obey someone who treated them as adults.

He returned to the monastery in the usual way, through the door, knowing the flies had been no random attack. The insects would have had a much easier time getting into the stable if they were only after blood. Ramiro considered the tray under his arm. Thankfully, something else seemed to be on their side.

But if miracles drew instant retaliation, should they hope for more?

Which force would prove the stronger? He very much feared he was soon going to find out firsthand.

CHAPTER 6

Clouds—perhaps heralding the long-withheld summer rains—obscured the moon and stars. They robbed the world of light and rendered Julian's four companions, walking beside him, as vague shadows. Yet, Julian didn't need to see them to know he remained the most outwardly controlled among them. Monitoring his appearance was a trick Julian had long mastered. One didn't survive a lengthy period in politics without it. The others, however, had less practice with control and gave away their emotional turmoil.

Beatriz pulled her arm from his to readjust her shawl for the thousandth time since they'd left the monastery to stumble over the uneven ruts on the road. The resettling of her clothing wasn't the only sign of her confusion—her hands were actually warm. Julian could count on his fingers the number of times that had happened, notably when she labored to birth their sons. Without being able to see their features, Julian guessed that each of his companions continued to suffer from shock. Father Telo clutched the stub of his arm to his chest as he walked, the priest's eyes would still be darting, never settling. His ambassador to the witches, Teresa, muttered soft bits of words that drifted to Julian's ears as she argued with herself over something about the Northerners. And Ramiro no doubt continued to wear a look of bemusement, gaze turned inward and half stunned, even as he would start and remember to search the area for threats. Ramiro led their horses—insistent they not ride in the dark and risk breaking vulnerable legs to a rut in the road. Ramiro's horse followed, the reins looped over its saddle and an ordinary-appearing kitchen tray lashed to the leather along with his son's armor. All four humans exuded a tightness and a reluctance to speak aloud, as if doing so would bring trouble upon them.

From experience, Julian knew his companions must throw off their devastation in their own way and time, even as he worked to recover from the struggles he himself hid. Struggles that beat upon him no less hard for his composure, making him as jumpy as a lizard with a hawk floating overhead. For one thing, he could remember little since the battle started around Aveston until he'd been reborn and the swarming flies attacked. A time period when, apparently, much had happened and left him clueless. And that was just the start of his uncertainty.

He flexed his left hand, stiff and clumsy from his previous stroke, and it now responded with full mobility as if he'd never been ill—that was certainly enough to stun a person. But on top of that, his memory insisted, their greatest threat was Lord Ordoño. Now, not only did his family tell him Ordoño was dead—murdered by the priestess Santabe—but that the Northern army could no longer be their top concern, compared to a rampaging god. He found it difficult to adjust to such a change of threat.

Equally distracting, he could vaguely recall incredible pain and being unable to move any of his limbs, and getting more and more distant from his own body as he faded into death. It was as if the world had left him behind while he'd been dying and now he had to scramble to keep up.

So while his face remained even and his stride sure, his inner landscape appeared to have been wiped clean, like a slate, to leave him with nothing.

What had been a tumbled emotional landscape of canyons and chasms filled with rocky boulders of doubt since the Northerners arrived had grown smooth and flat but blank and empty—rendering him with nowhere to turn and nothing recognizable—as if he were set down in another world. With the Northern army there were always angles to tackle, possibilities to access. With their new opponent an invisible god who struck without warning, he knew not where to start or how to react, left at a loss for answers to share. Adrift in an alien world.

Even his healing, which the others considered a sign of his importance, didn't give Julian the impression he was given a second chance for a reason. What did he have to contribute compared to the others with a better understanding of what they faced?

Only his tearing grief that followed Salvador's death had somehow turned to a new perspective on faith and left him with a glimmer of hope, providing the sort of belief that Beatriz had always wished for him. Julian touched heart and spleen. He prayed if miracles could occur then anything was indeed possible. In a single bright spot, Julian no longer doubted that a time would come when he would see his son Salvador again. Beatriz was right. There was a time for everything, even reunions beyond the grave.

Unwilling to concentrate only on his own uncertainty anymore, Julian scanned his surroundings. The road remained empty and the five of them alone. Beatriz had insisted they send the army boys with a few scouts to join the refugees from Aveston. He believed the boys had as much right as any to know about their foe, but Beatriz held tight that the children would be safer in Crueses. And after they'd been singled out by the flies, Julian couldn't disagree that being around the five of them might be more unsafe than other choices. So the boys joined the refugees from Aveston headed in another direction toward Crueses, while the deserting Northerners presumably went north. Beatriz sent the rest of the scouts from the monastery to Aveston to try and get an accurate count of the Northern army, leaving them alone for the moment.

Moonlight shown through a slit of cloud to highlight a great wall looming in the distance, where bronze gates hung warped and open. Julian jerked upright and stumbled to a halt at the sight. The others around him came to a standstill as well. Even the horses embraced the silence.

Colina Hermosa.

Broken and faded like a once-great lady whom time has passed by, now old and without influence or family.

Gaps in the stone breached the walls around the sides and rear of the city, where the great wall had been undermined to let the citizens escape. Julian hoped that did not mean this Dal could get at them inside. Once again, he had no information on the subject. No one else knew for sure either, so their consensus had led them to take the risk. After all, if blood called the *thing*, they weren't likely to attract its attention for the moment.

And they needed shelter and a place to regroup away from the monastery and the reminder of his almost-death. A breathing space to find their wits and pool their information before making crucial decisions. Where better than the empty city?

Home that was a home no longer.

The stench of smoke met them before they reached the gate and slipped inside in continued silence. Though even the hottest embers had grown cold, ash lay thick on every surface, charred beams and fallen buildings obscuring the avenues where the structures weren't totally consumed. In many spots nothing remained but ash-coated dirt and charcoal. Beatriz pressed her shawl across her nose and coughed.

A home of haunts and ghosts now—certainly no place for the living.

"This way," Julian directed. He'd read the many reports of the soldiers he'd sent in to explore the city even before it was safe to do so. Those soldiers had created a slender path through the debris running along the wall. A quarter of a mile later, it brought them to intact doors in the wall and a well that had been uncovered. Buckets and ropes still lay around the stone housing of the well.

"Storage rooms three and four," Ramiro said in wonder.

Julian gave a nod. "They escaped the inferno, though the guardhouses, storerooms, and stables near the gates burned." He leaned against the wall, his strength still uncertain and his hunger pangs stronger, as wasn't unusual in a man not long up from his sickbed.

Ramiro opened one of the storeroom doors, revealing a dark space, and Julian said, "They'll be empty. We salvaged everything from them before the people left for Crueses."

"One room for people and one for horses," Ramiro said, taking charge. He rummaged around in the bags on his horse and then handed a bag to Beatriz. "My lantern and firestarter are in there. See if someone can get some light. The rest of you go rest. I can see to the horses and start pulling up some water."

"As a wandering friar, I'm used to making my own light," Father Telo said, taking the bag and hunching over it on the ground.

Julian stared into the darkened chamber of stone where they'd take their rest. There were no beds or pillows, just a dirty floor with scattered mouse droppings.

Father Telo held up the flint and tinder in his remaining hand. "I'm afraid I forgot, this is beyond me now."

"Allow me, Father." Beatriz bustled over to help, and Julian watched, taken aback. His wife filled many new roles in the last days: politician and now servant. But they needed to focus beyond creature comforts.

"We should make a plan," Julian said. He didn't want to discuss what everyone else called a miracle, and he didn't believe they could rely on that sort of divine intervention again. Better to seek elsewhere. But where to start? Logic said to attack this problem—no matter the immensity of its size—like any other. When in doubt it helped to lay out the facts and plug the holes in his knowledge. The saints had provided him with perhaps the only people with information. The least he could provide in return was the ability to organize. "As I understand it, this Northern god strikes during the day and outdoors, as far as we know. Blood draws its attention, otherwise the appearance is seemingly random. There seem no limits on the number of people it can kill. What else?"

"Its priests use blood from the massacres to change their Diviners to red," Ramiro offered from where he unsaddled his mare. "I saw them doing so to dozens by Aveston."

"For a purpose, I assume, that is unknown to us," Julian added.

"Aye." Teresa stepped closer. "Father Telo and I saw one of the red Diviners as well, but we've no clue of their function. I get the feeling they are much prized. We were warned not to say . . . the Northern god's name. It apparently was expected to return on a consistent schedule, but has returned five hundred years early—"

"My fault." Ramiro stopped in his work. "I brought Claire and ordered her to sing about . . . it."

Beatriz made a noise of protest, but Julian spoke

first. "*My fault*," he said forcefully. "I sent you to get a witch."

Father Telo cleared his throat, handless arm clutched against his chest. "And I gave them the knowledge of the Northern god in the first place to put in the magic."

"If I hadn't needed rescuing," Beatriz said, "the magic might never have been used."

"And so we all had a part," Teresa said reasonably. "I was the first to talk to the witch girl and attempt to change her from prisoner to ally."

Julian shook his head. "There is no reason to cast blame. Or rather I should say, there is no blame at all in this case, only unintended consequences. If the witch had been too frightened to sing. If Ramiro had never found her. If I'd never sent the mission to the swamp. If the Northerners never came. If, if, if. One thing is true, we'd all be dead now if we'd made other choices."

Ramiro looked away. "Instead, others are dead in my place."

"Our place," Julian said sternly. "I took our troops to Aveston." He remembered them as winning, pushing back the Northerners in a glorious charge. Oh, the joy of it . . . Then this Dal came and cut everyone into tiny pieces and he remembered none of it. Instead of hanging his head, Julian swallowed hard. "We cannot go back in time, only forward. It cannot be coincidence that all of us who had a part in bringing this . . . terror into the world are gathered in one place."

"The Lord has a place and a plan for everything," Father Telo said from where he held the tinder for Beatriz. She struck flint and steel and the priest caught a spark, blowing softly on the tinder until a tiny flame grew. He applied the lint to the lantern wick. "Ah. Do you see? Light comes from base materials. Wonder of wonders, metal and stone gives us heat and comfort. So much more can we expect from the base materials inside ourselves."

"Aye, Father," Beatriz said. "It's too soon to give up now."

"What else do we know?" Julian asked. He might have a broader perspective on spiritual matters, but he didn't believe that would save them.

"That Da—our foe intends to snuff out the world." Ramiro stepped away from his horse to pluck the burning lint from the priest's hand and stomp it out. "That it won't stop until we are all dead, and soon enough it will be able to strike at night and indoors. That our instruments of battle are a kitchen tray and our bare hands. We don't know if steel can stop it, or magic . . . or anything."

"And you know this how?" Teresa asked. "You've witnessed it firsthand? Tried your sword against . . . it? The witch sang against it?"

"I . . . no," Ramiro faltered. "I . . . saw it in a dream."

Julian focused his gaze on his son but didn't interrupt.

"Little incidents of blood—a skinned knee, a baby's birth—will call its attention. Each one will make it stronger and stronger. It will take out the Northerners, the Women of the Song, us . . . all of the *ciudades-estado*."

"Dreamer," the priest and Teresa said together.

"Describe these dreams. What are they like?" Teresa demanded.

At the same time, Father Telo said, "Touched by our Lord. Shown things seen by no other."

"Dreamer?" Julian interrupted. "What is this?"

"Only the rarest of saints." Beatriz's eyes held fierce pride. "A prophet speaks with God's voice. A dreamer sees with His eyes." She dropped the lantern in her hurry to catch Ramiro in an embrace. "My child. It is from the Sight that runs in our family."

Julian could sense his son's embarrassment even in the dark, though to his credit Ramiro took the affection like a man and didn't squirm in his mother's arms. Julian hastily righted the lantern before the flame was drowned by the oil and turned the subject as Beatriz released their son and reluctantly stepped back. "So we know our foe, but not how to stop it."

"I can't speak to that," Teresa said, "but I do suspect that the Northerners know how to at least contain it. My guess is they kept it from the rest of the world for centuries, perhaps eons."

Priest and university-trained expert locked gazes. "Santabe," Telo said. "With Ordoño dead, she's the only one who reliably speaks our language. If we could interrogate her . . ."

"The murderer?" Julian asked. "That wild thing? She'd as soon bite out her own tongue as offer us information. You think to speak to her?"

"Without Ordoño, it's doubtful we can get near her," Telo added. "She'd kill us on sight. But she is of their highest clergy. She would know their deepest secrets. If we could capture her and if we could get her to speak . . ."

"Or maybe there is another way to find out more about it," Teresa said.

All eyes turned to Ramiro. His shoulders lifted defensively. "I don't think the figure from my dreams will help much. Not with stopping this dark god, anyway, or feeding us information. His hands are tied. He showed me what will happen and said I'd have assistance—but not from him."

"Then I agree that Santabe sounds like our best place to start," Julian said slowly. Though he didn't voice his doubts, worry for Ramiro grew in his breast. The lad wasn't acting in his normal fashion. "Santabe has met all of us, but one of us has spent much less time with her—enough that she might not readily see them as a threat. Only you, my son, might get close and be unknown to her."

Ramiro held up his hands. "I clunked her on the head with a rock. I think she might remember me."

"True, but it was in a battle, and barely light, and you were dressed as a soldier. You scarcely had a beard then . . . and you are not a Northerner. To her, you could just be one of many dark-skinned folk, and she might not be able to pick you out of a crowd. And remember she is a strong woman, tall and well made—only you have the necessary strength to match hers. We will help as best we can, but we need you to capture the woman so we can question her."

Julian expected a reluctant nod from his son, such had always been his influence before. Instead came a shake of the head. "My warning is too late for our troops or Aveston, but the other *ciudades-estado* must be told how to shelter from Da—it. Such I feel is the calling from the dreams. Then I must turn myself in to Captain Gonzalo as a deserter and take my fate."

"Nonsense," Beatriz said swiftly. "I am *alcalde*. I pardon you."

As Julian watched, Ramiro set his jaw. For the first time, Julian noticed how firmly his son stood, shoulders square, head up. His beard had filled in thick and full, though kept short. The set of his face was that of a man now. Gone was the indecision of youth.

"I thank you, Mother, but the decision isn't yours or mine. It belongs to Captain Gonzalo as the last *capitán*. It is to him I must go once I've given my warning to the other *alcaldes*. You'll need to find another to capture your priestess."

"Gonzalo is a stickler for the law," Teresa said. "I've met him. You'll find no favoritism or excuses given for honor won there. The penalty for desertion is hanging."

Ramiro didn't flinch. "Then so be it. Though . . . I would leave you a letter to deliver to Claire for me—in case I cannot."

Julian stepped into the breach of horrified silence before Beatriz could start wailing. As he'd feared, their son was troubled—perhaps wrongfully. Yet telling him so would only make his son dig in his heels— the boy could be as stubborn as his mother. "Yes, we could find another to go, Ramiro, but can I trust their commitment? And doing so quickly might be difficult. You've fought this Santabe before and won. Certainly in a time such as this—" Julian began, but his son cut him off.

"By San Martin, honor is all the more important in a time such as this. I shirked my duty and must pay for it."

Even before Ramiro finished, Beatriz wore a look of pure obstinacy. "Nonsense," she said. "I won't have it."

Julian rubbed a hand over his face as the others continued to argue. He would find the whole thing ridiculous if his son didn't obviously feel so strongly. Had he truly instilled such an unbendable sense of honor into his sons—or had it been their mother's doing? A combination of both, Julian quickly decided. Together, they had given Ramiro a double lesson on integrity, and he sensed there would be no change of heart here—no matter the persuasion used.

Then let there be a compromise.

"Hold," he said, breaking into a scripture quote from Father Telo on duty to elders. "Beatriz and I will take the warning to the other *alcaldes*. We are more likely to be believed in any case. We can go to Crueses and Vista Sur and the other *ciudades-estado* and meet you at Suseph. Help Father Telo and my ambassador capture this Santabe and bring her to Suseph for us. You can then surrender to Gonzalo there. Find and secure Santabe swiftly and you might be there sooner than if you rode with the warning to all the *ciudades-estado*."

Beatriz cleared her throat loudly and resettled her shawl across her shoulders. "Aren't you forgetting something? Who is *alcalde* now? Who makes the decisions?"

"I . . . I . . ." Julian stammered. He had indeed forgotten, too used to being the one in charge. "I am in the wrong. What do you think, *mi amor*?"

"I don't like this. It's too dangerous."

Julian didn't disagree, and a fear lingered in his breast for his youngest child. A father's protectiveness never ended. Yet for Ramiro to carry so much guilt wasn't healthy either. It was only reasonable for Julian as a parent to want to reach Suseph first and speak to Gonzalo, to use his influence on the man. He only prayed the saints helped them all live long enough to see the city.

To his mixture of relief and regret, Beatriz wasn't finished. "It's too dangerous," she repeated. "But I don't think we have a choice. I have to agree with Julian that this is the best option at the moment. As your *alcalde*, I have decided this is the path we must take."

Their son gave a nod and turned to his horse. Their journey together would last just a day. But that Julian could accept, because their next journey was more important.

Tomorrow morning, they began the task to defeat a god.

CHAPTER 7

Claire brushed at damp hair clinging against her cheek. Rain fell in little patters against the leaves. A calming sound that made it easy to curl up for a nap, if they weren't walking through a wet woods and if the wet wasn't starting to soak through her cloak. But she couldn't complain as they made much better time than she expected. Bromisto's scouting and ability to lead the way, while providing them with the occasional rabbit dinner, allowed her time with Jorga. The younger boy also managed to entertain Errol and keep him busy. They walked ahead, with Bromisto teaching Errol how to weave a leather cord into a snare.

"Again," Jorga demanded. Her lips pinched thin in a tart expression. Her higher position up on the horse gave her additional authority—not that her grandmother needed the help. "Keep going."

Claire rolled her eyes. "What do you think I'm doing?"

"Not Singing. Again."

"I can barely remember the words. I only heard them five minutes ago. It's hard to fix on a memory."

"Excuses, excuses. Are you a Woman of the Song or not?"

Claire huffed, but still drew her body up straight in her Singing posture. In order to get the Share Memory to work, she had to focus on a particular memory while Singing the words to the Song, all while holding strong to her will and intent. Not nearly as easy as Jorga made it sound, but her grandmother said this method was a shortcut that let a woman share images from her mind without having to create a fresh Song each time.

In fact, this magic and creating illusions, as when Claire had made herself and Ramiro appear to be deer to some Northerners, were very much related. Both times you shared what you wanted the target to "see." However, in Share Memory, the image had been real at one time—and thus should supposedly be easier to recreate—and wasn't meant to deceive.

Claire still felt like she juggled four balls while balanced on one foot.

She built a picture in her mind of one of her earliest memories: being among the branches of an apple tree and looking down at her mother's upturned face. She still remembered her infant feeling of triumph at being above and separate from her mother.

> *"Thus do you see,"*
> *"That which has been."*
> *"Given freely."*
> *"Memory shared is pain . . ."*

The next word faltered on the edge of her tongue. As she struggled for it, the image fractured, intent collapsing. The magic crashed around her with a snap of recoil like a physical slap. Claire flinched.

". . . lightened."

Claire rubbed at her cheek, though the sensation of being struck covered her whole body, not just her face. "What was that?"

"The punishment for failure," Jorga said. "Magic takes energy, power. When it can't go to the intended purpose, it has to go somewhere. Now focus. I got a little something that time. A tree? Again. Sing."

"I—"

"No excuses. Sing."

Claire bristled. If these were her grandmother's methods, no wonder her mother ran away. "I'm not a child. Stop treating me like one."

"Do you want to learn or not? You won't learn anything complaining and arguing."

No longer did she want to share a pleasant memory

with Jorga. Instead, she latched on to another recollection, discarding the bland Song whose words she could only half remember and seizing on the feelings associated with this memory.

> "Terror. Foes. Death."
> "Sweat so cold."
> "Heart stopping."

She formed the memory, quivering with the terror of standing weaponless and surrounded by the entire Northern army, knowing she was going to die, and flung it at Jorga. Then she enlarged the sensation as she switched to the moment her Song had first brought Dal to bear down upon her. Claire lost herself in reliving the passions that had been projected onto her, sending them at Jorga.

> "Evil. Hate. Contempt."
> "An ant squished under a heel."
> "All life to be wiped away."
> "Darkness within light."
> "Destruction."
> "Kill—"

"Stop!" Jorga had cringed down into a ball on the horse, hands over her head. "Stop! That's not possible."

Claire closed her mouth, shutting off the Song.

Before she could apologize for her thoughtless use of the magic, Bromisto and Errol came running with questions, but Jorga already struggled upright again. She waved the boys away.

"What did you do?" Jorga demanded. "That wasn't the image of a memory. I didn't see anything."

Claire bit her lip. "I think I sent the emotions from a memory. I'm . . . I'm sorry."

"Don't be sorry. That might be an entirely new use of the magic." Jorga gave a nod. "You are of my blood, after all. Hmm." Her eyes turned inward. "If we could merge the two, you'd have a powerful tool to impress those old brood hens at the Rose Among Thorn gathering. It will be triple the work and preparation, but if we practice it every chance we get, you should have it perfected before we arrive."

Claire stifled a groan. *Triple the work.* Triple the difficulty, Jorga meant. Claire didn't mind the work of using magic, but the balancing act was another story. She already felt drained from one attempt at sharing the emotions, wrung out and tired. Handling that much pure feeling daily was not going to be fun.

And yet, a smile of pride pulled at her lips for having done something new.

It wasn't such a surprise, after all. Women of the Song kept to themselves so much, private in the extreme, that they rarely shared their memories, let alone ever discussed feelings with each other. Claire got the sense from her grandmother that emotions were something to keep hidden, and probably considered shameful—while she had found it second nature to share her thoughts with her mother and then Ramiro. For the Women of the Song, doing so would be pure horror. Which led her onward to another worry.

"Grandmother, why did you call them old hens? How hard is it going to be to get their help?" She already knew the Women of the Song didn't like meddling with outsiders. If speaking to them about Dal was such a waste of time, maybe she'd rather deliver her warning and leave.

"They're 'old hens' because they tend to scratch around in circles, set in their ways and proud of it."

Claire closed one eye as she tactfully kept from saying that described Jorga very well.

"But"—Jorga held up a finger—"with Errol and the few others like him to back you up and the extreme nature of this challenge to our way of life, I'd say their taking you seriously are even odds. Showing you have the power of my family line will definitely help. Now try that again, but this time, direct it at a tree instead of me." Jorga sniffed. "Never thinks before she acts. We'll knock some sense in that silly noggin of yours. Try it again, girl, if you can remember what you did the first time."

Claire glared, suddenly filled with enough prickly anger again, and drew herself up straight. *Silly, am I?* It looked like gathering up the required emotions wouldn't be a problem with Jorga around to set her back up. Just from spite, Claire Sang a different tune Jorga had taught her days ago, relying on the moisture in the air to help carry the magic:

"Hear me across the void."
"Distance is no bar."
"Heed my call."

The Speak on the Wind Song was short and easy enough to remember. For the last line, she inserted Ramiro's name. The longer she held the notes on the ending, the more powerful and on-tune her Singing, the better the range of the magic, though she knew well enough her call would never reach him in the desert, no matter how perfect her voice. She put her all into Singing his name anyway, letting the notes belt from her tongue with power and holding them as long as her breath held out—all the while making sure not to make the message a cry for help. Instead, she used her earlier trick of inserting emotion, adding a touch of satisfaction and well-being. If Ramiro should happen to receive her call, she wanted him to know she was fine and in no danger—for the time being.

Bromisto and Errol turned to watch, their eyes wide with astonishment. Bromisto whistled. Errol put his hands over his ears and hunched his head. Her uncle was deaf to magic and likely tone deaf as well.

His discomfort didn't shake her voice, but she did reluctantly let the Song die.

Claire quickly vowed to do the same every day that separated them. It might not do anything to reassure Ramiro, but it made her feel better, closer somehow. She had a feeling she was going to need that encouragement in the future.

"Satisfied?" Jorga snapped with a scowl. "Got that out of your system? Now, how about we get down to business? Sing."

CHAPTER 8

Teresa found sleep visited her but fitfully during the few hours of darkness they had to rest. She lay with eyes open long before the dawn, having discovered she entirely lacked the nerves of a solider to take repose while she could. The others slept the sleep of exhaustion, while she tossed and turned, rendered too restless, anxious for morning to give her a view of Colina Hermosa.

As light crept into the storage room and all stirred, she couldn't stop staring at her first glimpse of the destruction, but it failed to settle her, rendering her unfit for conversation and with no appetite for breakfast. The company of others set her teeth on edge and she knew she'd be fit for nothing until she sought out the university and found her peace. She had to be sure.

The new *alcalde* and old had yet to emerge from

the storage room, but Father Telo fed sticks to the fire and Ramiro stood at the well, filling water skins in preparation for their departure.

She sidled up to Ramiro. "Cousin, I would take a little walk and satisfy myself the university is truly gone."

He stared at her, then frowned. "I saw the towers fall on the night it burned."

"I understand that. It is just something I *must* do. Like you must turn yourself in." His face folded in on itself that she would use such against him, and she rushed on: "I will walk to the gate and take the main avenue. I can't miss the way with that route."

He set down the bucket he held. "Then I'll come with you."

"No!" she almost shouted. "This is something I must do alone. If you come with me, who will guard your parents?" She couldn't explain why she didn't want his company—not even to herself. She couldn't even explain where the determination came to go in the first place. Only that it would ease her mind that her home was truly lost and give her some task. Plus she sensed her short absence would give Ramiro time to speak alone with his family before their inevitable split.

She gestured at her shorn hair and round figure. "What Northern is going to care about harassing me? I've nothing to steal. And I don't believe looting means much to our enemy since . . . *it* appeared."

"I will go with her," Father Telo said. "I'm not much protection, but no one should wander around alone."

She didn't anticipate Father Telo's resolve to walk with her, but she welcomed his company nonetheless. In the few days she'd spent with the priest, she found his companionship both valuable and calming, without being intruding. He often achieved the resolve she lacked, and she very much feared that going into the heart of the enemy to capture a madwoman would take all the determination she could muster.

Hurt filled Ramiro's eye that she preferred the friar's company over his, but he shrugged. "If you must, then hurry. And be careful."

"I will." She smiled and clapped a hand on his shoulder, realizing her friend had changed in their time apart. Gone was the constant questioning of his judgment and the emotional reactions. He'd grown into the beard he now wore so well.

By the time they reached the main gate, the sun had climbed higher in the fresh, new sky, sparkling among the ruins of Colina Hermosa, and Teresa drew in a deep lungful of air, despite the taint of smoke that lingered. Even in death, there was a painful beauty to be found here still. Gaping towers and charred upright posts lit by the first rays had an eerie elegance as she picked her way through the rubble. In places, only ash and a timber or two remained, while other structures had escaped the full force of the fire and lay in a toppled sprawl. Somewhere a desert wren called, the sound haunting in its solitude. It resonated and echoed the emptiness she'd been feeling all night.

She was the only member of their small group to see the destruction for the first time. All the others had been there when the city burned. When they'd arrived, the night had stolen the scene from her. Now, escape from the truth proved impossible. And it seemed that one reality hitting her in the face invited others upon her in an inescapable tide.

The loss of a home and the only family to sustain her over the last years since the passing of her parents had left a giant hole. She missed the pace and flow of the university with an ache that never truly left her. And since the role of motherhood had been thrust upon her in the form of a hundred refugee children, she had discovered exactly what else she was missing. Their childish hugs and needs had satisfied something inside she'd never expected existed. Then that too had been taken as she'd set the children aside to be of more use in stopping the Northerners. Even now, she wasn't sure which way her regret swung heaviest, but seeing the charred remains spread out around her brought loss to the forefront of her thoughts.

"Do you think it could be rebuilt?" slipped from her mouth before she could stop the wistful words.

"All things can be accomplished with God's grace," was her companion's predictable reply.

She let her lip curl, but at herself and not the priest.

Hadn't she witnessed two possible miracles the other day? And yet she still felt doubt. Not even being in the midst of the rarest and most prized phenomena of her civilization—returned from history—could make her put aside her skepticism. She found herself humming a nursery rhyme, the words playing in her head.

> *Saints above,*
> *Saints below.*
> *God's hand spiritual,*
> *God's rule made flesh.*
> *Covet not the miracle,*
> *It brings death.*

Common sense warned those blessed with miracles didn't savor God's favor long. Like Alvito, her soldier friend who made a miraculous return to health only to die within the fortnight while saving a group of refugees—including Teresa. Wielding such powers led to martyrdom and worse—a warning she intended to heed.

A toppled wall of loose brick and stucco blocked the path forward, covering the whole avenue. She sighed. Wisdom said to turn back. Instead, Teresa crouched on all fours to crawl over the obstacle. Despite the destruction, she recognized that they'd passed the shops that lined the street nearer to the front gate and had entered the affluent neighborhood outside the walls of her former home. Just a little farther and surely she could see the first building of the university, though the towers should have been visible long ago. She couldn't stop now.

"Be careful. Don't cut yourself." With that warning to avoid shedding blood, Father Telo gamely staggered up the hill of shattered stone after her, despite his handicap, arms spread wide for balance as debris shifted under him. "But perhaps what you should really do is ask yourself about the wisdom of holding on to the past and what you expect to find when we arrive, child."

Teresa froze, wiping a soot-stained hand across her brow. Her already worn and dirty poncho and trousers had added numerous dabs of ash and cinders to their collection of dirt and dried sweat.

The priest saw right through her. She couldn't deny that a tiny part of her whispered that another miracle could have spared the university—that the buildings would be whole, the community of people intact and waiting for her. No matter how much louder the rest of her shouted that it wasn't possible, the tiny voice remained. What was this mad quest across a burnt and dangerous city, but a last-ditch attempt to prove the hope correct?

She sat on the pile of whitewashed stucco, now shattered into a million pieces—too much like her soul. "You're right, Father. It's a waste of time better spent in other ways—and dangerous as well."

The priest caught up to her. "That's not what I

meant, child. I suggest you examine your soul on whether seeing will put your ghosts to rest. I didn't mean to imply the journey unnecessary." He glanced at the stub of his arm. "I'm the last person to say closure is worthless. I took you on a feckless quest to kill Ordoño, only to lack the heart at the last minute."

The weight of the sky pressed down. What clouds had gathered during the cool of the evening had disbursed without a drop of rain, leaving an empty blue to the horizon. The air hung stale and still around them, promising more heat. The bird no longer sang. Teresa reached the top of the pile, getting a view of more destruction, stretching as far as she could see and surely encompassing what remained of the university. A larger section of rubble topped across the space must have been the astronomy tower. There lay the twisted iron of the ornamental scrollwork gate. A tear gathered in her eye and then another as all came crashing down around her in the space of a heartbeat, and with the tangle of emotions, indecision bloomed. She caught at the words tumbling from her gut.

"Father, can we sit for a minute? I'm not quite ready to go back."

"Of course." He sank to a lumpy seat beside her to the clink of stone rearranging.

The tiny voice of hope choked and died within her, while the man waited beside her, his presence as restful and patient as though he sat at a deathbed.

Which it was in a way, she chided herself.

The sun beat upon her uncovered head and she cared not. Finally, Father Telo shifted.

"A long pilgrimage for silence, my child." But his eyes crinkled in amusement to show he was teasing and not rebuking. "I find from experience that it helps to speak about it. Loss comes to us all." He held up his arm that ended above the wrist. "Sharing with a fellow human or even talking to our Lord or the saints—"

"No . . . I don't know . . . maybe." She had not confessed to a priest in years. Not since the last had bid her repent or burn. First Wife Beatriz had confessed shortly after she arrived at the monastery, and Teresa believed *Alcalde* Julian—or former *Alcalde*, she corrected—had, not long after his cure. But she had never felt the need—had always kept her life private out of necessity, lest she be judged. Had spent her life hiding and not only from priests, but everyone around so they wouldn't spy out her secret. The part of her no one would accept.

The tiny voice sprang into action again, accusing her in a whisper that secrecy had only ever gotten her loneliness.

The loss of hope slapped her in the face with other deficiencies. Her life at the university that she thought held so much contentment seemed as empty as the sky at this moment. What she had believed to be her friends and family were reduced to their true sphere of business acquaintances—people to share a drink with and speak about their day, but with neither side really listening to the other. Drawn together because of their shared location and experiences, but with feeble connections. Had she given much thought to any of them since learning the city burned? Worried over any of their fates? Their names had become as faded and empty of meaning as if she'd been separate from them for years instead of weeks. She saw the flimsiness of her relationships clearly for the first time.

"I have no family, Father. Parents dead. No siblings. With an exception or two, no one in the whole wide world to care whether I live or die." An unexpected sob caught at her throat and she ducked her head.

"Ramiro is your cousin, surely he—"

"A joke, Father. From our first meeting. No real kinship exists. My parents died eight—no eleven years ago. I've fooled myself since then. There is no one. Spending time with the children made me see the truth." She found it less and less easy to laugh as the days wore past and the bad news grew. Gone her normally cheerful attitude, replaced with a troubled heart and a frown.

"The refugee children you mentioned?" He took her hand with a gentle smile on his face. "Yes, the young have the ability to bring truth before us. The Lord sayeth, 'Suffer the little children.'"

Bitterness stabbed Teresa from a thousand directions at his words. Long ago, she'd convinced herself she wanted nothing to do with having children or a family life—that work could be enough to plug a void that shouldn't exist. Now that twisted like a knife, for her choices had left her with no one.

Self-loathing renewed for being born different from everyone around her.

A truth she'd only confessed once before and been shamed for it. A lesson in never putting trust in anyone, even those supposed to be supportive.

Yet, Father Telo's strong face showed only concern as he waited for her to speak. He'd had compassion for even the worst of the Northern murderers, refusing to kill Ordoño or condemn Santabe. Here was a good man.

And what had hiding ever gotten her besides loneliness?

"I can never have children of my own—a family."

His answer came quickly with the ease of long practice in quelling doubt. "I don't know any who haven't spoken so at some point. You are young. You mustn't fret about these things. Love will come to you in time—once these dangerous threats have passed. Unless you mean, your health. Has a healer given you cause to doubt?"

"No, you don't understand." She hesitated, wanting to grasp at the escape he provided. Her differences could remain hidden if she drew back and let him believe his first instinct.

Somewhere stone fell against stone. Once again she forced herself to really see the collapse around her. To rebuild was possible but the city would not resemble what it had been in her lifetime. Dwelling on false hopes and dreams only kept her from achieving her true objective of being herself and not pretending.

"It's not that, Father. I . . . I don't see men in that way . . . for marriage. I . . . see women."

"Ah." His face cleared. "A difficult road, indeed, as a specialist in studying cultures must know." His hand squeezed hers. "I thank you for sharing your heart with me. Even when two blind men stumble down the street, it helps if they lean upon each other. I am not sure I can help, but I'm here for you to lean against."

She tightened her hold on his fingers, and his shoulder brushed hers. He spoke first, "Always I've felt that a child, whether born in the slums or a palace, is loved the same by our Lord. That a man with a crippled limb is looked on as kindly as one with straight. That women are favored with the same gifts and talents and intelligence as men. For nothing happens without intention from our Lord. Nothing. Do not feel shame for being what the Lord made you, though not all in the church agree with me on that. Another reason why I swore my oath to our Father and not the church. I don't know why they see so often with the eyes of intolerance."

He shook his head.

"But," Telo continued, "I do know that what the heart desires steadfastly and with humility to our Lord, He provides. If you wish for family with all your might, it will be found. And I think you do Ramiro a disservice, being so quick to deny his kinship. I'm sure he would claim you are *sangre* kin at the least—a sister to his heart, more likely. If nothing else, this unworthy priest counts you as family. You may always speak to me."

"Thank you." Teresa nodded, feeling like the newest novice at a debate, struck dumb from an overflow of emotion, and they sunk into companionable silence. This time the quiet brought repose instead of self-incrimination. She looked out over the loss of her home and former life and slowly let it go to embrace the new.

May it bring me better things.

She sniffled and rubbed at her nose with her sleeve. "I don't know what came over me, Father. I apologize for losing control."

To her shock, he pinched her cheek, beaming at her. "That is what family is for. We are all bruised in spirit, like fruit dropped by the tree, but all the sweeter for our bad spots. We make one juicy pie."

She laughed. "I will speak to Ramiro. You are right that I did him a disservice."

Father Telo shivered, eyes cast toward the sky. "I feel we will need all the kinship we can pull upon."

"Amen."

The air smelled of rot. Not the first time on their outing when buried bodies must be hiding in the ruins. But then the light dimmed as though a shadow sailed over them.

Teresa glanced up, but saw no clouds or obstructions. The sunlight had simply . . . become less.

"What?" Her question sounded thin, like a child's toy whistle in the street. Her shoulders hunched, knees curling to her chest. Instinctively, she knew the failing light meant Dal. Somewhere he struck. Her heart pounded and her body locked rigid as if she were a rabbit with a dog sniffing nearby.

Father Telo froze at her side, neither of them daring to breathe. Thrice she counted to twenty, her mind incapable of any other effort, then a breeze ruffled her hair and the sunlight expanded back to normal, beating upon her exposed skin once again.

She gasped, but the priest was already scrambling to his feet. "Hurry," he said. "We must check on our companions. I pray that was not aimed at them." He turned to totter down the pile of stone and she hurried after him.

CHAPTER 9

Ramiro gripped the rope as he watched Teresa and Father Telo leave on their exploration of the city. He hauled the bucket out of the well with too much vehemence, so that water slapped over the rim, wetting his feet. He cursed, though it was really his friends' going without him that had him worried. Then a dry nose on the back of his neck swung him around to find Sancha, emerged from the storage room.

"Sorry, girl." He set the full bucket on the well casing, then stroked her dapple-gray neck in apology that his mood had reached out to the mare. "I didn't mean to take you away from your breakfast."

Sancha's ears pricked forward, and she stamped a hoof.

"I don't think they should go, but I don't have any right to order civilians around." Or any right to order anyone while he waited to receive judgement from Captain Gonzalo. As a deserter, he was less than qualified to be an example, let alone to force his choices on a friend. And he couldn't refute that Teresa had been right that his parents required protection as well. Somebody needed to stay. That didn't keep him from feeling torn in two. "I'm sure they'll be all right."

He turned to check the narrow pathway along the wall, but Teresa was already out of sight. Logic said they couldn't hide inside all the time. They'd already voted to brave the sunlight and leave on their separate tasks after eating and packing up. Time pressed and some risks had to be accepted—that didn't mean he liked seeing his friends' and family's lives in danger. Claire, Teresa, his parents—he couldn't be with all of them. Soon enough his parents would be on their own; staying with them now was the least he could do. It all came back to letting those he loved make their own choices. He had enough wisdom now to know all of them had to decide for themselves— eventually.

Sancha blew at him, as his thoughts turned to someone else he'd left unwillingly. "I'm sure Claire's fine, too." Claire risked the sunlight as well. The swamp was treacherous enough by day, she couldn't always travel by night. He could no longer protect her either. It seemed that all their choices had shrunk until only the most dangerous remained.

Like going to a Northern encampment to find and

kidnap an unwilling—and incredibly powerful—priestess.

He set his jaw. He'd managed the same sort of task with taking Claire from the swamp and it had turned out for the best. He pictured her wheat-colored hair shining in the sunlight and a challenging light in her blue eyes . . .

More than the best.

"Claire *has* to be all right," he told Sancha. He didn't think he could get through the rest of his life without her. Knowing she waited for him was about all that held him together, and no six-foot priestess was going to slow him down, no matter how many people she'd murdered in the past. After that, he'd find a way to prove to Captain Gonzalo that his desertion was warranted. His mother might think he had a death wish, but that was far from the truth.

He put his hands to the task, filling a water skin, and allowed his mind to concentrate on their strategy. Though he hadn't fully voiced his doubts, he didn't find going after Santabe a solid plan. How were they to get inside an occupied city, find one priestess, and spirit her away without the entire Northern army chasing? And all of that would be the *easiest* part of the job. He didn't have the slightest idea how to get Santabe to tell them how to stop a god she worshipped with blind intensity.

Their whole plan hinged on her knowing something *and* sharing that knowledge.

Impossible.

And yet, he wasn't sure there was a better option open to them.

That thought, perhaps more than anything, bothered him. Because while Ramiro wasn't beyond helping himself when the need called, the fact was, the figure from his dream promised him help. So why had that dried up? A hint would have been timely. Yet, he remembered no dreams from the night before, just a mix of nightmares that left his teeth on edge.

But maybe this lack of help was entirely the point: He was being left to make his own decision without guidance so that he could learn . . . well, something.

Julian came out of the other storage room, stretching his back and yawning. "An early start for you, my son."

"A late one for you," Ramiro teased. "The benefits of no longer being *alcalde*? But then Mother isn't up either, and she hasn't that excuse."

"Oh, your mother is up." His father scratched Sancha under the chin by way of greeting the mare. "Awake enough to give me an earful this morning about my idea for us to separate. I do believe if I hadn't just returned from the dead, she'd have rejected the notion. As it is, I was spared the worst."

Ramiro frowned. "Then she's saving the worst for me."

"'*Prevenido vale por dos*,'" Julian quoted.

"I don't think any forewarning is enough preparation to overcome Mother."

Julian clapped him on the back. "Welcome to
adulthood, my son, welcome to being a man. Keep
repeating yourself and she'll wind down—that works
forty percent of the time."

"Or I could remind her it was all your idea."

His father gave a mock shiver. "Never that. Blam-
ing others riles her up more. I tried that over the
silk-dress misunderstanding in the fourth year of our
marriage and it backfired. I do believe if she hadn't
been pregnant with your brother, she would have
moved to your grandfather's house."

Ramiro had heard the story enough to know the
wisdom of his father's advice.

"I don't think she'll go into our separation in front
of others." Julian looked around. "But where is the
priest and our ambassador? Not left us, I hope."

"In the city, settling some ghosts."

Julian touched mind, heart, liver, and spleen, the
motion awkward and unpracticed. "We all do what
we must. Speaking of which, do you want to talk
about Gonzalo? I've known him some years, I could
advise you." Julian scratched his beard. "Your mother
can pardon you, by the way—it is an *alcalde*'s preroga-
tive. In truth, the difficulty might be in stopping her."

"I keep forgetting Mother is *alcalde* now. So
strange."

"Your mother will do very well as *alcalde*—when

her family can stop stealing her away from the job. What about her offer?"

The offer tempted, but what sort of man let his parents solve his difficulties the whole of his life? The decision to dodge his military duties had been no one else's. "I'll stand on my own two feet. I'd not have her first act be showing favoritism to me."

"So like your brother. I told her your answer wasn't going to change, but I also promised to ask you anyway. That's why she's sulking—never let her hear I said that." Julian clapped him on the shoulder and strode over to the fire. "Put me to work. What can I do to get us moving faster?"

"You can divide the food remaining between those five saddlebags." Julian nodded, and they worked in silence some moments. Ramiro finished filling the water skins and added them to the growing piles of readied supplies, then refilled the bucket for the horses to drink. By the time he returned from tending the animals, Julian had dealt decisively with the food and brought the blankets from the storage room. His father sat by the fire, eating dried figs.

As Ramiro joined him, Julian said, "All set?"

"Hi-ya." The question wasn't directed at the completed work surrounding them but the task before them. A sudden influx of nerves, striking now that Ramiro's hands were no longer busy, threatened to trip him up, making fewer words easier to manage for both of them. In a flash he realized such must have been Salvador's feeling before his brother led them on a hunt for a witch that had resulted in Salvador's death and finding Claire. Ramiro had learned then that leadership had its price. The grim reminder shut off any other desire for conversation.

"God go with you, my son." Julian ate his figs and that would have been the end, except Beatriz came bustling out of the storage room. Every button done, her hair gleamed smooth and perfectly arranged without the benefit of a mirror, though Beatriz had set aside her mantilla for a simple black veil hanging limp around her face.

"Enough of this manly attitude. I will have a proper parting. Hug your mother."

He complied, squeezing her hard enough to force the air from her lungs. She gave him a swat. "Are you ready? Do you have enough—"

"I've plenty of socks, Mother. Every time I tried to throw some away, Claire put them back in my bags."

Beatriz smiled like a cat with cream. "I quite like that girl. I didn't think I would, but then I saw her use a plank. She put down that Northern deserter with spirit to spare. And she speaks her mind. Fronilde and her quiet ways suited your brother. He needed a traditional wife. You, always with holes in your clothes, never settling still, could never be satisfied with such tameness. You take after your father in that. A wife who rolls bandages and sits at home won't do. You need someone more outspoken and adventurous, like me. I told your father so."

"I don't remember any such—" Julian started.

Beatriz held up a finger. "Don't start with me or I'll remember who decided we needed to split up. Who is *alcalde* here and should be making the decisions?" Julian's mouth closed, and Beatriz rolled onward. "I didn't know about a witch at first, but I've changed my mind. And when she brings the other witches, they'll find we welcome a woman in charge also."

Ramiro had a sudden vision of his mother as the most determined and single-minded leader ever elected from Colina Hermosa. His people didn't know what they'd gotten themselves into with their vote. It might be the saving of them. But Beatriz wasn't finished. She gripped Ramiro's chin. "Have you settled things properly with Claire?"

"Well, I . . . we . . . she knows how I feel."

"And?" Beatriz prompted. "It's war time. There's no sense in taking our time. You let her know you love her. How did she answer?"

Ramiro found he couldn't meet his mother's eyes. He sensed the disappointment coming already. He pulled his chin from her relentless grip. "She felt the same . . . but"—his mother's expression sharpened—"I never asked her as such. It didn't seem like the right time with treason hanging over me."

"Nonsense! She feels the same. You're sure." Beatriz gave a sharp nod. "Then Father Telo will say the first banns and he can do the second from inside Aveston tomorrow. This is no time for half measures. I let one son put off a wedding, and I'll not let that happen with another."

Ramiro opened his mouth to insist that he'd never spoken to Claire and hadn't an answer on whether she would marry him and leave her kind, then let it go. Claire would never know banns had been read unless he told her—likely she wouldn't care about an antiquated religious tradition—but the empty ritual would mean much to his mother. It cost nothing to let her be happy in this.

"A very good idea, Mother."

"Father Telo. Where is the man?"

"Gone for a walk," Julian said smoothly.

"A walk?" Beatriz huffed. "When we are ready to leave? What was the man thinking?"

"Most inconsideration of him, I know," Julian teased. "He should anticipate his *alcalde*'s every want. *Mi amor.*"

Beatriz's hands flew to her hips, but then she laughed. "Now and forever."

Ramiro sensed an old joke between his parents being revisited and escaped to saddle Sancha. The other horses were already done. Beatriz followed him to the well. "Horse, you will watch over my son"— her voice broke and recovered—"and see he comes to no harm."

Sancha whinnied and scraped a hoof across the pavers, and Ramiro left off adjusting straps and buckles to embrace Beatriz again. "It will be fine, Mother—Lady *Alcalde*."

She hid it well, but how could she not be suffering? Last time they parted like this, she'd sent out two sons—just one had returned. Now the world was trying to end. The brave face she put on was a thin mask.

Ramiro squeezed harder as it was all he could do. Promises could come to nothing. He knew that well enough.

A stink of rotting bodies filled the air. The sunlight dimmed.

Before he could get a solid look at the sky, a force of despair and worthlessness buckled their knees and sent all of them cringing in the dirt. *Hatred. Disdain for life. Desire to wipe creation away.* All slammed into Ramiro. The horses within the storage room screamed in panic. Sancha's ears lay flat, her front knees folded on the ground and her neck stretched out. Beatriz trembled beside him on the ground, her eyes leaking tears.

The edge of Dal's power hit them, not his direct malice. Ramiro quickly realized the difference, but could do nothing—even the periphery was enough to show the god's strength. Not a muscle twitched, not even to crawl toward his mother to drag her to the safety of the dark storage room. His body shook and his thoughts tumbled. The fear of drawing Dal's direct gaze so terrified him that he could not so much as lift his head.

Their will was nothing to the merest brush of Dal's intent.

Worthless. Powerless.

They had no more chance of stopping this demon than an ant had of lifting a boulder. Not with a thousand ants. Not with a million.

All would perish.

Like Salvador. Like all his companions in uniform. Soldiers. Women. Children. Humanity would end. Darkness would swallow the light, to rule forever.

Dust clogged his nostrils. Stones gritted under his hands. Oh, to be as lowly as the earth so as not to draw Dal's attention. Lower than a blind worm, crawling undetected and so spared.

Worthless. Unimportant.

Ramiro spat out a mouthful of dirt. Why was he doing the work of the dark god for him? Dipping his head, abasing himself without a struggle. For what? To earn a few more moments of life?

Pure stubborn determination bloomed, instilled in him by two proud parents, followed quickly by shame.

Not this soul. He was no worm. A tiny unafraid part of Ramiro refused to bow down and cower to evil. He braced his arms against the ground and shoved upward. Then his knees locked, putting him on his feet. His back slowly straightened, every inch gained a strain by locked and uncooperative muscles. Tears of terror still flowed, but he stood upright, chin raised. If his throat was to be cut, let it be as a man, not a worm.

He stood alone, teeth bared to the wind.

The sunlight flared to full strength. The demon vanished, and left him panting as if he'd fought for his life. Sancha shook her entire body like she'd rolled in dust, and scrambled to her feet. Ramiro turned to help his mother up as Julian stood more slowly. Somewhere, people had died, torn apart by the wrath of an insane god—he prayed the malice was turned on no one he loved—but his family had survived this day. Somehow, they'd survive the next and the next, and put an end to this. Help or no help, he'd find a way, even if he had to do so with his bare hands.

CHAPTER 10

Father Telo looked at the massive sprawl of the Northern camp around Aveston and noticed nothing unusual, despite what Ramiro said about his last visit.

"Do you see the change?" Ramiro asked. An entire day had passed since Teresa's confession to Telo and Dal's forcing them to grovel in the dust, and they'd all managed to put aside the effects. Their split complete, they'd reached Aveston with good speed.

Telo checked the scene again. The tents and wagons looked to be arranged neatly, much as they had been when he'd been a captive to Ordoño. Black-and-yellow uniforms filled his vision, going about ordinary tasks. No soldiers weaved around drunkenly today. The flow of refugees exiting Aveston had slowed to a steady trickle from the flood Ramiro described—that was to be expected. The only thing new was a row of white-robed priests spaced fifty feet apart around the perimeter of the camp and the gates of Aveston, all holding red Diviners—arranged like a living wall. Telo's eyebrows rose for that, but the thirty or forty priests simply stood there in perfect formation, doing nothing and ignoring what refugees or soldiers moved between them. In fact, they looked bored.

"Do you see it?" Ramiro asked again. They hunkered low among a jumble of boulders in the sand. He'd led them through a grove of olive trees, where they'd left their horses tied to take a quick look before they approached the *ciudad-estado.*

"The priests?" Teresa asked, picking out the most obvious incongruity.

"No, beyond that. I figure the priests are there to keep more troops from deserting."

"There's no confusion among the enemy anymore," Telo said, chewing on that information. "They've recovered from Ordoño's murder. From the emergence of Dal."

"Exactly. Which means somebody has taken charge of the military again," Ramiro added. "Put them in order. Making sure no more desert. And do you see anything else?"

Telo sat on his heels. "People only go out of the gates. They don't go in the city."

"Right again," Ramiro said. "Which makes our job of getting inside that much harder."

Who would willingly go into an enemy enclave? They'd stick out like a late arriving parishioner on a feast day. Telo rubbed at an itch in the healing skin of his left arm. The pains of his phantom limb had ceased days ago, except for occasional twinges, but what remained still hurt him, though the flesh had healed. "You're sure the priests are inside the city and not the camp?"

"They came from there before. I think we start there." Ramiro eased into the trees and stood once all three of them were under cover of the branches. "Do you still think your plan to get inside will work?"

Telo shrugged. Since the healing of Julian, he no longer worried in the same way. Gone was the doubt, replaced with a new tranquility. He felt as though he had passed some test in sparing Ordoño, and the Lord had their backs. They had witnessed unmistakable miracles for the first time in centuries. He had perfect serenity for his future. Heaven waited to receive him, and he would not fret what came before—even if that should be martyrdom. That did not mean they should take foolish chances, but he felt some risk had to be ventured. "Madmen and the simpleminded. I think I'm about to be a slice of both. My idea has the same chances as before. Will you trust me?"

"Do we have a choice?" The younger man began untying the horses. "The rest of us don't have the glimmer of an idea on how to get inside, unless you want to fight our way in."

Nobody bothered to answer that foolish suggestion.

"What about the priests outside the walls?" Teresa demanded. "Are they going to bother us? Maybe Santabe is among them. That would save us a whole lot of time looking for her."

"Sorry to disappoint you," Telo said. "Whatever they are up to, they all wear the single sun earring or none at all. I think we can safely assume nobody of high rank is among them. From their boredom, whatever their task, it would be given to the most junior among them. Our prey isn't there. Saints," he muttered, "I wish I knew what the red Diviners meant."

Ramiro turned from the horses. His face looked grim. "I've seen this before in my dreams—a line of Northern priests outside a city—all with red Diviners. Only in the dream, it was one of their cities, not ours, before the town fell . . . to *it*. Keeping people from fleeing perhaps?"

"But the refugees," Teresa pointed out.

"Right . . ."

Telo puffed out a breath. They had enough burden without the threat of Dal starting another massacre here. Best to take his companions' minds off that. "'Trust in the Lord because I've seen miracles,'" he quoted from the blessed Santiago. "As well have we, my children. Onward."

Telo placed the limp circlet of flowers and greenery they'd made a few hours ago around Ramiro's neck and then put the other around Teresa. A quick stop at the deserted monastery had supplied them with what Telo needed. "Remember, smile and hold hands. Look happy. Kiss when you hear the signal." He put a crown of wilting saguaro blossoms and woven barley stems on Teresa's shorn hair.

Ramiro's armor and sword were all hidden under bags packed on Sancha. One sword was as useless as a priest at a brothel—more likely to draw only ridicule and unwanted attention than to convert any unbelievers. Even a thousand swords would be too few, so better to show none. In addition, they didn't dare leave the horses outside the city, so Ramiro held their reins in one hand while gripping Teresa's hand with the other.

"It'll work," Telo insisted, as much for his benefit as the other two, as they headed for the road before Aveston. The idea had come to him in a flash when Lady *Alcalde* Beatriz insisted he read the banns for the witch girl, Claire, and her son. Put that together with the Northerners' superstition and they might have a chance.

Telo gave a nod. They would do.

They looked the part. The problem was, they didn't have an idea how the Northerners would react. None of their knowledge of the Northerners including anything about how their culture viewed weddings or even if they had such an equivalent—but, as Ramiro said, they had nothing better.

Telo wished he didn't have the sinking feeling his companions' trust in him had more to do with their ingrained childhood lessons in following priests blindly. Nobody questioned a priest, with the possible exception of fellow priests. A little doubt might have found flaws in his idea.

Too late now.

He whispered a quick prayer, reassuring himself that Ramiro had said Dal overlooked the insane and the simpleminded. His plan had an element of both. The ten or twelve refugees on the road blinked in surprise as the three emerged from the olive grove and headed *toward* the city instead of away. A group of twenty or more Northern soldiers at the gates drew to attention, hands on swords, as they approached, but Telo stopped and held out an open book of scripture with his one good hand, using his booming voice.

"Good countrymen, I publish the banns of marriage between Ramiro Juan Alvarado of Colina Hermosa and Claire of Mortífero Swamp. If any know of any just cause or impediment why these two are not to be joined in holy matrimony, you must declare it. This is the second time of asking. Let us not say that fear of the unknown put us off from following the Lord's will."

Telo lowered the book. Technically, banns were supposed to be read in the place where the couple lived, thus the first reading in Colina Hermosa. But with nobody there to hear the words in the burnt-out city or Mortífero Swamp, Aveston was as good a place as any for the next reading. It felt enough like a farce to have only one-half of the participants available and the other represented by proxy.

And if maybe a very religious people like the Northerners saw another people practicing their beliefs, a little goodwill could be gained. Telo would take all the advantage he could get.

While the Northern soldiers watched, puzzled, the refugees from Aveston broke into scattered applause. Ramiro landed a quick kiss on Teresa's cheek, and the tiny crowd came forward to clap them on shoulders and backs, the women hugging Teresa, who wore a bemused expression pasted on her face. The round woman gamely grinned and nodded as if she were truly the bride, while the bridegroom looked entirely too tense for a wedding. Ramiro had his eyes zeroed in on the soldiers at the gate, too much calculation and evaluation evident on his face, unable to leave behind his training. The boy would give them away.

Telo poked Ramiro with the book. "Smile," he whispered. "You're about to be married."

Ramiro's shoulders dropped slightly and a crooked grin spread over his face. The boy would win no awards for acting, but he looked shamefaced enough for a groom at least.

Telo led the way to the gates, tensing when he had to walk between the two priests with their red Diviners posted on either side of the road. Neither of the

STEADFAST 119

priests moved, however, and their threesome made it to the soldiers at the gate.

Telo tugged at his triple-rope belt and held the book before him like a shield. In some ways it felt a little like being in the monastery to be among so many beardless men—if it wasn't for all the light-colored eyes of greens and blues. Sweat slid down his back. "Church," he proclaimed, knowing the Northerners could understand nothing he said. "Wedding." He pointed at his companion's joined hands. "Man and wife. Inside, in a church. You follow me? We go inside." He tucked the book under his arm to panto-mime walking through the gate with his fingers, then pointed to the flowers on his companions. "Inside. I have a wedding to perform."

The puzzled expression on their beardless faces faded a little as they realized the goal behind the words, and several of the Northerners answered him with words equally incomprehensible. One made a shooing gesture toward the road.

Telo shook back his sleeve and held up both arms, displaying his stump for the first time. Lazy tolerance changed to shock. All the soldiers spoke at once and several pointed. A man went running inside Aveston.

"What is that about, priest?" Ramiro whispered through gritted teeth. "What's with that reaction?"

"They've never seen a dead man walking," Telo hissed in return, still holding up his arms. "Hurry, before they think about it too much." He'd counted on the superstitious indecision his stump would create, certain the Northerners had never seen anyone escape their priests' famous executions as the Northern priests favored cutting off hands and then their victims' heads. They could only hope the soldiers took missing one hand for having been forgiven, pardoned, and welcomed into the fold as his head was still attached. Telo walked swiftly forward, drawing the other two in his wake. The soldiers' muttering picked up, their faces showing hesitancy, but no one tried to stop him as he went past them and through the gates, hustling across the threshold of the city.

Then a most commanding voice shouted, "Stop," as sharply as a sword thrust decisively between the ribs to take the heart.

Telo did a slow turn, still with a smile pasted on his face, to peer past their horses. A new pack of uniformed Northerners had arrived, and one stood ahead of the others. Telo judged him to be their officer: a tall man with his black jacket cut longer and rolled cuffs of yellow on the ends of his sleeves. Of middle age, the green of his eyes was bright enough to pierce the distance between them instead of being a muddied hazel like so many of the other Northerners.

Teresa hissed. "I've seen that man. He was with the elite command around Ordoño when we first encountered him. One of their generals, I think."

The man wore his hair longer than Teresa's, but something about the command in his face drew Telo to a halt more readily than his barked order. Some part of him recognized to run now would end their quest before it began. Ramiro stirred uneasily at his back and Telo quickly said, "Let me handle this."

Instead of having them dragged off, the officer came to them, followed by at least twenty men. Telo had his smile ready. "What can we do for you, my son? I commend you on your command of our language."

"Priest," the man slurred. "I have seen you around our Lord Ordoño." He spared a glance for Teresa. "Her also. The game players. That was you?"

"Aye," Telo admitted. "You have taken Ordoño's place?" The blasted man gave nothing away on his face and the other Northerners all looked confused. Telo would bet his last extra sandal strap none of them understood a word spoken. One man fingered his weapon and another slapped his hand away. No doubt a tribute to their fear of Dal and desire to avoid bloodshed in the open. However, as Telo understood it, nothing stopped those surrounding them from dragging them inside to end them or from killing them after dark.

The officer spat—apparently a universal gesture—showing the first signs of emotion yet. "The next life comes. The priests say Ordoño was given his prize—no, how do you say—not prize, reward. Yes, that word. No one else wanted this task. Why are you here?"

Telo's appreciation rose. This man obviously cared too much to let his people fall to chaos. "Following law. Some things must be done in a church. Wedding, you see." At the man's frown, Telo tried again, pointing to Ramiro and Teresa, then glanced at the bright sun above them. "Husband and wife. They seek to join their lives together before the . . . next life. Must be done in a church."

The officer shook his head. "Weeding? I don't know this word. 'Church' I know, but we let no more in. We have laws, too. Food is short. There are enough of your churches outside of this city. Go there. You are a brave man, companion of Ordoño, I let you leave. Go now." He said something in his own language, and the soldiers shuffled around them, starting to herd them toward the gate.

Thrown out.

Telo set his feet. They'd reached the limits of his ideas. He had no other plans for getting into Aveston and finding Santabe. Ramiro turned toward his horse, saying something quickly, and the beast kicked out with her heels, showing her training as a warhorse and driving the Northern soldiers back. Shouts rang out. Telo sensed Ramiro shuffling under the saddlebags for his sword. Teresa had out a knife from a hidden spot in her clothing.

All around them changed to turmoil in an instant. Flowers fell from discarded wedding adornment.

Whether Dal came or not, they would die here.

Only Telo and the officer had not moved. Something lifted in Telo's heart as if a curtain had been peeled away. Truth came rushing out, and ever always afterward he would credit what he said into the chaos as the will of their Lord's hand.

"Wait, my son. We are not here for a wedding. We . . . we come to stop your god."

Telo had never seen a man choke over his own tongue before. The officer's face actually turned red. One of his men put out a supporting hand, but he brushed it aside. He shouted out commands in his own language and all went still, quiet returning, though sharp metal blades surrounded them, held back only by Ramiro's pathetically outnumbered defense.

The officer straightened his coat. "You would say this . . . aloud. But this is . . ."

"Blasphemy," Telo supplied. "Aye. I guess for you it is."

Telo stared at the man, into the fierce green of his eyes, trying to weigh what he saw. Instead of an enemy, understanding spread, and their foe turned into a fellow human. Suddenly, Telo fell into the green eyes, slipping past normal defenses and beyond to a world he'd never entered—to peer directly into another man's soul. He saw the city of Zapata unburned, and the officer wading into the turbulent waves to enjoy the sea for the first time. He experienced with the officer his joy and fear as the shift and ebb of a violent high tide tore at his legs and even drew the sand from under his unstable footing, attempting to drag the man under. Realized the man felt the same panicked instability now in being unexpectedly in charge of so many men.

The sharing of emotions went deeper, transferring to Telo the utter unpreparedness of this man to have *the* nightmare of all the Children of Dal come to life. This man never expected Dal to visit in his lifetime or indeed the lifetime of his children or great-grandchildren. The shock and horror of absorbing that information could never be understated. Despite their talk of a next life, this man only wanted to live and see his family again. He grasped for any savior—no matter in what form.

A name rose up in Telo's head: Rasdid. Somehow, Telo witnessed Rasdid's soul and it wanted to live.

The connection shattered into a million sharp shards, like a goblet crashing against stone. Telo reeled, the book of gospel dropping loose from under his clenched arm. The officer's eyes had gone round like coins.

"What . . . what witchcraft is this?" he stammered. His men muttered and sword points rose. More soldiers from the gate came running in support, weapons drawn.

Teresa shrank down near the horses, but Ramiro stood balanced on his toes like a dancer, sword high. The light in his eyes spoke of one prepared to go down fighting.

Telo waited, unable to answer what he didn't understand, but his heart said he'd witnessed another miracle. He touched heart, mind, liver and spleen.

The officer swallowed hard. "You can do this—what you said? Stop Dal?" Other soldiers cried out as the name was spoken. Some flinched from the sunlight, while others covered their head with their arms. Swords dropped from men reduced to frightened children with a word.

Telo stooped to recover the book of sermons, letting his determination swell. "For such have we been sent. It is our task to save this world or die trying. Our wrong to set right, Rasdid."

The mutters of the soldiers took on a sharper tone at this second use of a name—a name they couldn't have known. Several pulled at their left eye in some unknown gesture.

Rasdid recovered more quickly than his men, jaw setting. He jerked his chin toward the city. "Then go. Stop the sun, if you can."

Santabe kept her right hand firmly on her Diviner as she strolled through the plaza of the Ninth Sun, clasping the weapon tightly. The shoppers in the market might give her a satisfyingly wide berth, but she had been free to walk without companionship as an Enforcer for only two moon revolutions yet. She did not trust her ability to reach the Diviner before one of the Disgraced. The other priests of Dal would laugh if she admitted her fear of dying to her own Diviner, so she did not tell them. Her training to become a priest had been hard, and she had learned quickly to keep her mouth shut to avoid the strap or worse punishment.

But on patrol, punishment was the least of her worries. She knew firsthand how deceptive a Disgraced could be. They would do anything to save their miserable hides, so frightened of being sent to another life. She wouldn't put it past them to stalk a searching Enforcer for the chance to kill first by taking their Diviner. She might have patrolled as an apprentice only for one sun revolution, but she had heard the rumors and seen much of the Disgraced's trickiness. Sadly, one could not spot a Disgraced simply by looking. If that were true, there would be no Enforcers.

The people at a fruit stall moved aside as her stride slowed to look at the melons on display. With Dal high in the sky and hours of walking behind her, the sight of the melons made her mouth water. The man at the stall hastily held out a mango. "For you, Honored One. My gift." He bowed with an oily smile that made her check him again before taking the mango.

"Walk with the sun on your face," she snapped testily and the man flinched. His customers suddenly found other places to be. Such cringing still irritated her. How much easier it would be to ferret out the Disgraced for sacrifice if she didn't need to dress as a priestess. Then the people would speak freely around her and her moon-revolution number of sacrificed would be held in awe. She'd earn her first Sun-Blessed earring in half the time.

Blasphemy, the trained part of her mind shouted.

To hide from Dal was the choice of a Disgraced. Only an Enforcer of the highest level forwent the sheer-white clothing of their calling and only with permission because they hunted. She did not qualify for that honor. The bite of mango in her mouth tasted as dry as dust and she dropped the fruit to the cobblestones. She did not deserve a reward this day. She would confess her faults at the temple when her shift ended and accept the strap with head high.

Even as she turned her back, her eyes tracked furtive movement among the passersby. A child bent as small as a rat slunk for the dropped mango among the many feet. It held an arm outstretched and eyes down. Santabe took a step away, then spun lightning quick, coming up with the child fast in her grip.

"Thief," she snarled, eyes blazing.

The child sniveled in her hand, not even attempting to escape. Scrawny and underfed, it stared at her with hazel eyes under matted hair.

"Thievery is forbidden. You know this."

"Yes, Honored One," it wheezed, spreading its breath upon her hand and arm. She almost dropped it then and there. It probably crawled with fleas as well as being filthy. Its tiny body hadn't the blood to fuel two Diviners. But the law was clear, she couldn't wait for this one to grow up and become more of an offense to Dal.

Almost casually, she freed her Diviner from her belt and had mercy on the child, sending it to another life with a touch. All its muscles locked for an instant, the eyes staring at her with shock, and then she let it drop lifeless at her feet.

A shame.

Her act of mercy to spare it from sacrifice meant she couldn't add this Disgraced soul to her moon-revolution totals. Only a full blood sacrifice of hands and head counted. She would never earn her earring of rank this way. A kick of her foot turned the body so its dead eyes no longer looked her way.

She had no patience with those who pitied the poor. The poor could abide by the laws of Dal the same as everyone else. If they starved, then they should do so lawfully and have the satisfaction of passing to the next life.

On this, the church agreed with her. The priesthood didn't go so far as to condone that poverty or disease was the hand of Dal casting judgment on a soul and showing them as undeserving—yet. When it did, she would find it much easier to produce sacrifices for the cause.

She nodded at the body. "See that is cleaned up," she told the owner of the fruit stall.

He knocked his forehead to the ground, and she rolled her eyes. She didn't remember her mother or aunts being this servile. Most shoppers entering the fruit market turned around and went the other way. Santabe gazed suspiciously at any who did enter as they could be Disgraced trying to appear normal. Then she realized the people not so much rushed from her as toward the fabric market with excited whispers.

She secured her Diviner in her belt and set off that way. Where the people found excitement, there was often a Disgraced waiting to be discovered. High Priest Jemkinbu had recently completed many new

Diviners; she would earn much praise if the provided the blood to initiate them.

She followed the crowd through the fabric market, ignoring colorful silks and damasks, having no need for such extravagance anymore. Yet, out of habit, she glanced at the corner where her mother and aunts set up their stall. Empty. Summer was undeniably the best time to travel to the smaller *huets* without any merchants of their own, and she hadn't really expected to see her kin. The summer journeys could mean the difference between profit and loss. Her kin could not speak to her first in any case, unless they visited the temple at the celebration of Dal's Ascension, when the sun stood highest in the sky. No one from her kin had visited in the last two years and she did not expect them at this year's ceremony, in three weeks' time. Her family was the priesthood now.

She sniffed. Her kin might travel the roads between the towns of the Children of Dal, meeting new people and seeing new places, but she was the one who would please Dal and progress to the next life. So what if all she ever saw was the Ninth Sun market and the inside of the temple? She did her duty.

The crowd increased, though people gave way before her, shuffling back at seeing a priestess holding her Diviner sheathed in her belt. A gap opened, letting her discover the cause of the distraction: a brown man in brown clothing.

Santabe blinked even though she stood in shade.

He had skin as brown as if he'd rubbed his flesh with mud. His eyes were of brown, too, cloudy like dirty puddles. Against all law, he let a brown and ratty beard cover his face from Dal. For clothing, he wore not a proper coat, but a long piece of cloth with a hole cut out of the center for his head. Stings of leather crisscrossed his feet, leaving his brown toes exposed like a savage's. He sat upon the speaker platform reserved for priests and ate a piece of cheese.

For a minute, Santabe ground her teeth. This stranger had been many places that she couldn't even imagine. Then she realized where he sat for his rude picnic.

Blasphemy.

The foreigner spoke and her anger grew as none of the Children of Dal shouted him down or turned away. His speech was broken and imperfect as a toddler but she could understand a word or two.

". . . Strong people . . . much fight . . . wealth . . . rich for the taking . . ."

Foreigners were not exactly forbidden among the Children of Dal, but Dal did not welcome them. Sometimes scholars or politicians from other lands approached, seeking benefits or treaties, but the priests always sent them on their way unsatisfied. What did this man want here?

And why had Dal led her to be the first to discover him?

She elbowed her way past two slack-jawed soldiers

in black and yellow and strode right up to the stranger, already with her Diviner free of her belt. "You!" Her eyes blazed. "Stand up! That is the speaker platform. It is not for you." She yanked upon his arm in case he didn't understand.

Her strength moved him not at all, though he looked entirely ordinary in size and build, and she had been trained to handle much larger opposition.

Instead, he regarded her from head to toe, his weird brown eyes expressing only confidence. Seemingly coming to some conclusion, he rose and pointed to the wooden platform, getting slowly to his feet and letting the foreign words slip slowly from his tongue. "Petitioners. Speak here. Law. I petition to learn of Dal."

The people gasped and fled in earnest. Santabe's anger went white-hot. Tricked. She was used. The man obviously picked this spot, knowing full well that to encounter a priest here gave him this advantage. No petitioner who asked to learn of Dal could be turned away or sent to the next life until *the petitioner* decided they had satisfied their curiosity about Dal. Who was this foreigner to manipulate their laws? And how had he known?

"Woodsmen," she sputtered. "You spoke to the woodsmen outside of town." It could be the only way this stranger could have known how to protect himself. They must have taught this man to speak their language as well. The woodsmen, who rarely saw a priest of Dal, had started to develop offensive attitudes along with their care of the trees. Priests didn't want to bother to chase such a scant population through the hills and woods for days, only to see their prey slip away again and again. The woodsmen took pride in being difficult. They had informed this stranger how to circumvent the law.

"I would learn of Dal," he repeated.

Her bottom lip jutted out. She would be considered a fool by her superiors for giving this man a chance to speak—and now she had no choice but to escort him to the temple with safe passage. "Then come." She rammed her Diviner into her belt with extra force. This was not how her day was supposed to go.

He pointed to himself. "I Ordoño. And you?"

What kind of barbarian name is that?

The pleasant smile on his hairy face only increased her burn, but a petitioner asking to know Dal could not be refused on any question, except for the most sacred mysteries. Not that she had been taught those yet. She shoved her braid over her shoulder. She would give as little as possible. "Santabe."

"You priestess of Dal?"

"Yes," she bit out.

"You teach me?"

"No," she said much too quickly. Her flesh creeped at the suggestion. His eyes looked at her the way a man looked at a woman, much too familiarly, and not the way people should look at a priestess: with fear. His eyes traveled over her tall body, lingering on the muscles of her arms and her long braid. "You go to the high priests. They'll teach you."

His smile strengthened at her denial. "I think you teach me Dal. I teach you speak my words. We be great friend. Children of Dal like me very much. I learn you ways. We change world."

She forced a laugh at his insane words even as a shiver ran up her back, though Santabe could not say why. "And I think I'll be the one to end your miserable life and send you to the next life."

The Great Dal let that time be soon.

CHAPTER 11

Claire and the others pushed through the last of the raspberry brambles, where the fruit was beginning to ripen, to encounter a stretch of scattered cottonwoods. The dark ground was so soggy it squished underfoot. Claire took one look and shook her head, then turned to her companions and saw the same recognition in their eyes. She'd encountered places like this before: hidden death traps, worse than quicksand. The rock here was limestone, and in places centuries of erosion had turned the stone into pits of all sizes, from an inch wide to several feet across. But the pits were not the greatest danger—often only a thin crust covered caves full of groundwater where one unwary step would break through and send a person tumbling twenty feet to break their neck or drown.

Without a word being said, Claire and Bromisto

headed straight for the nearest tree on safe ground to cut branches for staffs. When Errol tried to follow them, Jorga put him to work picking berries, then slid down from the horse to ready the rope. They would have to feel forward on each step while tied together for additional safety. The treacherousness of this terrain couldn't be overstated, as unlike quicksand, here there would be no clues to give warning, just a quick drop and then inescapable water, with only the rope to pull them out before their lungs filled.

Luckily, they knew what awaited them and could prepare. Claire didn't think Ramiro or anyone unfamiliar with the swamp would have fared very well here alone.

Bromisto whistled as he swung their small hatchet among the tree limbs. The boy had scrambled up the tree like a squirrel, and Claire left finding the right-sized branches to him, busying herself with catching the tree limbs he threw down to her and striping off leaves and twigs so they wouldn't catch on clothing. Despite the danger, she hummed along with his tune, quite glad to have a break from practicing the magic. Jorga had worked her hard over the last two days and it felt good not to be under scrutiny, if only for a few minutes. Once they crossed to safer ground, however, it would be back to projecting emotions and images. Most of the time, she could hold the magic until a collection of emotions was shared, and she'd even been able to teach Jorga to match her efforts. Yet, all her work and exhaustion had earned her only a few sniffs and a grouchy "Try again."

"Gallant," Bromisto shouted to Errol in a carry-over of their earlier conversation.

Errol looked up with a mouth full of raspberries. "Buttercup."

"That's girly stuff. Thunder."

"This again?" Claire rolled her eyes. "Her name is Horse and that's the end of it. *Thunder.*" She sniffed. As if Horse looked like a Thunder. The animal shied when clouds crossed the sun, the mare afraid of shadows, and certainly was no warhorse like Sancha. More like a plough horse. "I tried two names and I'm going back to the first." Ramiro had made fun of her for calling the animal Horse so she'd changed it to Jorga, which didn't work out for obvious reasons.

The real Jorga arched a brow and Claire readied herself. The woman hadn't been happy to find a horse named after her and even less to hear they'd attached that name to a goat as well. "Your hands might be busy, but you can still do something more *useful* with that mouth than talk about flea-covered animals. Sing. Share Memory again."

Arguing would be futile so Claire didn't bother to try. All it had earned her was raps on the knuckles or across her shoulders if her grandmother rode on Horse. She drew her shoulders up straight and tall to lift her diaphragm for the Song, and Errol promptly dropped to his knees and clamped his hands over his ears. Her first note died half done as her uncle screamed.

"Enemy!" Errol shrieked.

As her muscles tightened, Claire searched the area and saw nothing threatening, getting only a shrug from Bromisto when she looked to him. The boy had a better vantage in the tree, yet found no signs of danger. Bromisto shimmied out of the tree and beat her over to the other boy.

"What enemy?" Jorga was already asking. "How soon?" But Errol only shook, eyes scrunched shut, and refused to answer.

A glimpse of the future then and not an immediate threat. Her uncle's talent continued to make Claire uneasy. She couldn't help scanning the skies, though there was nothing to see. Nobody was bleeding. They shouldn't be in any danger. Her heart beat erratically anyway. Did Dal seek them out? Would the god attack? Warnings were all well and good, but not if they didn't provide any details.

Her uncle could be incredibly stubborn at times, more like a child of two than nearly an adult. She crouched down on his level and put an arm around his shoulder. "What enemy, Errol? We need to know."

"Enemy," he repeated stubbornly in a shriek that made her ears ring. "Destroyer."

She repressed an angry huff while rubbing at her ear. No wonder danger found them with all his yelling. "Yes, but what?"

Bromisto swooped in and the smaller boy shoved Errol, causing her uncle to topple over. His hands slid off his ears as he moved to catch himself, and he looked up, his mouth dangling open with surprise. Jorga gave a growl and moved to grab Bromisto, but Claire got between them, putting up her hand.

"Wait, grandmother. It's working. Look."

Instead of curling up again, Errol wore a scowl.

"Stop acting like a baby," Bromisto insisted. "Speak up like a man. What sort of enemy?"

At first Errol's brows drew down like he didn't understand the question, then he blinked as if listening to a voice they couldn't hear. "Soldiers."

"When?" Jorga asked.

"Soon?" He shrugged, then pointed off vaguely into the batch of raspberry bushes.

Jorga turned to look at Claire. "That's the best we'll get from him. Looks like you'll get to practice your Death Song again."

Claire's spine stiffened. "If I have to"—she looked out at the cottonwoods—"or maybe not. I have another idea."

They set the trap on an area of stable ground in front of two massive cottonwood trees. The sogginess prevented anyone from actually sitting and appearing relaxed, but they scattered enough items around to make the area look like a campsite. Errol and Bro-

misto stood close to the fire at the rear of the pretend camp with Horse, feeding sticks to the flames. It
smoked abominably from all the wet wood, but that
was just as well. They wanted to draw the soldiers in,
not blunder into the Northerners accidentally.

Bromisto whistled a tune and Errol tried to imi-
tate him, blowing out more spit than noise.

"How long do you think this will take?" Claire
asked her grandmother. The two of them crouched
in a patch of tall grass.

The words barely left her mouth before Errol
shouted, "Enemy! Destroyer!"

Everyone jumped, but settled quickly. Errol had
shouted the same in a seemingly random pattern
since the first warning, often slapping his hands over
his mouth afterward as if he couldn't stop himself.

"Enemy!" Bromisto hollered in imitation, obviously enjoying the romp. Errol yelled again in return.
Both boys laughed until they wobbled unsteadily,
shouting their new chant whenever they got enough
breath, like a bizarre new form of Scream Tag.

"Long enough to give me a headache," Jorga answered the almost forgotten question. "It's not a
game," she called to the boys and then said to Claire:
"Not all of the enemy will go down in the trap. Are
you ready to use the Song?"

Claire gave a nod. She'd already set herself to do
what had to be done, though butterflies became bats
in her stomach.

"On my signal then," Jorga said. "We'll do this together." Her eyes continually scanned the landscape and jerked back as a line of men in black and yellow emerged from the raspberry bushes about two hundred yards away. Not a long wait after all. Ten soldiers . . .

Wait. Twenty-five.

Claire managed to keep her breathing steady and even, at the right depth for Singing, though her hands shook.

Errol and Bromisto gave one more shriek and then took off running as directed with Horse. They'd prearranged to go to the next nearest group of cottonwoods, the ground already checked and double-checked for safety.

The lure worked, as twenty-plus Northern soldiers barreled in their direction, drawing their weapons as they came. Claire took in three breaths before they halved the distance and reached the trap. She stood. Her nails cut into her palms as she waited for them to go down when they hit the thin ground. The lead man ran right past the tree branch they'd left as a marker. Ran right past it and kept going.

Claire stepped backward, eyes widening. One. Two. Three . . . then finally twenty-five. All twenty-five thundered across the trap without failing or slowing, cutting the distance. Their faces contorted with hate as they sensed victory over the helpless victims.

"Impossible," she gasped. *How can this be?* Her feet

wanted to run, get away, but she pushed the debilitating panic away and held firm.

Think.

The ground was so thin and crumbly in that spot, it wouldn't hold up a bird, let alone twenty-five full-grown men. She expected a few to get through, but not all.

Jorga clutched at her arm. "The magic. Use the magic! I'm still too weak! You must stop them!"

What happened to doing it together?

The men pounded closer. The dull sunlight glinted off swords coming for her blood. Claire's pulse raced with adrenaline. It all depended on her. She drew up tall for her Death Song, the words ready . . .

Wait.

It didn't make sense. At least one should have plunged through the earth and into the cave inches below the ground. Jorga was well able to use the Song again. A trap . . .

A trap in more ways than one.

By the Song, if she'd guessed wrong, they died. Fifty yards away.

"Hurry!" Jorga shouted.

Instead of letting the words of the Death Song slip from her lips, Claire fed all her anger and resentment at being used into a Song of emotion, holding it in a sphere-shaped bubble around her body, layering in intent and depth. With a last scream of competition, she thrust the magic containing nothing but passion, not toward the soldiers, but in every direction. It exploded outward with a vengeance, cutting through rock, stone, earth, and tree.

Jorga cried out and dropped to her knees. Dozens of answering cries echoed that first from behind trees and in clumps of brush. The Northern soldiers wavered, flickering, then vanished like the illusions they actually were. Nothing but a figment in her mind created by the Song.

A Song fashioned by others.

"Tricked," Claire shouted. "You can come out now! I figured it out." How dare they use her this way? There were never any enemies but what she saw in her mind. Their manipulation would have worked, too, if she were the same frightened girl who'd first run into Ramiro. But she'd been tempered in a hotter fire since then.

Somehow, the Women of the Song had even fooled Errol into giving his false warning. A trap indeed, only set by her own kind to test her. "Is this how you greet everyone?"

"Only daughters of a certain age," Jorga said as she climbed stiffly to her feet. "And only on their first visit. I don't think my bones could take it more than once."

"You knew," Claire accused.

"Of course I knew. Ever has it been this way. No true Woman of the Song would give our secrets away."

"And Errol's warning."

"A surprise indeed. He sensed the initiation, yet also the form the illusion would take in your mind. Each woman sees her own deepest fear made flesh, making each initiation different. Errol is more attuned with his family than I expected."

Other women appeared now, most with fair hair cut short or worn in a variety of styles of braids or even loose and rippling down their backs. But one or two had dark skin like Father Telo, taking after their fathers. They emerged from their hiding spots. The majority appeared middle aged or older. Some few looked more ancient than Jorga, clinging to canes or other women.

"Welcome, Daughter," the closest said, one of the older members.

Welcome," the others all called their own greetings.

Claire held tight to her irritation, figuring she'd need it for whatever came next. "Did I pass your test?"

The first woman smiled, cutting sharp wrinkles around her lips and eyes. She rubbed her elbow as if it pained her. "With power to spare, Daughter. Welcome to the Rose Among Thorns gathering. Share our Song."

"Destroyer!"

Everyone jumped, sparing Claire from having to give these women a friendly greeting in return.

What now?

Errol hurried into their midst with Bromisto hanging on to one of his arms and trying to drag him back.

With his free hand, her uncle pointed straight to Claire. "Destroyer!"

CHAPTER 12

Claire sat at the center of a mud shack that looked like it had been added onto repeatedly over the years to enlarge the space. In places the clay and mud coating had cracked and crumbled to reveal the branches within the framework. The floor was of plain dirt, swept tidy, and the single window had an oiled sheet tacked over the frame to keep out the rain, yet still allow in a thin light. Chairs made up the only furniture, the room bare except for the simple necessities needed for a gathering of women. A lantern hung on one wall and smoked with an oily smell.

Claire wiped her hands free of sweat, which had nothing to do with the stuffy heat of the room and everything to do with the scrutiny upon her. Her three-legged stool was surrounded by the plain-backed chairs of four other women—the Elders—

and Claire felt rather like a newborn lamb being inspected to see if it was healthy enough to join the herd—or the stew pot.

All four women were large, but the one facing her outmatched the others. She had three chins and no neck to speak of, while her heavy cheeks pushed up her flesh to make her eyes tiny. Her bust projected forward like a shelf, resting on a stomach that had no waist. Short white hair hid under a lacy cap. For all her size, her composure reminded Claire of Ramiro's mother. The Elder might have matched Beatriz in unyielding authority, but with none of the ability to laugh at herself and none of Jorga's soft spot for kin. It added up to a woman Claire had no desire to know better.

The piggy eyes stared down a bulb-like nose with a flat expression. "You bring a man to our most sacred enclave."

"Bromisto is ten, hardly—"

"I allowed it, Eulalie. The blame lies with me." Jorga sat wedged in the corner where Claire couldn't see her grandmother unless she leaned half off her stool. "It was to help Errol—as a companion for my son. I am an Elder here as well."

"Not when it comes to your own kin," Eulalie snapped. "You know the laws. Be grateful we allow you here to listen. But you will *not* speak again." She tented her hands across her vast stomach in satisfaction of scoring a hit, and Jorga hastily looked down and settled against the wall. "Now then. Our sister Jorga is not on trial here—yet. We can deal with her later. What do we do with this flibbertigibbet?" Her mouth pursed like she'd swallowed a gnat.

"She passed the first test, Eulalie," another Elder said. "That deserves some consideration." This woman looked a score of years younger, her hair dark and worn loose. She had brown eyes and brown skin, and her eyes twinkled with concealed amusement. When she smiled, as she seemed to do often, a dimple stood out in her cheek.

"I know that, Muriel. That's as may be." Claire found herself fascinated by Eulalie's waggling chins. "We put the girl through the Thorn trial and see if she passes. Rachael, do you agree?"

"I think you all misunderstand," Claire said, gripping the edge of the stool. "I don't care about your trials. I came to give you a warning, and also to get your help. You're in danger. We all are."

"We know what we face," Eulalie said. "We don't need any untested girl's help with that. My Amos gave us plenty of warning."

The Women of the Song all glanced at the only man in the room. As large and neckless as Eulalie, he stood by the door, staring down at the tips of his boots. Of all things, he wore a plain canvas apron over his clothing. Like Errol, he refused to meet anyone's eyes and he had the same soft, vacant expression. Unlike Errol, Amos was a man grown into middle age, in need of a shave, his hair curling and months past due for a trim. Somehow, despite their differences in age, both sons managed to give an appearance of waiting. They lacked the edge and alertness carried by Ramiro and it made them seem half alive.

"Destroyer," he said in a surprisingly deep voice.

The last two Elders traded looks as they waited silently for Amos to say more. Claire found nothing distinctive about the other two Elders with the exception that the one called Rachael was missing a bottom tooth and the other had the sort of tanned skin she saw frequently on the desert people. When no more proved forthcoming from Amos, they all turned to Claire. She suppressed a shiver, unused to so much attention since leaving Ramiro's people.

"I'm known for speaking my mind," Rachael was saying, "and I think we need to get to the bottom of this. Perhaps the Thorn trial can wait."

Claire jumped on the opportunity. "You might know about the Northerners hunting Women of the Song in the swamp, but were you warned about their god? That's twice as dangerous—"

"Malarkey," Eulalie interrupted. "Stuff and foolishness. The Great Goddess is the only real god. This is Rosemund's daughter, and we all know how flighty Rosemund turned out. She defied her own mother *and* the Elders." Her emphasis made plain which was the bigger affront. "Thought the magic should be shirked and avoided. Remember her final trial?"

All four Elders huffed, eyes narrowing.

"What about it?" Claire squeaked. Unlike the Rose Among Thorns trial for young girls, the final test of a woman's magic came well into adulthood, when a Woman of the Song was considered for entering the path to be an Elder. It usually involved women of high talent with the Song.

"Just stood there, my dear," Muriel admitted. "Wouldn't use any magic."

"A disgrace, that's what it was," Eulalie cut in, muttering under her breath. "We can't trust a girl from that sort of mother to put our best interests first. I'm surprised she followed the law enough to have a daughter. Perhaps this one doesn't belong to Rose-mund at all."

"I do so," Claire sputtered. The nerve of these women. "My mother can't defend herself. How dare you talk about her that way?" She stood, but Elder Rachael pushed her down with a firm hand.

"Look at the girl," the fourth Elder said. "She's the very image of Rosemund. I don't call her birth into question. Her motivation, however. Why, look at how she hangs around with . . . men."

"Bromisto is ten," Claire said once again, but her heart wasn't in it. "And the *men* I hang around with have treated me a sight better than I got here." At least Ramiro believed in her. She couldn't let him down. That alone was enough to keep her from saying more and spoiling her chances further. Jorga had advised her to be respectful and that was how she'd been raised as well.

It was just so hard with these . . . *women*.

"It's true we can't know her loyalty," the milder Muriel said, her smile slipping into a worried expression.

Claire's attempt to say "but I am loyal" was talked right over as all the Elders began speaking at once, each one coming out with yet another discrediting story about her mother. Against orders, Jorga jumped in, though Claire couldn't tell if she argued for or against. The noise rose in volume as the women disputed until Claire hunched her shoulders.

"Destroyer," the deep voice said again, and this time, if any tone could hold disapproval and still sound neutral, this one did. The Elders fell silent.

"There's that," Muriel said in her musical voice.

Claire wanted to ask if they knew what it meant, but stayed silent. Speaking now would rile them up again, and the answer couldn't be anything good. Whatever it meant, the warning hadn't gotten her thrown out. She'd hope for the best and investigate later.

Rachael picked at the buttons on her sleeve. "I'll vote for the Thorn trial—assuming we move it up and hold it right away."

"But to jump over the other girls," the fourth Elder said, "It isn't fair."

"Fair be hanged." Eulalie jerked her head. "Muriel?"

The woman gave a nod. "So voted. Her trial is tonight at sundown."

"The trial," Claire said. "I told you I'm not interested in your trial. Unless, you'll hear what I have to say now that it is decided?" Perhaps she could say her piece and leave before their test.

"Initiates are given an opportunity to thank the Elders," Jorga said from her corner, "right before."

Claire took the hint. If pretending to undergo a test of magic was the condition of getting to explain the seriousness of her warning, she'd have to take that option. "Yes, thank you very much for agreeing to speed up my trial. I—as well as all of you—will need to be as strong as possible considering what we face. Because I still don't think you understand the significance of what's happening. The Northern god will kill the Women of the Song just as he does the desert people. Maybe the Women of the Song can think of a way to stop him. If we all worked—"

"Demon," Amos interjected, causing them all to jump.

Eulalie shook her head, her expression stony. "We've heard about this demon and we are taking it seriously. We have a plan all prepared. And we don't need a snit of a girl, daughter of a failure, to tell us how to run our business. Give us your opinion when we ask for it."

Spots of warmth bloomed in Claire's cheeks. "If

you took this seriously, then we wouldn't be sitting around besmirching my mother's name. You wouldn't be worrying about a silly test, rather than preparing for a fight that is surely coming. The thing is, I don't think you do take it seriously because, well, you haven't seen the slaughter. If you did, you'd be wetting yourselves. This god kills and kills. That's all it does. You haven't felt it. You think the soldiers are the threat, but they are a splinter in your finger compared to the true danger. We can't protect against it. The god's power wiped a squad of soldiers out in the blink of an eye. This is not a joke. We need to be marching out of our swamp to help stop more killing. Even a 'snit of a girl' can see that. But unfortunately, that girl is talking to a bunch of old hens, clucking around instead of acting! Stupid and worthless! If we all die, it will be your fault!" In her passion, Claire found herself on her feet with her hands clasped against her chest. She looked around defiantly, and sour expressions and set jaws glared back at her.

"I think you've said enough," Muriel said. The sparkle had gone from her eyes, replaced with disappointment. "I was a friend of your mother. She might have disagreed, but she was usually smart enough to remember to respect the Elders. And she saved her disrespect until she was grown. You must learn that lesson, too."

"By the Great Goddess, she said more than

enough." Rachael's face had gone red in a match for Eulalie, who looked like she was having a stroke. "Stop excusing her, Muriel."

"Out," Eulalie choked through tight lips. "Get out."

"Gladly." Claire walked from the shack with as much dignity as she could muster, shutting the make-shift door of strapped-together branches silently. Once outside, though, it dawned on her she might have made a serious mistake. She had let their petty words about her mother overcome her good sense, and her tongue had gotten the better of her—that wasn't like her. Even when Beatriz provoked her with comments about witches, she'd managed to stay calm. Though there *was* a difference: Those remarks had been directed at herself, not at someone she loved.

It didn't change the fact that she needed the Women of the Song's help, and that chance might be long gone.

Happy with yourself, Claire? You've ruined everything.

The Elders would never listen to her now. They had enough prejudice against leaving the swamp and helping in the first place—what with their religion and the Great Goddess preaching noninterference and their distrust of men—and now she'd made her task that much harder.

She should go back and apologize—grovel a little. If she sucked up to their status and claimed ignorance, they would forgive. Maybe not forget, but hopefully enough that she could start over. Maybe they could see things her way if she aced their trial.

The meeting shack stood separate from the rest of the camp, surrounded by scraggly clumps of evergreens. She stopped next to a pine, her eyes seeing yet not taking in the trail of sap running down the rough trunk. Her back stiffened.

Grovel to those condescending women? They dismissed her because of her age, believing only gray hair gave you wisdom. The dismissed her because of her mother, believing wisdom only came from compliance.

That wasn't wisdom. That was servitude. And even though they eschewed men from their society for that very reason, their own hypocrisy probably didn't dawn on them.

Couldn't they see that their petty concerns about precedence and their overconfidence doomed them all? Dal certainly wouldn't wait for the Women of the Song to make up their minds. How silly to let four Elders control the fate of an entire people—and not just her people, but perhaps *all* people. Annoying old busybodies . . .

Her eyes opened wide.

Or at least the Elders *thought* they controlled everything. Claire didn't have to let them.

She swung around, heading past the meeting shack and toward the clearing where the Women of the Song gathered to eat and sleep and gossip. Her walk turned into a purposeful march, her heels beating the ground, each step ratcheting up her resolve to show them what's what.

People looked up in mild interest as she crossed the clearing to Errol, pulling the boy to his feet. Leaving Bromisto, she took Errol with her to the center.

"Have the Elders told you?" she asked in a loud voice. More heads came up. The majority of these women were girls, young women, or mothers, instead of grandmothers. "Maybe they told you about the soldiers entering our home and hunting us like animals, burning our houses, killing Women of the Song, but have they told you the rest—the worst?"

"Demon," Errol said right on cue.

"Exactly, Errol. There's a vicious evil loose on the world. One we can't even see. The Northern god can kill without warning. Blood attracts it. Dozens die from a force no one can stop. It's only growing and it won't halt until all life is dead." Heads dropped as girls resumed their tasks. A group walked right past her, swinging buckets on their way to the stream.

"That's the desert people's problem," said a woman bouncing a toddler on her knee.

"We're safe in the swamp," came from another.

"Let it kill them," said a third with a laugh. "Suits them right."

Claire frowned. "But . . . it will kill us, too." Her

voice faded as the last of the women turned away. "They didn't listen to me," she said to herself.

"Demon?" Errol said.

Bromisto tugged at her sleeve. "Now what, *sirena*? They won't help. These *sirenas* are very full of themselves. While you . . . you are like Osoro."

"Who?" Claire asked absently.

"Osoro. The low man in my father's hunting group. Nobody listens to him either."

Claire blinked stupidly at him for a second, then her jaw firmed as truth seeped in. Nobody here knew her or trusted her. She had nothing to recommend her words. Well, her mother was stubborn and she'd show the old hens she could be twice as obstinate. "Then I'll just have to prove that I'm no Osoro."

CHAPTER 13

Ramiro leaned against the wall of a tight alley to get his breath, wheezing from more than their close shave with the Northerners at the gate. The alley smelled of shit, and not the mellower stink of barnyard animals fed on grass and grains, but the riper smell of human animals. Even the roof-high piles of straw grouped around a sort of lean-to shed that had been a chicken coop couldn't cut down on the smell. It would be easy enough for the inhabitants to have spread the straw around to clear the air—for their own benefit, if not for his—but no one had. He covered his nose with his sleeve and cursed.

Sancha showed her distaste by raising her upper lip. "Easy, girl," he soothed, feeling unrestored himself.

Not a good sign if even the small conventions of

society had gone out the window—literally in this case, judging by the casements above them.

Yet, his small group had lived past the gate. Society's collapse didn't necessarily prove they would fail. In any case, he'd never expected to get this far—hoped—but not expected. The stress of their situation weakened his body, making his head ache. Hope and despair had struggled in his breast in an excruciatingly painful war for too many days, wearing him down. With all he'd been through, he couldn't blame the remaining people in Aveston for letting niceties slide, knowing full well finding the courage to believe in a positive outcome was the harder choice.

If asked, he'd never be able to explain it: how hope could be such a drain upon the spirit. Every wild dream of what might be, like seeing Claire again, become a taunting stab to his soul as another part of him mocked what would likely never be. Giving up and feeling nothing would be so much easier.

Teresa gripped his sleeve, standing shoulder to shoulder with him against the rough stucco, and pulled ever so slightly. "I've been meaning to thank you, cousin."

He looked at her in surprise. "Whatever for?"

"For being you . . . and my friend." Her face twisted as if she would cry. "For making me a cousin in truth, even after I pushed you away."

He squeezed her hand. "I don't recall any such thing. It is I who should be thanking you. I would have never held myself together in the swamp if not for you." When they'd first met Claire, his heart had been consumed with anger for his brother's death. Only Teresa had made the difference, reminding him of his soul—reminding him to give people a chance. He bumped her shoulder. "When this is over, we'll see the university rebuilt."

"When this is over, I'll settle for a long talk. I've much to tell you—personal information that I hid from you—and I hope you'll think the same of me afterward."

He leaned heavier on the wall. "Let me save you the trouble right now. Nothing could change my kinship for you—I see who you are—but I look forward to a chance to talk."

"You see? You know?" Her grip on him became more insistent.

Amusement tinged his concern. "You are not so hard to read. You didn't fall prey to Alvito's charms. Or my brother or Gomez. Or my own lesser ones for that matter, but I've seen your eyes follow a pretty woman—Bromisto's sister—remember her?"

She dropped her gaze, her face heating. "You knew."

He shrugged. "You didn't seem to want to talk about it. I figured if you needed to, you would."

She shook him by his cloak, but a deep smile covered her face. "You are a trying man, Ramiro Alvarado. You and the rest of male-kind, but surprisingly wonderful."

"If you wish to see wonderful and kind, you have only to look in the mirror, my cousin. You make the world a better place by being here."

She wiped at her cheeks and his eyes were not so clear either. "So what happened back there?" she asked, turning the subject. "They let us get away."

"I was there, and I have no idea," Ramiro said, ready enough to follow her lead, and looked to the priest as Father Telo caught up, bringing with him the other two horses. Father Telo stepped carefully to avoid the filth as he joined them in the middle of the alley. As soon as the commander at the gate told them to go, they had wasted no time, hastily putting distance between themselves and the gate, turning around corners, and twisting and hurrying through a den of alleyways. Unwilling to chance that the Northerners might change their minds and come after them.

"'Let each man manifest God's will to benefit all,'" Father Telo quoted, "'and the saints most of all, but the least man as likely as the first.' Or woman," he amended quickly. "No disrespect intended."

"None taken, Father," Teresa said. She released Ramiro to stand on her own two feet again.

"'The spirit of goodness lives in all of us, for deep down, we are all the same,'" Telo finished.

Ramiro grimaced. "I never noticed any goodness in a Northerner before. They never had second thoughts about taking off my head."

"Did you ever give them the opportunity to show a better side before?"

Ramiro shoved off from the wall, mind recreating a day in the swamp. "Actually . . . there was a time they had me surrounded. Could have taken me down in a rush . . . or used their bows to end it quick. Maybe you're right, Father." He could still taste the metallic tang of fear on his tongue as he'd stood over Errol, outnumbered and about to die, but unable to leave the boy. Faced by a handful of soldiers, but only one had stepped forward, while the rest stayed back. An honor among enemies. Chills chased up his spine as he remembered calling all Northerners barbarians. Had he been any better—judging without understanding? "Their ways are so different from ours . . ."

"But still human," Teresa finished for him.

Ramiro felt any so-called Northern goodness was mingled with their self-interest, but refrained from saying as much. The soldiers in the swamp hadn't intended to spare his life. They still planned to kill him and a defenseless child. Should he honor them for doing so with humanity? However, Ramiro found his own hopes too painful to crush his companions' fragile peace. Let them believe the Northerners could be human.

"Or I've spent much too much time being outnumbered and about to die lately." As intended, the tension in their bodies all slacked a fraction at his weak joke.

Teresa huffed out a laugh. "Too true, cousin."

"Amen," Telo added.

Ramiro stepped closer to Sancha and secured his sword, lacing his shield onto his left arm, feeling more complete with the metal in his hand, then gestured at the alley. "Where do we start looking for one Northerner? How do we find her?"

Father Telo shrugged his burly shoulders. "How does one find anything, my son? We ask people."

"Like them?" Teresa said. "Trouble."

Ramiro swung around at the tension in Teresa's voice, sword held before him to see a patrol of Northern soldiers approaching. They shouted and gestured at him, pointing at the ground for him to release his weapon. Everything happened at once. Father Telo dropped to his hands and knees, head lowered to the ground as if in prayer. Arms up and hands open, Teresa backed in the opposite direction. With a shout, she broke into a run and two Northerners bolted after her in chase. The horses, left to their own devices when Telo dropped their reins, broke and stampeded in the opposite direction, running straight at the Northerners and slowing them for an instant.

Three men came at Ramiro, spread out in a line. His vision blurred, blocking out details of their appearance and focusing on the weapons in their hands, watching their feet and shoulders for clues of their intentions. His training kicked in, and he sidestepped in front of Sancha as the mare squared up to be by his side, careful to stay on his left. She bared her teeth as the Northerners closed, grabbing the nearest man. Her teeth sunk deep between the man's neck and shoulder. Ramiro threw his shield at the two men on his right. He spun to thrust his sword—once, twice—into the man Sancha held. Such a move left him open, but protecting Sancha was always his first priority.

The long muscles in her neck bunched as she flicked the wounded soldier away. Her teeth tore out a chunk of his flesh in the process. He hit the wall of the building with an audible thump and rolled into one of the straw stacks.

Ramiro jumped to the right as Sancha surged forward in a move they'd practiced hundreds of times. Her forefeet beat the ground as she charged the soldier in the center and he went down under her dancing, razor-sharp hooves. Not even watching, Ramiro swung on the last soldier, sword spinning high, then low, as he dropped to cut the man's legs out from under him. Even as the man fell, surprise on his beardless face, Ramiro bounced to his feet in a leap, using the momentum of his return to earth to drive his sword through the soldier's chest.

He hurried to Sancha to finish the other man, but the soldier had been reduced to lumps of pulp and blood under her nearly two tons of weight.

Father Telo had his arms wrapped around the knees of the remaining Northerner. As Ramiro stepped forward to help, the priest scrambled away and the soldier toppled over. Red slashes revealed themselves across the rear of his calves as he twitched across the ground, unable to rise. Hamstrung. Father Telo held a small hunting knife in his hand.

"I thought I'd need some protection against Santabe." The priest's face twisted in grief or remorse, Ramiro couldn't tell which. "I didn't expect to use it."

"We never know what to expect in this life, Father." Ramiro leaned on Sancha's heaving ribs and pointed to the soldier Telo had defeated. "He'll live." He avoided saying the man might live, but he'd never walk again. Blood dribbled down Ramiro's cheek from a cut by his eye, unfelt until now. Something else stung in his side—a shallow stab wound—likely received when he'd turned to protect Sancha. Nothing too serious for the moment, as his thrown shield had proved enough distraction, but the bleeding would weaken him or possibly lead to an infection if not treated soon.

First things first.

The priest appeared to be uninjured. Sancha had a few cuts on her legs and chest, but nothing serious. Ramiro's gaze traveled up the alley but there was no sign of Teresa or her pursuit. Ramiro ground his teeth. His knees wobbled as he fetched his shield and wiped his sword on his cloak, smearing blood everywhere, though the familiar movement helped and his joints were firm by the time he finished and sheathed his sword. No need to draw more attention to themselves. He tucked sword and shield under the cloak.

"Let's go, Father. Teresa went this way."

"We can't," the priest said with regret in his voice. "Thousands live in this city and we must protect them first. The blood. Quickly." Father Telo hastened to the nearest pile of straw and began spreading it over the alley floor, tossing handfuls on the dead body Sancha had trampled.

"Shit! Shit!" Ramiro touched mind, heart, liver and spleen as panic began to build. Eyes he hoped were imaginary touched his back. He sniffed the air for the scent of rot, the feel of evil, and got nothing—yet. No sign of Dal. They were lucky so far, but how could he be so thoughtless?

Better than anyone, he knew the amount of blood needed to draw Dal was small indeed. His dreams had shown him that. But that was all they knew. Not how often Dal could or would strike. Not how often his attention would be drawn or what might be dividing the god's notice.

Ramiro used his already bloody cloak to clean the cut on his forehead and then bent to wipe down Sancha's legs and feet as Telo continued to cover the evidence of the fight. They had a massive job, to remove all traces of the blood, including bandaging the disabled Northerner or dragging him inside somewhere. Ramiro bundled up his cloak and thrust it into the abandoned chicken house, under some shelving, then turned to grab the first body and stow it inside also.

By the saints, Teresa would have to wait, and the thought tore him apart. Father Telo was correct that the thousands of people in this city came first, and it was his fault they were in more danger than before. *Yet Teresa.* He'd met few people smarter or more capable than Teresa, but he still very much feared what had become of her.

Teresa ran, hardly paying attention to direction, only knowing she needed to keep a gap between her pursuit. If the Northerners closed, their swords would be the last thing she'd see. She'd suspected Aveston was under some kind of curfew, the remaining people shut inside even in daylight.

The alley abruptly opened up on a square surrounded by houses and with a large well at its center. *Think. Think.*

She needed to use her brains, because her strength or speed wasn't going to stop the Northerners. Unfortunately, her head refused to cooperate, ideas driven away by the sharp edges of the blades behind her, and all she came up with were the words of a childish nursery rhyme. The one that warned of what came of meddling with miracles.

She was going to die like Alvito. Death was the only reward for performing miracles.

"Help!" Teresa cried repeatedly as she reached the far side of the well, placing it between her and the

Northerners. Gibbering panic reduced her to the coherency of a two-year-old. Her heart beat so hard her chest throbbed. Several buckets sat on the well housing and on the ground around the structure. Hardly knowing what she did, she seized one, heaving it at the soldiers' heads and succeeding in making them duck. Shutters on upper floors cracked cautiously open as she circled in a wary dance, keeping the well between her and death. "Help!"

She flung another bucket and another, her aim poor, but the soldiers had already deduced they needed to split and come at her from both sides. She froze, trapped by her own mistake of lingering, as they divided. Her choices shrank to bolting again, but she'd not surprise them with that this time, and her bulk made her an inefficient runner—soon caught.

"Help, please!" The last bucket earned her another second. *Oh saints.* She had no more options. The Northerners closed in . . .

. . . and a stream of sewage emerged from a window to splash over one of the soldiers, followed by the chamber pot, which caught him on the shoulder. "Get out of our city!" a voice shouted. A shoe came from another window, striking the other Northerner squarely in the face.

Teresa gasped.

More windows cracked open. A silver-backed hairbrush flew at the soldiers. Pots and pans followed. A child's wooden block. All around the square, sashes went up and household items poured out. Some fell well short, but others made their mark.

"Leave!"

"Get away from our homes!" Other shouts followed with much coarser sentiments. The barrage intensified as a chair knocked a soldier down.

Teresa retreated to the nearest house, leaning against the door. It sprang open, almost dropping her on her butt. Hands grasp her tight, promising security, comradeship. She sobbed in relief at not being alone anymore.

Men—fathers and grandfathers, boys without beards—rushed from doors all around the square, carrying brooms or mops. Some held kitchen knives or firewood hatchets. They fell upon the Northern soldiers with cries of righteous rage. The oppressors had become the oppressed.

Teresa's tears grew harder and she cried on someone's shoulder as strangers awkwardly patted her. "What were you doing out there?" a voice demanded.

She tried to answer but all that emerged was the childish nursery rhyme that kept repeating in her head:

> *"Saints above,*
> *Saints below.*
> *God's hand spiritual,*
> *God's rule made flesh.*
> *Covet not the miracle,*
> *It brings death."*

Yet, she hadn't died. She'd lived! That brought a new fear all its own along with a flood of guilt. *Ramiro and Father Telo*. She'd run and left them behind. Perhaps they'd died in her place.

"I have to go back. I have to find my friends. My friends! Oh! The blood!"

The sun beat down out of a clear sky.

Dal!

Someone pushed a cup into her hand, guiding it to her lips. The drink sent a shock through her body as the hard liquor burned all the way to her stomach, making her cough and gag, but driving away the fog in her brain.

"Now, woman, what are you doing out? Are you simple?"

Teresa focused on the speaker—a nearly bald grandfather, missing all his bottom teeth and wearing a nightshirt in the middle of the day. Suspenders held up his pants, though the grayish bed gown hadn't been tucked into them. Absently, Teresa noticed he was barefoot. She gulped and got her mouth under control. She knew what had to be done.

"The blood! We must cover it!" She shook off the hands holding her and ran into the house searching frantically.

"What are you doing, woman!"

"The blood! We mustn't draw it onto us! Quick, if you want to live!" She'd entered a kitchen and a heavy cloth covered the table. She seized it and yanked with all her might, sending dishes flying to smash on the floor. "Cover the blood! You!" She grabbed on to a tall young woman who looked old enough to be married yet still wore her hair down. "Get all your blankets! Quick!" The girl stared at her. "We must cover *all* the blood! Do you hear me?"

Teresa rushed to the door, but the old man got there first. "What is wrong with you?"

"The blood! Did you not hear what happened to the army? You must have seen the burned pile of their bodies outside your gate."

"They're saying it was a demon from the pits of hell. Those rumors are true?"

"Yes, a demon." She seized on the simple explanation. "It will kill us all! The blood draws it! Do you want to die? It will destroy this whole city!" Shock slowly grew over his face. She shoved the elderly man out of the way and rushed to the well, draping the first soldier's body she encountered with the tablecloth. Vaguely, she heard the old man calling for blankets as she turned to grab an upturned bucket. "Water! Clean the streets! Quick!"

The water level lapped too low in the well to reach without a rope, but several already hung in the water. Teresa heaved a bucket up and turned to send a stream of water over the blood on the cobbles. A large group of men joined her in washing the streets, thinning the blood with water and diluting the red to pink and then to clear. As they did this, women bustled forward with blankets, towels, and sheets until the two bodies lay covered in mounds several feet high. Boys were assigned to stand around the piles with buckets, waiting to jump on any more blood that should appear.

Only then did the pounding of Teresa's heart ease, though her breath still came in little pants and her hands shook. The entire city of Aveston might have been purged because of her careless actions, not that they'd given her a choice.

"As soon as it's full dark, find a place to bury them and make sure you clean up everything, do you hear?" The old man nodded at her. "Stay inside during the daylight. Walls hold some protection from the demon. Darkness also." She added *for now at least* in her own head. "Whatever you do, don't bleed or let your blood show if you do."

"Who are you?" the old man asked

"Specialist of Cultural Anthropology, University of Colina Hermosa. I'm here getting information for the *alcalde* of Colina Hermosa."

"Ain't no Colina Hermosa no more," the man said, eyeing her doubtfully from shorn hair to worn poncho.

"Your *alcalde* sent a woman?" another asked.

"Our new *alcalde is* a woman."

The old man let that pass. "You're a spy then."

"Well . . . yes, I suppose so."

"And what do you plan to do, spy? Are you going to stop this demon?"

She gaped at him and the people so obviously deferring to him. Her little group needed to stop blundering their way through this mission and start planning. "Do? I intend to get back some of our own."

A smile crossed his wrinkled face, showing his missing bottom teeth. "Why didn't you say so sooner? What else do you need?"

Teresa smiled in return. "Help finding my friends. And the Northerners in white. Where are they staying?" The time of miracles had returned, though whether she lived or died had yet to be determined. All the more reason to act while she could.

CHAPTER 14

Julian's flesh creeped. He could tell right away that the village they approached had changed, and he slowed his horse accordingly. Beatriz followed his lead and pulled her own mount to a walk. Having been here a few days ago on his way to Crueses and Suseph and overnighting as their guest, he already sensed the difference. No delegation waited to greet him today—and this before they had even known him for the *alcalde* of a major *ciudad-estado*. No, they greeted every traveler, and the lack now spoke volumes.

As the hard-packed street entered the village, the road rang with a hollow emptiness. No children played. No men kept watch for bandits. No women loitered by the wells to share gossip. His stomach tightened.

"Look." Beatriz pointed past lines of hanging laundry, where Julian spotted dapple-gray horseflesh—*caballos de guerra*—standing outside a building. No one rode such animals but the *pelotónes* of Colina Hermosa. His tightness eased.

"Captain Gonzalo has evacuated the village is all," Julian said as much for his own benefit as his wife's. Yet, his unease didn't lift.

"Oh." Beatriz covered her nose with her shawl. "Do you smell that?"

The cloying stench of death filled the air. Julian swallowed hard before reason took over and reminded him that nothing stirred. No sign of trouble remained. No sense of evil pressed down. Such a smell would take days to grow. If there was a fight here, it had long ended. He drew reassurance from the warhorses again. Experience had taught that the animals didn't linger after the death of their masters. He had seen as much with his son Salvador's stallion, Valentía.

Yet, why would soldiers remain in an empty village?

Here and there lay the traces that the place had been abandoned in haste. A dropped toy. Bread and olives scattered across a porch. Stable doors left wide open.

They turned their steps to the building where the animals gathered. Julian slid gracefully out of the saddle. "Wait here while I investigate." As he started to tie his reins to the iron ring in the post set for that purpose, Beatriz snorted.

She joined him on the ground. "When have you ever stayed in the background and waited, Julian? I am *alcalde* now. You must let me act the part." She tied her reins off besides his and dusted off her dress, then squared her shoulders. "We'll see what's in there together."

His admiration rose. "Now and forever," he answered, taking her hand. Her cool touch reminded they had nothing to fear when they faced it together.

The stench worsened as they reached the porch. Thick shade covered them as they climbed the steps to the meeting house that had hosted Julian for his evening meal. The people of this village had brought their best food, eager to impress him and to hear news of the Northerners and the loss of Colina Hermosa. Then, he had nothing to fear but the loss of his status as *alcalde*, homelessness, and an enemy army. Who could predict he'd ever long for the simplicity of those problems?

The doors stood open, letting out the smell. A man came to their side before they got all the way into the building. "Lady *Alcalde*." Captain Gonzalo took a knee before Beatriz, helmet hanging from one hand. The dark skin of his face was entirely too devoid of emotion. "Our sentries said you approached. We are happy to have you here, though it pains me you still go about without protection. Now I can assign a guard to you."

"The sooner, the better, Captain," Julian said. "My wife should not have left her guards behind when she heard of my illness. Make it happen. Trusted men who will cling to her like a burr, if you please."

"Julian!" Beatriz snapped. Her face had gone red, but she held his gaze. "That is not up to you! I will let Captain Gonzalo know when I need guards."

He barreled onward. "There can be no question in this time of needing protection—"

"And how does that make me look," Beatriz insisted, "to be buried by guards? What sort of impression would that give to our people? To the *concejales*? How does that make me an *alcalde* to trust? To follow?"

"Sir. Ma'am," Gonzalo said lamely, looking from one to another.

"I apologize," Julian said with a stiff bow. "My wife is right. She is the *alcalde* and makes the decisions, Captain." The words tasted bitter on his tongue, but not from anger at Beatriz. She was right to speak so. No, the anger was at himself. As her husband, he should be aiding Beatriz in her new role, not hindering her. "I'm sorry, *mi amor*."

"Leave the orders to me, if you please. I'll have no more guards than would be given during a normal time." She slipped her arm in Julian's to show there were no hard feelings, but Julian feared he would need more lessons to get over a habit of command ingrained in him for over twenty years.

"Of course," Captain Gonzalo said, looking not at all happy for this order. "I'm pleased the rumors of your ill health were exaggerated, former *Alcalde* Julian."

The soldier stepped aside to reveal the room, and Julian felt as though he'd slipped from reality, leaving him unable to speak. The composed tone of the captain could not be at more odds with the sight unfolding in the meeting house. Tables and chairs had been pushed against the walls to give floor space to dozens upon dozens of corpses covered with sheets and blankets. Dark stains spoiled the white-painted floorboards under them.

"What has happened here?" Beatriz demanded with a rising voice. "Who are they?"

"The villagers, ma'am." Gonzalo shrugged, looking to the two soldiers waiting among the discarded tables. "Your guess is as good as mine. Looks like they massacred each other. The survivors arrived at Suseph with . . . their stories yesterday. We came to see for ourselves and stayed to do burial detail. The wagon should be coming for the next load soon."

"How many?" Julian heard himself ask. Then glanced at Beatriz to ensure he hadn't stepped on her toes again. She gave him a nod as if in thanks.

"Nearly a hundred, sir." Gonzalo gave a shrug. "The survivors say it came out of nowhere. Thin air killed them. Lies, of course—they obviously fought over food or just went mad." Gonzalo frowned. "Though we found no weapons around them. No sign it was the work of bandits or Northern soldiers either. Nothing has been looted—no property damaged. Damn odd—forgive my language, ma'am."

"They didn't lie, Captain," Beatriz said slowly. "We have a new adversary."

Julian walked to the closest corpse and lifted the sheet. Staring brown eyes gazed emptily back. He jumped and dropped the sheet, but not before recognizing the head woman of the village. A graying grandmother, twenty years his senior but with a soul of kindness, she'd served the meal he'd eaten here with her own plump hands. He lifted the sheet again, taking in the cuts crossing her face and neck. Her midsection had been laid open from pelvis to collarbone, ribs forced apart, and her insides diced into small pieces. Julian shuddered and retreated.

"Tell me, Captain, were the only survivors those who were inside when the attack came?"

Gonzalo stirred uneasily. "So they claimed, sir. We found all the bodies outside—left to lay as they fell. Do you know what this is?"

"We do. You know of the Northern god?"

"The time of miracles has returned," Beatriz said before the captain could answer, "and with it the time of trial."

Julian gazed heartsore at the covered bodies, many

of them child sized. Between what the surviving villagers had witnessed and the menace of the Northern army, no one would ever return to live here—at least not for many years. Who could return to a place where your loved ones had been slaughtered before your eyes by a ghost? How many other small villages would go the way of this one—dead and empty, never to return to life? How many cities?

"I'm not sure I catch your meaning, ma'am," Gonzalo said.

Beatriz lifted her chin, though her expression remained more mournful than angry. "I mean there is a force loose in the world that seeks to end every human life, Captain. The way it ended every one of our *pelotónes* but yours. I'm sorry to have to tell you, Captain, that all your fellow soldiers are dead, including the ones from Aveston and Suseph. You are our last military force remaining."

For the first time in his life, Julian witnessed the steady Captain Gonzalo speechless and without the correct response. Julian stepped to the man's rescue. "A shock I know, Captain, but I was there at the time and survived, thanks only to a miracle. The Northern army is now a fly compared to our true foe." Julian winced at the rude comparison, all too aware of the welts he still bore from the flies sent by Dal. He gestured at the bodies. "What you see here is only a small part of his power."

The tall soldier fumbled his way into a chair, fingers plucking at his beard. "Sir?"

"I think—no, it's not up to me. The *Alcalde* can tell you more," Julian said.

"Outside if you please," Beatriz said, "in the fresh air."

She waved a hand in front of her face as if that could help dispel the smell, then got an arm under the captain and helped him to totter out to the porch, leaving Julian with the dead and the two living guards. He looked out over the rows of bodies again and felt a small relief that they'd learned Dal still could not act inside structures. He calculated quickly in his head, taking out the time he'd assigned to go to Suseph—as now Beatriz could send Gonzalo there with the warning—and came up with three days to reach Vista Sur, the farthest of the *ciudades-estado*. Saints, let there be someone remaining there to warn.

Julian's first instinct was to follow Beatriz outside and talk to Gonzalo, but he remembered that responsibility was no longer his to own.

Instead, his eyes turned inward to his landscape of self, the unrecognizable place, as he brought up his left hand and idly opened and closed his fingers, watching their freedom of movement, so changed from days ago. Why had he been wholly healed and these children left to die?

Slowly a white-hot rage formed. Too many children had suffered already in this war. Yet, to blame God was a fool's errand. God helped those who helped themselves. It was his job to prevent their deaths, to protect children and their parents—or it had been his job. No longer. The people had lost faith in him, just as he'd lost faith in himself. But you did not throw away what you'd spent years creating. The burden of protecting his people had been carried for too long to set aside now. Beatriz would make the hard decisions, but he could be there to help her. And with that realization, some of the building blocks of his mind's landscape rearranged themselves, becoming familiar once again. He was the one who saw to the safety of the weak. His job to see those with few opportunities were treated fairly. That could still be his task, though from the side instead of the center.

The world righted itself a fraction as he clung to that lifeline. He was proud the title of *alcalde* had passed to Beatriz—but his involvement and dedication did not need to be less or his part in the fight any smaller.

They sought for a way to stop this Dal. He approved that determination, but they needed a backup plan in case removing Dal proved impossible. A strategy that would protect their weakest and most vulnerable. It would no doubt be costly.

Julian nodded to himself. Sometimes to be truly brave required sacrifice.

Ramiro stood in the gray world of fog, though this time it was not entirely featureless. Tall buildings poked through the covering mist, which thinned and shifted enough to show cobblestones under his feet and the close walls of the same buildings on either side. The dream had found him in the desert, in the swamp, and now in a city—but not Colina Hermosa. The buildings were unfamiliar, their tops too rounded, the streets too narrow. The designers of Colina Hermosa had favored wide avenues and open spaces. This *ciudad-estado* pressed down, claustrophobic. Aveston then. It made sense, as that was his location in the real world.

Or was it?

For a moment, the world spun as Ramiro considered the implications of this being the real world and his life the dream.

He shook himself. Such speculation was better left to scholars or stray thoughts on rainy days when nothing else occupied him. Now, he had things to do. The gray world always meant a message of some importance.

The streets ran uphill ahead of him, and when he turned around, they ended in a cliff-like drop that was only imaginable in a dream—or a nightmare—or here. After all, if he could walk among the clouds as he had before, then anything was possible. Behind him, the *ciudad-estado* simply stopped, one building sheered right in half, to become empty air—a void. Somehow, Ramiro knew a fall backward would be a fall forever. He moved some steps away from the edge, but felt little relief.

A glance around revealed an opening in the fog and the one constant of the gray world, the expected sight of his brother. Sure enough, Salvador was there, standing at the top of a set of steps leading into a great church. The roof of the church was dominated by one mighty bell tower peeking through the fog and lording over the rest of the city. Once again Salvador wore the robes of a priest, but without the triple-rope belt of their order. No helm covered his brother's face. Once again Ramiro's heart jumped with joy only to drop in disappointment. The figure looked the same as Salvador: his eyes, his beard, his build—but this was not his brother.

"Why do you bring me here?" Ramiro asked. Even as he tried to draw nearer, his legs bogged down, dragging and resisting his efforts. He ceased trying as it became clear he would not be allowed to get close this time.

As always the figure refused to speak, lifting his arm and pointing over Ramiro's shoulder. Ramiro whirled. Northern priests came boiling from every direction out of the void, running on thin air. All carried the killing white Diviners lifted high with unmistakable intent. Ramiro tried to flee but his legs remained unresponsive, moving like a man traveling through quicksand. He reached for a weapon but wore only his smallclothes.

"Oh saints!"

The more he struggled, the more his panic grew. The Northerners converged on him. Diviners pointed at his heart. He cringed from the killing touch . . .

And woke with a gasping start, heart beating like a rat's in a trap. His limbs scrambled out of his bedding before his brain could even pull free a clear thought, tearing the stab wound in his side. He spun to look behind him.

An unthreatening whitewashed kitchen wall returned his stare. Their packs and bags sat against the wall on the hard-swept dirt floor with the wooden kitchen tray from the monastery leaning against them.

No Northerners. No danger. No Salvador.

And no message that made any sense.

Why take him to the gray world if not to relate something of use? He already knew they were outnumbered.

He rubbed his jaw.

Stupid head. Overreacting. He was as jumpy as a frog with a heron wading across the water. There was never any danger in the gray world, he reminded himself, and the message would come with time—or maybe he'd woken before it could be delivered. He adjusted the bandage wrapped around his torso where his wound had been stitched and dabbed with honey to keep off infection. It still took his heart long minutes to settle into a normal rhythm, helped by the unconcerned snoring of Father Telo on the floor nearby.

Thankfully, there had been no one to see his panic. The man slept like the dead, pulled up close to the banked hearth for warmth. Ramiro envied the peace the priest had found since the healing of Julian. He wished he could leave aside his fears and doubts as easily and trust in God to bring them though their trials. Faith came harder for him. Or maybe he felt he had more to lose.

Ramiro left the priest to sleep and headed out the back door for a glimpse of the stars. His nerves refused to let him attempt sleep again yet, and he was reluctant to go traipsing around this house in the middle of the night to wake Teresa for a chat. She slept in a spare bedroom upstairs. No, crashing through their house in the middle of the night was a poor way to repay the people who had come to find them when they were separated from Teresa, helped them bury the soldiers' blood, and opened their house to them. Ramiro didn't intend to put them at risk for long. He hoped to be out by morning now that they had a destination—the Northern priests were apparently holed up in Aveston's grand cathedral. A fitting enough place, especially since their story to the guards at the gate was supposed to lead them there anyway. With that information, the sooner they were gone, the safer these good people would be.

The open door let in the chill midnight air, as even in the height of summer, the nights could be cold in the high desert. Ramiro shrugged a blanket around his shoulders and looked toward the stars, reflectively nudging aside hair that had become stuck to the cut on his temple and getting a dab of honey on his knuckles for his pains. Clouds muffled the sky, blocking out everything but the thin shine of the moon trapped behind their layers.

When one lived in the desert, clouds were a welcome sight. Often hoped for. But these were too insubstantial to bring the needed summer rains.

As useless as his dream.

Had the gray world been a message to be careful? That they were doomed to fail in their pursuit of Santabe?

None of those questions felt right. A nagging along his spine said the message was there—he just couldn't see it.

From out of the clouds came a haunting sound, like an unseen hand trailing fingers drawn across his bare skin.

"Ramiro."

He blinked and took a step forward. "Claire?"

Whatever it had been, it was already gone. A wisp of magic carried by the clouds. But real, unlike the gray world. Claire, or her voice, had spoken to him. In the too brief instant, he felt her well-being but loneliness. She missed him.

"I'm here," he said to the empty clouds.

I miss you, too.

His face clenched and his throat worked, wishing there was some way to send word that he felt the same. But he had no magic. Just tasks to perform before they could be reunited—as did she.

"Until then."

Time to get some sleep so he was fit for those tasks. He stepped inside, closed the door, turned, and stopped as his eyes landed on their bags. *Wait . . .*

And then the message of the gray world became clear.

He hurried forward to jostle Father Telo awake. The man looked up at him, rubbing sleep from his eyes.

"What is it, my son?"

"I have an idea. We're going to the cathedral now."

"Now?"

"Yes. It's time to get Santabe."

CHAPTER 15

Ramiro balanced covered dishes on the kitchen tray, feeling like a fool. Teresa kept throwing him accusatory glances as she lugged along her mop and full bucket. Water sloshed over the edge as they hastened to follow the priest.

"I understand why we're going to the cathedral at night—because of the Northern curfew on daytime travel—but why this?" Teresa asked.

"How better to get inside then as the cleaning staff? They may be overlords of evil, but I assume they still prefer to live in a tidy house." In a move that made actual sense, the Northerners had installed a curfew during the day, no doubt to try and ward off Dal. The toothless grandfather who ran the house where they'd left their possessions and Sancha said the soldiers were lax about enforcement. And despite the action yesterday, Ramiro had the bad feeling that the soldiers they'd encountered would have walked right past without trouble if he hadn't been holding a sword. Someone might be in control of the army again, but a soldier who expected to die screaming and begging for his life soon wasn't going to care much about anything. Still, Ramiro needed to be more careful.

Which was why he had no weapon with him for their reconnaissance of the cathedral other than his knives.

Teresa struggled along. "Then how about I carry the tray and you take the bucket?"

Ramiro looked away. He could blame his wound for having her take the heavy bucket, but that would be a lie. A small adjustment to his stride meant the puncture barely pulled or caused him pain. How could he explain the tray had been the first thing he saw after his dream and he felt he was meant to carry the blasted thing? He'd sound crazy and at the least be teased relentlessly. "Go ahead and dump out the water. We can get more when we get there."

Teresa gaped at him for a moment, then rolled her eyes, but upended the bucket to send the water splashing across the cobblestones. Father Telo looked back, put his finger to his mouth to shush them, turned around, then simply stood in the middle of the street.

Ramiro sidled forward to shake the priest. "Father?" The man looked a thousand miles away.

"Sorry. Got distracted. So many associations with this city. It's why I moved to Colina Hermosa. I wasn't exactly a . . . good man here. This way."

Ramiro shook his head, unable to believe Father Telo was anything but virtuous—ever. He shook his head again. Everybody was too distracted. Too little sleep and the smell of desperation oozed from all three of them. It was his plan, and yet he had a bad feeling about it. About the city itself. *We need to grab Santabe and get the hell out of here—the sooner the better.* His own need to get to Suseph and turn himself in to justice for desertion pulled at him.

Just in case things went truly bad, he had forced promises out of several small boys back at the house to see Sancha set free outside the city if he didn't come back within a day. He didn't trust the tooth-less grandfather not to salt and pickle the mare. That kind was practical to the core and food was already growing scarce. But, again, he had to have a little faith—if worse came to worst, Sancha could take care of herself. The Northerners had already found out her hooves and teeth were deadly. She'd sense danger and could kick her way out of the flimsy barn if necessary.

That thought, at least, calmed him a little. And when one of the dishes on his tray slid perilously close to the edge, Ramiro refocused on holding the tray level.

"Almost there," Father Telo whispered.

Ramiro hoped so. The priest had already taken them to the house of an old woman, where various herbs hung all around inside to dry. The place had made him sneeze. Father Telo now took them through what seemed like little-used alleys but that the people of Aveston probably considered thoroughfares, ending at the caretaker's house at the rear of the cathedral. If they had one advantage, it was in exploiting what the priest knew about the city of his birth—and more important, *who* he knew.

The caretaker's house looked like a cottage transplanted from the country into the heart of the city and left to lean up against the rear wall of the greatest structure in Aveston. In other words, it looked like a slum beside a mansion.

Ramiro recognized the church as the one from his dream in the gray world.

"Father Ansuro is a humble man," Telo said, "yet very proud of his home. He's very protective of the cathedral."

"We'll leave the talking to you," Ramiro promised. "Just get us inside and off the street."

They crossed a small covered porch with rotting boards. Telo gave a soft knock on the peeling paint on the door. Ramiro shook his head. If the owner was proud of his home, he had a funny way of showing it—which didn't include basic maintenance, or else his definition of *home* didn't extend to the cottage where he actually lived.

The door opened to reveal a wisp of a man, the brown of his coloring faded so pale, it appeared he never spent time in the sun. His skin had the fragile appearance of the paper surrounding an onion, but his face quickly widened into a beaming smile. He wore a dark robe of fine linen material like a man given high status in the church, but his rope belt was made of simple twine like any lesser priest. "Little Telo from the streets."

Ramiro eyed the wrestler-like shoulders of the man beside him in bemusement as Telo towered over the caretaker even while standing down a step on the porch, but Telo only grinned in return. "Father Ansuro. It's good to see you again. These are my friends, Ramiro and Teresa."

The tiny priest shuffled into the one-room cottage. Small windows made the room dim and dusty, yet his enthusiasm was infectious. "Come in! Come in! What brings you to see me?"

Father Telo waited until the door closed to say, "We need some help and more than that—information. Can you still get into Her Beauty?"

The old man limped to a rocking chair and fell more than sat into the wooden seat. "Her Beauty. Oh, aye. I tend to my magnificent girl as I have for fifty years." One brittle fist came up and shook at the air for a moment. "No matter who lives inside her, the Lord dwells there still. We fade and pass, but Her Beauty is the legacy we leave behind us."

"Amen," Father Telo said gravely. "What's happened inside since the Northerners came?"

"Only ill, which I hesitate to speak about, but they need their chamber pots emptied the same as anyone else. But sit, sit. And we will have a long talk." Father Ansuro gestured at the cramped room and to two chairs near the hearth. "I'll tell you all I know. Little Telo." He shook his head. "Of all the priests to return here during these dark times, to think it is little Telo, who used to brawl in the streets so his unrepentant friends could steal from the markets undetected. But my dreams said someone would be coming, and for Her Beauty and my dreams, I refused to go to our Lord yet, though my time is long due."

Ramiro paused in taking the three-legged stool from the corner. "Dreams? Have you dreams—about the Northerners?"

"Dreams from our Lord. They've been coming to me all my life, young man. They come to you, too, I see." Before Ramiro could answer, the thin voice went on, "You are only the second I've met to share the dreams." The old man shook his head. "A soldier and a holy man. The Lord uses what He will."

"How did you know I'm—"

"A soldier?" A gentle smile put a thousand laugh lines around the old man's eyes. "You don't have to be an observer of people to spot a soldier's carriage."

"You do have a way of standing, cousin," Teresa said.

Ignoring her comment, he asked Ansuro: "Your dreams. What message do they send?"

"What don't they say would be a better question. As I grew in years, so, too, did the dreams become more numerous. Now they haunt me constantly. Sometimes I can feel them pressing behind my eyes even when I'm awake. But they always told me my place was with Her Beauty and someday the reason for it would be clear. Lately, they've said that I wasn't alone. And here you are . . ."

"Aye," Ramiro said. Wonder rose in his breast. This frail old man had been visited by the dreams all his life, while he'd been struggling with the weight of it only a handful of weeks. No wonder Ansuro looked as if a stiff breeze could blow him over. "They told me the same. They promised me help."

"'Ask, and it will be given to you; seek, and you will find; knock, and it will be opened to you.' There are many fighting in the cause, whether they recognize as much or not. Alone we can do little; together we can do much. Help comes from all directions and in surprising forms. Have you not succeeded where you expected to fail—and lately? Good souls will recognize one another."

A shiver rode up Ramiro's spine, and Teresa wiped hastily at her eyes. "We have had unexpected help. But, to be clear, I've never been particularly religious," she said. "It just seemed like common decency to me."

"Call it what you will." Ansuro looked at them with a calm expression, not in the least put out at the skepticism. "Names have no meaning. Our Lord. The saints. The swamp women's goddess. The universe. Justice. The spark of humanity. It is all one and the same. Such has the wisdom of age taught me."

Father Telo cleared his throat. "I'm the last one to stop a discussion such as this, but Her Beauty. What goes on inside the cathedral? How fares the bishop?"

"Dead." Father Ansuro touched heart, liver, and spleen. "God forgive my anger. Most of the souls who lived inside Her Beauty are gone. The occupiers have tarnished her purity. The bishop, good man that he was, tried to reason with the enemy. They were only interested if we would forswear our own oaths and pledge ourselves to their god. As each refused to take this Dal into their heart—"

Teresa winced. "We were instructed not to say their god's name aloud. A warning for our safety."

Father Ansuro showed a frail smile. "An old man with little time calls out evil when he sees it. When they refused to take *Dal* into their hearts, they were murdered with a white staff. I never saw anything like it."

"A Diviner," Telo said, touching his body's centers of emotion as well. "So they are called in our language. God, take their good souls to your side—they might be the lucky ones to go quickly. Usually the

Northerners are not so kind." He tucked the stub of his arm close to his side.

Saddened as he was by the cruel murders, it was something else Ansuro said that struck Ramiro. "The Northern priests spoke to you?" he asked, feeling excitement rise. "How many of them could understand our language? What did they look like? Where are they now?"

"Slow down, young man. Soldiers have ever been so hasty." Ramiro quieted, though the chastening did little to quiet his mind as Ansuro continued. *He could be speaking of Santabe—we could be so close!* "Three or four of the occupiers could speak to us. One more than the others."

"A strong woman?" Teresa interrupted, as eager as Ramiro felt. "A hand taller than Father Telo and about thirty winters old. With short hair. She is called Santabe."

"Aye. That is she. A cold soul for one so young."

"Where is she now?" Ramiro asked again, his heart beating harder with sudden anticipation.

"Here, in Her Beauty, with all the others in white robes. It was she who interrogated me and she who let me live." He pointed to a small door set beside the hearth. "I told her I served only this glorious house and she saw that someone must light the fires and bring in the coal. I suppose they could have ordered their soldiers to serve them, but she was quick to see leaving some few alive who knew how to run things would make all go smoother. So I remain. Directing the few servants who haven't fled, such as they are, and putting these old hands to tasks long given over to others with more physical strength. Doing what I can to mend the tarnish they inflicted on Her Beauty. Me and mine are allowed to come and go inside as we will, and are mostly left alone."

Ramiro tensed, feeling the time had come to enter the lion's den. "Father Ansuro, you've found three more servants to add to your cleaning crew."

"Good. Good. I trust you seek this Santabe for the benefit of all. I'll ask no more." The old priest shuffled to the door beside the hearth. A map of the cathedral showing all its levels hung on the wall above a chest. From the chest, he pulled out three sets of soft-soled slippers such as he wore. "Then let's waste no time. We tolerate no boots or sandals inside Her Beauty, though I have little control over protecting her anymore. Still, I do what I can. You'll have to change. Young man, let your shoulders slump and your spine bow some. Cleaners display more humility, or to put it plainly, they display their fear more openly. Pretend you are tiptoeing around your mother."

Ramiro tried to follow the directive, but only succeeded in feeling ill at ease. "Tiptoeing around my mother would be a sure way to get her attention."

"Our Ramiro is no great actor," Teresa said with a tolerant smile. "He made but an indifferent bridegroom as well. Transparent as glass, but solid as the foundations of this great church, right, cousin? It's a trade-off we are forced to accept."

Ramiro frowned as he balanced on one leg to remove a boot. "You should not mock someone who tries. But I am a solider no longer—something my mind never forgets, though my body refuses to heed."

"Circumstances change," Telo said, fumbling one-handed with his sandals. "They don't necessarily change the man. Some are born to be soldiers, my son, and such you will be until the day you die. Circumstance cannot undo what is in the heart. Just as even in my lawless early days, I was still a priest on the inside. It simply took a little longer for my brain to recognize myself as such."

Father Ansuro turned from a shelf with a pile of polishing cloths in his arms. "As I recall, your vocation was certainly buried deep twenty years ago. No one would have guessed you were headed here—to the church."

"I think you guessed." Father Telo looked up from sliding on his shoes. "You, and others like you, wouldn't give up on me. You brought me back from my criminal ways."

"Those are some stories I must hear," Teresa said. "Father Telo as a most unsaintly youth."

"And I'd be happy to share them. But what is this?" Father Ansuro squinted in the dim light as Ramiro retrieved what he'd brought. "You'll have to leave your tray, young man. The occupiers don't trust us to pre-pare their"—his words cut off and the cloths fell from his arms as his gaze shifted to Telo for agreement—"little Telo! Your hand. I don't see as well as I used to, but I see something is missing."

Telo held out his stub. "A gift from the woman we seek, though not the reason we seek her. Over and done now. As I said, a man's circumstances change, but what's inside remains the same. Do not fret, Fa-ther—I have made my peace."

"We all bear our scars," Father Ansuro recited at rout, but the smile had gone from his eyes. "We are all touched by the evil that has come upon us. Lord, hear our prayer. Be with us in our need." He subsided into silence, though his lips moved in an unheard communication, until suddenly he said, "Little Telo, remember you are not that person anymore. Don't let anger or despair drive you back to old habits."

"It's been difficult—so much killing—but I strive to remember."

"Don't let *them* tarnish your soul as they have tar-nished Her Beauty."

Ramiro bowed his head for a moment, stricken by their words. The Northerners had put a tarnish on everyone—or had they made the tarnish them-selves in their rush to react to the Northern army? A sick feeling rushed over him, and he quickly slid the dishes from the tray with a clatter and took the pol-ishing cloths from the floor to arrange them on the wooden surface, feeling much too uneasy. If the Lord wanted to truly help them, He could have sent them five or ten fighting men, instead of two priests—one who could be knocked over by a gust of wind and the other disabled—and a scholar. "This goes where we go, Father. It's proved useful before. What else do we need? Time speeds. We should get moving."

Ramiro had to repeat his question twice more before the elderly man came out of his supplication with the Almighty and pulled some grayish smocks from a basket. "All my workers wear these. They should allow us safe passage inside Her Beauty." Father Ansuro waited the few seconds it took them to pull on the rough clothing, then opened the door.

The space inside led, not to a tiny bedroom as one might expect in a normal cottage, but to white marble floors and polished columns the diameter of a thick man, which climbed well above the roof of the simple house of the priest. The massive columns had been painted in blues, golds, and reds. A single oil lamp revealed a fresco of San Pedro, who, scripture claimed, chased the snakes from Aveston. In a niche, a reliquary of gold sat on a marble plinth beside a font. A few steps took them from rude poverty to palatial wonders. Ramiro carried the tray of polishing cloths and Teresa her bucket. Father Telo closed the door behind them, and Ramiro tried to drop his shoulders and stoop, though there was no one to see. He fingered his medallion.

"There are many saintly artifacts kept here. Rumor says, they include the armor of San Martin. He is my patron." Of all the saints, only San Martin had been a soldier at one time. Oh, others had fought, like San Jorge or even Santiago, but none had war as their profession until San Martin—he who divided his cloak with a beggar.

Father Ansuro smiled. "That's one rumor I'm sad to say is untrue. The Armor that Glows Like the Moon vanished so long ago it is only legend—if it existed at all. I can show you the preserved body of San Pedro or the robe of Santiago himself, but no armor."

Not far from the door the light faded, leaving them almost in the dark until they reached the glow of the next lantern.

"We've had to manage with less since the invasion," Father Ansuro whispered with a gesture at the oil lamp. "Less than a tenth of Her Beauty is now lit."

"That will only aid us," Father Telo answered in the same whisper. "Where do the Northerners stay?"

"And what use do they make of the cathedral?" Teresa added.

"Little use, though vile," came the answer with a sigh. "They treat Her Beauty like a hostel or a tavern. Their lesser priests and soldiers sleep in her transept and the nave. They bed down in her chapels and the choir lofts. Their more important members have taken the bishop's quarters—God rest his soul—and the other living quarters as well. That's where I take you."

Teresa switched her bucket to her other hand. "Where do they practice their worship if not the nave?"

Father Ansuro stopped. "I don't know about worshipping, but they do their killing in the inner atrium that was our reflection garden."

"It is unroofed?" Teresa asked. "Open to the sky?"

"Aye. They have spread a great carpet upon the stones among the rosebushes." Father Ansuro resumed his walk and they clustered around him. "They gather everywhere, even in the kitchens, but it is there they seem to have their formal conclaves. The entrances to the garden are kept guarded and there they store their white weapons—what did you call them?"

"Diviners," Telo supplied. "Such did I witness before—that they worship outside."

"You must tell us of anything like religious practice you have seen," Teresa said. "We need to shift through it for clues about their god."

Ramiro gave the conversation only half his attention. His eyes kept sliding around to inspect every dark corner, automatically checking behind a massive statue of Santiago hefting the staff with which he split the rock where Aveston was built. He left it to experts to hash out the inner workings of the Northerners. His job was the protection of their small group—a job at which he felt inadequately prepared without his sword or his armor.

Well did he remember that the only defense against the Diviners was to be encased in metal. And even then the protection preserved the wearer's life only. The Diviner's touch still incapacitated, rendering flesh numb.

How do I protect my friends from weapons such as that?

No longer did he have to pretend to stoop. His shoulders drooped on their own. Paranoia had him trying to look in all directions at once, as twitchy as a pack rat under the open sky, despite the cathedral being as empty as a tomb thus far. He gripped the tray tightly and tried not to panic over his responsibility for four fragile lives.

Glamorous trappings began to give way to more homey touches. A carpet runner now softened the marble floor of the much narrower hallway that Father Ansuro took them down. The lanterns grew closer together. They passed a few other souls also wearing the grayish smocks and received silent nods. Wooden doors often had some memento pinned to them to differentiate them: the faded prayer scarf of a woman, a paper with verse scrawled on it, a wilted flower.

Once they saw a man in the white sleeveless robe of a Northern priest down a cross corridor. He went on his way with barely a flicker of the eyes in their direction. Ramiro hoped the rest of the Northern priests slept like normal creatures and wouldn't be roaming the halls at late hours.

The two priests spoke together in a whisper of the most likely place to find Santabe. Father Ansuro believed the bishop's apartments to be given over to several of the more venerable Northerners, much older than the woman they sought, and suggested they check the rooms nearby instead.

Ramiro kept his eyes on the floor and tried not to break into a run as two Northern soldiers stood half-asleep on their feet below a marble arch that led to the grander apartments. Proof that the Northerners found someone worth guarding ahead. They eased past the dull stares of the soldiers and continued to the other end of a long hallway. Here, the doors were farther apart and silver placards on each proclaimed the names of the now-deceased original occupants. The old priest slid open a panel in the wall to reveal a heap of irregular lumps of black rocks. Teresa squatted to fill her bucket as the other two worked out the details of delivering coal to each room as an excuse to get inside.

Ramiro took a polishing cloth and idly ran it across a piece of crown molding. "Let me check the rooms," he whispered. He tried to hand Teresa another cloth, but she glared at him.

"I'm just as capable."

"It's too dangerous," he hissed back, trying to take the bucket from her as the two priests stared. "I'm the one with training. Let me be the one to risk myself."

She drew her bucket back when he reached for it. "No. You made me carry it. It's mine."

"We don't have time for this," Telo said with a shake of the head.

Teresa gritted her teeth, then relaxed and clicked her tongue. "You're right. This is silly. We'll take turns. But I think they are more likely to dismiss a woman like me as no threat. You give me too little credit."

Ramiro took his hands off the bucket as if stung. She had a valid point. His mother and Claire would both scold his sexist ways. "I'm an ass."

A smile crept up her face. "Not so much an ass as an overprotective nanny goat."

He grinned in turn. "I'll let the name-calling slide. Equal turns, then. You can go first."

"Now you are an ass." But she squeezed his arm as she chose a door at random and slipped her head inside. Ramiro held his breath as the others seemed to do the same, counting slowly in his head as thoughts tumbled on what he should do—could do—if something went wrong.

The answer was a frightening nothing.

"Not her," Teresa said breathlessly, easing the door shut. "It was a man. Sound asleep."

Ramiro gave her the tray and took the bucket, then went to the next door. A glance inside showed a large canopy bed with the hangings left open. The priests of Aveston lived a richer life than most of their people. He shook off the intruding thought and focused on the snoring occupant—gray hair, mouth open, chest hair—another man. "Not her," he said simply as he backed out and inched the door closed. Ramiro touched his medallion of San Martin as he traded the bucket for the tray again, cracking his neck to cut the climbing tension.

By the saints, this could take all night.

He didn't know if his nerves could take it. A clearer message in his dream could have made this so much easier and faster, not to mention less dangerous to their health. Annoyance mingled with fear to make the sweat dampening his hairline that much thicker.

Anyone could walk by at any minute and find servants clustered in the hall, most definitely not doing their jobs and in obvious need of punishment.

Teresa opened the third door and dodged back out fast. Her face burned with a red blush and her eyes were round with shock. "Hell's bells. Not asleep." An angry shriek came from behind the door. "And not alone."

Before Ramiro could open his mouth, the door burst open and a naked woman launched out, a Diviner held in her upraised hand.

Their plan fell into chaos.

CHAPTER 16

Indecision held Ramiro frozen in the hallway while their plan of stealth crumbled around them, taking their opportunity for flight.

Teresa managed to dodge under the naked woman's wild swing with the Diviner by falling to the floor and scrambling away. Her bucket went rolling, spilling lumps of coal. Ramiro hesitated as his other companions, the two priests, receded to a safe distance. Self-preservation screamed at him to flee, weaponless and therefore helpless, but it got scant notice behind the urge to protect those weaker.

No longer stuck by uncertainty, Ramiro jumped in to intercept the next attack on Teresa, sweeping the tray around to give him time to pull his knife, sending polishing cloths flying everywhere.

The solid staff of the Diviner hit the back of the

wooden tray with an audible whack. Ramiro cringed, expecting the thin tray to fail and split. Instead, the Diviner burst in a spray of splinters, the solid weapon flying apart.

Saints!

Ramiro's eyes closed as fragments cut into his face. His wasn't the only gasp of astonishment. Someone screamed. He overbalanced when the resistance against the tray vanished and found himself falling before he landed hard on his left elbow on the relentless marble floor in a burst of pain. When he reopened his eyes, he stared in wonder at the tray, but it looked no different, though it felt a touch warmer.

In the intervening time, Father Telo had shot forward, leaving Father Ansuro by the coal hole, and grabbed the naked woman around the neck, pulling her down. Her stiffened fist made contact with his middle, sending the air rushing out of Telo's lungs in an explosive cough.

Barefoot and hair tousled, a man burst out of the sleeping room, adjusting his white robe around his hips and brandishing another Diviner. Ramiro managed to stick out his leg. The Northerner's feet caught on it, and he stumbled across the hall to bang into the wall. As Ramiro fought to his feet, Teresa jumped on the man's back. They bumbled across the hallway with the Diviner flailing, the Northerner unable to quite bend his arm to reach Teresa for the kill.

Doors opened all along the hall. Ramiro's heart

sank as more Northern priests poured out. There wasn't time to worry about the fresh threats.

Ramiro swung the tray in an upstroke to push the Diviner away. The barest brush with the tray and the white staff cracked apart like the first, showering them with bone-like shards.

"Saints!" burst from Ramiro's lips, aloud this time, then, "hold him still!" he shouted to Teresa to little avail. But years of training from the time he still wore his mother's apron strings had taught him many things: how to fight or defend, how to survive, and how to be lethal in an instant. He punched out with his tingling left arm and landed his fist squarely in the Northerner's throat, hearing fragile bones and cartilage break. The man folded, hands grasping his neck as he choked, taking Teresa down with him.

Father Telo had his legs scissored around the naked woman, holding her captive. He fished a small brown bottle out of his pocket that Ramiro recognized from the herb shop they'd visited earlier. He splashed the liquid inside onto his handkerchief and doused his robe in the process. He held the cloth over the naked woman's nose and mouth as she struggled and struck at him until her body went limp.

"One out," Telo panted. He twisted and found the choking Northern man with his handkerchief. *Another out soon*, Ramiro thought. But more Northern priests and Diviners rushed them from both ends of the hall.

Tray held tight in both hands, Ramiro spun like when he'd fought the biting flies, fanning the tray to strike as many Diviners as possible. The Northerners aimed for the tray with a single-mindedness that bespoke an anger and obsession with an obstacle never encountered before. They weren't used to seeing their weapons fail and it showed on their faces.

Yet, the Diviners failed again and again.

Bone-like weapons shattered in every direction, chips of them cutting into Ramiro's arms, his back. The knife-sharp splinters, however, fell hardest on their opponents, taking out eyes or gashing throats. But not enough. With each strike, the tray grew hotter to hold as if it absorbed the power into itself and could not be rid of it.

Disarmed Northerners fell to fighting with empty hands. Ramiro drew his knife, while Teresa had found the coal bucket and swung it to good effect against Northern priests' heads, allowing Telo to dose them with the knockout drug. The tide began to turn and the numbers to go their way.

A Diviner reached for Teresa as desperation to destroy turned to killing rage. Ramiro despaired he'd be too late to save her when he saw frail little Father Ansuro leap between them. The Diviner touched the priest's shoulder and his muscles locked for one terrible instant, then he dropped to the floor, eyes staring and empty.

Teresa stifled a scream behind her hands.

Something snapped. Ramiro didn't bother going for the Diviner. He attacked with the knife, leaving the blade embedded when he lost his grip on the hilt and hitting the Northern man's head with the tray—once, twice—putting all his strength behind the blows. The man crumpled, breathing raggedly. His outstretched arm fell across the dead body of Father Ansuro in an eerie embrace of murderer and victim.

Bile rose in Ramiro's throat.

"Look out!" Telo shouted.

Ramiro turned to find one last Northerner.

"You!" they both said in recognition at the same time.

He faced a tall woman, easily able to look him in the eye. Wiry muscles stood out along her arms and confidence surrounded her like an aura. Santabe looked the same except for hair cut off raggedly short and two sun-shaped earrings. She flicked a strand of hair from her face, standing perfectly balanced among shards of Diviners, lumps of coal, and unconscious Northerners. A white Diviner was held ready in her poised hand and another of red waited belted at her waist.

Her face twisted with hate. "The boy with the stone. This time you die."

"A boy no longer. This time we take you again." Ramiro spat to seal his words, seeing his message hit home. She feared capture more than she did death. But his words were bravado. Already he panted, fatigued from the fight, recent wounds aching, while she was fresh and ready.

Plus, wiser than her companions, Santabe held back, making no extravagant thrusts with her Diviner, but staying cautious and away from his kitchen tray as they felt each other out, measuring determination and finding not a hairsbreadth of difference between them.

"Why would you come here?" she asked as they circled, stepping warily over the clutter in the hall. She motioned at Father Telo with a flicker of her Diviner, even outnumbered, holding her cool with impressive calm and employing a sneer. "I let you go and still you return. You are stubborn like a *frigmet*. You think to kill our chief priests and make us retreat from your land? It will not work. We shall never go away."

Teresa looked up from where she struggled to pull Father Ansuro's body to a safe distance, but it was Father Telo who huffed and answered, "You tell us why the Northerners invaded in the first place, and we'll tell you why we're here. Why do you stay? Surely, you got what you came for. Your god is loose among us and away from your people. Why else kill Ordoño?"

She barked out a laugh. "Ordoño? He was ever always . . . what is the word? A cata . . . catalyst. That is the word. Still you think of him. You are as stupid as the rest."

Ramiro saw his opening as her eyes wavered from

him. "Now!" He charged in with the tray held before him at chest height. She swung at him, powering forward to meet him using all her strength. Diviner struck the miraculous tray, and for a moment the balance of power lay even, then the heat in the tray spiked to an unbearable level. The tray split with the sound of a thunderclap, growing instantly cool.

As it gave way, Ramiro didn't waste time on regret, twisting to the left and feeling the shadow of the Diviner pass along his back, actually touching his smock—like an invisible finger. The near miss raised chill bumps along his spine. He had avoided its deadly touch . . . and then his foot came down on coal dust mixed with blood, and the floppy shoes slipped, betraying him. He braced for death.

His muscles didn't lock, and the charge like lightning didn't come.

Father Telo had ahold of Santabe's arm, forcing her Diviner aloft. She raked her fingers down the priest's face, tearing his skin and scraping at his eyes, trying to force the priest to let her go. Ramiro used the time to scramble to his feet, reaching for his knife only to realize it was long gone. He looked about for something else, but then remembered he still held the split tray. Moving forward, he clapped the two halves of the tray around the deadly Diviner and squeezed them together, pinching her hand in between. Santabe howled in pain. Teresa leaped into the fray, grabbing Santabe's free hand and pulling it down.

Stymied, Santabe kicked out, catching Ramiro with bruising force on the thigh. In return, he drew the tray pieces with her arm clamped between closer to his chest just as she wrenched her other arm free from Teresa.

Ramiro grunted as he swung their whole group around and slammed Santabe's hand, clamped in the tray, against the wall until the Diviner clattered free. He kicked it away and it shot into the coal hole.

He dropped the pieces of tray, but Santabe had already used his second of delay to punch Telo in the kidney, sending the priest reeling off.

It was still three against one, however, and while the priest fell, Ramiro grabbed Santabe by the throat and squeezed. Her eyes rounded as anger surged through him. He might be exhausted, but right now he had one of the reasons for all his losses in his hands. For this he had strength to spare.

She beat useless at his arms, unable to find purchase, and he elbowed her off when she went for his eyes. "Why?" he demanded in a growl. "Why is your kind doing this? Every time we meet, you kill another of my friends—my kin!" Sweat and blood trickled into his eye, stinging, yet his gaze never wavered from hers. He tightened his grip on her neck, uncaring if she could answer him or not. Tired of the killing—tired of the dying.

Father Telo was abruptly there with his drugged handkerchief as Teresa spoke unheard words in

Ramiro's ear, fighting to pull his hands away from the Northerner's throat. Santabe sagged in his arms and Ramiro slackened his grip with great reluctance as their common purpose flooded back. They needed her alive. He let Santabe crash to the floor, wiping his hands on his pants.

Father Ansuro's empty eyes stared up at him in accusation. His body even more shrunken. Another soul let down. Like Gomez and Alvito. Like Salvador. Like all his fellow soldiers.

Ramiro tottered away to a bare spot against the wall to sink to the cold marble and cover his face with his hands. What good did it do to fight when good men could die in the time it took to snap your fingers?

Even if Santabe lived and talked and they found a way to stop Dal, what good did it do? It wouldn't recreate Colina Hermosa or Salvador or free Aveston from their occupiers. Even without Dal, they lived at the mercy of an unstoppable army in their midst.

And most likely there was no way to stop a god.

He scrubbed at blood and grit on his face, pushing the foul away as he pushed away the despair in his gut, trying to shake off bitterness. Wisdom claimed revenge was hollow, and so he struggled to look past retaliation and vengeance. The three of them had succeeded for the moment. If he only looked at the present and not ahead, he could keep faith and keep going. He could only pray in the long run that he didn't regret this act of mercy and letting Santabe live another day.

He clung to the fact that there was a job to do. *One thing at a time.* He wished to all the hells there was someone else to be in charge and give the orders. He looked over the jumble of bodies and knew they needed to act fast before they were discovered.

He spoke his worries aloud. "What do we do now? How do we get her out of here without being caught?" The priest and the scholar had planned and bluffed their way through so far; they needed a little more of that magic.

Father Telo looked up from where he said last rites over the little caretaker and spoke as if he hadn't heard. "He was the best of men. I'd be a bandit or dead if not for his intervention."

Emotion tightened Ramiro's throat. "Father Ansuro got involved when he didn't have to." Ramiro touched his San Martin medallion in silent salute to a brave man who deserved better. Who would take care of Her Beauty? Somehow the great cathedral being empty and uncared for sent a stab to his heart—another part of normal life wiped away. He choked off a sob before it could start and the last scrap of him that still stood firm could fall apart.

Teresa continued to stand with her face against the wall.

"Father," Ramiro pressed. "I'm sorry, but we have to move on. Try and hide this to give us time to escape."

"I know a way." Father Telo levered himself from the floor as if all the heart had gone from him as well and went a few feet down the hall to slide open another panel in the wall. "Laundry chute."

Ramiro nodded. The space was wide enough to thrust down an armful of bedding with ease. They could drop the living and dead down to the cathedral cellars, swab up the blood, coal, and splinters with the polishing cloths, and drop those down, too. He glanced down at his blood-splattered smock, feeling the sting of each cut on his face and body, and knew they'd never pass through the building unnoticed. They'd have to take the laundry chute as well and hope the bodies they pushed down first broke their fall.

A piece of the tray lay nearby, and he touched a corner with his foot. It didn't take a dream to tell him the kitchen tool would save their lives no longer. And he'd never get a chance to talk to Father Ansuro about the dreams.

He said a thank-you to both in his head and touched mind and heart, tightened his jaw, and forced himself to his feet. There was a job to do in this moment. He'd meet what came later and so get through the now. But by the looks of things, they all be as broken as the tray before the end.

CHAPTER 17

Claire lay looking upward at the rough finish on the ceiling of the one-room structure, while the pit in her stomach slowly grew. Her Rose Among Thorns test would be first thing this morning. Dread kept her in her blankets and unable to move.

Her fingers curled, gripping helplessly. She'd rather have had the test last night and gotten it over with, but another applicant had been promised that time for her own test, and so Claire's had been put off. Her sleep had been pitiful. She'd even gotten up in the middle of the night and spoken Ramiro's name on the wind, for all the good such a childish action did. He might not be able to hear her, but her venture had given her enough comfort that she could ignore the startled faces of nearby sleepers and go back to her bed for a little rest.

But now she was lying here with nothing to do but think, which only made the worry worse.

With a sigh, she pushed upright from her blankets, only to jump as she found Errol staring directly at her. "Demon," he said, then pointed a twig at her. "Destroyer."

His eyes dropped, and he resumed poking at the heel of his boot with the stick.

She slapped a hand over her mouth and dashed out of the little shelter to heave the contents of her shriveled stomach into a buttonbush. Did he have to bring that up when she felt at her weakest?

Three empty heaves later, she passed a shaky hand over her face. The anger quickly turned toward herself. It did no good to be upset at someone who for all purposes might as well have been an infant.

When she returned to the shelter, Errol sat poking at his boot, paying her no mind. He'd been doing the same before she went to sleep and every time she woke up during the night. Jorga had already taken a small knife away that he'd been using to try and cut apart his boot, but he seemed as satisfied to use the more ineffective stick to worry at the leather. Bromisto still lay curled in his blankets in the corner, able to sleep through almost anything.

"Good, you're up," Jorga said by way of greeting. "We should practice. We have a few minutes and a warm-up might do you good."

Claire's face tightened into a scowl. "No more

practice. What else haven't you told me?" If Jorga kept the ambush by the Elders a secret, there was no telling what else she held back. Claire still felt enough resentment at the trickery that she'd kept the Diviner they carried in her belongs instead of handing it over to the Elders as she'd planned.

"I've told you everything that I'm allowed to share." Jorga's face looked as sour as Claire's stomach contents had tasted. "If you spent a little more time practicing and a little less time worrying, you wouldn't be afraid of failing."

"I'm not afraid of failing. I'm afraid this is a waste of time."

"Spending time with your own kind is never a waste of time."

Claire rolled her eyes—internally, of course. It always seemed to come back to that with her grandmother. They were both up, though, so she asked instead, "What happens to girls who fail?"

"Never you mind about that. It's not going to happen. Not to my kin."

"How do you know? Maybe I'll be the first."

Jorga merely shook her head and didn't respond. Claire eyed the older woman suspiciously. Since when had Jorga passed up a chance to shoot down her hopes? Jorga seemed to enjoy taking her down a peg at every opportunity.

"Why are you so sure I'll pass?"

Her grandmother looked away, and for a moment,

her face slid to pure mulishness, then her expression relaxed. "Your magic is too strong. It's a rare ability to Sing a Death Song at your age—or any age."

Claire's curiosity grew. "How rare?"

Jorga shrugged. "Rare. One in twenty, if that. I doubt your mother could have Sung such a Song at seventeen."

Clare's eyes widened. "One in twenty. Why . . . that would mean only two in the camp."

"Myself and Muriel," Jorga said with a smug twist of her mouth. "Until now. Eulalie never did live that down. Mind you, more gain the strength by middle age; few have it in their youth. So that sets you apart even more."

Claire found she had nothing to say and so dusted off her clothing as best she could. Jorga had reported the girls spent months creating a new outfit for their testing, sewing each stitch by hand. The only thing she had to wear were the clothes on her back. She lifted her chin. That's as may be, but she'd rather go to her test smelly and dirty than beg and borrow clean clothes.

She was nearly two years over the normal age for this trial. That should have given her some reassurance she was better prepared, but it only made her fret more. Standing out, whether among her own kin or in the desert, never got any easier.

"Where do I go for my test?"

Jorga got laboriously to her feet. "I'll show you. As

an Elder, I must witness." They paused a moment for the older woman to wake Bromisto and give the boy strict instructions to keep Errol inside, and then they were on their way.

Walking seemed to help as their destination turned out to be a good way from the gathering, no doubt for safety reasons. Sixteen-year-old girls using new magics and forcing their talent to the highest edge of their ability—what could possibly go wrong? Despite the sarcastic thought, Claire's nerves slowly settled with the exercise of simply moving. She would do well or she wouldn't and no amount of fretting would make the outcome positive.

They were the first to reach the clearing where Jorga said the test was held. Nothing marked it as of any importance except a small pile of rocks with a baked clay figure atop it, which could have been a woman sitting on folded legs . . . or just a lump of sun-dried clay, as time and weather had so worn the statue as to make it nearly featureless. Still, Claire sent a quick appeal to the Great Goddess for a favorable outcome, or at least to be spared making a fool of herself.

Soon other women joined them, silent in the mist of early morning as if reluctant to speak. The clearing held that sort of sacred stillness that only occurred when few people were yet stirring. Claire recognized Rachael and then Muriel, and stood alone as Jorga went to join them. Muriel had lost the dimple from her cheek and Rachael kept pulling her scarf closer about her throat, their faces awash in such seriousness that Claire's stomach complained to her again.

The rising sun had begun to break up the mist before Eulalie arrived, carrying of all things a live chicken by its feet, and causing the other six or seven women to look up expectantly. Apparently, Eulalie felt quite happy to keep everyone waiting because she wore a pleased smirk in her piggy eyes. The Elders rotated the top responsibilities, with each taking turns being the leader for a term of three years, and Claire had just missed being under Muriel's milder governance.

"Well, let's get this trial over with," was Eulalie's inauspicious opening. "I expect it will be a right hash with Rosemund training her. You may guide this trial, Muriel."

To Claire's consternation, Jorga refused to stand up for her and she had to bite her tongue to keep from more hot words. She'd already resolved not to rise to their bait, but Eulalie's decision to stand as judge instead of officiant burned. She suspected Eulalie would vote for her failure no matter what.

"I think we all heard her Speak on the Wind last night. It was quite impressive, despite being sent to a man"—Muriel's dimple appeared for an instant—"so we can skip starting with that. Show us your Share Memory, Claire."

Claire drew herself up tall, clasping her hands

before her. She'd practiced that enough to be fairly confident and felt thankful to Muriel for starting off with something easy. She quickly Sang her memory of Ramiro's city burning, remembering to add the sparks that flew upward and the height of the flames. With a few short words, she added the emotion of the heat beating against her face and driving her back, and the great sadness she'd felt, mixed with awe for the power of the fire.

More than one Elder gasped as she shared the emotion along with the vision, and Claire hid her own pleased smirk as Eulalie's faded to annoyance at the proof of her innovation.

"Fancy feathers don't necessarily make a swan," Eulalie huffed in a false whisper and many of the Elders nodded their heads.

And sheep don't necessarily make great leaders, Claire thought, but kept to herself.

Next, at Muriel's suggestion, Claire Sang an illusion by making them see her as a deer, and demonstrated the strength of her Hornet Tune. Their dismissal of her made it easy to harden her determination and summon a magic that sank deeply into their minds. Two of the Elders actually bumped heads while flailing at the air, one of them stifling a bloody nose with her sleeve. Eulalie had to grab at her squawking chicken at the last minute as it almost worked itself free from her fingers when she swatted at nonexistent bees.

Jorga gave her a nod of approval, and Claire's spirits soared.

"She seems very well prepared," Muriel said, her dimple again in evidence.

Rachael cleared her throat, brushing at a strand of hair that had worked loose during the Hornet Tune. "I'm not one who can't admit when I'm wrong, and this girl is better trained than I expected. I give the credit to her grandmother. Jorga always had a fine hand for training."

"Strength runs in families, I'll admit that," Eulalie said with narrowed eyes. "But so does flightiness and foolishness. Jorga boasts the girl can manage a Death Song. I say we move straight to that." She gave the chicken a shake to stun the poor thing and dropped the bird, stepping away from it. "Prove you can manage a Death Song. Kill it."

Claire stared at the bird wide-eyed as her mother's warnings about relying on the magic reared in her head. Death magic was meant for defensive purposes—to save her life, to protect others—not for a whim.

She looked down. A plain old brown hen, it lay unmoving among the tangled grasses. No doubt intended for the stewpot anyway, like dozens of others she'd killed with her own hands and eaten. The magic would give the poor thing a quick and more painless death than a hatchet or wringing its neck. If she used the magic for killing just this once it didn't form a pattern or make her any less principled. After all, they weren't asking her to take a human life.

Silly. It's just a hen.

Completing the Rose Among Thorns trial would give her standing and make her a peer. Her words would be heeded. But why couldn't Jorga testify that she'd accomplished this magic? Why must she prove it?

They looked at her expectantly. "Go ahead, dear," Muriel said, but her dimple had vanished.

The animal would die for their food supply anyway. Cold washed over her, but she gave a nod to show she would play along. The decision might have been made, but she had to work past a lump in her throat to get out the first words, adjusting the Song to fit the much more unsophisticated victim.

> *"Icy shakes.*
> *Strength flees.*
> *Suffering.*
> *Will dies.*
> *Loss, Emptiness.*
> *Heart fails.*
> *Let go.*
> *Go in peace.*
> *Inevitable.*
> *Nothingness."*

This time as she invoked the magic—unlike with the Northern soldiers when she'd been scared out of her mind—she could feel the life fade from the bird as its heart slowed. Her determination focused the magic upon the chicken, stifling its breathing, the flow of blood. The beats becoming fainter, slower.

The hen already smelled dead. A malice pushed against her skull. Hatred. Evil.

She jerked as something split the hen into two chunks of flesh. A slicing cut ran across Claire's thigh. She cried out. Another stinging pain hit her back.

All around her the Elders shrieked as the attack fell upon them, parting their flesh.

Dal.

"The demon!" Rachael shouted.

Claire gasped. They'd shed no blood. What had brought the god?

"Our plan. Time to bring out our strategy." Eulalie gestured, and the other Elders hurried to line up, arm in arm with her. Jorga took her place at the end of the line. "Together."

Plan? What strategy?

The Elders blended their voices in a Song that Claire recognized. The same Song Jorga had used to try and induce Ramiro to kill himself. That Song had been powerful enough to force him to put a knife through his own eye, only Claire's desperate refusal to allow him to die had stopped the nightmare, awakening Ramiro from her grandmother's magic.

Taken together, the combined Song lay Claire out on the ground with her hands clamped over her ears. No matter how much she knew the Song wasn't aimed at her, she had to grasp her hands together to keep them from tearing at her face, her heart, and attempting to injure herself.

This was the Elders' response to Dal.

Despite the force of the Song, Dal's malice didn't falter. The hatred and malevolence beat upon Claire as hard as ever. Another incision opened down her forearm. She watched in shock as blood slowly welled to the surface of her skin in a precise line as long as her hand. Jorga cried out, losing the thread to the tune but groping her way back to the Song, only to fail again. One by one, the other Elders fumbled and lost their concentration as wounds grew. In desperation, they switched to another Song that Claire had never heard before. Muriel dropped to the ground, clutching her belly.

It wasn't working.

A god wasn't a chicken or a human. Its mind must be too alien to comprehend or influence. Did it even have a heart to stop or breath to still?

Illusion.

If Dal couldn't be stopped, perhaps it could be fooled.

Words tumbled from Claire's mouth, growing into a new Song. A Song not to defeat or weaken but to hide. With words and melody, she built a picture that washed away herself and the Elders. Frantically, she fought against a force that shouldn't exist, to blot out evidence of their existence—to let the god see an empty clearing. Her will fought to strengthen the Song and send the illusion out farther and farther to cover as much ground as possible.

The hatred against life wavered as if puzzled. Dirt near Claire's ear poofed into the air as a strike went wide. A form appeared in the sky about ten feet above their heads, bulky and elongated like a grossly swollen caterpillar—if a caterpillar could be the size of a goat. There and gone before she could get a sense of details. Then Dal's presence receded to become more distant—still there, but focused elsewhere.

For an eternity, Claire lay where she had fallen, not daring to move, continuing her Song of illusion until it became a hoarse whisper. Her lips cracked and her throat ached, and still she Sang. She clung to the words as to a lifeline until her voice gave out and all that persisted was another woman's whimpering cries.

Claire clutched her bleeding arm to her chest and sat up, wondering if the death blow was about to come. After a few tense seconds, it was clear Dal had gone. Worked his evil and moved on. Instead of relaxing, her heart pounded. What had it *done*? A killer must . . .

"Amos," Eulalie said weakly.

A breeze rippled the feathers on what remained of the chicken. Claire climbed stiffly to her feet, wounds protesting. When she attempted to assist Jorga, her grandmother slapped her hands away.

"Errol. Go find Errol. Hurry."

The Elders were in no shape to rise with any speed, their age and bulk working against them. Claire stumbled away from them in the direction of the camp, gaining swiftness as she tore through the trees. Disaster met her eyes before she even entered the camp. The illusion she'd conjured had saved their lives in the clearing, but her magic hadn't reached to the camp. Bodies of Women of the Song lay sprawled everywhere, broken and bleeding. The large shape of Amos lay near a fire pit with his throat sliced open. His arms and legs were scattered three feet away from the rest of him.

Claire retched until bile landed on her shoes, but she couldn't unsee the sight or the others around her. Women and girls lay dead everywhere, having suffered in the most gruesome ways possible. A very few of the older women moved, and Claire wondered if they too had used illusion.

She covered her eyes, wanting to run away. But Errol and Bromisto had been inside. Perhaps they survived. Claire made herself walk to their shelter with her eyes open but mind closed to the slaughter around her. The door was shut. She pushed it open with a trembling hand to find that Dal could work inside walls now.

The boys' flesh had been torn apart, making it impossible to tell one from the other.

Rage bloomed in her heart and spread from the

top of her skull to the tips of her feet. Wrath traveled through her, pushing out loss and grief, leaving no room for love or kindness.

Errol had named her Destroyer.

Destroyer is what they would get.

CHAPTER 18

"I understand that, ma'am," Gonzalo repeated for the third time as the afternoon sun faded into the weakness of evening. Shadows from the saguaro cactus stretched across the road to Suseph, looking like flat men throwing their hands into the air in surrender. "But I still think a stronger-worded message with clear orders, not suggestions, is needed."

"*Alcaldes* are not soldiers." Beatriz slapped her fan against her chest, a sure sign of exasperation, though Julian watched her make decisions and receive reports as if she'd been doing so all her life—from horseback no less.

He'd agreed with her quick arrangement with Captain Gonzalo for his men to act as messengers and visit every village, small town, and city with warnings about Dal, in addition to a suggestion for their *alcaldes* to attend a large convocation in Suseph in five days. All of which freed the three of them from the time-consuming necessity of visiting each settlement. Although it remained doubtful if the more distant *ciudades-estado* like Vista Sur could make the meeting in time.

We'll take what we can get.

The newly made messengers only waited the word to go—the letters written—as Beatriz and Gonzalo hashed through the finer points one last time. Julian prayed his wife kept her temper. Debate was a healthy opportunity for a leader to make her decisions stronger, but Beatriz was unused to viewing opposition as such. However, it was her lesson to learn, and not his to teach—at least in public. He must walk a fine line of advising without influencing.

Beatriz's words did nothing to diminish Gonzalo. "In times such as these, exceptions must be made," he said. "The other *alcaldes* do nothing. They must be ordered by those with more vision."

Her fan flew, disarranging her hair, then gradually slowed to create a more gentle flow in the still air. "I thank you for your words, Captain," she said. "I continue to disagree. You can't treat *alcaldes* as hirelings. You cannot command politicians to keep their people sequestered inside, nor can I demand they appear at a *convocación*." Julian bit his tongue to force himself to stay out of it until invited. Beatriz went on without a glance his way. "It must be their choice. We must persuade, not order."

"But there is no law as such against doing so," Gonzalo said.

"Julian, tell him what you told me."

"Actual there is at least one," Julian said, happy to go for the surest argument against the straitlaced captain. "Our law states a convocation can be invitation only, unless a quorum of *alcaldes* has declared support. In normal times, it would take a dozen sevendays to organize enough support to send invitations alone and still some would stay home to show their strength. Now—with no gentle feelers ahead of time—possibly half will come. The rest will send surrogates or no one at all. I have to agree with Beatriz that ordering will only put their backs up. I'm afraid, in the case of politics, unwritten rules are as important as those on the books."

Julian knew Beatriz had to stand on her feet as *alcalde* without any help from her spouse. Yet even he had taken counsel daily from the *concejales* of Colina Hermosa—often learning and benefiting from their experience and wisdom. With those men absent, he'd do his best to fill the void of experience and give good advice when asked.

With a half smile, he chided himself that from what he'd witnessed, Beatriz needed very little help from himself or any other. She'd managed a citadel with hundreds of servants and run the rumor mills of Colina Hermosa for long enough years to be perfectly capable of making excellent decisions as *alcalde* with minimal advice from him. Yet, he knew the difficulties she'd have would come from others' reaction to her leadership. A woman in charge would be second-guessed. If hearing the same words from his mouth would make people accept her directions, then he'd gladly back her up. Soon enough they would see her good sense, as he did.

A glowing pride in Beatriz's commanding presence easily overshadow the tiny part of him that missed being the one to make the hard choices.

"Hi-ya," Gonzalo said reluctantly, finally giving over. The man meant well, but he'd never acted as advisor in this capacity before. The news of the death of all the other *pelotón* captains had the remaining captain champing at the bit like a horse eager for action—even if no one had any idea what—any action would do. Still, Julian was the one to encourage Gonzalo to speak his mind and act as an advisor—at least until they reached Suseph, by tomorrow morning. The man was straightforward, experienced in his own field, and used to leading men; his thoughts in other areas besides political maneuverings would be invaluable to Beatriz.

Julian rubbed at tired eyes and stifled a yawn, amused in a strange way that being raised from the dead didn't make one less subject to exhaustion or free a person from the ravages of increasing age. The gentle sway of his horse acted like a lullaby to send him to sleep. Despite Captain Gonzalo dancing attendance on them, Julian looked forward to a real bed.

Selfish.

How many citizens would never enjoy a bed again? His own son was out there entering the den of the jackals to find a madwoman who might or might not tell them of a way to defeat Dal. There might be no such information to find—no way to stop the killing. They were truly hanging from a spider web—their hopes as flimsy as a thread.

Gonzalo showed no such signs of being weary or discouraged, making yet another protest. Thank the saints for military men and their sense of duty. "Then I would urge caution on the last part of your message. Telling the common people the truth about this god not only goes against the precedent, but will lead to chaos in the streets. Law and order will break down. Looting. Thievery. Even murder will result."

"Then you have less faith in our people than I," Beatriz said with force. "People will find their faith. The truth will bring them together. They deserve to know, to have that chance to make their peace with their families and their god, and protect themselves in the meantime."

"I have some experience with controlling a civilian population in dangerous times. It doesn't always work out as one would hope." Gonzalo's spine snapped straighter, if that was possible. Julian could see his knuckles whiten on his reins.

"I agree with you both," Julian said hastily. He thought Gonzalo likely right about the chaos, but the side of honor leaned toward Beatriz. "If I might, there is no right answer, as there are bound to be some who react badly to the news—possibly a majority. Society could destruct further. Precedent is against revealing too much. But precedent has never put us under such deadly conditions. Like Beatriz, I want to believe that this test will bring out the best in our people."

"God works through us all," Beatriz said simply. "I might be overly optimistic, but the more people who know what we face, the greater the chance that someone rises who can stop it. If we miscarry, perhaps someone else won't. What would the saints do?"

Gonzalo touched mind and heart, his dark face solemn. "'Ever do we speak truth,'" he quoted from Santiago's famous sermon.

"'For all to hear,'" Beatriz finished. Her mouth twisted sourly. "Besides, that is not my call, except in Suseph. Like the rest of the message, acting on my suggestions is up to the *alcaldes* reading the letter. Some will be wise and some will let their feet stick in the mud out of cowardice. Like you, I'd rather order, but some things cannot be forced."

Beatriz sniffed. "The *alcalde* have always reminded me of small children, with their petty pride squabbles. *What* alcalde *should lead this? Who gets right of preference?* A woman would not care about such things, and yet now I have to. I can only hope that the group who actually come to the convocation will also reveal the truth publicly. The more who know, the better our chances."

Unlike Beatriz, Julian couldn't find faith that someone else would save the day. The task fell upon them to devise another way in case their plan with Santabe faltered. So if Dal couldn't be destroyed, could the god be bribed or distracted or somehow made weaker?

The answer stared them all in the face. Julian gazed at the shadows crossing the road without seeing them. Nobody wanted to be the one to broach the solution because it was equally devastating. Even letting his mind skirt the words turned his blood to ice.

Coward. How can you refuse to face the truth? It must be done, and sooner rather than later.

"Blood," he said.

"What's that, Julian?" Beatriz asked.

"There is something else we could prepare," Julian said, causing all riding close enough to hear to turn in his direction. "A last alternative plan. The Northerners use blood, *mi amor*—"

"Later," Beatriz snapped, her face becoming closed. "We can talk about this later."

"There is *no* later." To say the words brought only sadness. To force the issue in public hurt more. "We must face the fact that we may not be able to stop the deaths. But we also know the Northerners have given us clues to their god and we must take advantage of that gift."

"What are we talking about?" Gonzalo's face registered suspicion. The captain stuck to Beatriz like a queen bee to its honey, refusing to leave her without protection. No doubt he saw any subterfuge as another trick for Beatriz to blunder off defenseless.

Julian, however, wanted this off his chest and out in the open as much as Beatriz preferred to deny it. "Blood summons the creature. Blood fuels their weapons. Their executions are nothing but a bath of blood in the name of their god. It is the common theme at every point. If blood is what starts it, what if only blood can stop this monstrosity and end it?"

"What are you saying?" Gonzalo looked sick and Beatriz hid behind her fan.

Julian reached across the space between them and took Beatriz's cold hand. She'd shut her eyes as if to shut out his words. "*Mi amor*, you must face it. We all must. Better the choice be on our terms than that creature's. Giving it the blood the thing desires may be the only solution." And if the amount of blood it had taken so far hadn't been enough—the weight of two armies—Lord save them from what they would need to do. The sacrifice would be tremendous.

Gonzalo made a horrified sound.

Slowly, Beatriz's eyes opened. "I have thought

about little else. Santa Ildaria and the bandits has been on my mind since I learned of this Northern god."

"A minor saint?" Julian asked. "I barely remember her from catechism. What about her?"

"She saved her village by sacrificing herself, going out to face the bandits armed only with her faith. She and her followers slowed the bandits at the expense of their lives, enough that the villagers could escape to the protection of Zapata.

"At the convocation. I will present that at the convocation, but for now, I would not speak of it." Her throat worked. Always Beatriz had cried freely when her emotion required such relief. Now, she resisted the tears. "Some things one must have space to absorb and take in before accepting. I need that space. Captain, send out the messengers. We are done discussing. I've decided, and we will move forward.

"Let the Saints save us."

"Mi amor?"

"We have our fallback plan if we can't find a weakness. In that case, we will try martyrdom."

CHAPTER 19

The stench of burning human flesh was inescapable. No wind was needed to carry the reek to Claire's nose and no amount of cloth worn around her face could shut it out, or the roiling smoke. Crusted blood covered her hands past the wrists from doing her share of placing the dead on burn piles, but every Woman of the Song had been given a dignified send-off, their spirit set free by fire to rise and mingle with their ancestors.

Smoke and flame rose from twenty shacks. There had simply been too many dead, so they had used what was available and placed the bodies inside the log cabins and set the dried wood alight.

Claire looked around, too tired to do more than sit on folded legs before the shelter releasing Bromisto and Errol's remains. Heat scorched her face, but she refused to retreat or rub at stinging eyes.

Jorga had collapsed within touching distance, yet her grandmother's presence offered cold comfort. More than the drifting smoke filled the space between them. Self-recrimination robbed the living of speech. For Jorga and the other Elders it was the knowledge that they'd refused to speak about her warning, had created a plan of action which hadn't worked—inside Claire burned with the sorrow of not having done enough. If she'd been faster, stronger with the magic, thought of illusion sooner . . .

None of that could bring back their kin now.

The flames danced and moved, consuming the wood eagerly, giving the illusion of life where there was only death.

She saw Bromisto again—scrawny, shirtless, his face beaming with pride when he'd showed Ramiro the Northerners' trail in the swamp, the skepticism in his dark eyes when they'd first met, and his wariness of *sirenas*. She remembered how that uncertainty had melted over time to the bossiness that only a child could manage. How he had been determined to act the man, though in a child's body.

And that brought her to Errol. Her uncle, the opposite, a child in a nearly adult body. She dwelt on the few times he'd met her eyes and she'd felt a real concern from him. His utter adoration of Jorga. The way he spit when he tried to whistle. His simple delight in even the tiniest things, such as jumping puddles. They had that in common. He, more than anyone she knew, exhibited the innocence of a child. Yet being special had not saved her uncle this time. Nor had his ability to see the future foreseen this outcome.

Her eyes burned with more than pain from the heat and smoke. Instead of tears, though, her blood-crusted hands curled into fists. A scream ripped from her throat, expressing frustration and grief all in one and scattering the silence. The release felt so good she screamed again until her lungs ran out of air and the clearing echoed with the sound. The others turned in her direction, their faces blank—too deep in shock to issue either reprimand or consolation.

Thirteen.

Thirteen Women of the Song remained. Eleven of them Elders and past childbearing age. One already pregnant. And herself. Plus, a few scattered more in the swamp who had been too busy or uninterested to attend their annual gathering.

Her people. All gone. All wiped out by Dal.

How much more loss could she take before the beating left her broken?

Her fists tightened until fingernails cut into skin.

Not today.

Not today would she let the world shatter her. She would not fall apart and let them win.

She knew where she had to be and it wasn't here.

Claire rose on wobbly legs and tottered to the pile of possessions behind her, hastily shoving them into bags. Horse had vanished in the chaos of that morning. Perhaps escaping from Dal by bolting, perhaps lying dead somewhere. Gone either way. She'd have to take less baggage this time, only what she could manage to carry. It was a long walk to the desert.

She shook dirt and leaves off her blanket, then put the few mementoes of her mother on the fabric, adding the short knife that had belonged to Bromisto and a whittled chunk of wood that vaguely looked like a face, which Errol had carried. It was all she had of them but the memories.

The items blurred and she moved to rub hastily at betraying eyes with shaking hands before remembering the filth that covered them. Gone already was her earlier bravado of being a destroyer. Nothing but a scared girl remained. A lost soul drowning in quicksand and grasping at reeds. She had to hope Ramiro had managed better with his task.

Seeking comfort, the words of her Goodnight Song dropped from her lips in a whisper:

"All is well.

"All is safe . . ."

And died, providing no reassurance or relief because nothing was well or safe.

No time for that.

She hesitated only a few breaths before rolling up the blanket and thrusting it into the bottom of a saddlebag. She'd pack and then find water to wash. The possessions beside her moved as another bag was filled. Claire turned to find Jorga beside her.

"Are we going to the desert, granddaughter?" Jorga's voice had gone hoarse, becoming a rasp drawn across raw wood.

"Aye. That's where we'll find them," she answered, not knowing whether she meant Dal, the Northerners, or Ramiro. Or all three. Their magic may not work against Dal, but the Song could take her revenge against the Northerners and it was they who had caused all her pain. They had started events in motion and brought Dal here.

Her packing finished, she stood to layer the bags across her shoulders. Eulalie, Muriel, Rachael, and three others hefted their own bags. When she attempted to meet their eyes, they avoided her gaze. Like Jorga they appeared flat, deflated. The blow had knocked away their confidence, leaving clay figures behind, and Claire could not resist needling their raw wounds—if they had listened instead of obstructing perhaps their kin would be alive.

"Now you believe and will help."

Shame flashed across their faces, to be replaced with a stubborn outthrust on at least one jaw. Eulalie stepped forward. "Do you want our help or not?"

To say no flashed through Claire's heart, but that would be childish. They had all suffered. She had been as unable to stop Dal as the others and the Elders had tried—had fought and lost and yet still stood ready to go and fight again. To deny their help out of pettiness would be foolish.

"I would take your help," Claire said, "but I go to the desert people. I will be allying with men. Can you handle that?"

Muriel stepped forward, brown eyes warm. "We understand that and see no choice. The Great Goddess put us here for our protection, but there is no safety anywhere anymore, is there? We choose to go so those who stay may live."

Claire nodded and looked toward Jorga. "Then there are no more Elders—you are not in charge. My voice has as much say as any other in making decisions. You will take my lead."

"Rather more, I'd believe," Jorga said under her breath. Louder she said, "Singers?"

Rachael used dirty fingers to push at a gray clump of hair that had worked loose from her bun to dangle over her eye, leaving a red streak on her skin. "I always speak my mind and I say we all do the same. But"—her eyes shifted, her mouth puckering—"I say we take this child's lead for the time being—as long as her advice works out, anyway. I always said age was no indication of wisdom. There's many a fool who's an old fool."

Other heads nodded, though most reluctantly.

"My Amos called her Destroyer." Eulalie's chins drooped on her chest with her disapproval. "Maybe she will destroy us or maybe our enemy. His word is good enough for me. I insist we follow her now. She needs further training in our ways and we can't do that if we aren't with her."

A gasp escaped Claire's lips. They'd find a way to twist everything she said into being their idea and would seek to control her at every turn. More than that, they'd actively try to shape her in their images, down to even changing her way of thinking to theirs. For a moment, the thought infuriated her, then she shrugged. *Let them try.*

"Then let's go take down our enemies, Singers," Claire said, taking the title from her grandmother and watching determination spring up among them. Not one Destroyer would there be, but eight. Let the Northerners make their peace with their vicious god for she was about to bring them hell.

ing the Children of ... ...

Five Years Ago

In the long years past Santabe had learned the two
ways an Enforcer of Dal walked. The first and most
often used was a walk of pride—assured, confident,
never hesitating for a crowd to part before one of the
most dreaded and feared persons among the Children of Dal. The second, lesser way of movement was
one of stealth and deception, Diviner hidden, as the
Enforcer hunted for a particular member of the Disgraced for punishment. That walk was reserved only
for Enforcers of the top rank. Out of habit she fell into
this walk now as the exhilaration of putting people in
their place filled her. She threaded through the venerable trees of the park at the heart of the Great Palace
of Dal with her footsteps light and her eyes darting to
watch for other walkers. Her work would go better if
unnoticed, and she hoped to preserve secrecy, despite
how the white of her robes stood out in the darkness.

Some habits, like the way she moved, couldn't be
unlearned even after passing beyond the rank of Enforcer and earning her first Sun-Blessed earring——a
reward not given for her numbers of captures as an

Enforcer, but as a prize for her handling of the outlander, Ordoño. It was she who had earned his confidence, learned best his language, and taught that skill to other Children of Dal as Ordoño had gone from hated foreigner to fascinating vault of wisdom, showing the Children of Dal new mysteries first in secret and then openly. And all the time, she had been at his side, indispensable and keeping his feet on the path to the next life, ensuring he never stepped wrong and earned punishment or committed blasphemy.

A rare smile curved her lips. Yes, as he rose in popularity, it was she who had advised him what the people wanted to hear. Her Sun-Blessed earring was a just repayment, and Ordoño's whispers in the right ears had gotten it for her. Now she returned the favor and cleared his path forward.

Four assignments had been her duty this day, and now three lay behind her and one remained. She could take a nice hot bath after this one. Impatience grew and her pace increased.

A small cottage of stone loomed through the trees, isolated and alone. Master Jemkinbu had earned the reward of solitude with his mastery of creating Diviners long years before she'd been born. He'd asked and received, not just a room to himself, but an entire house. He claimed it necessary for his art as he must be alone to hear Dal—a claim no one could dispute.

Santabe had never heard Dal herself and doubted anyone else did either, a belief she very carefully never expressed aloud as she was not ready to be sent to another life.

She knocked softly at the cottage window and then entered, having requested this visitation days earlier. Master Jemkinbu awaited her at his table with the tools of his carving trade spread around him. Chisels and tiny hammers, planes, and files, along with pieces of *einhorn*, lay scattered across the stone table. He held one tool hidden in his thick fingers. He had changed his silk robe for wool in the comfort of his home.

The years had not been kind to the Master. His bulk had only increased, putting extra strain upon his joints and making it near impossible for him to rise unassisted as rheumatism wracked his legs. Veins that had been spiderwebs had become ropes at his ankles, and his once sparse hair had vanished altogether. Yet, his skill at carving the *einhorn* remained unsurpassed—no matter how many apprentices he trained.

No doubt Master Jemkinbu was careful not to teach his students everything. The glory of Dal was important, but not at the expense of losing one's place. She admired him for that as she would have done the same if their places had been reversed.

And though his body failed, his eyes remained shrewd. He noted quickly that she carried no Diviner and allowed the tension in his shoulders to ease. Her time as Enforcer had taught her to read the slightest body display, especially those that benefited her.

"Walk with the sun on your face, Honored One," she said pleasantly.

"And you, daughter. How may I help you this day? Does Ordoño wish to watch me carve again?"

"Not this time, Master. He wishes something a little . . . more."

Jemkinbu set down a thin-bladed chisel. "Oh yes. I've heard that the rallies of his followers grow ever larger, and that you took him on a tour of all our cities and even the smaller villages—several times in fact."

"Ordoño is very interested to learn all there is to know of Dal—and of his children."

"So it seems. Five years and he hasn't tired of us." The Master pushed some invisible dust to the floor where a small heap of *einhorn* shavings gathered over his foot. The sale of that pile would have fed a clan for years. "His speeches have raised the national pride. The common people are happy to be Children of Dal again. And I've heard rumors of more: hints of a whisper of marching upon the southern outlander blasphemers and bringing them to Dal."

She faltered, forgetting her prepared words. None of the others she'd approached had heard anything. "Indeed. Well, that saves some time. We have many friends in the priesthood now. And that is why I came to you today, Master. We want you for our friend as well."

"That depends on your definition of friend. I believe I always have been. I assigned you to Ordoño in the first place."

"I remember." Her hand darted to her hidden pocket. As if she could forget. She had thought that the end of her dreams for advancement. Instead, the results of that one day had set her on the road to everything she wanted—travel, adventure . . . power. Yet, Master Jemkinbu hadn't planned for that to happen. He'd always sought to keep her down, the same way he ensured his apprentices failed. On top of that, she also remembered the many beatings he'd given her before her rise to full priestess. "I never thanked you for that." Her hand tightened in her pocket and she had to make herself let go. Her orders still stood—no matter her own feelings.

"But we would know where you stand now," she prompted. "And eventually, yes, we'd like to take the southern lands—for the glory of Dal, of course."

"Of course. Though to take so many priests from the cities and from Dal some would say is blasphemy. While to use Diviners as weapons against the unenlightened is a crime. So it is written."

Ordoño had anticipated these arguments. Securely on solid ground again, she moved closer to his table as one driven by enthusiasm. "But Dal does not return to us for over five hundred years, and we would raise many more priests before taking any out of the country to war. The priests would take their

Diviners as self-protection only. That is hardly the definition of a weapon."

He nodded and she allowed a smile in return. Well did she know that beauty could often fool and distract the elderly or the young. Ordoño had taught her that a pleasing face could be a powerful tool. But his next words stripped the smile away.

"I see this is more than rumor. Your invasion is already a well thought out plan, not a dream." He tapped the floor with his priceless cane of *einhorn* and touched the sun-shaped gold in his ears. "But I would expect nothing less from one so young. Without both Sun-Blessed ranks, you do not comprehend all the mysteries yet. Your plan is dangerous."

"What do you mean?"

"Child, Dal never rests."

She could only stare for the blink of an eye, but then she laughed. Why must the old be so off target? His brain wandered. "What are you saying, Master? All know that Dal rests for twenty-five hundred years. Never has that pattern been broken. No amount of blood can call Him early. Some have tried."

"That's not what I'm saying." He looked down, studying his lap with unseeing eyes until she fidgeted, shifting from foot to foot.

"Old man, this is not—"

He held up a thick hand. "Wait. This is not something you should know yet, but Dal doesn't truly rest. Rather, he moves between lives—between times.

When He is not here, He is in a prior life or skipping ahead to one of the lives to come."

"That makes no sense."

"It *is* mystery. But you must remember: Dal is a god. Time cannot hold Him."

Her patience broke. This meeting was taking too long. It should have been over long ago. The Master kept trying to distract her. Why? Was someone coming? "That changes nothing, makes no dent in our plans. Do you stand with us or no? We want your wisdom and your skills on our side, but I would have your answer now."

Laboriously he pushed, grunted, and heaved his bulk to his feet, leaning on his priceless cane. His back was bowed and curved like the arch of a beautiful woman's brow. "It's a lesson, child. As Dal can travel between our lives, so what you do in this life has consequences for all the rest of your lives, even in the past. As you know, we were given this charge to keep Dal to ourselves for our part in waking Him. It is our curse and our blessing. So it has been and so it will always be, in this life and all others. The red Diviners give us the means to trap him among us and protect others. Over time that warped to be a matter of pride—only we could have Dal.

"To go from our lands. To seek out others to use as sacrifices to Dal . . . It goes against our ways. You are doomed to fail. Your plan is blasphemy."

He yanked on the top of his cane. It tore apart in

his hands to reveal a staff as long as a forearm, smooth and bone white. A Diviner. "I must stop you."

Her eyes widened, and her hand drew forth what hid in her pocket. Age slowed and made him clumsy. She had no such handicap. As he turned with the Diviner, she ducked and let the killing weapon go over her head. She thrust the chisel taken from her pocket at his ear. Haste drew her off slightly, and the bright metal cut across his skull, peeling up skin. It didn't kill him, but it was painful enough to slow him even more. He tried to bring the Diviner in again, but her aim was true this time. She stabbed the tool into his brain, pushing with all her strength to drive the chisel to the hilt. Blood bubbled over her hands.

He twitched and twitched again, eyes filled with an emotion she could not identify. Scorn? Betrayal? Disgust? It mattered not. His hand sprang open and the Diviner fell. Then the life in him died and his body went limp.

She drew out the chisel and let Master Jemkinbu drop to the floor. The collapse of his body sent the pile of feather-light *einhorn* shavings scattering to every corner, a fortune lost.

That didn't matter, either.

Breath rushed to her lungs, threatening panic. He was supposed to be defenseless, weak. That had been closer than she liked. She pushed the adrenaline away, forcing her body to relax.

"So not a friend after all, Master. I've been looking forward to that for a long time."

She cleaned the blood from the chisel on his wool robe and set her weapon on the table with his other tools. She'd taken it months ago in anticipation of this very day, though she would have followed orders and let him live if he'd been amenable. But Ordoño didn't send her to meet with those likely to be agreeable to their side. No, others got that job. All four of her meetings this day had ended the same way.

They should have listened and seen where the future of this life was headed.

But done is done. Let Master Jemkinbu enjoy his new life while they changed this one, making over the Children of Dal.

She carefully scrubbed all the blood from her hands onto his robe, then left the cottage. People might suspect her work in the murders, but they would also expect her to use a Diviner, and there would be no proof. Her mind dismissed the night's activities, already dwelling with pleasure on her bath.

CHAPTER 20

Telo stared at each vein, knot, and scarred knuckle of his remaining hand as if memorizing every detail. The flickering light of torches revealed the specifics but fitfully; however, the sight was clear enough. Strange how flesh remained largely the same even as the soul changed. And Telo feared he was much changed inside.

Father Ansuro's warning not to go back to the man he had been rang in his head.

He pushed the thought of transformation away. By the saints, studying his flesh was better than examining his soul and much better than staring at Santabe as the Northern priestess lay on a tomb, sleeping off the effects of the drug they'd given her. After they'd survived the laundry chute and left the cathedral, Telo had taken them to a forgotten hidey-hole of his childhood. A place deep underground and another part of his shelved past—an abode of tombs that were centuries old. While Ramiro fetched his horse and Teresa took a light to read epitaphs to lost souls long dead, he stood guard over their unconscious charge.

Bits and pieces of the living lay scattered all around from past refugees hiding from other troubles—a bent spoon too valuable to discard and meant to be retrieved but never recovered, a rag doll so rotted as to be barely identifiable, ashes of campfires between the stone sarcophagi. All remnants of those who were as cast off as the dead. Once upon a time Telo had been one of those castoffs—maybe against all his best intentions he was again. His life become a loop.

A soldier, his father had died before his birth, killed in some meaningless border battle between Aveston and Colina Hermosa. His mother had joined his father just a few short years after Telo's birth, worked to death in supporting them both, while alone and kinless. Telo had grown up running in the streets—a street orphan—hiding from authority and stealing to feed himself. He had spent much time below ground in such hidey-holes until he was old enough to work in the brawl pits and learn a more sophisticated style of fighting. From there it was a small step to stints with bandits, harming others in a larger way.

He would have stayed there if not for two things: His small memories of his mother all revolved around her praise of the priests—he'd promised her to go to them for help—and the concern of a few such priests, like Father Vellito and Father Ansuro, who helped him without judgment. They had seen something of value in him when he could not. Various other priests had repaired his education and instilled enough values in him to bring him out of his sinful life. Perhaps they had fed upon his guilt, but for that he cast no blame, as it had saved his life. In return, he'd eventually joined them to make amends for his criminal past, to do good for others instead of harm.

In the priesthood he'd been content, not seeking fame or importance, choosing the life of a wandering friar rather than the political risings of the Church. Never part of anyone's life in a permanent way, or connected to one acre of the world for long, or key to the center of events—until now.

Somehow Beatriz Alvarado had seen in him a counselor fit to help her husband. Julian Alvarado had found in him the courage to fight for the lives of children held by the Northerners and his role had grown from there. And Ramiro Alvarado had trusted him enough to follow his lead in capturing Santabe. Each step forward small and natural until he'd been yanked from his self-imposed humbleness into a battle to stop a god.

Ah, pride, he chided. *As if you are more important than the rats hiding in this darkness. Yet here you are, back where you started.*

He shivered, eying the shadows around their

small fire, but without fear of the rats. No, he'd spent too much time with such creatures to fear them. But the air down here had an icy touch; moisture dripped in slow plops in an unseen corner, enough to chill anyone. All the chambers for the dead led to three or four others, doubling back on each other, resulting in a tangled web of interconnected rooms that would be a maze to anyone unfamiliar. The ceiling spanned high above, lost to the darkness. Too chilly for spiders, the catacombs were part natural cave and part man-made. The stone coffins—chest high, some plain and others covered with designs and lettering—took up just about all the space, meaning barely enough room existed between them for a person to sprawl out straight. Telo sat on one of them with Santabe on another—the carving an uneven lump under him.

In his fearless youth, Telo had traced out less than half the space in this catacomb with the sort of unheeding bravery only children were capable of. Others of his friends had learned many more of the twists and turns. And some had died here of hunger and neglect, their small skeletons hidden by the larger tombs of what had once been Aveston's most wealthy citizens—the unwanted and the rich, now mingled together in holy equality.

Telo touched mind, heart, liver, and spleen to drive away the gloom that had entered his soul. *God will provide.* He always did.

But the confidence and peace of mind Telo had

gained from witnessing miracles had been snapped by the death of Father Ansuro and his violent reacquaintance with Santabe, leaving him feeling emptier than before. Why had a God who worked miracles abandoned one of the best of souls to roam this land? Father Ansuro hadn't deserved to die. And Santabe didn't deserve to live.

Telo had pondered the unfairness of life many times, yet never felt it more keenly than today. Faith faced with concrete evil seemed like so many empty words, and gone was his sense of prevailing over depravity. Suffering had stripped from him the one virtue that had always saved him: the ability to laugh at life and himself—leaving his heart unable to sense truth. It hurt to acknowledge that his humor had been subsumed under so much grief, and he wondered if he had the will to face the world again when they might fail. If only a source among the living or dead could provide answers.

Santabe lay still and Telo strained his ears for a holy word, but the only noise came from Teresa some feet away as she struggled to read in the faint light. As he'd feared, the Lord would send no answers to him. He was no saint. No one worthy of God's time. Just a man doing his best in a world breaking down.

His eye lingered on Santabe as the epitome of all cruelty. Telo had witnessed enough cruelty and immorality in his lifetime to recognize the real thing when he saw it. Dal and the Northerners were no group of bandits selfishly grabbing for what they needed without thought of consequences. Instead, they were a deliberate evil with a vocation to harm as many as possible.

Eyes downcast, he rubbed his thumb over a callus in his palm, seeking something real.

"So, you understand now," a thin voice asked.

Telo jumped before he recognized the voice as Santabe's, and noticed her eyes had opened. She held one arm flung across her forehead, eyes squinted as though pained by the small light.

"You've seen Dal's work." Her pained laughter rubbed unclean fingers on his soul. "Your eyes have a freshly haunted look. You've seen. Killing me will not stop Him."

"You must have noticed you're not dead," Telo said. "Nor am I interested in torture. I leave that to your kind." Telo shook his head. How easily she goaded him into anger. He wondered if she ever dealt in any other emotion. Instead of fury, then, he embraced pity for her. The Children of Dal had been trapped by their god's depravity for thousands of years. No wonder they were twisted.

"But I would seek truce, my child. You'll get no rancor from me." He held up what remained of his left arm. "You have taken a piece of me and I have abducted you twice. Can we call it even and speak to each other with civility?"

She moved to sit, and Telo reached for the white

Diviner at his feet, her gaze tracking his movement as they regarded each other warily. Two street dogs, each waiting for the other to bite first.

"It hurts to think. What did you do to me?" she demanded. "Why does my head feel like this?"

In the hope honesty would bring a return, he said, "A drug. A mix of herbs that renders people unconscious—but does no lasting harm. It is used for surgeries and other procedures. The pain will clear in a few hours." They could dose her no more without refilling their supply. He'd spilled the entire bottle down his robe or on the cloth in his haste during the fight in the cathedral. Besides, they needed Santabe awake. "Drink. That will help."

She eyed the water skin next to her on the tomb but made no move toward it. "It's untainted," he said. "My word to my god."

"Your god is weak." She snapped the words with little venom and reached for the water, letting it splash over her chin as she drank.

He didn't want to argue with her about the various kinds of strength and the value of kindness. They had gone over that subject before and no minds had been changed. What they needed was information, not spiritual discussion—as fascinating as that would be. "And your god is strong. Strong enough to get to us underground?"

She paused in her drinking to eye him over the water skin, then the tombs around them. "With time . . . yes. You want to know if hiding your people underground will save them. It's been tried—and failed."

He nodded, hearing truth in her words for once, then waited, hoping for more.

"That is why you took me." Her laughter rang out stronger this time. "You scared little people want what I know of Dal. Then you shall have it: I know *He* will send you back to your last life to try again. Weak. Untried. You have not been tested like the Children of Dal."

"And if we find the way to defeat him, when you failed?"

Her laughter cut off sharply. "There is no way."

"But we have a power you do not," Teresa said, coming out of the gloom. "We have miracles."

"Miracles? What is this word, ugly woman? You speak in riddles."

Teresa frowned. "A miracle? Why a miracle is . . . well it's . . ."

Telo took over. "It's a helping hand from God to bridge the impossible, for He can make the dying live and the despairing have hope."

Santabe snorted. "There is no such thing." She tossed down the water skin. "Keep faith in your 'miracle' when Dal flays the flesh from your body."

"Then what would you suggest?" Teresa said. "Your people managed to survive. You have nothing if not numbers."

But Santabe crossed her arms over her chest, looking smug, and pressed her mouth closed like a spoiled child.

"Finding a way to stop this killing is only to your benefit," Teresa pressed. "Your people would live, too." She waited to no avail, then huffed out her breath.

Santabe's eyes roamed the space around them, flicking from one point to another as if in search. A crease formed across her brow as if disappointed. "He'll be here soon, if you are looking for Ramiro," Teresa said quickly. "But there are still two of us and we have your weapon. Don't try to escape."

A glare was their only answer, and Telo wondered at their prisoner's ability to keep silent. She had always been easy to goad before. When Santabe's head began to droop, though, he realized she was in no shape for a physical attempt at escape. As if in proof, Santabe retched up the water she'd swallowed over the side of the tomb and then lay back down. So she was not noting their numbers in order to escape.

It also meant she hadn't been looking for Ramiro. Why would she? She had seen Ramiro only for a brief stretch. Always before she had seen just him and Teresa. Just the two of them alone should be no surprise to Santabe.

So who was she looking for . . . or better yet—what?

Unless . . .

Telo jumped from the tomb where he sat and

turned sideways to sidle between two sarcophagi to their bags. He drew out the red Diviner. Even in the darkness surrounding them, it somehow seemed darker. Santabe's eyes snapped open, latching on to the implement like a magnet.

A painful hope grew in Telo's chest. He'd brought the thing with them out of curiosity when Ramiro suggested they hide it with the bodies. Teresa had sided with him and they'd packed the strange Diviner away—clueless as to its uses.

"This!" Telo exclaimed. "You were looking for this. *Why?*"

CHAPTER 21

After the first day of walking, Claire stared into the campfire as she tried to empty her thoughts in the dancing colors and the random movement—the flames so wild and without connections or heartbreak to weigh them down. But unlike fire, she had troubles, and she and her seven companions all had heartbreak. The heat stroked against her cheek, drying her eyes, and becoming almost unbearable, but to look away was to risk making eye contact with one of the other Women of the Song. Since dusk had begun to gather and the bustle of setting camp ended, conversation had died to only necessary words and movements. What had been endurable during the light of day became, not something that brought them together, but a shared grief that drove them apart. As darkness prepared to arrive, each woman had withdrawn into themselves and closed the door on their companions to nurse their loss alone.

Sometimes it was easier to bear a single grief than shoulder a mountain of it.

So Claire pretended not to hear the occasional cut-off sob, because to acknowledge one would be to let her own out. And her suffering was nothing compared to the women around her who had lost their children.

They would have sat silent and aloof until the stew finished cooking and they curled in their own blankets if not for a sudden movement. Claire blinked and looked away from picturing Errol and Bromisto in the flames as the woman Eulalie had left on guard knelt next to the Elder to whisper in her ear.

"What is it?" Jorga asked sharply.

"Swamp cats," Eulalie said. "The smell of our dinner must have brought them. Muriel, we'll need your trick."

"I don't know what you mean," Muriel said.

Eulalie's face puckered. "Now's not the time to play coy. I know your great-aunt Milly had this skill, and she wouldn't have passed on without teaching it to all her kin. Do you want swamp cats keeping us up all night?"

"For the Great Goddess' sake," Rachael huffed. "Just do it, Muriel, or we'll have no more peace this night."

Muriel stood, smoothing her dress. "Very well.

Plug your ears." The other women put fingers in their ears. Claire stared transfixed until Jorga jiggled her arm. She hastily followed their example of plugging her ears.

Muriel drew in a deep breath to her diaphragm as if to Sing, but instead put two fingers in her mouth and produced a piercing whistle that was more like a scream. Even with her ears blocked Claire winced at the sharp sound, scrambling to her feet.

Angry roars came from outside the camp, and Claire could picture the big cats running. The creatures were fierce but they had keen hearing. The whistle would have been twice as painful for them.

"Thank you, Muriel," Eulalie said with all the graciousness of a scorpion.

"What was that?" Claire asked as Muriel settled back by the fire. "It was the Song? How did you learn to do that?"

"Every family has their own tricks and innovations," Rachael said, "passed on through the years."

"Every family makes certain innovations to the Song over the years," Muriel expanded. "Like the way you added emotion to the Memory Song. We don't ask and we don't share. That's how it works. Anything a family learns stays in that family."

"That's the stupidest thing I ever heard," Claire said. "Look at us. Just look! Eight Women of the Song—that's almost all there are left of us! If ever there was a time to share knowledge, it's now."

"It's not how it's done," Eulalie said flatly. She looked like a fat crab with her head drawn inside her shell and her pincers up.

Claire's indignation grew. Silly women with their feet stuck in the mud. Any grief she felt was replaced with anger. "And maybe that's why there were only fifty of us. Now there are less. How has that attitude been productive?"

They stared at the ground, unwilling to meet her eye.

"Are you telling me you're not prepared to share secrets about our magic that could save lives?" Claire insisted. "That's insane! Who are you saving them for?" She turned to fix Rachael with her glare. "What about your family? What skills do you keep to yourself?"

Rachael stared back at her, unsure how to respond, when Jorga answered for the other Elder. "What's the matter, Rachael? Don't want to talk about how you can Speak on the Wind?" Rachael glared at Jorga, but Claire wasn't about to give her a moment of righteousness.

"Why are you angry with Jorga? For revealing a secret that could *help* us? You know a trick to Speak on the Wind and you won't share it with me? After you've seen me using it every day!"

Before Rachael could speak, Claire turned her focus onto Eulalie and the women who hadn't spoken yet. "And the rest of you? What are you hiding?"

Muriel sat with her spine stiff. "Violet can make double-bite spiders do simple commands. Rumor says Eulalie can direct a Song at a single target in a way that should not be possible. I'm not sure what Anna and Susan can do."

"Muriel!" Eulalie gasped, her chins wagging.

"What of it?" Spots of color stained Muriel's cheeks. "If one is unmasked, we all should be unmasked. That's the fair thing to do."

"I agree." Rachael nodded, a fierce look in her eye. "If our secrets are shared in front of everyone, then everyone's should be, that's what. What's good for the goose—"

Whatever else she said next was lost in all the women speaking at once in ever-increasing volume, climbing to their feet and getting in each other's faces.

"Stop it," Claire said, gesturing for them to cease. Nobody paid her the least heed except to push her out of their circle of argument. "Would you stop it!" she finally had to scream.

Voices cut off and heads turned to stare at her in astonishment.

"Let your elders speak, child," Eulalie said. "This isn't a matter of leading us. We didn't give our internal governance over to you."

"No, I won't be silent. Not when you sound like a pack of rats caught in a sack. You're going to shut up and listen! Elders? You haven't the sense of this rock!" She stamped her foot against a stone. Women gasped.

"We are one force now," Claire persisted. "With one goal. If we are to succeed in that goal, we must work together, like one body, as soldiers do. We have to train like soldiers do. Learn to work as a team. Share *everything*. Become an army. Become a team. Become a *family*. Our foe has destroyed us exactly because we keep secrets. The time for secrets is over."

She looked at them, unsure if she wanted to say the rest of what was on her mind. But it seemed important for them to fully understand the depth of their situation, so she continued.

"I know how raw this wound is, but you're arguing about secrets like you have any kin left to share those secrets with!" She ignored their gasps and said. "There's just us!

"Just me."

The air went out of her lungs. She was the biggest part of their future and she feared they'd never let her go. Even if she wanted to leave the Women of the Song for a life with Ramiro when this ended, these women wouldn't let her go. "There's just me," she whispered.

Rachael wiped at her eyes with the corner of her dress. "I'll teach you, child. I'll show you how I can make Speak on the Wind carry farther." She managed a weak smile. "With sass like that, you'll learn it in no time."

The others gave weak nods, eyes down.

"An army, huh," Eulalie said. "If it pays them

back for what they did to my Amos, then I'm listening." Her small eyes filled with determination. "My granny taught us how to narrow an attack to hit a limited number of targets. To single out the men in the crowd for the magic. Not everyone in my family could manage it, and it'll take lots of practice, but I think this group of Singers can handle it—if the Great Goddess wills it—an army we'll be!"

"An army!" the others echoed, followed by a ragged cheer.

"An army," Claire said so quietly no one heard. They clapped her on the back, jostling her around, but not really seeing her. She would gain more power with the Song.

Destroyer.

The tiny fear in her heart grew just a little more sharp, but she'd do what needed doing to stop the Northerners.

"No time like the present, I always say," Rachael said, pointing upward. "A just-right night to get started. See all those clouds?" Half the sky was filled with great fluffy masses, outlined by the moon, moving slowly to the east. "Instead of spreading the magic all around in every direction and squandering the power, we're going to stream it all into the clouds to be the messenger." She grinned, showing her missing tooth, and they followed her a few steps from the campfire.

"That sounds like the trick Eulalie has with directing the magic to limited targets," Claire volunteered.

Rachael blinked and all the watching women behind shifted and muttered to each other. "Maybe. Possibly. It could be related."

"It's rather fickle, isn't it?" Claire asked. "I mean you need clouds first off. And what if they're going the wrong way?"

"What do you expect?" Rachael snapped, grin fading. "Nothing's perfect in this life. I said it's a way to enhance Speak on the Wind. I didn't say it was flawless. It carries the magic much farther than without my trick. Do you want to try it or not?"

"Of course. I apologize. I didn't mean to complain, just to understand."

"Well then," Rachael said, sounding mollified. "Place your hands like this." She cupped her hands on either side of her mouth, lifting her chin up toward the sky, and turning east. "It helps put your mind in the proper place. Aim your Song at a cloud. Concentrate real hard. Picture the magic going into the cloud instead of all around you. And add these words, 'Cloud, carry my heart.'"

Claire choked back an inadvisable reply of *That's it?* and focused on her Song. What did she expect? They were simple homespun tricks, not ground-shattering revelations about the magic. Her discoveries had been made with the same small steps. She readied the Song, feeling more than a little self-conscious to be shouting Ramiro's name at a cloud in front of a handful of watchers. But an image of him with a brow raised for worrying about what a bunch of old aunties thought soon made her forget about her audience. Suddenly, all her grief and loneliness rushed over her.

The loss of the boys. Errol's prediction.

She wished so much that Ramiro was here. As she let the words free, the emotion bubbled out of her and attached itself to her Song, vanishing into the cloud.

The women behind her clapped at her success, but Claire drooped, wrung out like wet laundry, and then slapped a hand over her mouth. "I didn't mean to send him that." She'd meant to send reassurance with his name, the sense of well-being such as she always sent. How could she have been so careless?

"It's gone now," Rachael said cheerfully. "There's no getting it back."

"Great."

"Likely it'll never reach him anyway," Jorga said, coming up beside them. "Too far to travel. Or he could be dead already."

Claire's eyes widened and she gagged unexpectedly, bringing tears to her eyes. "How . . . how could you say such a thing?"

"He's just a man," Jorga retorted. "Better than most maybe. But a man. We don't need their kind. Your place is with us, not moping over some man."

"Someone's got a real dose of puppy love," Rachael chortled.

Muriel came up and draped an arm around Claire's

neck. "Never you mind them. Any love is a beautiful thing. I'm sure your young man is perfectly fine. We'll be at the edge of the swamp tomorrow night, and then who knows? We may run into him sooner than you think."

Claire drew in Muriel's offered comfort and the world slowly swam back into focus. They were right about one thing: Done was done. Much as it hurt to admit it, they had a point. No sense worrying about something she couldn't fix. She had to keep believing Ramiro was safe.

"Violet, your turn," Eulalie called out. "Let's see the next trick. Then Susan and Anna."

The next woman came forward to share her tip on controlling double-bite spiders, and Claire let them shuffle her into the center of their pack, glad to no longer be the focus of attention. Or almost. Jorga shot her a glance to make sure she was paying attention.

Aunties was right. She'd become the center attraction simply by being alive and the only focus for their considerable attentions. If she didn't watch out, they would nitpick her to death. Then and there, she vowed again to stand on her own two feet and not let the Women of the Song control her.

One by one, they all shared new ways to enhance and expand the magic of the Song. Even Jorga shared the Hornet Tune. Claire did her best to memorize each twist and trick. Some required learning a Song like the one for controlling the spiders—others provided a new layer on an old Song like Rachael's. Muriel's whistle tune to counter predators, whether on four legs or two, would take days of practice, as Claire had never learned to whistle. Eulalie's secret of selecting targets for the Song would take even more work, as it involved a difficult form of complex concentration and visual focusing, along with inventing new wording in each Song used to suit the intended target. As one couldn't stop sound from traveling everywhere, a partial description of a victim had to accompany the words at the start of the Song.

It couldn't stop the Song from going everywhere, but if the target had ears, it could make the magic a sharp spear instead of a net.

Already Claire could see how to adapt this to her Death Song. Eulalie's family had used this method to attack only men in a given situation, but with practice Claire could make her focus even more restrictive, to mark Northerners. And luckily for her, they had days of walking ahead of them in which to master the skills shown today.

Her feet throbbed just thinking about it.

Each demonstration of another unique magic brought applause, praise, and grateful thanks for sharing. And as the last woman finished, Claire pulled at her braid. They had all displayed something, given up their secrets, except for her. The Elders had already seen her add emotion to Songs—she'd done it again tonight with her Speak on the Wind. She had nothing else to offer.

Or maybe she did.

"Wait," she said as the group began to break up. "Just a minute. I have something else for you to see." She hastened back to the fire and grabbed one of her saddlebags, rescued from inside their cabin before they burnt the small structure. Claire had been reluctant to take anything out of that place of death, but the more practical Jorga had insisted they recover their belongings despite the blood spatters on them. Claire had taken her bag and layered it inside another and never opened it since.

Inside lay the white Diviner. The weapon taken from a Northern priest in the swamp village by Ramiro and that had turned from bone-white to a bloody red color after the massacre of the Northern soldiers by Dal. The Diviner had turned white once again when Errol had directed Claire to use the staff as Jorga lay dead. The red had drained out of the Northern object as life reentered Jorga.

Claire's fingers faltered in opening the bag.

Errol would never be there again to direct her with his uncanny glimpses of the future.

"What is it?" Eulalie demanded in a suspicious voice. "A root? An herb? Or something of men?"

Claire pulled herself together and dumped the bag upside down, shaking it to dislodge items. "No. Something of the Northerners—used for killing." Ramiro's shirt holding the Diviner lay wedged in the bottom. She extracted the bundle with some difficulty and more care, not trusting the weapon within.

The Elders of the Women of the Song gathered over her in an anxious circle to see what she would produce as she set the shirt on the ground and peeled back the fabric.

A staff a little longer than her forearm and much thinner than her wrist lay inside. Claire gasped. The moonlight didn't reveal bone white but the eerie crimson of fresh blood.

CHAPTER 22

Ramiro dismounted Sancha outside the crypt where Telo and Teresa waited for him. He debated removing the mare's tack and saddle to make her more comfortable, or leaving it in anticipation of a quick departure, finally deciding to just remove the saddle. He let the reins dangle and Sancha responded with the horse equivalent of a human yawn by turning her head away from him.

"I know. You'd rather be doing something, going places. We can take care of that soon enough, right?" She looked about as convinced as he felt. The desire to settle his fate for his desertion pulled at him, making him pace. He could easily give Teresa and the priest a quick good-bye and be on his way to Suseph. Let them interview Santabe and try and draw information from the Northerner. That was their mission—

not so much his now that they'd captured her. Or better yet, they could follow their earlier plan, take Santabe along, and all go to Suseph. Turn her over to his parents and let the authorities handle her. He could meet with Captain Gonzalo and find out his fate as far as the military was concerned.

He lost himself in a daydream of what he would say to them in his defense. Would a court martial punish him or exonerate him? Or some combination? With a shiver, he jerked himself from what-ifs. Time to deal with the here and now, not possible futures.

Would he leave alone or with his friends? Either way, he should be leaving soon.

That *had* been the original plan.

He had a feeling Teresa and Father Telo's version of the plan had changed. He wasn't sure he blamed them, either. Getting Santabe out the gate of Aveston was going to be a problem. They risked getting caught with her, captured, and learning nothing if they left before interrogating her. Added to that, Teresa and Telo would want to be here, among the Northerners, in case they got any information they could act upon. They would not be in a hurry to go. With his part largely over, he didn't have to wait on them to head to Suseph. Yet, he certainly didn't like the thought of leaving them.

They were adults. They certainly didn't need him, right? He had equally important tasks to accomplish that couldn't be done in Aveston.

He tugged the reins idly, thoughts conflicted. Sancha turned back to him, nosing at his chest. "Go or stay?" he asked her.

She winked one liquid eye at him and jerked the reins out of his fingers.

"That's what I feared you'd say." Sancha might be chaffing for action—like he was—but she had her own opinions, and on rare occasions she'd expressed a different view from his. Twice before she had refused to heed his orders. Once on the first day of their bond, just to show she could—that she was the bigger and stronger of their pairing and had a will of her own. The second time when he'd drunk too much, taken a bet, and been about to break his neck jumping a canyon much too wide to handle. Both times, he'd been young. Not old enough to grow a beard, let alone earn one.

Restlessness rose in his chest, confirming that wasn't the answer from her that he secretly desired. He'd hoped Sancha would reinforce his decision, so he could share the blame when he told Teresa.

"Who is the master here?"

She turned away again, giving him her answer. Sancha might not like standing idle here, but she'd decided this is where they should be.

"That's not what I wanted to hear." He huffed and walked off a few yards, then swore in a shout that made the rats outside the abandoned buildings nearby scatter with dry rustles. He did something he'd never done before: attempted to force his *caballo de guerra* by seizing her bridle and pulling her forward.

Sancha casually moved two steps against him, dragging him along as easily as a dog knocks over a kitten. Her lip lifted from her upper teeth, and then she butted him in his chest with her head, hard enough to make him gasp, but not with enough force to crack a rib, clearly letting him know he was the fool.

"Saints. What am I doing?" Was he that desperate to clear his name . . . or go to his death? He released the bridle.

Before he could recover, like the touch of a butterfly across his flesh, his name carried on the wind. Sadness. Hurt. A longing for comfort that was there and gone as fast as a rock newt.

"Claire?"

Something was wrong. She needed him.

Sancha blew horse slobber across his face and gave a true yawn, a sure sign of stress. He scrubbed the slobber off angrily, then subsided against her warm bulk. He'd upset Sancha needlessly and his horse had sensed Claire's call before him because he'd been lost in anger. All because of his fired-up hurry to get to Suseph. And for what—pride?

Pride in doing the right thing and appearing to have more integrity than anyone else.

All his desire to fulfill his duty and turn himself in imploded, leaving only the yearning to get to Claire.

How could he be focused on his duty to a military brotherhood that didn't exist anymore at the expense of other responsibilities? Claire. That was the true importance. But he didn't know where she was. How far away . . .

Ah saints.

He'd lost her—for now at least.

The burn in his chest turned to regret, his noble purpose of carrying a warning to his people and then handing himself over more like a fool's errand. If only he'd stayed with Claire in the first place, but he couldn't regret coming to warn his people about Dal.

He'd thought that speed would save him. The sooner he admitted his desertion and pled for mercy, the more likely it would be granted to him. That they'd be more open to take him back into the military fold if he came to it quickly. Then he could get leave to go to Claire and everything would have a happy ending.

Stupid.

Much had happened since he'd first made that decision. Namely, a god that killed without mercy.

Church bells rang in the distance. The mournful sound reminded him of Father Ansuro and the dreams. That priest had given his entire life to the service of Her Beauty, cleaning and swabbing and worrying about a building. The priest had given back in that way. His service seemed trite, but it was no less important than the bishop's work. And when the moment came, Ansuro had sacrificed his life for theirs.

Ramiro thought of all the people who had given them help in the last days. The Northern soldier who'd let them through the gate. The people of Aveston who'd put them up in their homes. And longer ago, Jorga and her willingness to abandon her home to support Claire. Father Telo and Teresa who had left everything they'd known. His father giving up his place as *alcalde* to do what was best. His mother who took on an additional burden of being *alcalde* so soon after her child died. People large and small who all served in their own way.

And here he was trying to hold on to what he cared about—his pride, his honor, a belief in a system rapidly disappearing—when all others had given up what they loved—even their lives.

He wanted to rush and solve his own problems, forgetting about what might be best for all. Patience and self-deprecation had always been difficult for him. He should be practicing them now and not being so selfish.

Ramiro scrubbed a hand over his face, then touched his sword hilt. Everything revolved back into focus with a snap. He was a man, and yet he allowed himself to act like a *bisoño* throwing a tantrum. He had to see past insecurities. Past his desires.

He had to look forward, not back.

Focus on what you can do—what you should be doing.

If he couldn't get to Claire, then stopping Dal mattered most. Other friends needed him as well. Friends he did know how to find. Who he shouldn't be abandoning. The choice was clear.

"To hell with it. I can't fight what's right." He buried his face in Sancha's mane. "I'm sorry, girl. I was being stupid—and selfish. I thought old dreams of military honor and what I owed to them mattered more. Life has changed. I've got to let that go. I'm sorry."

In reply, Sancha nibbled on his hair, proving all was forgiven. Some of the burden lifted from his chest.

"Wait for me, girl. I've got to sort something out. I'll be back soon. Then we can find a better hiding place."

Sancha sniffed, and he walked inside.

Ramiro entered the underground chamber and shot a quick glance at Santabe, reassured to find her still sleeping. He threw a lump of blankets and several leather straps he'd grabbed from their bags on the nearest sarcophagus. The inside of the hiding place Father Telo had found them was as bad as the outside—he needed no gloomy reminders that everyone died, as mortality pressed on him hard enough. In addition, their presence among the dead felt like an invasion of privacy. And on top of all that, the spot was cramped and uncomfortable. The sooner they found a new location to hide, the better.

"I've some news," Ramiro called as Father Telo and Teresa came to meet him, looking ghostly in the gloomy light so that he half expected them to go through the tombs instead of turning their bodies sideways to slide between them. "The wells have started to run dry. Aveston is swirling with it. It happened so fast they are calling it another sign of the end of days." The wells had only been a little low a few days ago. He could dimly remember a drought had caused such a panic in his sixth year when the summer rains failed. The adults had gone around with pinched looks of worry for several sevendays, until the rains came two moons late. The rains were at least that late now. He'd always associated thirst with a touch of fear since.

Teresa clicked her tongue at his news, and the priest said a short prayer. Ramiro had no prayers left to say. Either the saints had heard him already and knew what needed to be done, or their hands were tied like the figure from his dreams. He hadn't time to spend on seeking their influence. No heart for it either.

He ran one of the leather straps through his hands, checking for worn spots.

"We have news as well," Teresa said. "We got a little information out of our prisoner before she went to sleep again."

Father Telo looked away. "It appears I overdosed our prisoner. She woke up once, got sick, and passed out again. I must have applied too much of the drug in my haste. She'll be fine—eventually."

"Then it's a good time to do this." Ramiro had scant sympathy for Santabe. He slid between two tombs and started tying Santabe's limp hands. "What did she say? How long do you think she'll be out before we can question her again?"

He reached for the other strap to bind her feet, but Teresa drew it away, eyeing him worriedly. "You are content to stay here, cousin? I'd thought you'd be the one clamoring to leave, and we'd have to try and convince you."

"That transparent, was I?" Ramiro grinned sheepishly. "I did want to go to Suseph. I still do, actually. But Sancha helped convince me otherwise. She reminded me that what needs doing is here. Though I do want to find a better place to hide—Sancha is too exposed."

Teresa handed him back the strap to secure their prisoner's feet, and Telo said, "I think I know a better place. We can try it. As for our news, while you were gone, Santabe let slip her people tried hiding underground and it didn't work. I believe her on that. Hopefully, we can keep learning more. The effects of the drug shouldn't linger much longer, and we'll be able to get back to interrogating her soon. I have an idea where to start." Telo clasped Ramiro's shoulder.

"I understand your hurry to reach Suseph, my child. We'll do our best to get you there as soon as possible."

Teresa smiled. "I much prefer you stay and help us, then go to Suseph and languish in a prison, awaiting a trial that shouldn't be happening, but are you sure? We were going to insist that you go ahead of us. As your friend, I wanted to put you first. I wanted to do what would make you happiest. Sending you to Suseph seemed the right course."

He tried to speak, frowning to keep from betraying how her words touched him. She took his arm, and the warmth of her eyes felt good in this cold tomb. "Can you blame me, cousin? You didn't shun me when I revealed my secret. Whatever your decision, I support you.

"It's what friends do."

Speaking his heart had never come easy, and for a moment his throat was too swollen to talk without shaming himself. The strength he felt from Teresa added to his own, and he finally said, "I feel torn into a thousand directions. Claire is pulling on me . . . and you. My parents. My duty to Gonzalo and the *peloton*. And I'm realizing the last should be the least of my duties. But Claire . . . ." His voice broke. "I guess I just have to hope she stays safe or finds her way to me, because I would stay with you instead, to do what needs to be done. I think that's what she'd want of me."

Relief washed over Teresa's face, rounding her cheeks, too plain to be denied. "Perhaps if we get some information from Santabe and they don't need us anymore, Father Telo can take the message and I can go with you to look for Claire. But I'm glad you're staying with us, where I can know you're safe—if hiding in a tomb with our enemy's high priestess is safe." She laughed. The sound a peal of pure light in the gloom.

"All is well then," Father Telo boomed in his powerful voice. "I tried to tell you forcing him to go to Suseph without us was foolish. We can be done with this talk of splitting up. We are a team again. As the Lord sayeth, 'Work well for thy God and I shall work through you.'" He clasped Ramiro in a brief embrace.

Ramiro cleared his throat, wanting to be done with this touchy-feely conservation. "You said Santabe spoke already. What else did you learn from her?"

"This, my child. Come and see. I think we have a clue." Father Telo drew him to a corner, where their possessions lay. He pointed to the two Diviners on a sarcophagus far enough away from Santabe to be out of reach. "When she woke, she ignored the white weapon in my hand, closest to her, and searched for its twin: the red. Why? Is it the two together, or does the red do something more? We need to know. Unfortunately, she passed out before we could question her further."

"Likely it will burn us all to cinders." Ramiro rubbed at his chin, feeling the scratch of whiskers dragging on his fingers. His instinct said he needed to be the voice of dissent in their discussions. That Father Telo and Teresa would be too likely to rush into risk without seeing all sides. "A weapon like the other."

"I agree," Telo said with a grudging smile. "The Northerners are capricious in some ways, but knowing the Northerners, a means to kill is the safe explanation. But what if it's something more? Why else have separate colors? The Northern priests stand before the front gate with these red Diviners, when before, we always encountered them wielding the white ones. Why? Santabe's first glance around was to search for it. It must be significant."

Teresa's good humor had faded, her eyes filled with dread again. "I feel anything significant is likely to be on Santabe's list of things *not* to discuss with us. If she speaks at all it could be to mislead. She says her people weren't safe underground and could find no way to stop Dal—it seemed candid, but it might not be the whole reality. We need to press her a bit harder."

"Yes—and find out what the red Diviners do," Telo repeated.

They all turned to look at the woman who had caused nothing but cruelty in their lives and the lives of so many others. Father Telo had explained how she'd order the deaths of children. The peacefulness of her breathing seemed out of touch with the brutality of her soul.

"Or you could be reading too much into where an ill woman was looking," Ramiro pointed out. "She had to look at something. You claim she is crafty. Her gaze could have been meant to deceive, exactly as her words."

"Logically, the only one who could help us sort truth from lies is another Northerner," Teresa put in. "Surely, though they might not have all the facts about Dal, they would all know about the red Diviners."

Ramiro shook his head. "I take your point, cousin. But we can't just ask a Northerner his thoughts," he pointed out. "They'd hardly answer us freely even if they did understand us."

Father Telo's eyes lit up, and Ramiro braced himself. "I know one who speaks our language," Telo said, "and might even be sympathetic to our cause— the officer from the gate. After we question Santabe thoroughly, I shall go to him alone, and with the Lord's help, I'll try to get confirmation for anything we have discovered from Santabe. At the same time, the two of you can go out the gate and get our news to those waiting."

Ramiro touched mind and heart, hoping to bring them into balance. His mind said all his friends' plans made sense. Their ideas sound and logical. Unflawed. His heart said otherwise, warning it could never be that easy.

CHAPTER 23

Julian held himself straight and tall at Beatriz's back with Captain Gonzalo and a few others, his gut pulled in to flatten his stomach. Well did he know the value of appearances at times. Occasionally the façade of confidence had been the only thing that made a vote swing his way when the *concejales* should have opposed his choice. His best help to his wife on this day was steady eyes and a neutral expression while she spoke to the combined people of Colina Hermosa and Suseph.

His companion caught his eye. As a soldier, Captain Gonzalo had long mastered a similar art, projecting solid reassurance while fading into the background. By necessity the captain of a *pelotón* must be a man of many talents—able to lead and command at a moment's notice, but also to take orders in turn. Julian gave the captain a nod of approval as Beatriz's speech drew toward its close, and got a quirk of the head in acknowledgement.

The faces in the packed church showed a mix of incredulity and horror. They had visited so many churches already that Julian had lost count after a score. Each church was in a different district of the city so that every person could hear for themselves the words of their *alcalde*. Words to prepare for the worst. Beatriz had decided to offer hope, but not to shirk truth:

We will oppose this Dal, yet might not be able to succeed.

So far her message had been received as well as could be expected, though word had surely run ahead of Beatriz as they made their slow way through the city, and to be fair, no amount of preparation could brace a person for the details spelled out from an actual authority figure.

Yet the speeches to the people had almost not happened—or not by Beatriz. The *concejales* of both cities had tried to dissuade her and then insisted they'd be better to speak to the people—that the people needed to hear such dire news from a man. The scene outside the first packed church replayed in his head.

Beatriz had been surrounded by fourteen councilmen, all trying to protect her from herself.

"Let someone with more experience talk to the people," Osmundo the potter had suggested with a patronizing smile. "We would not stress you."

"I concur," had said a landowner from Suseph whose name Julian always forgot. "To speak at so many venues all over the city would be tiring for anyone. Let us handle it."

"For *anyone?*" Beatriz had snapped. "But not for you?"

"Beatriz has been in front of crowds since I got into politics," Julian had said, hoping to defuse the situation. "I daresay she has done this more than any councilman."

Beatriz's eyes had narrowed. "Thank you, Julian, but today I need no one to speak for me." She had given him that glare he know so well and he had stepped back. "I am the *alcalde* here. Duly elected by not one, but two cities. It is clearly the duty of the *alcalde*—"

"And our duty to advise and vote," Diego had said. The elderly man had lifted a hand to stroke his white beard. "And to spare the *alcalde* when possible. You may verbally delegate this unpleasant task to us. This needs to be handled with care to avoid a panic."

Beatriz's expression should have spit sparks. "And you think I'm not the person for it. That I need to be spared *unpleasant* tasks?"

"You are new to it," Diego had agreed. "Untried. Better if one of us takes the podium so things don't get . . . emotional."

"*Emotional?* And would you suggest the same for someone in pants or do you speak to me in this way because I can't grow a beard?" The *concejales* had been unable to meet her eye at that. "Thank you for your *concern* for my welfare, but I will delegate this task to no one. I daresay I've been handling *unpleasant tasks* since before some of you were born. If you ever try to patronize me like this again I shall not be so discreet about it, if *you* get *my* meaning."

Beatriz had turned from the councilmen, still muttering about not needing their help to get elected and certainly not needing their assistance to do her job. Julian had left his smirk in place, and had given the councilmen a cold, *"Caballeros,"* before he had followed Beatriz to the first pulpit and her speech. Reminding them her popularity far exceeded their own had been a masterful touch—he couldn't have managed better himself.

And she had managed each speech just as masterfully, getting stronger with each performance, conveying the same details each time while giving each message a personalizing touch. Yet still Julian felt for the people receiving that communication.

Who would want to believe that their entire family—an entire *ciudad-estado*—might be slaughtered and left nothing but a pile of corpses by an uncaring god? A myth come to life.

It had been hard enough for Julian to face the loss of his eldest son. The unbidden image of an entire city's death almost shattered his composure. He quickly schooled his face back to stillness, touched mind and heart, and turned to Gonzalo as a distraction.

Here at least was one who hadn't tried to dissuade Beatriz. He had more brains than the *concejales*. The dark-skinned captain was a good ten years older than Salvador had been. "Have you any family?" Julian asked.

For a moment, Gonzalo's throat worked before he answered. "A wife. Four children. Two sons and a daughter here in this city."

"Evacuated?"

"Aye. With the same group as your good wife, the saints bless her. They shared stories with me of her leadership on the journey here."

"That is Beatriz," Julian said with a glow of pride. "Times of hardship bring out the best in her."

"My eldest son rides with the grooms and squires beside me," Gonzalo confided. "I haven't had a chance to see my wife and other children yet."

Julian nodded in understanding and allowed himself a small smile as remembrances flooded him. "Your son has answered the calling. Both of mine did the same. They would have it no other way, right from the beginning. They had one-track minds. The military was the only place for them."

"Duty to our people runs in your family," Gonzalo said.

"And in yours. When our tour of the city is over, you must go to see your wife. I insist upon it—and

I know Beatriz would as well. Consider it an order, Captain, from one no longer able to command you."

"Hi-ya, sir. It is my privilege to serve."

Julian sensed neither of them felt easy speaking of their private lives. The situation with Ramiro's abrupt departure from his duty stood between them. He turned the conversation. "Have you troops in place in case of rioting?"

"What troops are available to us are ready. We are spread very thin. I doubt we can do much good if the whole city erupts, let alone a quarter of the people take to the streets."

With one regiment and a few squads of gate guards, Julian agreed. So far the people's reaction had been quiet, but he was pretty sure they hadn't fully absorbed the news yet. They would reach the real precipice as light faded to night, when inhibitions weakened.

Beatriz finished her prepared speech and blank silence greeted her and stretched to an uncomfortable count before being broken.

"What should we do?" asked a woman, holding an infant to her chest.

Beatriz's fingers, which had been clamped on to the podium until the knuckles turned white, slackened. This is where his wife excelled: speaking not to a crowd but to an individual. He knew well Beatriz dreaded public dialogues, but interaction was another story.

The first question broke the flood and more poured from every direction, too many to hear or answer.

"Silence!" Gonzalo shouted in a booming bass. "Silence for the *Alcalde* so she can speak! Silence!" The crowd settled with a reluctant final drone of noise.

When quiet prevailed, Beatriz said, "You can pray. Pray that we prevail." Beatriz pulled herself taller against the lectern. "We have taken many steps to protect you. There will be a *convocación* of *alcaldes* soon. I have the advice and experience of former *Alcaldes* Julian and Ramón. Our scouts and spies are among the Northerners, looking for ways to stop this god. Scholars, historians, and clergy have all been instructed to examine every scripture, every document, and history for clues. The best minds of our military have been consulted, including the retired members. Indeed, we have requested those members and any who left for other professions to form a new *pelotón*. We have put word among merchants and other travelers who have visited foreign lands for any rumors they have heard of the Northern god. Be assured we have left no stone unturned, nor will we."

Julian nodded to show the people he agreed. He had snatched perhaps two hours' sleep since returning to Suseph, and Beatriz had gotten less. Everyone on the inside had been tireless in doing everything that could be done, including the councilmen of

Colina Hermosa and of Suseph, though he noted Beatriz left their names out of her praise.

"The best thing you can do now is wait and be ready. As I said, darkness and shelter are our protection. We have plenty of food and water. Go back to your houses and be with your families. Seek solace at your church. Let no one suffer fear all alone but include those without kin at your hearth, just as the people of Suseph took in their cousins of Colina Hermosa."

Julian looked up. He had not heard these words at any of the other events. Tears stood in Beatriz's eyes. "The Northerners are a people of violence and bloodshed. They took our city—my child—our children. I would not have us be like them. I would have us show them the meaning of kindness. Embrace the lost. Tend the sick. Soothe the panicked. If you have plenty of something, offer it without price to those who need. Let us take no money in these days of trial, but help each other. Stand together and stand for compassion. Be not angry or hopeless, but find strength in family and courage."

Her mantilla trembled atop her head with the force of her conviction.

"I trust in you. Enough to share with you everything I know. I wish I had more answers to give you, but for now, like you, I wait. Let us wait with kindness. If these be our last days, let it be said we filled them with benevolence and showed the world the true meaning of humanity! Let us not be like them!"

Beatriz stepped down from the pulpit and the people, swept up in her emotion, rushed forward. Gonzalo tried to dart in front of her, but most people merely touched her arm or the edge of her dress, murmuring words of thanks or promises to be kind. Tears stood in many eyes, and Julian dashed his hand across his cheek to wipe away his own.

As a large matron crushed Beatriz in an embrace, whispering blessings, he managed to get close enough to his wife to smile at her across the distance and mouth the words. "*Mi amor.* Now and forever."

Her return smile was filled with sweet sadness. There and gone as she went from belonging to him for an instant to back to belonging to the people. How many years had she been the one who stood back and gave him over to their city, offering her quiet support? He gladly took his turn being her strength.

"No emotion, *caballeros*?" Julian couldn't help putting forward that dig to the members of the council close enough to hear.

Gonzalo cleared his throat beside him, having worked his way through the crowd. "I think those words will travel to every corner of the city. We will have a quiet night. Unless I miss my guess, there will be no riots."

"No," Julian said in agreement and gestured to a table in the corner where a priest scratched words on parchment as another dictated. Other clerics wrote furiously on their own papers, making copies of the speech. "I don't suppose there will be."

"They love her," Gonzalo added.

Julian had no answer but the swell of pride in his throat and heart. Beatriz had become the parental figure of old and young.

Law and order would be maintained tonight. All due to the will of one very extraordinary woman. Another miracle of sorts. Let the morrow bring them more blessings.

CHAPTER 24

Telo stared at Santabe as she sat on the ground, her back against a pillar. Leather straps bound her there—her arms pulled backward and pinned against the stone, while the girth of the pillar ensured her hands didn't meet. While he was loath to see anyone so restrained, having suffered his own captivity at the hands of the Northerners, he agreed with Ramiro that she was much too dangerous to be free. With relief, his conscience gave over that worry to the Lord. God would have to judge if necessity outweighed morality in this case and tally the results against his soul. For now, he was willing to live with this treatment.

I can ask for forgiveness later.

"What does the red Diviner do?" he asked Santabe for the hundredth time.

A gloating smile remained his only answer.

Ramiro took a step closer, eyebrows raised in inquiry, and Telo gave a small nod. The young man knelt slightly behind the pillar, close enough to breathe in Santabe's ear. Her gloat wavered, looking far less certain. It vanished altogether at the rasp of Ramiro's knife leaving its sheath.

"You have rightly pointed out that a man of my calling is by nature too kind," Telo said. "Too quick to forgive, as I forgave the taking of my hand. Our job is to council and absolve. But Ramiro is of a different calling."

Ramiro passed a sharpening stone over the knife, leaving a hiss of stone against metal to hang in the air. "A soldier learns to put aside conscience. You burned down my city. Ordered the death of *children*. Maimed the good Father. Helped cause the deaths of thousands . . . including my *brother's*." He leaned forward so she could see him out of the corner of her eye, then set the knife against her wrist, drawing a thin mark of blood. "We have a saying here: Treat others as you want to be treated. But we have another one, similar in nature, yet slightly different: What comes around goes around." The knife bit a fraction deeper.

"You would not," Santabe hissed. "You bluff. Your religion forbids it."

"Does it?" Ramiro said into her ear. "Sorry to disappoint, but a lot goes out the window in a time of war. I learned field interrogation in my training. You would be amazed what I can do with a knife and a fire. The fire will make sure there isn't enough blood to bring down your Dal. The knife will make sure there's enough blood to at least make that a worry. And if you're concerned about our religion, the good Father can take a little walk if he doesn't want to watch. But I'm not going to have *any* regrets."

"Tell me something about your god—the Diviners—and I'll call him off," Telo said.

Santabe's lips pressed together, and Teresa stepped forward. "Did Ordoño teach you the symbolism of a man's beard? On a soldier it means they've killed. Ramiro earned his beard particularly young."

"Thanks to you," Ramiro purred in Santabe's ear and she jumped. "They taught me all kinds of ways to inflict pain without causing death. But I've never taken off a hand—yet."

"How do your people get the demon to leave?" Telo snapped quickly. "Give us something or I leave it to Ramiro!" Telo nodded and Ramiro dug deeper with the knife. Blood ran down into her hand, dripping off her fingers.

"The moon," she gasped. "It is no secret. Any could tell you that with each visit Dal stays another turn of the moon."

"How many months?" he prodded, but the gloating smile had returned. She had confessed that much not out of fear, but as a dig—to get under their skin, not to save hers. Or possible she lied, but at least she was speaking. They could sort out truth from fabrication later. "Tell us about the Diviners!"

"No—I think not. Wait and you'll find out first-hand."

Teresa growled with frustration and darted forward to slap Santabe across the face. The crack of flesh brought Telo half off his seat.

"Stop!" The same frustration ate at his insides, but he couldn't condone this anymore. Not yet. They had only been at the questioning for half a day. He would give more peaceful methods at least a full day. Besides, he doubted intimidation or torture would work. He waved Ramiro back and the young man faded to the edge of the room as they'd agreed. Teresa returned to her seat in front of their prisoner as well. Today Telo was in charge, but tomorrow would be a different story.

I will not fall into my former brutish ways. But the day I cross over that line might very well be coming soon . . .

Instead of letting Santabe's obstruction anger him, Telo allowed his focus to drift to calmer ground.

Their new accommodations, where Telo had led his friends, allowed them much more space, including concealment for Sancha. Still underground, still full of the blessed dead, but some long-ago smugglers or others hiding from law and order had moved the heavy tombs aside, clustering them around the edges of this room or crowding them into other chambers. This place gave them area to move around and stretch out without having to squeeze between blocks of stone.

A few smaller sarcophagi had been left for seating, and the walls had been decorated with centuries of graffiti, erasing the original murals and covering the remaining carvings. Hooks in the walls let them space oil lanterns for much better lighting. Pillars covered with carvings gave them a convenient place to secure Santabe, who had eventually recovered from her overdosing. Telo even believed this location was a little less chilly than the other. A good thing, as the damp of the first location had caused severe aches in his amputated limb. A ring of broken rocks formed a place for a fire, and the flames added a cheerful glow entirely out of place with their purpose.

Their new den hadn't been empty when they arrived, but the transients had taken one look at Ramiro's weaponry and the sullen captive, Santabe, and made for the door, sped along by some coins from Teresa. Taken altogether, it made for a much better living situation—while perhaps a worse interrogation chamber.

We'll see about that.

"Magic or science," Teresa mused. "Which creates these Diviners? Though isn't science always like magic to those who don't understand? Do we perhaps misrepresent magic of, say, the witches, because we just don't have the tools to explore what's really happening? Fascinating thought. Could that be the case here also with the Diviners?"

Father Telo cleared his throat, hiding his expression, though Ramiro looked annoyed at the digression. "Yes, well, my child. Shall we stay on topic and leave the philosophy for another day?" They had enough trouble with Santabe without confusing the issues. Telo was no professional interrogator, but he understood that concept at least. Though as a priest, he found that getting people to talk meant getting them to relax, so perhaps Teresa's off-topic asides helped with that.

Getting people to talk.

An idea clicked. A method that always brought people out of their shell.

He held up his stub to his companions in a warning to stay quiet for a moment. Santabe's eyes narrowed. "I just realized how rude we are being to you," he said. He moved next to her long enough to place a bandage on the cut Ramiro had inflicted. "We pepper you with questions, but don't give you the respect of offering to answer any. Perhaps you have questions about us, our goals, our people. What do you say? I will do my best to answer truthfully anything you want to know."

He could see her struggling against the temptation to speak. Temptation won. "Hypocrites. You preach of kindness, but how long do you intend to hold me before you kill me?"

"A complicated question. That has yet to be decided," he said without offense that she would jump to such a conclusion. Her response was the logical query to spring to her lips. "But you saw what happened with Ordoño. I was unable to go through with my decision to eliminate the Northern leader. If I have any influence, you will not be killed. Nor will we hold you long." God forgive him for letting such a one loose on the world yet again, but he was guilty of that already. "I have come to hold more firmly as the best of us preach that retribution is not in my hands. But as I say, it isn't totally up to me, and my companions might feel differently. After all, there are many levels of violence before reaching killing."

Ramiro cracked his knuckles.

"See?" Telo added. "It is not entirely in my hands. Our goodwill does depend on your cooperation. Keep in mind I am only in charge for today. And as to our kindness that so disgusts you, it is not hypocrisy, as we are also a people of justice. We have only been defending what is ours, hoping to find a way to protect our people so we can return to a life of harmony." He refrained from pointing out that her kind were the ultimate oppressors. Casting blame would not lead to good feelings. "What else would you know of us?"

Santabe seemed to be a woman of strong opinions combined with a volatile temper. In his experience as a traveling friar, Telo had never found that a recipe for a human who kept silent when given an opportunity to express themselves. Each conversation could be brought to lead to one more, and perhaps—eventually—reveal useful information.

The key was patience.

Luckily, he hadn't long to wait this time, either. "Justice. You say you value it, but your society reveals you do not. Where is your punishment for those who break the law? Again you pick kindness"—she slurred the word into sounding like an oath—"over sending criminals back to their former life to learn better ways. Kindness doesn't help those who break the law. Punishment does. You believe your society superior, yet you don't even allow women among your priests. You restrict half your society with some misbegotten view of inequality. Your people deserve to fall to Dal. You are the barbarians! Inferior!"

Telo sat back on his stone seat, strangely calmed by her anger. "I do not claim we are a perfect society. We have our faults, as you have found—on the issue of women most definitely—though I disagree with what you said about our justice. But let us discuss equality first, because it's something I'm eager to learn more about from you. Before we do, though, it might be worth mentioning that unlike Aveston and other *ciudades-estado*, Colina Hermosa has never had an actual law preventing women from joining the clergy. Indeed, there have always been a few female priests—six or seven added in the last year or so. Yet I know we can do better at that, and I'm curious what you might suggest. For example, what are the other roles of women among the Children of Dal?"

"I noticed none in your army," Teresa added when Santabe didn't respond.

Instead of appeasing her with his concession of fault, the red spots in her cheeks spread and grew larger. Telo stepped in swiftly. "Here women become healers, or educators, scholars and professors"—he waved at Teresa—"they work in shops and family businesses, they take their turn to sit on panels as judges and act in juries to judge their peers. They have even become leaders of our cities. But most choose traditional roles of marriage and raising families. Many give their time to the church as laypersons. They are restricted from our military as seems to be the case with your land. But again, what about you? What do women do besides working for your god?"

She wanted to resist—he could see it—and yet she also wanted to speak.

He could see that, too.

"We are merchants—farmers," Santabe finally said. "Women own the shops, the properties. Generate the money. We are not forced to stay home with children. Our children learn to take care of themselves or they perish. We are not subservient, lazy thralls as your people make them. We have power!

"And you worry too much about the poor. Soup kitchens. Bread lines. Blasphemy! They should be left to starve as suits their worth! How else are they to learn in the next life?"

"Fascinating," Teresa said, her eyes glowing. "What a treasure trove of directly opposite lifestyles. I wish we could learn more from each other. Tell me more about the next life and what happens in your afterlife. I really must know."

"You only want to *know* how to stop Dal, ugly woman," was the sharp reply. "There isn't any way to stop him. You will die as you deserve and learn nothing from me."

"You mistake us," Telo said. "We are an open people—curious. We always crave to learn more." A great weariness sunk into his bones. He had gotten her to talk, or to cast blame more accurately, but it wasn't leading to a better understanding. Still, he could only press on. "You don't pay taxes or donate to support your poor—your elderly then?"

Santabe's eyes flashed. "Why should we?" And she proceeded to tell him exactly what she thought of that idea.

Ramiro groaned and settled against the wall as the conversation turned to the topic of economics—the Northern version was a most bigoted and heartless system according to their prisoner's words—while Teresa tried to redirect the talk to religion. He could see where Father Telo attempted to go with this general talk, but it wasn't going to work and Ramiro found it hard to keep his attention where it belonged. He really didn't care that the Northerner's largest crop was wheat, nor that they burned half their yield rather than give the grain away—that fact didn't matter here unless they could bury Dal under a flood of grain and be done with it. His part in this farce was over for today, though it hadn't really been playing a part on his side. He expected to use some sort of coercion eventually, if not truly chopping off her limbs. He hadn't been lying about what he could do with a knife and a fire. Now, boredom and the fact that he'd run on short sleep for days made his eyelids heavy.

He blinked, jerked awake, and blinked again as the urge to sleep hit him from nowhere and everywhere. He shook himself, standing more upright. Never had he fallen asleep on duty—

The world of gray fog floated into existence as he closed his eyes again.

"Leviathan."

He jumped as gray fog surrounded his waking eyes, revealing Salvador's form—his brother's face—in the distance. Too far to reach without sprinting and yet too near to mistake. Experience with the gray world of fog had taught him not to try to get nearer, as he would not be allowed. He recognized the narrow, alley-like streets of Aveston. The figure who was not his brother waited at the opposite end.

"Leviathan."

The word drifted to him from a dozen voices at once. Each sound coming from a tiny window gaping in the fog—each perhaps the size of a book. All showed a fresh perspective. Priests in their pulpits. Scholars sharing cheap bread and olive oil at a tavern. A monk pointing a tapestry out to a group of pilgrims. Too many windows to glimpse before they faded, covered with fog again. A single word came from every fresh window to elsewhere before they closed.

"Leviathan."

"Leviathan."

"Leviathan."

"Leviathan!" Ramiro shouted as the gray fog vanished, having never existed in the first place. "Leviathan!"

Teresa and Father Telo swung around from Santabe with concern on their faces at his shouts. Part of him filled with relief that the help from the dreams continued, while the other felt only dread for what the vision could mean. "My dream says Leviathan. I remember that vaguely from church. But it's dead, right? I'm sure the lesson said God killed the Beast. That's what it is—a sea beast."

His companions exchanged a long look. "Not exactly," Teresa said. "A sea beast is a label that grew over time. It's not what is recorded. 'God smote the Leviathan with a flaming'—or in some translations shining—'sword and so defeated the darkness so He could create the worlds.'"

"Worlds?" Ramiro asked. "There's just one world."

"It translates literally to worlds," Telo said, rubbing his bare chin absently. "This is bad. This is very bad. The name came from your dream? You saw something that can help us?"

"Not saw, no. Heard. 'The Leviathan.' It's got to be what's behind the Northern god. What is it?"

Father Telo looked thoughtful. "Simply put, it's *the* Beast of Darkness that God fought in order to use his power of creation at the dawn of time. Fought and won, back when only two things existed: good and evil."

"Then the dream is wrong. It is dead and not what's causing the massacres."

"Not exactly," Teresa said. "You can't kill the Beast. Leviathan was the first monster and the father of all the rest. It is the Darkness as God is the Light. Neither can be wholly defeated."

"What?" Ramiro said blankly. "That's not what I remember from church."

"It wouldn't be," Father Telo said with a quirk of his lips. "The Church doesn't exactly go in for reminding people that there was something out there our Lord couldn't defeat for all time. God has no weakness. He's all-powerful, remember? But there are hidden scriptures that say otherwise."

Teresa nodded. "The Heretic Scriptures. Recognized

as authentic, but banned by the Church for one reason or another from public mention. You can believe the clergy talk enough about them privately, though. You have to be a full professor to even hear about them, let alone see them. They all confirm the same thing: Simply put, the flaming sword of God cut the Darkness into chunks. Each piece kept a share of the life and strength of Leviathan in proportion to their size."

Ramiro shook his head. "That's hardly simple. Spell it out for a blockhead."

"Monsters," Father Telo said. "It means monsters. The sword cut Leviathan into sections and the smaller pieces became manticores, sphinx, griffins, dragons, and others. The weaker sort of creatures that saints or even mortal men could take down with mortal weapons. These could die and eventually became extinct. Do you remember the legend of San Jorge and the Dragon? Well, it's not exactly a legend. It was a smaller section of the Leviathan. San Jorge persevered, but died of his burns."

"And the bigger pieces?" Ramiro made himself ask.

"What do you think?" Father Telo turned his back, looking too shaken to continue.

"Not good," Teresa said. "More monsters. The immortal kind. God couldn't kill them, but He supposedly locked them away where they could only occasionally revisit the world."

A shiver crawled down Ramiro's back. "Like every twenty-five hundred years."

"Apparently."

"Then we can't kill it."

"No," Teresa said. "If your dream is correct, we can't kill it or destroy this thing we're facing."

"As I told you," Santabe said, laughing. Ramiro jumped as he had forgotten she was there. "Now maybe you will hear me. I know not this Levethorn—He is our Dal, not a thing belonging to you or from your writings—but Dal cannot be stopped."

Father Telo faced them again to say, "The Darkness doesn't think—doesn't feel. It has one purpose and that is to smother life. To kill. To wipe out existence. It always was and always will be. There before the dawn of time. The opposite of God."

"Dal kills." Santabe agreed, showing her teeth. "It has been killing the Children of Dal for millennia. Now He kills all."

Ramiro stalked over and seized the Northerner by her robe, shaking her. "But the Children of Dal survived! How did you do it?" She only smirked at him, until he shoved her hard, smashing her against the pillar. It quivered, rocking slightly. "Tell us or I'll knock your teeth out!" Rage swallowed him.

When he'd cut and taunted Santabe before, he'd been the one under control, knowing that his threats weren't going anywhere—not on this day at any rate. But this was different. Now he wanted nothing more than to end Santabe for all time.

Teresa was quickly there, peeling his fingers from

the priestess. "Ramiro. I don't think this is the way to face down the Darkness. If that's truly what we face, matching it with anger isn't the answer or even possible."

"Let me handle her," Father Telo said, stepping forward.

Ramiro backed off, his reactions cooling. How had his temper slipped his control? The pseudo-Salvador from the gray fog never displayed this kind of negative emotion, not even when he had exhibited images of entire cities devastated, all the people killed. Always the figure of the gray world had been a well of compassion, exhibiting sorrow for the victims and the enemy both. He sensed that the man from his dreams loved even the Darkness.

That was something Ramiro could never do.

It might have been a mistake to choose me to have these dreams. I am too imperfect, unfit for the job.

Deserter, a tiny voice reminded.

"Fool," he whispered to himself. "Stop that."

It wasn't easy, but he knew he couldn't simply succumb to the doubt. He might not have that sort of control over his behavior or love for all, like the figure in his dreams, but he was hardly worthless. He could at least manage not to kill Santabe if nothing else. A fair fight would be a different story, but she was tied and bound, helpless. He was better than that.

Teresa still held his hand and he turned to her. "Thank you for restraining me. Truly we are in this together. However, some of this still doesn't make sense. My dream is trying to tell me Dal is a piece of the Leviathan—"

"If your dream is right, a *big* piece," Teresa agreed.

"So Dal *is* the Darkness. Then why do the Northerners call him a sun god? He works his killing by day and not at night. That doesn't fit with my vision of evil. Shouldn't it be the other way around?"

Teresa's cheeks rounded with a smile. "I don't think it's a literal darkness." She sobered and patted his hand. "Religion is full of paradox, cousin. Why did some pieces of the Leviathan become dragons and some sphinx? Each monster is different. Perhaps there's another out there that dwells only in night."

"Lovely. I think one monster is enough." He drew his hand away to rub at his face, leaning against the wall. Somehow it had been easier to accept when what they faced had been unnamed, some unfamiliar Northern god. But his dream put truth somewhere squarely here at home, though so ancient an evil as to be all but forgotten. It bothered him even more because he'd been trained to fight human enemies, not myths. "Monsters. By the saints, there are no such things as monsters. But then there are miracles again. I suppose . . . where do we get a flaming sword?" he joked.

Swords he could understand.

Teresa thought for a moment. "Well, Santiago mentioned the weapon from the dawn of time once during his lifetime. He said the Lord created it from a piece of flesh off his own arm and blew on the unshaped mass to give it substance and fire. He used his own flesh probably because there was only God and the Darkness available at the time. Chopping up the Leviathan apparently destroyed the sword. But I don't think that helps. Even to *look* at the Sword of Creation would kill us."

"Good to know. I'll remember not to ask for the flaming sword that's the only thing that could save us." Ramiro felt frustration building. "An immortal monster out of legend. Sure. We can tackle that with our two hands—or in Father Telo's case just one."

"Cousin!"

His head snapped up, to see anger in Teresa's eyes.

"Do we have a choice?" Teresa said. "We do what has to be done by someone. Someone has to step forward. Right now, we have the knowledge, so God must have chosen us."

Ramiro took a shuddering breath, then acknowledged her words with a nod. "Well-spoken. Someone has to. We helped unleash it. We can die trying to end it." He got his feet under him and stood. "No point sighing about that. We need to get a message to my parents, the rest of our cities. They must know about Leviathan. Hear what we've discovered, cousin."

"I don't think any of us should leave." Teresa gestured toward Santabe and Father Telo, and Ramiro had to allow the soundness of her words. "Can we inscribe a message to Lady *Alcalde* Beatriz and find a messenger to take it?"

"I believe so," Ramiro said. "Let me take care of that. That's a task that fits in this world and doesn't need a miracle."

Unlike defeating this impossible monster . . . .

The Leviathan had been broken into manageable chunks. It reminded him of his decision made in the cathedral to look at the path forward as just one step at a time. One action would lead to the next.

Right up until the part where they all died.

CHAPTER 25

Telo left his companions to talk and resumed his seat, watching Santabe. The small block of stone under him could only be the sarcophagus of an infant. A soul robbed of this world before it had a chance to experience life. What mother had lost her hopes and dreams on that day? What family had been reduced to misery? Of all the unfairness in this world, surely the death of a baby was one of the most grievous. To lose out on so much.

The Lord had a plan, but that didn't make death any easier. Even when the victim was an old man who had lived his life, like Father Ansuro. By the saints, how many millions more would be cut short of their time? Yanked from contented lives? Killed in a way to cause the most suffering?

In attempting to save life, Telo and the others had brought about the monster who would extinguish it.

He more than anyone here knew what they had unleashed. His background and study should have been a warning. Should have insisted they not mess with the profane. Interfering with an unknown god. He had taken his skepticism of Dal's reality for security when he suggested Claire sing about Dal. Something not real could not hurt them. And now the truth was much worse than some petty and unknown godling.

Leviathan.

The origin of darkness. The source of all evil. The ultimate destroyer of life. Telo had no illusions that the darkness would stop at removing human life. They already knew it extinguished animals as well. Given time it would consume plants from large to small. Wipe the entire world from existence. Take down the stars. Erase everything until only the Light and the Dark remained again.

Then try to swallow the Light.

"I didn't know." Telo slumped, his head lowering until his face pressed against his knees. As if ignorance was an excuse.

A heartless chuckle met his ear.

"You will all die!" Santabe cried out. "When I get free I will not even bother to kill you. Instead I will enjoy seeing Dal take you all! Take all the unworthy and rid this world of them." The gleam of truth in her eye was unmistakable.

No anger rose in him. Instead a sick feeling grew in his stomach. Could she really be so detached from humanity as to celebrate the destruction of countless innocents? Could anyone be that depraved?

On the other hand, could a human be defined with such simplicity? Reduced to one element of personality?

His training said no. That there was more to Santabe than anger and hate, just as there was more to everyone than what appeared on the surface.

Telo said nothing, just continued to watch, as his emotions emptied, really looking at the woman before him. Not at her physical strength or the clean lines of her features that many would call attractive, but seeing *her*. Another human with all the complexities that implied.

Everything else ceased to exist: Teresa, Ramiro, the room around him, the stone under his feet. All that remained was the woman before him. Layers peeled back before him as they had at the wall with the Northern soldier, Rasdid, allowing him access to all.

"Why do you look at me like that?" Santabe shifted uncomfortably in her bonds, for the first time exhibiting real unease.

The packaging of outward flesh slid back and Telo saw as with other eyes into Santabe's soul. Saw a streak of cruelty as deep as it was wide. A desire to bully and to hurt and to control. The Santabe he had encountered and that she showed the world. Yet, her downright spitefulness was mixed with a righteousness that the unfit be sent to another life to try again.

He finally saw what she'd been saying all along: a twisted justice without compassion drove her, of a sort Telo rarely encountered—that to punish with death was for a person's *benefit*. To Santabe, death was not the end, but just a voyage for the soul to be cast into another life to learn the lessons of truth missed in this existence. She saw most humans as failures who must repeat in an endless loop until they bettered themselves.

And if Dal could wipe away the failure all at once . . . he could see how that'd be appealing to Santabe, instead of the nightmare it appeared to him and his companions.

It was a dizzying prospect, and yet not what Telo needed to focus upon now. That was still something on the surface—something she'd basically shared with them. If he was going to truly understand her, he had to go further.

He looked deeper than her cruelty and found another river—this one of wounds that a mother, aunts, cousins would turn their backs and no longer care what happened to her once she entered a new family at the palace of Dal. Betrayed by her own kin. And deeper still beyond that, a child's longing, so hidden he could barely find its source. But there it was: a girl on the bed of a wagon heaped with silk and cotton cloth, examining a fresh city, never seen before, with shining eyes.

The heart of an explorer, yearning for new places, new situations. The unknown. Capable of joy and excitement just as any other human heart. A heart of innocence and wonder before it had been knocked around and buried under years of calluses. Now pumping the blood of those she'd killed, rather than that which gave her life.

He moved forward to kneel at her feet, gripping her face to turn it to his. "Look at me."

She resisted, fought to jerk her head away and hold her eyes from his, but eventually she was forced to see. To go past his defenses and encounter his compassion—his desire to save lives, even hers. To go deeper, where his steely determination waited.

Then the sharing ended with a painful jolt like the shattering of a mirror. Walls came down and the outer flesh was all he saw. Whatever insight he'd been granted by this miracle ended, but not before they understood each other.

"You know, child, the evil that comes. You don't really want it," he said. "You can help stop it. Talk to us."

Her face curdled, and he pressed onward, his words slow and gentle, but as inextricable as a boulder sent down a mountain. "Your kin—your mother—

she didn't want to leave you in that place. She did not mean to turn her back upon you. You must know that she thought it the best way for you to survive. She would reach out to you if she could, as I have done. Do you not know, she still thinks of you every day of her life? As any mother would. You know she does. Her lost child—taken from her."

"Stop!" Santabe shouted. "Do not say these things!"

"She will always love you."

"Shut up!"

"As does your entire family."

"I will hear no more of this!"

"They love you. As do I. As does a true god. We are here for you. You are not alone."

"Stop," she whimpered. "I will not hear you." But tears hung in her eyes. One liquid drop trembled on the edge and fell, then rolled down her cheek. "It's not true. I am alone. No one cares."

Father Telo whisked the liquid away with a gentle finger, then pulled at the knots of the straps binding her to the pillar until they fell away and left her free. Ramiro moved forward as if to protest, but Teresa pulled him back, shaking her head. *Thank you, Teresa.* "You are wrong, my child. I do."

"You do not."

"I would stop Dal from killing your family. You. All. But I don't know how. You can help me. How many moons?"

She closed her eyes to avoid him.

"Telling us this betrays no one. Help us fight. How many?"

"A lie," a whisper so low to be hardly audible. Again stronger. "That was a lie. No one knows why Dal leaves."

"Thank you, my child. And your people survived how?"

The so-odd light eyes opened to pin him down. "You cannot kill Dal," she said with conviction, but no heat. "It cannot be done. Though the Living Diviners, the red. They both repel and hold Him."

Telo sat back on his heels. "Repel? Is that why you were looking for it? Why you said Dal's name aloud and in the open? I noticed, my child."

She shook her head, refusing to say more.

"In Zapata there were the most beautiful gardens. Their mild climate allowed practically anything to grow there. Roses. Orchids. Plants impossible for a desert. All manner of exotic bloom and leaf. The smell. To walk in the gardens is to walk into a perfumery. Such color. A paradise for the eyes. Did you see it before it burned?"

When she kept her head down, he continued:

"But you saw the sea. That you couldn't miss. I saw it once. A sight I will never forget.

"Near Vista Sur there is a canyon so wide that clouds obscure the other side in winter. Even in summer the opposite side is like a mirage. So deep it takes an entire day's climb to reach the bottom. A river has cut through the stone for millennia, revealing so many colors of rock. A tapestry of shades that takes the breath away, I'm told. Oh, to see the wonder of it. Can you picture it in your head? Does it draw you? But it cannot be seen if we are all dead. So many opportunities lost.

"What do the red Diviners do, my child?" he coaxed. "We, too, cherish the beauty and mystery to be found in *this* world. I have this same yearning to see more. We are not unalike. Tell us what we need to know."

Her hands twisted in her lap. "The red . . . the red keep Dal away. Enough reds together can surround and hold Him. Not for long. But it can stop an attack."

"And you make them with the blood of the murdered. Of course." Telo flashed onto the line of priests around the army encampment. Not there to keep deserters in—or not entirely. There to keep Dal out. There to protect the Northern army from massacre. How effective was it?

Before he could voice the question aloud, Telo's thoughts leaped ahead, seeing what Santabe did not say. The more who perished, the more the Children of Dal could save. They could pick and choose who they wanted to ensure would live. Telo did not believe their choices would coincide. The Children of Dal would surely save the priests, those in power, while someone like *Alcalde* Julian would offer such gift to the most helpless—actual children.

So the Children of Dal had survived all these centuries by protecting their elite and letting the rest perish. No wonder they had developed such a belief in other worlds and other lives. It balmed their consciences to believe the losers of life's draw simply went back to try again.

If a core always survived, he understood the panic of the soldier class at the gates and the calm he'd sensed from the priests in Her Beauty. Of course the people of Aveston would rate even lower. The priests of Dal literally held the difference between life and death.

He felt too stunned to feel anger for all those deemed too unimportant to survive. His mind ranged further ahead to what it meant for his quest.

Without question, the Children of Dal would not share their red Diviner protection with the people they conquered.

"We know where they are," Ramiro said, startling him. "Father Ansuro told us the Diviners are in an inner courtyard at Her Beauty. Let's tie her back up and we can talk about how to get to them."

"That doesn't make sense to me," Teresa said. "Why would they leave such a protection lying around when they could be using them?"

"Agreed," Telo said. "Remember how few of the priests we encountered carried red weapons with their white. They would hand the red ones out if they had them. The red Diviners are outside protecting the army or being worn by their priests. We need to question her some more."

Santabe hissed. "Let me go. You got the answers you want."

"And let you run off to warn them." Ramiro reached for a strap. "I don't think so."

Santabe's face firmed and Telo tried to shout a warning. She braced her back against the pillar and kicked out, making the pillar wobble, catching Ramiro in the chest, and thrusting him across the room. Telo leaned in to grab her, but used the wrong arm. His stub crashed into Santabe, sending pain rocketing up his arm. He overbalanced, falling into her, pushing them both against the pillar.

The wobble became a wild rocking as the top shifted out from under the ceiling. The bottom gave ground, sliding with a grate against rock. The top ring of stone broke free, crashing downward, even as the next level fell. Telo threw his arms over his head in a flimsy shield and glimpsed hollowness in what he thought was solid stone. The pillar was hollow. No wonder it collapsed so easily.

Teresa rushed in to seize him, tugging futilely before the entire pillar toppled in a rumble of stone and clinks of metal. Something hard crashed into his skull and he knew no more.

CHAPTER 26

"A short break, Singers," Claire begged. Bags and bundles, including full water skins, swung against her back and legs as she walked. The weight pulled at her shoulders and made her tire faster. She carried her own possessions as well as a large part of the Elders' share. Somehow they had twisted her around until she found herself offering to carry their provisions. But the break she requested was not from her load, but from the magic.

She felt less and less like they were an avenging army on the move and more like she'd been drafted into a work gang—one where she did all the work.

Life had been hard enough when she was the protégée of one Elder from the Women of the Song. Now seven Elders had taken her on, and she didn't get a moment to herself. Judging from her nightmares, one of them probably stood over her as she slept, waiting to pounce and say, "Try just one more time."

Eulalie assumed the expression Claire had nicknamed "prune eater" and grunted. "A short break. Rest until we reach the road."

Now it was Claire's turn to groan. The road began less than a mile away, even at their slow pace they would make that goal in under an hour, giving her practically no break at all. But then Eulalie was the most unyielding of all the Elders. Even worse than Jorga. Eulalie had taken charge of the red Diviner and rolled the weapon into her baggage—the one thing the Elder did carry. She continually waved aside opposition from the other ladies as if their words proved less bothersome than a fly.

If only the Elders had something to put their focus upon besides Claire's training. Claire appreciated their efforts and all—she most certainly needed the work—but what she needed now was time alone to practice what she'd learned, and not under the intense scrutiny and critical eye of seven meddlesome women. Confidence in her abilities wouldn't come with them ganging up on her and finding fault with everything she did.

So she hoped for some other distraction. An obstacle of quicksand to go around. The return of the swamp cats. A heavy rain shower to wash the magic out of the air and make it impossible to practice— though even then they would probably still make her

Sing the words. An Elder with the sniffles and in need of tending. Anything.

None of the Elders were what you could call fast walkers, and the scenery passed at a snail's pace. Add into that the fact that they stopped early at night and rose late, and took prolonged breaks for meals and in-between meal munching, yet expected her to perform for them while they rested. At this rate, it would take another sevenday to reach a city once they got to the road, Aveston being the nearest. And longer to find where the Northerners gathered now.

And locate Ramiro.

Her thoughts shifted from her own annoyances. He had to be well—and waiting for her. Surely, his people had found his contributions too valuable to lock him up or punish him. If she could see how much the desert people needed him, they must also. The banging of the bundles against her legs faded as she used the short break to recreate the *valuable* way his bottom looked in his pants . . . the shapely way his leg tapered down to his high boots . . .

Muriel shouted, "Smoke."

Claire startled out of her daydream with a gulp and turned to where the dark-skinned Elder pointed. A plume rose above the trees, a short distance from where they believed the road to the desert merged with the swamp. A very thick plume of blackish smoke, not the normal light gray.

"If it's not a lightning strike, it's an obvious trap," Jorga said.

"And a delay," Rachael added.

"But possibly some Northerners to remove," Eulalie said and heads nodded.

Claire eyed the low-hanging clouds. It had remained dry for the last hours—such a luxury during the wet months—but that didn't mean there hadn't been lightning. Heat lightning was just as possible with such unstable weather. Likely the smoke was natural. But exactly the distraction she'd been hoping for. "We should investigate," she said instantly. "It could be Northerners."

Eulalie's eyes narrowed for her eagerness in a way that made Claire step back. Somehow Claire had gone from being in charge when they left the Rose Among Thorns camp to not being allowed to have an opinion. "So eager, girl? But I see it as the perfect opportunity for you to practice the tricks we taught you."

"Yes," Violet agreed. "We can send the girl in to spring the trap, if that's what it is."

"Oh." Claire frowned. "Wouldn't it be better if we all—"

"Ten minutes' head start," Rachael said with a wave. "Get going. Impress us."

Claire stood stupidly, staring. "Tick tock," Eulalie huffed.

"My granddaughter will not disappoint," Jorga said. "Hear that, girl: don't disappoint. Run."

Claire dumped all the baggage, turned blindly, and ran toward the smoke, irritation growing with each step. *Don't disappoint. Run.* As if she were some lackey to do their every bidding. So much for her break. They were supposed to follow her directions—her lead.

How had things taken such a turn for the worst?

Claire ground her teeth. The Elders could manipulate a stump into doing what they wanted.

Well and good, she decided. Let them have their victory. When they reached the desert people, she would be the one making the decisions. There, she would hold them to their word and enjoy watching them twist.

Besides, she had wanted to be alone, even if only for ten minutes. Even if it meant running toward potential danger.

She slowed as she neared the smoke—she could smell the woodsy flavor of it now. Feel the nearness in the sting in her eyes. As she moved from tree to tree, she let a hum build in her throat, gradually adding in whispers of words, sending the magic in growing waves that would each travel farther than the last. Anna and Susan had helped her practice erecting the Song in such a gradual way that even birds wouldn't flee the magic before it could take effect. Now, she used illusion alone to make any human see a deer moving among the trees.

A harmless deer. Hesitant and cautious. Nothing to fear. Nothing to attack.

She tried to trust the Song, but the hair stood up on the back of her neck at her exposure each time she stepped into the open for an instant. Anyone strong enough of mind, like a Northern priest, could see through her illusion.

That was before, she scolded herself. Before she'd had seven Elders sitting in judgment and training her. Now she had to believe she could match even the strongest mind.

As the magic reached full power, she entered a small clearing. The fire had been arranged in the center of the open space with at least a half dozen green boughs laced overtop the flames to ensure plenty of smoke. A trap indeed.

But left by whom?

She held the Song with ease as she skirted around the clearing, seeking any signs of life. There! A shine of metal came from behind a buttonbush. She hiked her skirts in her hands to ensure their silence and prepared to creep closer . . .

And seven Elders came thundering into the clearing with seven different Songs flaring, blowing her cover. Their abrupt entrance knocked the Song from her lips, scattering her deception. Screams sounded from behind the buttonbush as Claire darted forward. Three men rolled on the ground. One of them wore bits of rusted armor. A few more crashed around in another bush. A second look revealed a young woman among their number.

She had seen them before.

"Stop!" she shouted. "It's not Northerners! Stop! I know these people!"

The Elders' Songs cut off, and Claire placed her hands on her hips. "That wasn't ten minutes. Did you even give me five?"

All of them except Eulalie looked away. "Who is it?" the largest Elder demanded.

"Villagers." Claire toed the one with armor with her foot. "This one is called Suero. He is their leader. I think they set this trap for the Northerners." Suero glared at her through tearing eyes, blood coming from his ears. She had stopped the Elders just in time.

"And it would have worked, too, if you hadn't shown up." The greasy little man had stopped rolling in agony with the end of the Songs and sat up. He spat even while wiping away blood from his face. "*Sirenas.*"

"Men," Eulalie said in the same tone. "You expect to kill soldiers with a few rusty swords and one rickety bow."

"We are hunters. We hunt from the shadows. And draw them away from our women and children. None of them will survive."

"We are both here because of the same enemy," Claire said heatedly to Eulalie. "Every man in this world is not against you. Some might even help you if you gave them a chance." Though probably not this man. Ramiro's opinion made it clear Suero was a cheater and a thief as well as greedy. Not one to show your back. She turned to Suero. "And you traded with my mother, so you know not all *sirenas* are out to hurt you. The Northerners are the true enemy."

For her attempt at peacemaker she got more glares. "Honestly!" She stalked to the fire to pull as many of the green-leafed branches off the flames as she could, kicking dirt over the rest. No need to attract more attention.

"I will never trust men," Rachael said.

"Where is my son?" Suero demanded. The bent little man clutched at a sword he retrieved from the ground. "You have stolen him."

Claire froze, her heart dropping. She had forgotten Suero was Bromisto's father. They were so different. The boy hadn't had a sneaky bone in his body . . . well, at least not in a vicious way. Bromisto had come with them willingly enough, but she had failed the boy. She could not speak of his death here, in front of so many, as if it were casual conversation.

"Gone," Eulalie said. "Like my son." She gestured at Jorga. "And hers. Their daughters. Sisters. Mothers. Aunts. Cousin. Almost all our kin. Taken by the enemy."

The young woman with the villagers had been silent this entire time. She wore her hair up and had on a simple tunic over deerskin pants, like the other hunters. But the features of her face reminded Claire of Bromisto, especially in the friendliness of the eyes.

She burst into tears at Jorga's words, then gave a keening wail. "Ermegildo!"

Bromisto's true name. The sister the boy had always complained about.

Claire's heart clenched for her pain.

Suero had gone white under the dirt on his face. Another villager clapped him on the shoulder.

"My son."

Claire wanted to disappear. "I'm sorry. I shouldn't have taken him with us. Our losses . . . only grow."

His face hardened with hate. He hefted the sword, and Claire feared she had made an implacable foe.

"Behind you," Suero said. He rushed forward with a battle yell, but not at her.

Claire whirled to see ten men in black and yellow step from the trees, swords held ready. A full unit of Northerners.

Too late. She'd put out the smoke too late. Rage sparked in her heart. Errol. Bromisto.

"Fool!" Eulalie called at Suero.

Rachael and Muriel tripped up the advancing villager, stopping his progress and dragging him sideways into the other women, but also foiling any of the Elders from acting.

"Get down!" Claire yelled, though no one stood between her and the soldiers. The Death Song burst from her throat between one breath and the next. She used Eulalie's trick to direct the magic at her targets, calling them by name.

> "Men of the North,
> Fear, panic,
> "Cold hands,
> "Icy shakes.
> "Knees buckle,
> "Strength flees.
> "The grave waits, men of the North,
>   darkness . . ."

Rage and determination fueled her Song. She might not be able to harm Dal with her magic, but she could damn well take down his minions. All ten men dropped before she completed a verse. Dead before their bodies hit the ground. Their hearts stopped.

She felt the life drain from them like a blow to her soul.

A joyous satisfaction flooded her veins, hindered only a moment by a nudge of doubt, reminding her she wasn't a killer. Until someone reminded her she *was*.

"Destroyer," one of the Elders said in a startled voice.

Suero ran forward to kneel beside the Northerners, touching here and there. "They're dead." He raised incredulous eyes to her. "*Sirenas* can do such things? How?"

"With desire and practice," Muriel said, "and a willingness to take the scars."

"Scars," Suero said. "I see no scars upon you *women*."

"Exactly. It is the unseen ones that cause the most damage."

Muriel's concern twisted in Claire's gut. Empty eyes stared without seeing from the bodies upon the ground. Brushes of blond hair lay on foreheads still wrinkled in shock. Enemies no longer. People. People she had killed—now stacked in a heap like so much kindling.

Brothers. Sons. Fathers. Husbands.

Suddenly, Claire didn't want to be in this clearing anymore. "We've delayed too long. We should get moving again. The road is this way."

Claire was walking before she finished the words, something in her chest trying to break, while she did her best to force the feelings away.

Jorga took her elbow and guided her more to the right. "This way, granddaughter."

She heard the buzz of other voices speaking, but couldn't make out any words. The pressure on her elbow increased, and Claire realized Jorga was worried for her. She gripped her grandmother's hand in her own and held tight.

"I didn't think to stop the Song before they died. It didn't occur to me. I just killed them . . . because of what they did to Errol. To Bromisto."

"Aye," Jorga said for her ear alone. "The grief can do that to a person. What you must decide is, is that the sort of person you want to be?"

"I did what had to be done."

"None can argue that," Muriel said, coming up behind them. She now carried the belongings Claire had dropped. "But don't try to live with it alone. Talk to us."

"Tonight. Another time. Not this moment." Claire released Jorga's hand. *Destroyer.* She couldn't stand to dwell further on it. "Not yet."

The other women faded back as an argument grew between Suero and Eulalie, with Suero intent on coming with them, while at the same time insisting his hunters and his daughter, Elo, go home.

Claire clasped her hands together, letting her nails dig into her palms, as the Elders ignored her to concentrate on Suero, granting her peace and solitude of a sort.

It had been only a handful of Northerners. She had acted in self-defense. The Northerners had been the aggressors—as always. She had protected the others. Saved lives. As the nearest, she had been the safest choice to use the magic so none of them would die. Of course it had to be her who used the Death Song. It only made sense. They had to be stopped.

Too, the Northerners had surprised her. If she'd had an instant to set the Song, she'd have cut it off early and tried to spare their lives. Killing had been an accident. Something that wouldn't happen next time. One slip didn't make her a destroyer . . . did it?

The words ran in a loop in her brain as she walked, justifications appearing and fading, none able to push

away the queasy twist in her stomach, until the plain
dirt of the road appeared under her feet. The tangible
line between swamp and not swamp. The first step
toward the desert.

A strange reluctance dragged at her heels.

She had taken this road before with Ramiro, and
she knew what to expect this time. She had seen the
cities and met the people. The desert people wouldn't
be outright hostile toward her. She looked forward to
seeing some of them again—Beatrice, Fronilde, possibly Teresa would be there, and of course Ramiro. Yet,
she couldn't deny her dampened enthusiasm—she also
knew the numbers of Northerners at the other end.

There would be no avoiding more confrontations.

Her mouth grew dry.

Claire halted to allow the Elders and Suero to
catch up. She waited. The first step would be easier
with kin at her side.

"Claire, haven't you been listening?" Eulalie wore
her prune face again, all three chins in a bunch. Her
vast expanse of a bosom heaved from her exertion
or irritation or both. "I asked you three times if you
vouch for this man."

"He wishes to join forces with us," Rachael added.
"Thinks we can kill more Northerners together. I
don't really see how he can be any help. What do you
say?"

"Women know nothing of fighting," Suero said in
defiance of the demonstration of killing Claire had

just put on. "You need me to show you better tac-
tics. Standing in the open like that. Rushing forward
unprepared. Only a woman would be so stupid. It's
unnatural, but you're unnatural. I can be of use and
show you how to remember deference to a man at the
same time. Make you tolerable."

All seven Elders snapped at the man at once, giving
Claire a chance to think. She didn't trust Suero. The
short man had a way of meeting their eyes without
actually looking at them. Not in the innocent, so-
cially awkward way Errol had done, but in a way that
implied he held unclean thoughts about them. It gave
her the creeps.

More than looking like a weasel, he acted the
part as well. He had twisted the deal he'd made with
Ramiro the second the minimum terms had been
completed, leaving Ramiro to be killed. All he cared
about was gain for himself. Greedy for weapons to
assure his own reputation. Even with the power of
their magic to fuel his dream of revenging his son,
Claire couldn't believe his word would hold from one
sunset to the next. He'd betray them and do it gladly.

Yet, it might be better to have him under their eye,
then behind their back. A no from them wouldn't
keep Suero from following the same path.

"Swear," Claire said so abruptly every voice shut
off. "Swear on the life of your family, on your soul,
or whatever vow will hold you most, that you'll stand
firm to us until all the Northerners are dead. *All*. That

you'll not betray us to the enemy when you believe it convenient for you, or try to take our lives or harm us in any way. Swear it or go your own way."

"I swear on my family's life and my good right arm, may it wither, that I'll hold true to you. That our interests will be one—our lives one—until *all* the Northerners are dead. I swear by my good right arm to part from you in harmony if you help me avenge my son."

Claire nodded. "Accepted. Singers, watch him like a hawk anyway." She stepped forward onto the road, moving in an even stride. She had a sevenday to find a way to put aside the doubts that haunted her. Too long. Too much time to think. Too much time to worry.

Too much time for Dal to cause more misery. For the Northerners to kill innocents.

Almost she was tempted to ask for a Song to practice just to occupy her mind, but couldn't decide whether the scrutiny from the Elders or the worry were worse. "Let's try to hurry."

False words. Already the Elders began complaining about their knees or their hips. They couldn't keep up this pace.

If only they could travel faster. Make the miles they had to traverse disappear. Might as well pray for the Great Goddess to appear and whisk them across the distance. Claire knew well enough that their deity didn't intervene. They were on their own.

But that didn't keep her from wishing for more speed.

Maybe the saints Ramiro always applied to could help. His people expected intervention and assistance. She felt too embarrassed with the idea of speaking to dead people to put the plea into words, though. Besides, the saints weren't of her people. Why would they listen?

One of the Elders shrieked as the bushes beside the road rattled and shook, parting to let a large form emerge. A huge dapple-gray horse paced delicately around the Elders and a gaping Suero to stop in front of her. It overtopped her by a good foot and pawed at the ground restlessly as more horses, some brown and others also dapple-gray, followed the stallion onto the road. None wore bridles or saddles.

Claire reached out a hand to touch the stallion's shoulder, unsure whether she saw a ghost. She thought she recognized the pattern of his coat, though . . . "Valentía?" She was certain she had seen this animal long ago, when she and Ramiro had still been enemies, right after he kidnapped her. The stallion had been carrying the dead body of its master, Ramiro's brother. Ramiro had said something to her about setting the horse free.

The animal turned to show her its side, where scabbed scars of frightening-looking injuries broke the perfection of its hide. Valentía had been gouged with a sharp object and recently, but the animal seemed to feel no weakness. He held his head high and his eyes were clear and bright. Whatever had injured the horse hadn't killed it. The stallion nodded its head at her and then at its back.

Claire looked around at the small herd of waiting horses and a delighted laugh slipped from her lips. "Hike up your skirts, Singers. We're riding to the desert."

"What?" Jorga said, her eyes wide. "On those things? With no saddles? They just came out of nowhere. We can't trust some random animals."

A gleam of avarice lit Suero's eye, but like Jorga, the other Elders held back from the horses. Claire was willing to bet none of them had ever ridden.

"Never look a gift horse in the mouth," Claire said. "Think how much pain they will save your feet and knees." Though the same couldn't be said for their rumps. Claire didn't care how much the Elders complained—they'd find something to moan about one way or the other. So they might as well do it while moving faster. She'd get her grandmother and the others up on the horses and on their way, even if she had to shove each one up on her shoulders. This would cut their time in half.

And possibly save many lives—if their Song could in fact reliably hide people from Dal.

"Enough," she said sharply, cutting off the protests. "Thank the Great Goddess, the saints, your lucky stars, or whoever, but we *are* going to ride these horses, and we *are* going to put an end to the Northerners."

CHAPTER 27

A feeling of dread and nausea gripped at Teresa's belly, coiling through every inch of her body and suggesting panic to come. A throbbing headache stationed right above her forehead added to her desire to sick up. It could only mean one thing:

She had to teach the pre-breakfast history class to the first years.

They cared nothing for the past or learning. Worse, as the children of wealthy families using the university as a stepping-stone to running their family business or marrying, they felt themselves vastly above a junior professor, especially such an ugly one and a woman to boot. She had learned fast to show them no weakness or they would tear into her like hungry wolves, working together to take down their prey.

She groaned, refusing to open her eyes. No matter how well she managed them, the dread returned to haunt her twice a week like clockwork. And experience had shown that the anxiety would turn to outright fear if she didn't get up and moving quickly. Lingering in bed only made it worse. Perhaps if she hurried, she could claim illness and get Lope to take her class.

A tentative opening of her eyes sent pain shooting through her head and down her spine as bright light stabbed into her eyes. Had she overslept? It should still be dark. She had to hurry. She was late.

Her mattress felt thin; something hard lay directly underneath it. This couldn't be her bed.

"Calm," someone said right in her ear. "You don't have class, cousin."

"Class?" She rubbed at her aching head. "Ramiro?"

"Yes. Each time you wake, you rant about getting to class."

Wait. Each time?

Her eyes reopened, squinting against light reflected off a mirror. She squinted more and discovered the reflection came not from a mirror but a breastplate leaning against the wall. A breastplate that shone like a sun, when every such piece of equipment she was familiar with had been a dull iron-gray color.

She shifted, and pain sliced through her arm. The limb was bound against her body in a sling. She also noted that the hardness beneath her thin mattress was bedrock. "Stone. Where am I?"

"Still in the tomb. It's been three days since the pillar fell on you." A damp cloth was set on her forehead, soothing.

Of course. Just a dream. A memory. She hadn't been a junior professor in a dozen years or been responsible for a class of first years in nearly as long. Not since she had first graduated.

Funny how such fears stayed with you. But she was here with Ramiro and Father Telo, trying to find a way to stop Dal. What had happened?

"My head. My arm. It hurts." A tear leaked from the corner of her eye.

"That's where the pillar hit you. Drink this. I got it from that herb shop Father Telo visited."

The bitter liquid in the cup thrust against her lips made her retch. She drank it all anyway. The agony began to lift slightly. A strong arm helped when she struggled upright. "Father Telo?"

"Not doing as well as you, I'm afraid. I can't tell you how glad I am that you're awake."

Sitting up, her eyes couldn't take in much around her, zeroing in on small details with tunnel vision from the pain. Teresa could see the fire had been allowed to die down to nearly embers, the coal merely glowing lumps. The room was dark except where the light reflected off pieces of armor lined against the wall. The metal shone like silver mirrors. Other sections of armor lay in a pile, covered in rust and the dark tarnish of age.

"What's . . ." The pounding of her head wouldn't let her finish. She pointed instead.

"The armor? It was inside the pillar. I tried cleaning it up for something to do and *that* was underneath. I've never seen anything like it." Awe rang in Ramiro's voice, but she couldn't bring herself to care. "When I sold my other armor, I never expected to find this."

Teresa leaned on his arm until slowly the pain faded from a raging river to a fast stream, and gave promise of dying to a dull ache. A glance at the pile of their possessions showed it to be much smaller. "Sold your armor? Why would you do that?"

"It took all my coin to pay for the healers and the medicine. There was nothing left to pay a messenger. Selling the armor, one of my knives, and a few other small things brought in enough for that and to buy food and more coal."

"But your armor . . ." How such a decision must have stung.

"Wasn't really mine anyway. That got left in the swamp. It was only borrowed. And I had all this time on my hands while you healed. I started working on the old relic armor from the pillar. I thought it was junk—too light. But it's strong. Stronger than anything I've seen. I can use it to buy the other armor back once this is all cleaned. The stone from the pillar didn't even dent it when it fell."

Teresa groaned at the reminder. "Unlike me. Odd how the universe sometimes has a way of evening things out. One armor for another." She touched her head gingerly. "Three days, you say."

"Aye. The healer bound up your wounds, and I fetched the medicine and more water. Got the message sent to my parents at Suseph. Then there was nothing to do but wait and try to clean that armor. It must have been inside the pillar for centuries."

"You've been busy. Three days," she repeated like a parrot. "I've been out for three days."

"The healer had me wake all of you every few hours because of the head wounds, but you've been out except for that."

"Father Telo?" she asked, surprised at the plaintive whine in her voice.

"Here." The arm around her back disappeared. His hands directed hers to a blanket-wrapped bundle. She touched the priest's shoulder and up his neck to find his cheek. Heat engulfed her hand. Beads of sweat coated Father Telo's dark skin, shining like dewdrops in the faint light.

"Fever."

"Aye," Ramiro confirmed. "I get the medicine into him, but it hasn't done much good. Just kept him from getting hotter. The healer said it will break tonight or not at all. But yours did, so that's a good sign."

Father Telo had been her companion for so many days. They had gone through so much together. She hated to see him suffer like this, seeing how he'd suffered so much already. He was strong, but his body had been through the wringer. A cold streak of fear pierced through her own pain. What if he didn't make it?

Teresa willed healing into her touch. Julian had gotten a miracle. Why not Father Telo? *Santiago. God, please. Heal him.* Her heart begged the words silently, but the priest's skin remained hot to the touch. No miracle followed her plea.

Sadly, she tugged his blanket up higher.

"You brought a healer here?" she asked and then felt stupid. Ramiro had already told her that. Her mind felt slow and clumsy. The rest of her helpless, nothing but a burden on Ramiro. Unable to help at all. She felt at her face, but detected no heat from fever. Nor could she recall such an illness.

"Had to. To start with, your arm is broken. The Northerner's legs. Father Telo had a dislocated shoulder."

"Santabe?" she asked.

"Alive," came a new voice. A harsh voice. "No thanks to you."

"*You* dropped the pillar on us," Ramiro said. "This

is your own fault. By rights, you should be the one lying there with a fever."

"I demand to be released! At least move me to the other side of the room."

"Get up and go there. Nobody is stopping you."

Teresa pulled herself all the way upright and took a clear look around the chamber. The same sarcophagi lined the perimeter. The fire still burned at the center of the space. The remainder of their belongings had been piled neatly at hand, some glass bottles lined up in a row—the medicines. Polishing cloths and various wire brushes that Ramiro must have been using were spread around. The red and white Diviners lay side by side near where Ramiro must have been working. Farther away, a mound of rock lay heaped in a random sprawl on the far side of the embers. Carving covered parts of its surface. The ceiling above it sagged noticeably.

The fallen pillar. Dimly Teresa could remember darting forward to try to drag Father Telo out of the way. She must have failed.

Santabe sat among the fallen stone, while she and Telo had been pulled away and taken to the opposite side of the room.

She frowned as understanding came. Without the pillar, that part of the tomb had no support. The ceiling over there could come tumbling down at any moment, and Ramiro had left Santabe in the fault zone.

"Move her."

"What?" Ramiro said.

"Are you unhurt, cousin?" Teresa asked.

"Stiff," he said. "A bruise on my chest where she kicked me, but I'm unhurt."

"Then move her out of danger. It's what the priest would want."

"The healer told me not to if she ever wanted to walk again. As I told many times." Ramiro raised his voice at the last part, and Santabe glared and looked away. "Actually the healer said her legs need to be amputated. He didn't think they'll heal, but said not moving could help."

"But the ceiling."

"Is not likely to change. Look close." Ramiro pointed to one of the intact pillars in the room. "They barely touch the ceiling. That's how it fell so easily. If it was securely attached and load bearing, it wouldn't have fallen with just her weight behind it. They wouldn't be hollow. They're just decorative. The ceiling must have been sagging before Santabe kicked it over. It could have been sagging for centuries. This place is old. So old I can't even read the writing on the pillar. It's more like pictures than letters."

He got up and went to their bags, picking up the red Diviner. "I think this is what she's actually worried about. I've been thinking about it. About how much protection they offer to keep off Dal. How far that stretches. She seems entirely too concerned with being close to us all of a sudden. Almost like she thinks we're going to need its protection soon."

Teresa turned from the intact pillar—which did have a small gap between top and ceiling, just wide enough to allow light through—to examine Santabe. The tall Northerner looked decidedly uncomfortable. She would have seen it herself if her head didn't hurt quite so much. "Smartly figured, cousin. I noticed the hieroglyphics also. I think these tombs may have been here long before Aveston came into existence.

"The pillars could be part of the tombs instead of built into the room. A repository for some treasure of the dead, like the armor. Concealed so no one would steal them."

"And if I could figure it out, so could she," Ramiro said. Santabe bared her teeth at them in a snarl. "Which means she wants the pleasure of our company, not because of the ceiling tumbling down, but because of this." He hefted the Diviner. "I'm guessing you need to be pretty close to it for it to keep Dal off. What do you think?"

"I think you're right, cousin." Teresa fingered her sling. Through the cloth, she could feel her arm and something long and straight on either side. Splints. Shaped shafts of wood bound on her arm to keep the bones aligned.

Something nagged at her and it wasn't a problem with the splint. She tried to brush the pain aside and clear her head. Something . . . something about what Ramiro had told her . . . not today but at another time. Something there that she couldn't grasp, unlike the wood of her splint. "The Northern priests wear the Diviners strapped at their waist," she said, thinking aloud. "The red and the white. They keep them close. What if they don't work much beyond the sphere of a person or maybe a small room?" She looked around at the chamber of tombs, big enough to hold a country dance inside. "That means it wouldn't protected the whole of this vault. The Northerners wouldn't leave any lying around if they need to keep them that close . . ."

"We already talked about that," Ramiro reminder her. "Remember? We decided there was no point in going looking in Her Beauty for more red Diviners. Not unless we wanted to take out their priests, too."

She waved him off. "I remember that. Just . . . There's something else. Something you said. I can almost—" She gasped. "If the red Diviners can keep Dal from killing—keep him away—but they don't have much span, much distance. Then the Northerners would want as many as they could get."

"Yeah. Obviously. I saw how they tried to make more of them outside of Aveston—where my military brothers died . . ."

The last piece clicked home. She scrambled to her feet, ignoring a moment of wooziness, and took the

Diviner from Ramiro. It felt cool to the touch but inert, lifeless. Just a thing. She expected it to be humming with life because of the magic inside. "You said the priests take the white ones and turn them red. That they had hundreds of the white ones. That they tried to turn them to red and failed. They use the blood of the people Dal murders."

"Yes . . ."

"Don't you see? They aren't protecting the citizens of Aveston. Couldn't if they wanted to. There aren't enough of these Diviners. What if it goes beyond not protecting the civilians? What if they intend to sacrifice Aveston to make *more* Diviners? To get more of their white weapons to turn red?"

"Nobody is that evil." Ramiro looked at Santabe. "Or maybe they are."

Teresa bent although it ratcheted up the pain in her head and dropped the Diviner as if it had grown white hot, scrubbing her hand on her trousers. She didn't want to finish her thoughts, but the words came tumbling out anyway. "By the saints. That would explain why they let some people leave and don't try to stop them. As long as enough people stay in Aveston to provide plenty of blood, why would they care who goes? The Northerners will cause another massacre to make more Diviners. They'll kill our people so *theirs* can live."

Her knees felt wobbly, and she went back to collapse beside Father Telo, taking in the reassuring bulk of his body against hers. "All they need is blood to start it, right, cousin? They intend to kill the civilians and let their blood bring Dal, just to make more Diviners. We have to stop them."

CHAPTER 28

Julian let the parchment slide through his fingers, catching the paper by the top folded edge and flipping it to repeat the process. His fingers, and perhaps his heart, couldn't seem to let the letter from Ramiro go—even during the most important meeting he'd ever attended. By rights he shouldn't be inside the tent with a seat at the table, but Beatriz had insisted on his presence as one of her three advisors, along with Captain Gonzalo and the Bishop of Colina Hermosa, so he got to hear what unfolded.

Though he was not sure what Beatriz hoped to accomplish with this meeting, he did admire her insistence on trying. This get-together would spread the warning—whether anyone heeded it or not.

But *alcaldes* tended to come to such meetings, with blinders already in place, to see only what they wanted.

Already, as usual with a summit of *ciudades-estado*, no one could agree on anything, with the possible exception of the existence of the Northerners—though Julian gave them the benefit of the doubt on that. If put to the test, he'd bet *Alcalde* Juan of Crueses would flatly deny the army under oath, even if it were at his gates. Reaching any kind of agreement would be nigh on impossible in the best of conditions . . . and the conditions were hardly optimal.

Everyone had seen the overcrowding in Suseph, made even worse by the influx of evacuees from Aveston. All the refugees had gladly helped till and plant new fields for extra food, but with no rains, it looked likely that all the crops would fail. Each family had accepted three to six more mouths under their roof and that created stress as well.

Such realities would influence this meeting, making the politicians particularly cagey. Over-crowding was a subject all attending wanted to avoid, as no one wanted to be asked to take in more people in these times. Yet they knew denying their help outright would make them look reprehensible.

No, the overcrowding would not come up for discussion, and that was just one subject they wanted to avoid—one of many. They had already branched out to a safer topic, and they would try to steer the rest of this conversation to items that didn't truly matter to make sure they didn't come out on the losing end of this convocation.

"Leviathan is dead," the Bishop of Crueses said stoutly in reply to Beatriz's recap of the letter from Aveston. "Our Lord destroyed the Darkness at the time of creation."

"Then what of dragons, griffins, and other such monsters?" the newly created bishop of Aveston demanded. Both the *alcalde* and bishop of that city had been executed by the Northerners, forcing a hasty election among the evacuees from Aveston to decide new leaders.

"Creatures of the flesh," Crueses insisted, "but mortal. Not part of the Darkness. The Darkness was banished."

The new bishop of Aveston was a large man with a large voice and quickly drowned out his counterpart from Crueses, proving even men of God had their flash points. "Poppycock. Scripture is clear. The Leviathan was sliced into scions to torment humanity. The Lord sent the saints to rid us of them." More than half the clerics in attendance shouted their support, while the other half shook their heads before shouting back. The tent threatened to erupt into chaos. Clean-shaven men of peace stood from their seats, some with fists raised.

"They are extinct. Destroyed by the saints," one shouted.

"Dreamers are naught but rumors. Heresy."

"Santa Margarita, who was swallowed by the dragon, was a dreamer—"

"—no proof."

"—faith—"

"The scripture of Menendo—"

"—inaccurate translation."

Julian halted the slide of the letter through his fingers, catching it by the middle and looking at Beatriz with concern. Less than ten minutes for a meeting to lose control. He knew clerics could get heated over details, but he had rarely witnessed such a vehement scene. Each of the eight *alcaldes* who had come in person took the side of their spiritual advisor as would the other five designee representatives of *alcaldes*, though they wouldn't be as vocal about their support. The *ciudades-estado* had always fought each other starting from the time when they had been wandering tribes, but he'd hoped they'd learned a little more civility over the ages.

He wasn't sure where that optimism came from.

The entire convocation could devolve if Beatriz didn't get control quickly. She had to see through their steering of the topics to useless areas. Yet he could not say as much outright where all could hear.

He cleared his throat with force.

As if she sensed his cue, Beatriz pounded on the table with the gavel. As the convener of the convocation, she officially led the proceedings. Elderly bishops with white hair and arthritic knees sank back to their seats, looking chagrined, like schoolboys caught pulling a girl's plait.

"Let us establish one thing at a time, gentlemen," Beatriz said. "Shall we get this out of the way? Is there a consensus on the existence or nonexistence of a Leviathan? Was it real or an invention?" Ten voices rose, all with different responses, and Beatriz used the gavel again. "The basics first, please. A show of hands, bishops. Is Leviathan a fact or a fiction? Those for its reality?" All hands rose.

"Well and good. Now, those for Leviathan"—her brow rose to quell another protest—"or a scion of Leviathan to exist today and be murdering our people?" She paused to count. "Those who have a different explanation for the Northern god?"

"I object," *Alcalde* Juan said angrily. "Misleading phrasing." The leader of Crueses would block Beatriz at every turn, still angry at her taking the election of Suseph from his kinsman, Ramón. No doubt he was thrilled they'd been sidetracked into this talk.

Beatriz sniffed, but relented. "Those who believe Leviathan or a scion of Leviathan could be murdering our people? Those who believe something else is murdering our people?"

The vote came out seven to three in favor.

"I don't see how this helps," the new *alcalde* of Aveston said. His former occupation had been as owner of a popular tavern at the heart of the city. "It's just a substitution of names. I saw what it did to two armies. What we call it doesn't matter. The effects are the same—death for all of us."

Julian's brows rose. The man with the least political experience had cut to the heart of the matter. He looked at Beatriz hopefully, but she didn't seem to sense the trap she'd fallen into.

"Perhaps," Beatriz allowed. "But we have experts on Leviathan who may be able to enlighten us. We have none on a Northern god."

Murmurs broke out again. The bishop of Colina Hermosa opened his eyes and rose. Julian had found the old man often slept through meetings and had to be prodded awake at the end, but as the eldest cleric in attendance, the others gave him the respect of turning in his direction and falling silent. "Leviathan, if it lives, cannot be harmed by a mortal. Possibly by a saint, though unlikely. I have seen no evidence the time of saints has returned. In summation, a large scion of Leviathan cannot be defeated by us." He sat. Silence followed his proclamation until the other clerics beat their hands together in rare agreement.

Julian looked at the letter still suspended between his fingers. Ramiro had written the same thoughts. Their spies in Aveston didn't believe Dal, or Leviathan, could be killed either, though Beatriz had not mentioned that fact. In a way, this declaration could be a good thing—maybe with that established they could move on to something more productive.

As for saints returning, Julian had told no one of the miraculous events he'd witnessed, and didn't believe Beatriz had either. Healings. An ordinary kitchen tray killing flies by the hundreds. Dreams providing truths. Myth come to life.

Julian had never been a man who believed in what he couldn't see. He preferred facts over fancy. He hadn't believed in the spiritual over the human until his healing.

But miracles aside, to his mind, the convocation of *alcaldes* should have been dominated by politics and military discussion. Instead they heard from historians and priests as the closest things to experts available so that they could talk about monsters out of legend.

He preferred they discuss something more tangible from the letter, such as Ramiro's interrogation of the Northerner, Santabe. Weapons you could hold, like these red Diviners. To get this meeting back on track, it was there they needed to go. It seemed he was not the only one who felt that way.

"This is a waste of time," Guter, of one of the minor *ciudades-estado*, said. His fiefdom had been growing for the last years, putting him on the edge of becoming a major power. With the destruction of Zapata and Colina Hermosa, his influence would grow even more, and so others listened. "I came here to discuss the army occupying Aveston. Not some mystical monster. Villages massacred. Armies destroyed. Where is the proof of this Northern god—or the deaths caused by it?"

"Yes," another agreed. "If we are not to talk about

the army, then I shall go home. I have better things to do." A stirring sped through the tent as agreement began to build among the *alcaldes* of the smaller holdings. With Vista Sur absent and the burned Zapata's spot empty, the minor *alcaldes* outnumbered them and might be able to take over the momentum of this meeting and force the topic on reluctant members like Juan.

"The Northern army," another smallholder *alcalde* said. "Let's talk about that."

Beatriz employed the gavel once. "Gentlemen, we are here to share information and to try to coordinate our efforts. Already we have reports of five villages destroyed. Look at the empty seats here. Many locations have sent no representative. No word that they wouldn't be attending. That is not normal. I fear they may have been attacked as well. I'm sharing—"

"We got your *warning*," Juan sneered, taking control once again. "Keep our people inside during daylight. Avoid bloodshed. Hide or wash away any blood. You want me to tell my people that and put everyone into a panic. What nonsense. Am I right?"

Again came the murmurs, but this time with nodding heads.

"The honorable *alcalde* of Aveston can bear witness to the truth of the massacres," Beatriz said. "He witnessed." Heads turned in his direction.

Unfortunately, the new *alcalde* had little practice with politics or public speaking. He had shared the tale of the death of the military of Colina Hermosa, Suseph, and Aveston far and wide at the get-acquainted luncheon before the meeting started, but in such a fanciful way as to rather harm his case than reinforce it. As a tavern keeper, he was used to embellishment to create customers. His story even made Julian doubt the facts, and he'd almost died on that field.

"Yes, we've heard it," Juan said in a greasy way that sent a flare of anger through Julian. Several people snickered. "I repeat, why are we talking about this nonsense? Why are we talking at all? The Northerners seem to be content with Aveston. They seem settled there. There was no reason for this convocation. This is nothing but feminine hysteria from our newest *alcalde*."

Julian sprang to his feet to shout a defense of his wife, only to snap his mouth shut. That would only hurt Beatriz's standing. On this day, even his advice must be kept to himself. With a start, he realized he'd crushed Ramiro's letter between his fingers.

Beatriz showed none of his anger, except in maybe the set of her jaw. "Second-newest *alcalde*, if you please. Not the newest. Nor the most feminine." Her eyes lingered on the curls in Juan's hair. Rumor said his manservant spent hours each morning creating them. "I wager I have more calluses than some." Ramón, the former *alcalde* of Suseph and one of Juan's three counselors, hid his plump, pale hands of which he was usually so proud under the table.

"I have more witnesses," Beatriz continued with a nod toward the soldier stationed at the tent flap as Julian retook his seat.

A man in a simple poncho, bag-like trousers, and sandals, holding a hat tightly with both hands, was ushered inside. The leaders in the tent remained grave as the villager shared his tale of watching his neighbors being slaughtered by an invisible force as he and others cowered inside. Villager after villager shared the same story. Finally, Beatriz signaled for the chief cook from the citadel of Colina Hermosa to stand before them.

"Lupaa was caught in what we believe was one of the first attacks just hours after the fall of Colina Hermosa. Tell them how you survived, Lupaa." The plump woman, wearing her brightest clothing in honor of the grand occasion, studied the toes of her shoes.

"It was as the others said. A bad smell. A sense of evil pressing down." She touched heart, mind, liver, and spleen. "So much hate. Cuts. Wounds that just appeared. Like our skin being sliced with a butcher knife. The screaming went on for hours."

"But did you see anything?" *Alcalde* Juan pressed. "Did you see what was attacking you as proof this happened?"

"I object at the insinuation," Captain Gonzalo said. "Military men saw the torn-apart bodies. This is no fabrication."

"But did she see anything?" one of the lesser *alcaldes* prodded.

Lupaa looked troubled and slightly sick, as well she might. The memories had caused a queasy roll to Julian's stomach, too. "No. I saw nothing. There was nothing *to* see, other than the wounds. I gathered my grandchildren close and told them to close their eyes. Then we prayed. We prayed so hard to Santiago, and he saved us. A peace. A love came over us. It protected us."

"The Darkness," the bishop of Crueses said, sounding startled. "That description fits with the Darkness. A hatred of anything living. A force that can only be opposed by its opposite. Perhaps it *is* Leviathan."

More argument broke out at the bishop of Crueses' apparent change of opinion. Julian's heart sank at retreating to this topic again.

Juan laughed. "So we are to love this thing to death. Pray for our survival? As if it exists at all and isn't some distraction to keep us occupied. Is that supposed to be our grand consensus from this meeting?" He stood, followed quickly by Ramón. "This convocation is over."

"Go if you want," Guter said with a dismissive—and insulting—wave of his hand. "We are here to talk about working together. I would that we join forces to take on this army of Northern barbarians at Aveston. Fight them. Keep them from taking any more of our cities. Steal from them these red-colored weapons that might protect us, in case these massacres *are* real. We kill two birds with one stone by destroying their army."

"That is suicide," the *alcalde* of Aveston said in his loud voice. "Much as I want my city back, you've heard their numbers. I'm no military man, but even a tavern keeper can understand numbers." Like any good soldier, Ramiro had included estimates of the size of the Northern army in his letter. Tallies that matched closely with what scouts and spies of the other cities had reported. All had heard the particulars. "I've witnessed how their white weapons kill with a touch. I saw *Alcalde* Martin die. You did not. The Northerners have thousands of these weapons. We cannot expect to steal their magic for ourselves."

"He is right," Captain Gonzalo said in his deep bass. "It cannot be done anymore. We have lost the help of the witches. We cannot match the Northern numbers or their magic weapons. Not with Colina Hermosa, Aveston, and Zapata gone. Besides the fact that any battle would draw the attention of the creature we are trying to avoid. The other captains concur."

Everyone present remained silent, and it didn't take a genius to know their thoughts all dwelt on the same conclusion. If they had worked together sooner, they might have been a match for the Northern army. Back before Claire had Sung and saved them at the cost of waking a monster. But it couldn't be done now. And of course, no one had been prepared to work together when they had the chance.

"A suicide mission," Beatriz said into the silence. Her voice was low, full of sadness, which touched a chord with everyone present. "That *is* what I propose. Not to send our remaining armies. But something else. I believe there is a way to take down the Northern army—but not with arms."

"Then how?" Juan sneered.

"With our blood. With our deaths."

Silence descended around the table.

"We ask for volunteers," Beatriz continued. "Those willing to give their lives. Those who have less to live for. The old. The sick. The orphaned. We'll need thousands upon thousands of volunteers. Enough to go to Aveston dressed as a formidable army and lure the Northern forces from the city. There to shed our blood and draw this Dal or Leviathan to cause a massacre."

She stood. A single figure dressed all in black, from the lace mantilla above her head to the slippers on her feet. "We draw them away from the people of Aveston and hope for a similar butchery. We do this so the children, the families may live. At the least we eliminate the Northern army. At the most maybe we give this creature enough blood to satisfy it and send it away. Perhaps its span of time here is judged by the flow of blood."

"That is insane," Juan said. "I want no part of this."

"It is sacrilege. Life is sacred, given to us by God Himself," the bishop of Cruses said. "Suicide is an evil and a sin. No one will volunteer for this madness."

Beatriz didn't give ground. "Is it sin if it's to save others? Isn't that the ultimate act of love? To sacrifice ourselves? Do none of you remember Santa Ildaria and the bandits? She stood before evil with hundreds of her voluntary followers, and they sacrificed themselves for their village. Hundreds saved thousands. The people believed. They came. I believe thousands can save a million."

"They came for San Jorge also," the bishop of Aveston offered. "His followers struck the dragon with rocks and distracted it enough that San Jorge could slay the beast, even though some of them died. Our people have never been afraid to give their lives to save others."

"Let me be the first to volunteer, even if I must go alone," Beatriz said. "We cannot kill Leviathan, and we can't beat the Northern army—we are all agreed on that. Perhaps, though, we can placate it and satiate it and so save those we love. What say you?"

In answer, Julian found himself clapping his right hand on his heart in the salute to the brave, though the *alcaldes* around him shouted in alarm and revulsion at the suggestion.

Once again the frail bishop of Colina Hermosa fought to his feet. "When the saints came to lead us from the desert and our nomadic ways, they had a purpose higher than establishing cities and civilizing our people or increasing our numbers. The Lord made sure they foresaw a time when all of us would need to work together. Something we couldn't do as small tribes of nomads. I believe that time is now. I am old and near my end. I volunteer to make this act of love."

"And I," Julian said.

"I would do this to save my city," the *alcalde* of Aveston added. All around, clerics and military men added their voices, some offering to make the sacrifice and others speaking against it.

"All in favor of putting this before our people and taking the resulting volunteers to Aveston?" Beatriz asked, cutting in.

"I'll not be a part of this," Guter said. "Do as you will and throw away your own lives if you want. You won't take my people with you." He strode from the tent. Only two of his counselors went with him.

"Insanity," Juan said again. He left, taking Ramón and most of the other *alcaldes* with him.

Julian wiped at a tear on his cheek. Life even in these days was sweet—no one wanted to leave it. But he would do so without regret if it meant Ramiro and the children, whether of Colina Hermosa or another *ciudad-estado*, could live.

Perhaps Beatriz replacing him as *alcalde* had been fated. She had handled this juxtaposition of myth over reality better than he could. She saw the need for taking this risk more clearly than he. At his advice, lives had been lost for little gain.

"*Mi amor,*" he said, going to Beatriz and placing his hand on her cheek. They had always guessed that the burden of this sacrifice would fall upon the people they ruled.

Beatriz cupped his hand in hers, squeezing. "Then this meeting is adjourned. We take two days to gather those willing and enough uniforms to clothe them, then we depart for Aveston."

Let it be done.

Let lives be lost this time for the ultimate advantage.

CHAPTER 29

Two days had never passed so fast. Julian stared out over the gathered crowd of volunteers as the sun crested the hills around Suseph, taking a moment to find beauty in the ordinary. The sun turned the hills red and orange and cast a golden glow over the wilted sprouts of wheat in the field. Despite the buzz of conversation from dozens of wagon trains that had arrived in the last day and the weight of Beatriz standing against his arm, Julian stored the sight in his landscape of self as a precious treasure. He had collected many such prizes over the last two days, enjoying all around him to the fullest until the emptiness of his inner landscape was filled with beautiful memories.

When he closed his eyes, instead of trembling with doubt, he immersed himself in his treasures.

How had he ever taken such things for granted?

His two days had been heavily involved in all the organization: procuring uniforms and supplies, giving suggestions, sorting out how much foodstuff was enough without slowing them down, arranging yet more wagons. Yet he'd found time to lie late in bed with Beatriz and savor the combined feeling of safety and comfort, while having no demands upon him. He'd walked gardens and smelled the scents of rose and thyme. He had marveled at the wheaty taste of hops on his tongue from his favorite brew of beer and slowly chewed a perfectly cooked tenderloin. He'd sought out old friends to tell them he loved them. All this he'd done and more, filling every span of the period available to him with wonder. The only wish of his heart denied to him was to speak to his sons one last time. He pulled Beatriz tighter against him.

One could not have everything.

"You need not go," Captain Gonzalo said to both of them. "You are needed here. Your skills and expertise are invaluable. You've taught me so much. We must have your leadership."

Beatriz reached out to take the captain's hand. "What kind of leader would stay? No, you're the one needed here. For your family and your country. We are just the sort to go. Our lives have been lived."

Julian nodded. Though their days together had been short, Gonzalo had grown close to them both. He'd been orphaned at a young age and Julian suspected he found a substitute parent in Beatriz's keen concern for him, and hoped his own advice to the younger man on being less strict in his outlook had helped as well. Gonzalo reminded Julian so much of Salvador. If he could remember to loosen his grip on the rules when needed, he would go far. "We go to be with our son, Salvador, knowing Ramiro can stand on his own. As can you. You are a man to be proud of."

"But—"

"You will do fine," Beatriz said. "You'll only be in charge until the elections are finalized. Just don't let that winner be Ramón." She smiled to let him know she jested—somewhat. "Tell your children to take good care of Pietro for me. Pietro will help them adjust to losing their home. There is nothing like a pet for giving comfort. I feel better knowing you'll be here with the *concejales* to give advice to whoever comes after me, but this is where we belong." All around them people in too-large uniforms greeted each other with the hugs of long-lost-though-never-met kin. Actual kin said tearful good-byes, but pride shone from all the volunteers. Pride and a sense of purpose.

Julian prayed that purpose would be fulfilled. They couldn't force the Northerner army to come out to meet them, though they would do their best to make it so. He and Beatriz had already decided that if the Northern army refused to leave the safety of Aveston, their army of elderly and misfits would go find them. One way or another, the threat of the Northern army would be removed.

"You have our letters for Ramiro?" Julian asked. They might not get to see their son again, and pencil and paper gave them a poor substitute, but it would have to suffice.

Gonzalo touched his jacket over his heart. "I do. And I will keep in mind the letter he sent to me. Be easy for your son. A trial there must be, but I will be fair and compassionate."

Julian forced a smile. Gonzalo had not offered to let him read that message that had come with the other letter giving the details on Leviathan, but Julian had no doubts it contained an explanation of Ramiro's reason for desertion. Julian created a vision of the future to treasure in his inner landscape of Ramiro and Gonzalo returning the military to its full complement and former glory. It warmed his heart.

"Light a candle for our success," Julian said, "and our memory. We go with joy to accomplish one last victory—for Colina Hermosa. I shall see my city rise again in my mind's eye, even if I'll never see the actual rebuilding."

"For both of you." Gonzalo held out recently minted medallions of Santa Ildaria. Many others in the crowd carried them already. Julian tucked his away with a smile of thanks, turned, and moving among the crowd, left Beatriz to say her good-byes to the captain alone.

People had come from every hamlet, village, and *ciudad-estado*, easy to pick out by the color of uniform they'd brought to wear. There the orange and white of Suseph. The gray and green of Colina Hermosa mingled with reds, browns, blues and blacks, among dozens of other colors and shades. Trains of wagons filled all the available space in front of Suseph, containing thousands. Like in the time of Santa Ildaria, the people had come. Enough to match in numbers the army they had lost. One had even come from Crueses, proving Juan could not stop the truth from surfacing. All had come to save their kin and offer their lives for others.

Julian halted to clasp hands with *Concejal* Diego. The elderly landowner and counselor sat in a carriage with the dozing bishop of Colina Hermosa and several other timeworn clerics as they waited to get started. By his side sat an even older woman, her back humped and teeth long gone. Julian recognized the mother of *Concejal* Lugo, his former political rival killed by Ordoño just after the burning of Colina Hermosa. Lugo had been her only child and he'd never had a family. She was alone in the world. Julian had known her and Diego for as long as he could remember.

For an instant, Julian's resolve wavered. The faces in the carriage took him back to a time in his youth when he'd just entered politics. They had already served the community for many years.

They and others had given him the advice of their experience and made him the man he was today.

"We must chat of old times during our journey, Julian," Diego said. An icon of Santiago holding book and staff sat upon the old man's knees, kept in sight as if to lift spirits and stiffen spines.

"That we will, old friend." And just like that, his world firmed at the prospect of another treasure to add to his inner landscape. Julian continued on with a nod to another *concejal* on horseback beside the carriage. Sarracino the weaver had always carried a torch for Beatriz and had never married or had a family of his own. Now he had decided to end his life with her. Well, Julian would not begrudge him the chance to speak to Beatriz. All who trod this path were heroes and they all had their own reasons for being here.

Even as Julian stepped away, the light dimmed. The sun becoming less. The smell of rot carried through the air and a force of evil pressed down. People cried out. Julian kept his feet under him by sheer determination. The force of Dal pressed upon the crowd but lightly; the real power must have been miles distant. Julian threw a look toward Crueses— could it be there?—and said a quick prayer for the ones under the full attack of the Northern terror. Somewhere in a village or a town people died, while here no one moved or spoke, as if in compassion with their suffering. Julian tried to keep track of the time by counting, but the terror went on too long. He soon lost track as his mind wandered into fear that Dal could be at Aveston with Ramiro.

Yet the new attack changed nothing—they would carry on as planned and do their best to put an end to this.

When the light returned, people looked a little paler—their voices a little more hushed. Their embraces held a little tighter and longer to make up for it. No one spoke of what had just happened.

There's your proof, Juan.

Julian shook himself and resumed his course. He accepted hugs and handshakes from familiar faces and strangers all the way to the front of the crowd. The wagon train of Aveston had begun to move, chosen to lead the way in honor of their sacrifice to save their own citizens. Two units of scouts would flank their progress and ride in advance to deal with any Northern spies they found. The scouts would turn around and leave them when they reached Aveston, taking the wagons and horses back to Suseph, and letting the sad army take the last steps on their own. Beatriz would have no one unwilling with them, not even beasts. Only minds that had chosen this of their own will would go forward to die.

But for now, there could still be joy.

A wagon from a grain mill waited with a place for him and Beatriz. Inside sat servants from the citadel where Julian had lived so long. Lupaa set a basket on the floor to make room for him on the hastily added bench seat. "*Alcalde*. I go to save my grandsons." The smile on her lips did not quite touch her eyes.

Julian squeezed her hand as he had hundreds of others. Some had been warm and confident—others cold as stones—like Lupaa's. She, unlike all the others, had been in one of Dal's massacres. She, more than others, knew the horror that awaited. "Bless you. You are welcome."

A slender girl in black sat beside the bulky Lupaa.

"Fronilde!" Julian said in shock at seeing his son's intended bride. The wedding had been planned and a date set, and then Salvador had died at the hands of an angry witch. "You don't belong here."

She held a black handkerchief to her face, though no tears flowed. Lupaa held tight to the girl's other hand. "Since Salvador's death my heart won't heal. I may breathe, but I'm not alive since he is gone."

"You are young. Your heart will heal and you will love again. Salvador would not want this. Go back."

"You are wrong," she said and there was steel in her voice. "Time will never heal this hurt. Maybe if there had been a child, but there is not. I cannot care. Not for my parents. Not for anyone. Life is but a shadow to me. Tell me you would want to live without Beatriz."

Now and forever.

He could not speak such a lie. He might live without Beatriz, but would he truly be alive? And hadn't Salvador's death left him in similar pain? Only duty to his people and Beatriz had kept him going. Wasn't going to his death a type of relief from his own heartbreak at Salvador's death?

"Welcome, daughter." Julian held his arms wide to take her in. She settled against his aching heart, and suddenly, Beatriz was there to join them in the embrace. Lupaa added her warmth and the other old friends and servants grasped on also.

Tears flowed but they were tears of healing and acceptance. They had all made their choice.

Then the wagon lurched and they were under way. Bound to a one-way trip to save lives. The cost paid freely. The saints be with them.

CHAPTER 30

Teresa had not battled such indecision since her parents died. It had been just a few months from the completion of her first degree. Her parents had passed within a short time of one another, leaving her penniless, until a family friend had offered her room in his household. She'd known very well his kindhearted goal was to shelter her with his daughters and marry her off to some man she might learn to like but could never love. He'd had enough influence in their small sphere to even manage an arrangement for a dumpy, awkward girl like her. No one knew at that time that her inclinations ran a different direction. They all just thought her odd in her ways. Standoffish and bookish.

She'd been violently ill each morning for months as she struggled to decide: security and comfort over being true to herself. Not only would she be expected to marry a gender that didn't interest her, but to take the offer was to turn her back on her other love: university and a life of study. Everything she'd argued with her parents to achieve. The family friend did not believe in educating women, even his daughters. She'd have to accept a sham of a life to guarantee herself a home or face an indifferent world alone, with complete uncertainty of earning her own bread and shelter. There was no guarantee a woman could get any kind of employment, with or without a degree.

Instead of resolving her hesitancy on her own, her time had eventually run out, forcing her to make a choice. For the second time in her life, she had taken the harder path, and both times she'd chosen the life of an academic. The kind family friend had shocked her with a tiny allowance and gradually she'd stood on her own two feet, finding teaching assistance jobs and continuing her studies. Indecision had rarely plagued her for long since.

Until now.

Now she couldn't make up her mind again. It was one thing to choose between marriage and a career. But now, with lives other than her own, those first two times seemed a flip of a coin in comparison. Resolving to save the people of Aveston had been the easy part. Deciding a way to do so and actually carrying it out frightened her to death. She and Ramiro had put such worries aside for the first few days to tend Father Telo, hoping to see him recovering before they acted. It had seemed promising as Telo's fever had broken the first night. Soon, they would have the advice of the burly priest again. But the heat in his veins returned the next morning. The fever continued to vacillate in an on-again, off-again fashion, and his improvement had stalled.

Teresa found herself spending her days and much of her nights sitting at her friend's side, holding his hand or bathing his forehead; but Telo did not wake, though he might open his eyes for long enough to take some nourishment or mumble a few incoherent words. While her body mended and the pains in her head dissipated, her friend got no better. Often he called for Father Ansuro and lamented over the old priest's death in a way that crushed her heart.

She'd prayed for another miracle, and been secretly relieved and ashamed of her feelings when it didn't happen. They'd been close enough to miracles already. Death always followed.

Sadly, they had to accept that God had other plans.

Father Telo moaned a little, and she moistened his lips. "Sit up, my friend. Drink." Whiskers had invaded his face, normally kept so meticulously clean shaven. Bristles more gray or silver than black. As if age had found him in a short time. Somehow Father Telo's growing a beard troubled her more than the loss of his triple-rope belt, cut away by the healer, or his much worn and mended sandals standing empty with their belongings.

Ramiro set down the piece of armor he'd been polishing and was at her side in an instant, helping her support Telo. Between them, they got some watery broth into Telo before laying him back down.

His eyes fluttered open. "Where am I?"

"Aveston. The tombs, Father. Remember? We have to decide on a way to save the people of Aveston from being massacred."

"Awh." Telo blinked owlishly at her and she wasn't sure if he understood, then he said, "Take . . . their incentive." His eyes closed and he fell back into a semblance of sleep. The healer said head wounds could be tricky, taking days or even months to heal. She'd hoped days would be enough. Vain wishes. Like in her past, their time ran out and her indecision showed no sign of lifting.

"Their incentive?" Teresa said. "The Northern incentive. The white Diviners." Father Telo had gotten right to the heart of the matter. Destroy the incentive for the Northerners to start a massacre.

She traded looks with Ramiro. They both knew getting back into Her Beauty and the cathedral's stash of Diviners should be their destination. "We can't leave him alone like this. What if we don't make it back?"

"You heard him," Ramiro said. "He told us his choice."

"He's too sick to make a choice."

Getting caught or dying while trying to stop the

Northerners would leave Father Telo stranded here alone with only Santabe as a companion. The woman would never help Father Telo, even if her badly broken legs allowed it. After her sudden confession about the Diviners to Telo, Santabe refused to do more than shout mocking insults at them. Somehow, the man had read the Northerner's soul like a book, getting her to reveal information they needed, but that advantage was gone like the man himself.

The loss of Telo had also left Ramiro and herself floundering. His voice and positive attitude had been the prop they didn't know was supporting them until it was gone. They couldn't seem to make a decision without him.

"If only . . ." she said. They both swung around to look at the pieces of the tray propped against the stone wall of the catacomb. Ramiro had wheedled some wood glue from a carpenter in the city, but the simple kitchen tray had been too splintered from their fight in Her Beauty to hold a repair. Teresa lied to herself that its power wasn't a miracle. After all, it wasn't a relic, just an ordinary kitchen tray. Nothing to do with the divine. Yet, she couldn't deny it had saved their lives twice, and its loss left them with no protection against the Diviners if they left the catacombs.

It didn't take a degree in human nature to understand its destruction influenced their indecision, increasing their lack of motivation.

She could almost feel time running out for Aveston while they remained safely tucked underground with a red Diviner to keep Dal away. They guessed nothing had happened yet because the Northerners would be putting their own protections in place to make sure they didn't die in the massacre they would soon create, but those plans could only take so long. Teresa very much feared they needed to act *today*.

It made Teresa almost as hot as the fever plaguing Father Telo. Yet it wasn't enough to goad her to move. They needed a plan with an actual hope of success.

Her skin seemed to itch. She couldn't sit still any longer, but scrambled up and paced over to one of the pillars to inspect the pictograms carved on the stone. Her studies had touched on ancient languages, but only lightly. Most of her time had been spent on learning more about relatively modern societies— two thousand years ago or less—the *ciudades-estado* after their nomadic ways had ended. Her training had taught her little or nothing to peruse the carvings, but she had to do *something* to occupy her mind.

This pillar, like all the others, sounded hollow. She had debated with Ramiro about pushing the rest over in a more controlled way to see if they also contained treasures, but they had decided it would be like opening a tomb—a desecration. Neither wanted to take such a step. It would be unethical and immoral to indulge their curiosity as the dead had hidden whatever lay inside for a reason. So Ramiro had been satisfied with restoring the armor they'd found, and she with uselessly looking at the carvings.

With one arm bound to her chest in a sling, she used the other hand to trace an uneven rectangle the size of a beetle carved on the pillar. She was drawn to the carvings despite being unable to read them. "San Martin's cloak," she said. She had found such a pictogram on all the pillars, including the toppled one. Her finger moved from one picture to another. "San Lucius's book. A cup that could be Santa Teresa's wine. It's full of images I recognize, but I don't know what they say."

Ramiro rested his chin on his arm draped across his bent knee. "Does it matter? They aren't going to tell us what to do."

"I know. But I don't like leaving anything unexplained. Perhaps they can tell us about the owner of the armor."

"Does that matter either? It's here. We can use it if we have need or sell it for more medicine. You heard what Father Telo wants us to do."

"Leave him," she said reluctantly. "Go try and save the city."

"Aye," Ramiro said. "I don't like it either. But we can't put it off anymore. I'll put on the armor and cause a distraction, draw the Northerners into the streets. You sneak into the cathedral when their backs are turned and take care of the Diviners."

Her stomach dropped. She knew what such a plan

entailed. They'd talked around the idea enough times already. "We'd be killed, cousin. We don't even know the Diviners would still be there. And how am I to manage with just one arm." She sighed as frustration built. And that's where they became stuck. Ramiro arguing for action. She expressing doubts. He realizing her doubts weren't wrong. She knowing that action was necessary. They were stuck in this circular argument with no end in sight.

"We'll leave this with Telo." Ramiro held up the red Diviner. "The priest will be safer than we will. One of us will make it back to care for him."

Before Teresa could tell him no, Santabe stirred across the tomb. "Bring it closer and I'll tell you what you need to know," she said. Teresa froze. She'd forgotten the Northerner was there. Unless the woman was cursing at them, her presence tended to fade into the background, as she often went for hours without speaking or moving. She took food from them but not much else, even preferring to sit in her own filth than have them tend her.

Santabe sat upright. Her legs stuck out straight before her. Her limbs were useless and kept her tied to one spot. For some unknown reason, the woman had removed the splints the healer had placed on her legs. Teresa supposed it didn't matter. The bones had been so badly crushed that they'd fractured into pieces. The healer said the bones would never knit together and the legs should be amputated otherwise the Northerner would die. Santabe had gone berserk at the idea, and Ramiro had decided to let her have her way as he had enough on his hands at the time. Teresa had felt guilt over that, but let it be.

Santabe had to be in considerable pain, but all Teresa felt was vindication. Their misfortunes were tied to this woman. That Santabe suffered as well was a small compensation.

"I don't think—" Teresa started to say in warning, but Ramiro was already up and crossing the room, holding the red Diviner aloft.

"This? You'll tell us what we want to know if I bring this closer? Like this? So speak. Where will your people keep the red Diviners?" There was a darkness in Ramiro's eye that Teresa didn't like.

"As you guessed: My people carry them with them. But you are right about what we are planning. The weak must die and leave this life so the strong can live. The unbelievers will perish. You cannot stop it. Give me the *einhorn* and I'll answer your questions."

"The what?"

"The Diviner."

Ramiro stood over the woman, holding the Diviner above his head. "Someone sounds desperate. Answer my questions and I'll think about placing this closer to you."

An uneasiness stirred along Teresa's spine. "Don't," she began to say.

In a flash, Santabe seized one of the abandoned

splints. Instead of using it as a weapon to bludgeon Ramiro, she employed it as a crutch, springing to her feet in a scream as she put weight upon her broken limbs. She didn't attack Ramiro, but reached for the Diviner with single-minded intent. Her hand closed around the staff.

Ramiro's scream joined Santabe's. His face twisted in an expression of agony. The air smelt suddenly of burning, as if lightning had struck nearby. They fell, strangely stiff like fireplace pokers, the Diviner clasped between them. Both their hands locked upon an end. The frightening blood-red color of the Diviner drained away between one blink and the next, leaving the Diviner bone white.

Before Teresa could react, Santabe scrambled to her feet. The Northerner lurched for the exit, knees buckling and swaying like one drunken—but legs holding her upright and moving with surprising speed. Her bones quite obviously now unbroken. Ramiro lay unmoving, his eyes closed as one dead.

Teresa tore herself from her stupor, heading to intercept Santabe, only for the woman to throw her shoulder into her and knock Teresa onto her butt. Stone bruised her hand as she landed. Pain burst through her broken arm.

She had no time to feel the pain, though, heaving her bulk up in pursuit. Santabe had used the opportunity to stumble through another room to reach the outer chamber where daylight shone. The North-erner appeared to be gaining speed, though retching as she ran. She dodged around Sancha and through the outer exit into the abandoned cemetery above.

Teresa pursued, but was forced to jerk to a halt as Sancha backed into her path. The mare threw her a glance across her back, blocking the path to the door-way and Santabe. Teresa lost precious time jostling around the horse.

By the time she reached the doorway and the late-afternoon sun, Santabe had gone. The tiny cem-etery lay empty. The gate to the surrounding city open. Headstones leaned at angles, some cracked or broken—a testament to their neglect. No one had oc-casion to visit the graveyard walled away and forgot-ten inside Aveston. Santabe could be hiding behind any of the hundreds of gravestones or even have gone into the city. How would Teresa find her? Where should she even start?

"Oh saints."

Ramiro.

She didn't know if he were dead or alive. Teresa's hesitancy fled. She turned and found Sancha had left the sunlight of the outer room and navigated down the few steep steps to the next, going to her master. Teresa hurried after the mare, but had to wait as Sancha squeezed through the next doorway.

Ramiro was pushing himself up from the floor

with the palms of his hands, shaking his head as one dazed. Her heart slowed in its galloping at seeing him alive.

"*Mierda*," he said. "That hurt. What happened?" His short hair stood up from his scalp.

"She used the red one to heal." Teresa kicked the now white Diviner to a corner. "Magic." She reached out to touch Ramiro and static electricity jumped to her hand and left her arm stinging with its intensity. Of course any magic done by the Northerners would involve more pain. They thrived on causing suffering, sweet as mother's milk to them. "She must have been waiting for her chance. Saving her strength. That would explain why she was so quiet. Now she's gone. Are you all right?"

"It's fading." Ramiro got his feet under him and lurched upright, taking a few stumbling steps to lean on Sancha. The mare gave a whicker and stamped impatiently. Ramiro rubbed at his head, eyes not quite focused. "Huh. Doesn't seem to be any lasting harm. She got away? Saints save us. Then we'll need to move."

"We could have helped Father Telo this whole time," Teresa said, hardly hearing. "We had the means under our noses. I'm so stupid."

"My fault. I got too confident." Ramiro pulled away from Sancha with a final pat, to stand on his own. "I should have known better."

"I couldn't stop her," Teresa said. She'd let Santabe

get away. A stupid scholar with no physical abilities. "You couldn't have known. I let her knock me on my butt so she could run past me. It's my fault."

Ramiro ran a hand over his beard. "Neither of us should go down that path. We did our best. Start packing up. We've got to get out of here before she brings back trouble. Maybe this was the kick in the pants we needed."

"You're right. If only the people of Aveston would find her and take care of her for us." A Northerner alone in the streets, unsteady on her feet. The people wouldn't hesitate to take some of their own back. Teresa scolded herself. That was wishful thinking. As if they'd get that lucky. She went to Father Telo and checked the man's cheek for fever. He was cool for the moment. She turned and began shoving items into a saddlebag, determination growing with each second. They'd take Father Telo to some priests. He'd be tended there until they could go back for him, and without their prisoner, they had more freedom. No longer needing to guard her.

She touched Father Telo's whiskered face again. "Hold on. Help is coming."

She turned back to Ramiro. He walked to the armor with hardly a waver in his steps and slung the breastplate over his head, settling it into place. He saw her looking and touched his sword. "It's time to try this out."

"Not necessarily. We have a weapon that doesn't

shed blood," Teresa said. His eyes fastened onto hers and she knew they were in perfect agreement. "We have a better way to fight. Together. Fight fire with fire, right?"

She left Telo and went to the corner, pushing back against the twist in her gut and a sudden coldness in her feet, and picked up the white Diviner. More than looking like an old bone, it felt like one in her palm— lifeless and chilly. If they hadn't the tray to block the power of the Diviners anymore, then she'd take one for herself.

Ramiro rolled their other Diviner to himself with his foot. "Fire with fire. And that gives me an idea." He took down one of their lanterns, brimming with oil she'd just refilled. "Now we're ready."

CHAPTER 31

Claire endured hours of conversation about aching backs, grinding hip bones, and sore shoulders with hardly a murmur. She let her mind dwell on other things when the Elders discussed herbal remedies, poultices, and steam baths. She nodded along in a bored fashion, concentrating on staying atop Valentía—bareback riding was harder than using a saddle, especially for people of lighter weight—as the Elders enumerated varicose veins, boils, and weight gain. But she drew the line at listening to stories of irregular bladders.

Suero had wisely maneuvered his horse back almost out of sight behind them at the first mention of swollen joints and tender breasts—good riddance to him. However, she had no such option. The Elders kept too close an eye upon her, believing she'd trip over her own feet if allowed on her own. That left her one option:

"Which desert cities have you visited?" Claire's voice came out rather breathless in her hurry to turn the subject. "A little knowledge of the geography could come in handy." When they stared at her in surprise, she added, "I've seen the area around Colina Hermosa. But as it's burned to the ground, that's hardly useful now. Have any of you been to Aveston? Crueses?"

"Cities? Who said anything about visiting cities?" Muriel asked.

"Why, my grandmother did. My mother told me stories of how she went to a city. That's where my mother was conceived. I thought all of you would have. Being Elders and all."

Heads turned to look at Jorga. She flushed, turning red and wobbling on her horse. "Those stories might have been embellishments. I never said Rosemund resulted from a city man. I said I'd been to a city . . . once. On a dare."

Claire blinked at her feeling like an owl. "What? That's not what I heard."

"It was a dare," Jorga continued. "I was young and foolish. And this person was an annoying, stick-up-her-butt, bossy know-it-all."

This time heads swiveled toward Eulalie, who also turned red. "Who's the fool who actually went to a city, huh? That was your choice." The others chortled.

Muriel saw the blank look on Claire's face and took pity. "It's too dangerous to visit a city. Too many people. Much too hostile. Too ignorant about us. We go to the villages when we need to have daughters. We trade with them. They are much more tolerant of us. Most of them know who we are despite our disguises and pretend they don't. We have an unofficial welcome there as long as we bring something to trade and some of us continue visiting the fathers of our children until they pass on. It can get lonely living alone."

Claire nodded. She'd always known her father came from a village—just not which one. She'd witnessed her mother go off to trade at several different ones. Was her mother secretly visiting with her father? Giving this unknown man updates on Claire's growth and development? Claire hadn't thought her mother lonely. Nor had she ever really pined over her unknown father.

She saw only her mother and that was just the way things were for the Women of the Song. It was nothing to feel disgruntled about. But now she wondered. With her mother gone, there was no one to tell her the truth about her father's identity. No one female, anyway.

Claire shivered and made a face. What if her father was a cringing little suck-up like Suero? In that case, she'd rather not know the truth.

"Disguises?" Claire asked instead. Of course, most

Women of the Song didn't look anything like the desert people, with their light hair and fair eyes, though Muriel might fit in at a village with her dark skin. "I thought you'd use illusion."

"As if someone could Sing for days—months. And during . . . well you know"—Eulalie's face puckered and she dropped her voice to a whisper—"sex."

"Walnut oil dyes the hair and skin," Violet said too quickly. "Lasts for quite a long time."

"Exactly how long did you stay in the city, Jorga?" Rachael asked overtop the others.

"Yes, tell us," one of the others prompted.

"Hardly long enough to count," Eulalie taunted.

"Five minutes," Jorga said. "You know very well that was the number mentioned in the bet. I Sang an illusion as if my life depended on it. Walked two streets in and turned around and hustled out like the boogeyman was on my tail. Almost soiled myself. I think I was all of fifteen. I won that bet, but it wasn't worth the risk. Let that be a lesson to you not to try it." She fixed Claire with a steely stare.

"You barely won it," Eulalie allowed.

Claire sat a little taller on Valentía. She was the only one here who had spent any time among the cities—even if that city had been a smoking heap of ashes at the time, it still counted. She had sat with the desert people for tea and been part of their gossip in sewing tents. She'd been noticed by the city leaders: Ramiro's parents. Slept near their tent. The Elders, for all their experience, couldn't outmatch the things Claire had done at just seventeen.

"So none of you has really been to a city? Or spoken to a desert person from a city?"

"My shoulder is sure throbbing," Rachael said. "Got any more of that ointment, Eulalie?"

Claire huffed. They wanted to dodge her questions; two could play games. "None of you've had *sex* with a city man?"

Squawks like a bunch of chickens greeted her question. "We could talk about sex," Claire said again just to see them blanch. Her mother had been quite open about the subject—happy to discuss anything that didn't have to do with magic—making sure Claire wasn't afraid to talk about it in turn. She might not be able to think about such intimacy when Ramiro was around without wanting to die of embarrassment, but she wasn't hindered from speaking about it when with old women. Though that wasn't really the topic she wanted to pursue at the moment. "Or you could answer my questions."

"We don't know anything about city people," Eulalie snapped. "There, happy? Chit of a girl. Thinking she knows everything," she hissed under her breath but loudly enough to be heard.

Claire ignored her. "And who has encountered the Northerners and Da—their god—the most often?"

"You," Rachael said, sourly. "What are you getting at?"

"That I should be the one in charge—as you promised before. Remember. The one making the decisions, with your help," she added. She glanced at the scenery, seeing how often barrel, prickly pear, and pincushion cacti replaced bushes with leaves, how most of the trees had vanished. The temperature had risen and the water in the air dissipated, making it easier to breathe, though drying the throat, nose, and eyes uncomfortably. They neared their destination. "I think you're forgetting who is running this mission."

They gave her dead-eyed stares, even Jorga, but she'd gotten her point across. They wouldn't forget again in a hurry. Good, as they'd made quick progress with the horses. They might even arrive tomorrow. Claire turned her mind from the unexpected way providence, or the Great Goddess, had put the horses in their path. That was a luck to be accepted and not questioned.

"And what do you intend to do at the cities?"

Suero's oily voice made Claire jump. Thankfully, she wasn't the only one. He'd held on to his bits of armor to keep them from clanking and giving him away. A rusting sword was thrust through his rope belt, bumping against his horse's flank. His gelding danced under him, apparently just as put off by the man as they were. When had the village man rejoined them? Had he heard her mention sex? Claire's skin crawled.

"What I must," Claire said with a firm voice. "What I must."

The brave words felt like the right thing to say to Suero, but each time she killed, the doubts swept back upon her. One moment it felt right to let her anger carry her along to avenge Bromisto and Errol. The next she worried and fretted about the means she chose making her as evil as her enemies. She might not want to think about her actions, but if she didn't contemplate the change in herself, soon there would be no more opportunities.

She'd demolished every Northern soldier encountered, but they weren't responsible for the boys' deaths. Or only indirectly. The Northerners had done many terrible acts, but not that one. They might be here against their wishes, coerced, or only following orders. Perhaps they had children and families back in their country and only left their homes from a sense of duty.

She was the one who'd Sung and brought Dal to this world. Her revenge should rightly be directed at herself.

Or was that right?

The rhythmic motions of Valentía couldn't soothe away the unrest building inside.

The Northerners had come here in the first place with aggressive intentions. They were the killers, the burners of cities. The slayers of children and the innocent. Not content to restrict their fight among other soldiers, they attacked anyone not Northern. Taking their need for blood to the populace at large. She could stop them.

Destroyer.

Errol's last prediction. Sometimes the word drove her onward, gave her strength and courage; and sometimes it made her want to hide, cringe away full of guilt.

She tried telling herself as she had Suero and the Elders that she did what had to be done. The truth, however, lay somewhere in between. Not black-and-white, but gray.

Why couldn't her fate be somewhere in the middle? Not kill or be killed. Not murderer or victim, but savior.

Valentía nickered as if the stallion could read her restless and conflicted thoughts. He maneuvered around the spear-sharp thorns of a barrel cactus. Ramiro had shown her how butcher birds impaled their prey upon the spikes—squirrels, packrats, even other birds—leaving the carcass hanging until the butcher bird or its offspring were hungry. Dozens of little dead bodies left hanging in the sun. A tiny open cemetery of animals. A macabre sight that had turned her stomach.

She was like those spines. Deadly.

Like that butcher bird. Piercing her prey, not on spines, but on the magic of her Song.

She revolted from such imagery. Dal was to blame. Not her. Sadly, her magic could do nothing against him, so she'd reveled in taking her rage out on his emissaries.

She captured her braid between tightly laced hands, pressing them against her mouth. Pulling on her hair. Sickened.

Did it have to be that way?

They would reach a city soon. Encounter many more Northerners at any instant. Could she handle those meetings differently?

Use a different Song?

An idea began to form around her latest magical discovery: combining illusion with emotion. Illusion had worked before in a spectacular fashion, chasing off a whole army when she pretended Dal was among them. What could it do if combined with emotion, passion?

Details cleared in her head, becoming fuller and more certain. Relief surged through her, pulling away her stress, telling her she was upon the right track. This could make her something other than a murderer. A Destroyer who didn't need to take lives.

Claire brushed back her braid. "Ladies. New plan. When we find the Northerners, this is what we're going to do."

CHAPTER 32

Ramiro had led Sancha with Father Telo on her back to a small, nondescript church of stucco where a handful of friars gladly took in their fellow priest, promising to tend him. Indeed, Father Telo showed more signs of recovery under their care and lying on a cot in one of their austere chambers. He stretched out in a real sleep, no longer mumbling. He looked haler somehow, less feverish, almost as if he knew he'd come home to his kind. Whether his improvement came from the friendly environment, the quick ride through the city, the surge of fresh air, or leaving the unhealthy atmosphere of the crypt—or all those factors—Ramiro couldn't say. He could only approve any advance in the priest's healing.

The friars also offered Ramiro and Teresa a place to hide until night settled over Aveston. Though additional people, including more Northern patrols, would be moving with curfew lifted as the sun disappeared, Ramiro still preferred the cover of darkness to hide their way to Her Beauty.

The moon rose and Teresa went to say her goodbyes to their friend, while Ramiro had some last words with the eldest friar—one of those men always immaculate in their dress and never ruffled by the panics of the flesh. Ramiro envied him. "If we're not back by morning, take Father Telo and get out of the city. I'll tell Sancha to carry Father Telo."

"The marvelous horses of Colina Hermosa. Smart as a child or so I've heard." The friar paused as if for confirmation, continuing when Ramiro said nothing. "But I'm afraid rumor says the main gate is closed, my child. Egress is denied everyone. I've had it from too many credible sources to dismiss rumor as anything but truth."

"And the other ways out?" Ramiro asked. The city must have other exits, even if just a sewer. A good priest would know them all, like he knew the heartbeat of his city. Ramiro judged these friars to be that sort of priests.

"The Water Gate appears to be still open. But it is only wide enough for one at a time and more difficult to access. It descends into a canyon, dangerous if there should be a flash flood. My bones say something is coming and it may be the summer rains. The weather is as uncertain as the times."

"It's not the summer rains." Ramiro stared at the sky where clouds had begun to form. The light silvery ones that did not portend precipitation. "It's something worse. Use the Water Gate. Get out. Warn who you can to get out, too, but do it without making a stir. We mustn't let the Northerners guess more of us are escaping. You understand, Father."

"I'm afraid I don't. We should warn everyone, my child."

"Normally I'd agree, but they plan for Aveston to die in the same way as the armies—in blood. If they sense an uprising or a mass escape they'll act immediately and everyone will die. I am going to try to stop it, but should I fail, this is a chance to at least save some. The key is, you have to be outside the city before the sun breaks."

Bushy eyebrows of black and gray rose. The only sign of the friar's shock. "Then we will make it so and take as many as we can, including your friend. And then there's another rumor I should share with you. I hear the Northerners are taking the curfew breakers they've been holding to Cathedral Square. I assume for executions."

"How sure are you of this rumor?"

"Only relatively, my son. Two different boys reported it to us. They hang around the prison and saw our people being led out by soldiers, taken to Cathedral Square. Frankly I'm shocked they weren't executed immediately, as they executed the bishop and

Alcalde Martin. The boys followed as boys will and saw the prisoners being kept in the livestock pens of the market. Is this what you feared?"

Ramiro sighed. He'd hoped to be ahead of the Northerners, but it appeared he had only half a step on them. They must be preparing for daylight. "Blood calls the demon who killed our armies. Don't wait. Take your people and get out now. Tell as many as you can so long as it doesn't delay you." To hell with causing a panic. He couldn't be a part of leaving anyone to their deaths when he could at least warn them. "The saints be with you, Father."

"And with you, my son. May the saints guide your aim and your steps."

"Amen." Ramiro went outside to find Sancha, the new armor settled on his shoulders like a second skin, barely weighing on him. He tried to have faith the lighter metal could turn a Diviner's killing blow as his other armor once had.

When the moonlight struck the armor, the surface glowed. In sunlight, the metal would be blinding. He knew why they had quit making armor in this fashion: He'd stand out like a beacon in daylight. Fortunately, the clouds obscured the moon for the most part.

The mare was waiting for him at the entrance to the lean-to the friars used as a stable. It housed chickens and a few goats and smelled of straw and faintly of the ammonia of chicken droppings.

He'd given Sancha a good grooming when they'd arrived yesterday, spending the hours with her instead of sleeping. Now he stroked her coat. The feel of her was almost as powerful a comfort as going home. She'd been the other half of him before his beard, before his growth spurt, almost half his life, since she was a colt. They'd truly grown up together like siblings. Closer in some ways than with Salvador, who was often too old to be bothered with a little brother.

Maybe I'll be bothering you again soon, Salvador.

"I need you to carry Father Telo for the friars and go to my parents," he told Sancha.

She whickered, ears laid back, understanding him too well. He rubbed her nose.

"It's not a parting—not really. I'll find you with my parents. We just have different paths for a short time. I need you to help get Father Telo out. And maybe I'll be back in time to go with you."

She leaned her weight against him in a sign she agreed but didn't like his orders, and his knees buckled, almost sending him to the dirty cobblestones. "Hey!"

Her upper lip lifted in a laugh.

"Not funny."

"What's not funny, cousin?" Teresa asked, adjusting her poncho around her round form. Her broken arm was bound under it. "I'm ready . . . I guess." She carried a Diviner in her hands.

He drew, not his sword—they couldn't risk

bloodletting—but another white Diviner from his belt. "Let's go. Stay behind me."

A crease appeared on her brow. "You don't have to protect me."

"No. I know that. It's so we don't touch each other accidently with these things." He gave a flourish with the Diviner. It felt all wrong in his hand. Too light. Too . . . unsafe. Unlike his sword, this magic weapon, born of blood, troubled him. It would be too easy to make a mistake with it.

"Are you sure we know how to work them?" she asked.

"No. I'm not sure of anything."

"Except we have to do this," she finished for him.

"Hi-ya," he agreed. "That we do. Let's go." He said a last good-bye to Sancha and they snaked their way out into the night, heading for Her Beauty. The great bell tower above the nave stood a dark guard over half the city, visible from almost every point. It acted as a beacon to them now. Guiding them. A holy place turned into a den of nightmares.

He only hoped they could rid the world of a few of them.

Occasionally they'd see a woman with a bucket, going swiftly to the well. A child played with jacks and ball close to the door of their house, while a girl across the way swung a rope as her siblings jumped. A man lugged coal home to his family. A family dug vegetables from a scrap of a garden. Normal city folk doing their daily tasks as best they could in an occupied city. The people of Aveston pretended to ignore Teresa and him, and they gave the citizens the same courtesy.

"I'm going to get one of those red ones for Father Telo."

Ramiro turned to see Teresa's face looking grim and determined in the faint light. "To heal him," she continued. "I can do it. I'm not afraid of the pain it causes. He's my friend."

"He's a friend to both of us," Ramiro said simply, intending to make sure it was he who took the punishment of healing Father Telo. "We'll find one for him."

"I can't stop thinking," she said softly as they kept to the shadows of the street. "Julian was healed, but others were not, like Father Ansuro. Maybe with Father Telo nothing happened because we had the means in our power to heal him ourselves the whole time. We just didn't see it. Do you think that could be it? The Lord helps those who help themselves and all that?"

Ramiro checked around a corner before leading them forward again, more than a little surprised she wanted his opinion. On matters of theology, she knew a hundred times more than he did. But maybe on the subject of miracles no one was an expert. "I dunno. Never thought about it. Possibly, I guess. We had the red Diviner. It could have healed Telo. But wouldn't I have had a dream showing us what to do, if that's what . . . God wanted?"

"I wondered that, too. It all seems so . . . arbitrary. Why a miracle here and not there? Why send a dream yesterday but not today? I guess I don't like how random it is. I always just assumed the saints had the Lord's help all the time."

"All the time? They died, remember? Unpleasantly."

"Until then," she said. "And the unpleasant part was part of the plan, too. I think they knew it was coming. To be martyrs, I mean. So they and their message would be remembered thousands of years later."

"I'd rather not be remembered then."

"Me neither," she agreed softly. They made the rest of the way in silence, hiding behind some abandoned crates once until a patrol of Northern soldiers passed. They slipped around the back of the cathedral to the cottage of Father Ansuro. All the windows were black as the night, the house as dead as its owner.

At least from the outside.

Teresa clung to his arm. "Do you think Santabe got back and told them we were coming? Set up an ambush? I *really* don't want to be a martyr."

"Only one way to find out." If they ended up dead in this cottage, Ramiro didn't think anyone would remember them. They'd just be dead.

He crossed the square before the cottage with

haste and leaned against the peeling paint of the door. Locked. Father Ansuro had locked it right after he let them in. They hadn't returned here, but had exited from the cellar last time. The locked door matched what he remembered at least.

The tip of the knife from his belt fit in the door seam. He wiggled it back and forth until the crack grew wide enough to push the whole blade in and force the latch up. The door swung open on a room unchanged from their last visit. No soldiers waited, at least.

Every inch of the place was a reminder of the frail, old man who'd lived here.

Ramiro moved on before regret could take hold. He put a finger to his lips for silence and darted to the map of Her Beauty on the wall. Teresa joined him there, pointing to the reflection garden on the drawing. Ramiro had seen the like in other churches: a small courtyard garden in the center of a building with no roof and surrounded by walls. A space that allowed for nature and gave a place to go for contemplation and quiet. The map showed this one as bigger than most, as aggrandized as the rest of Her Beauty.

According to the map, there was an entrance from the back of the nave. One that required walking through the heart of Her Beauty to reach. But another entrance started with a corridor on the outer wall of the cathedral. Ramiro traced it with his finger and it ran all the way around the building, right to the door to Father Ansuro's cottage and continuing around to the grand front portico.

"That's our way," Ramiro whispered.

"A pilgrim's path," Teresa whispered in return. "They come in the front doors, take the corridor where they stop to pray at each niche. By the time the pilgrims make their way to the reflection garden, they're supposed to have cast off their sins on the path and be purified, almost ready to enter the church proper. The corridor is meant to be isolated so the pilgrims don't have to meet anyone. There will be very few connecting doors."

Ramiro remembered the niches, each one supporting an icon or statue of a saint. They had used the corridor briefly before peeling away to the living quarters at one of those few connecting doors.

He left Teresa to her contemplation of the map and flipped open the lid of the chest below it. Inside were several pairs of floppy slippers and a pair of familiar boots with metal reinforcement. Ramiro lifted them out. "My feet have missed these." The replacement pair he'd bought had been used, broken in to another set of feet, and they pinched. Teresa shook her head at him as he sat on the lid of the chest to change shoes.

"Priorities," she said with a roll of her eyes.

"Happy feet, happy life," he said with a shrug. More important, the metal reinforcement was better in a fight.

"Let's hope."

He tightened his grip on his Diviner before going to the old wood door that would take them inside Her Beauty. Teresa followed, more hesitant.

Ramiro touched the wood of the door, but felt no heat, though whether it would feel warmer with a dozen soldiers waiting behind it was debatable. It creaked in a whine that shattered the silence when he opened it.

A single Northern priest in white rose from a nest of blankets on the marble floor in the niche opposite the door. His mouth opened to call out and his hand darted for his Diviner. Ramiro was upon him in an instant, bringing his own Diviner down to touch the soft flesh at the base of the man's neck. Ramiro felt a jolt to his hand, like the distant sway of a far-off earthquake or the rumble of an overloaded cart going down the street. The priest, however, flailed wide, muscles locking, then dropped with staring eyes to the blankets from which he'd begun to rise.

Ramiro retreated until his shoulders hit the wall of the corridor behind him. He stared at the Diviner. This weapon took skill out of the equation. It let any person kill without any training, preparation, or even giving them a moment to question intent. Not even the sharpest sword or most skilled swordsman could kill this cleanly. It sickened him.

"These Diviners all need to be destroyed," he said. "I don't like using this."

Teresa nodded. "Me either. But I can't think of any

other way, can you? Not unless we want to cause the massacre of the whole city. That's what we're trying to prevent. We have no choice yet."

"Aye," he said hoarsely. He felt unclean anyway. He reached for his San Martin medallion only to remember it was gone. He'd traded the charm days ago for more medicine when the herb woman took a shine to it.

He glanced at the Diviner in his hand as if drawn to it. By the saints, what would the figure from his dreams think of him for using a Northern weapon? Worse, what would his father say? Or Salvador? Would Claire turn away from him now?

Teresa snatched the priest's Diviner from the blankets. "We have to take this one, too. Can't let them keep it to turn it red. Look at it this way—we know they work for us now, and if the Northerners knew we were coming, there'd be more of them waiting for us."

"Aye," he said again, his unease only growing. "I don't think Santabe warned them. This seems like a response to our first break-in, when we took her."

"That's heartening."

"Not so much. It's worse than I'd hoped. If they had a man here, they'll have men stationed all along this corridor. All over Her Beauty. All it takes is for one of them to be more alert, or luckier. I don't like the odds. Maybe we could have done this if they weren't prepared like last time. We should go back."

"What?"

"You heard me, cousin. We won't make it this time. I'm being realistic. Maybe we should cut our losses and get out. Go to my parents. Or you should. I might be able to get through alone."

Her eyes narrowed. "Cut it out. That noble thing isn't going to work with me. Give me a second. We can think of some other way."

He shook his head. "Now who's trying to be noble?" If they just had some of that help he'd been promised.

A tendril of fog wound around his knee. He stared at it, eyes tracing it back to one of the marble columns on either side of the niche even as his mind tried to take in the appearance of the vapor. He took a step and saw more fog behind the column, hovering from floor to ceiling like a wall . . . or a door.

By the saints, the sight of the fog made him sweat as it seemed to beckon him. He didn't want to take that path. He wasn't meant for the supernatural. The mystical and uncanny always unsettled him. Even Claire's magic had frightened him. He preferred things he could understand, things he could touch, that were based in reality.

Then he remembered the people of Aveston: the old herb seller who always gave him some mint or a dollop of honey to add to his tea at no charge, for his handsome face, she said; the healer and the friars who could have left, but stayed to tend and support their patients and their flock; the little girls jumping rope in the dark because they couldn't play in the daylight; the little boys with a touch of wildness who ran through the streets despite the Northern occupation. So many others. Women still hanging out their laundry, tending their children. Men still trying to provide for their families when the wells ran dry. Faces becoming pinched with hunger. All of them would die.

"I think I found another way. Give me your hand."

Teresa stared at him like he'd lost his wits, then she saw the fog. "What . . . what is that?"

"Our way through Her Beauty without being seen. The dream world. Your hand." He held out his left. "I'm sure I can get in. Not so sure about you, but if you hold my hand, we can try."

She put her Diviner under her poncho and, he presumed, into her sling, then took his hand. Her face was twisted, as if he'd asked her to jump into quicksand. "It doesn't hurt," he told her as much to remind himself as for her benefit. "It's just strange . . . distant. Like a dream."

With his Diviner held before them, he approached the fog, but it pressed back against him like a shield wall during a practice bout, rebuffing his efforts to enter. Rejecting him. Which made no sense. Surely it was here to help them cross Her Beauty. "I can't—it won't let me in."

"The Diviners," Teresa said. "What if they're like magnets?"

"What do you mean?"

"There are opposite kinds of magic: one of creation and the other of darkness. What if they aren't compatible? They could repel each other like magnets."

"Then we have to leave the Diviners." He was wary to let go such a powerful weapon, and yet couldn't wait to set the evil thing aside. He tried the fog once again, and this time the resistance vanished. Teresa dropped his hand and removed the other two Diviners from her poncho, depositing them atop his. He pulled her toward the fog, but she held firm.

"We can't just leave them here," she insisted. "And if we do, we'll have no weapon that won't draw blood but our hands. Are you sure about this?"

"How can I be sure about anything?" But he didn't like using the Diviners and now he had an excuse not to. He pulled free his sword and hacked at the slim rods. They broke but reluctantly, dulling his sword and taking many strikes to come apart. Eventually, however, they lay splintered into dozens of pieces.

"Best I can do," he said, getting his breath back from the exertion. Teresa stood well back and he suspected neither of them wanted to find out if splitting the Diviners had removed their magic. Teresa took his hand again and the gray world of the dream soon engulfed them, taking them elsewhere.

CHAPTER 33

The wall or door of fog didn't part for them as much as allow them to move through it. The fog felt no different from ordinary fog: cooler than the air and with a slight dampness. Two steps and Ramiro pulled Teresa through to where the whiteness thinned. He glanced back to see that the wall of fog remained behind them—a way back to safety. There was nothing about the fog to raise concern, except for the vapor existing inside a building and being the size and shape of a door.

"Yep. Perfectly normal," Ramiro said. His eyes tried to take in everything at once.

"It's not so bad," Teresa said. "It's like being in our world, but not." Wonder shone on her face. "This is where you go when you dream?"

"A few times, yes. But I'm asleep then. I've never

gone there when I was awake before. It's like this, only a little different." He didn't want to put the differences into words. The usually thick, concealing fog had turned to thin streamers that seemed to blur everything without hiding objects, becoming stronger with distance so that nearer objects were the most clear. He could see the floor under his feet plainly, the walls a little less so, and the ceiling not at all. Still, everything felt more like a painting with some of the details washed away, robbing things of their texture and specifics. He could see the floor but couldn't see the cracks of the flagstones. The colors seemed more muted here, dull, especially things that were normally bright, like the lamps in their brackets.

No patches of fog opened to reveal glimpses of the future. He searched for Salvador's figure, but they were alone. The only things that stood out cleanly, as sharp as ever, were himself and Teresa—and the dead body of the Northerner behind them.

They both stared at it.

"Excuse me for being juvenile, but that's just creepy," Teresa said. She poked Ramiro with her free hand. "Where did the Diviners go?"

He looked, and sure enough, the pile of white chips that had been the Diviners didn't exist in this place. Nor did the blankets the dead Northerner lay upon. He didn't want to know what that meant. He shrugged.

"Let's go."

He followed the corridor. His boots made no thumps on the floor, as if the thin fog cushioned them. Now that he thought about it, their voices had been muted as well. Sound traveled differently here. And unlike the cloying response of his muscles in the real dream, he could move freely here, but his movements seemed slower, more deliberate, the world around him less steady. Like the way you reacted when you were just drunk enough to be concerned about hurting yourself, but not so far gone as to be carefree.

The corridor they traveled continued to be abandoned; the niches they passed empty except for reliquaries or statues. No Northerners. No humans. No life of any kind, not even a lost bee or a fly.

"We're completely safe here," Teresa said at his back. "There's nothing to hurt us. A miracle." She smiled at him as if they went to a picnic in the park.

He tightened his grip on her hand, surprised she didn't feel as he did. "This place isn't meant for the living. The rules aren't the same." It came to him suddenly that in addition to their physical movements, *time* moved differently as well. The distance between niches, which would take them a few minutes to traverse, now passed in half that time, requiring just a few steps. The longer they stayed here, the more convinced he became that this place was dangerous in a way he still couldn't articulate. It was just clear that wherever they were was not for the dead or the living. Humanity, as they knew it, didn't exist here, and if they stayed long, he was certain it would take all that made them human.

"There it is," Teresa said. "The reflection garden should be that door." She raised her hand to point, and for an instant his vision doubled, allowing him to see her arm still lifting, yet her hand fixed with the motion completed. She took a step toward him and her foot lifted at the same instant she set it down a pace ahead.

He blinked and cracked his neck to either side, and avoided looking at himself or Teresa again. Focusing straight ahead on fixed objects, he took them through the doorway. Stone flooring underfoot became pea gravel as they entered the garden, though he could tell more by feel than picking out the pebbles below him. Five or six stone benches were spread throughout the rectangular courtyard. Lanterns on the walls provided light. Shrubs and rare plants, like roses that required extra care and water, grew spaced well apart. Their leaves were a dull and faded green here. Their blooms looked washed out by the fog. No fragrance perfumed the space and the ceiling was only fog where the night sky should have been. As elsewhere the space was empty of life.

Some urgency pulled him to a back corner of the chamber behind the columns that held up the edge of the roof. Ramiro stumbled, and they burst out of the fog as the world returned to normal. Colors and details sprang back to life. The smell of roses almost overpowered, along with fresh air entering from the open roof. Lichens grew up the columns like spots of green and gray moss as bright to his eyes as the fiercest summer sun. The sound of voices crashed into his head as loudly as a dinner gong being rung against his ears. Everything stood out as it burst with life. The clouds had thickened over the moon, but here and there a star shone through as brilliant as a torch. He reeled for a breathless instant, then the world clicked and become ordinary again.

Teresa was holding her head. She opened her mouth, and Ramiro put a finger to his lips. He had heard voices when he came out of the fog, and although he was still a bit disoriented, he was pretty sure they weren't alone. Two columns, set inches apart, concealed them and allowed them to peek between.

Sure enough, the reflection garden was filled with people. Ramiro spotted two Northern priests with gold in each ear—so elderly he had trouble telling if they were male or female—and nearly a dozen soldiers in black and yellow. One man had gone to his knees before the two priests with his head bowed. Ramiro recognized the solider from the gate, the general who'd taken control of the army. He also recognized a dressing-down when he saw it. The two priests spat angry words at the kneeling soldier—

Rasdid had been the name Father Telo called him—while the other soldiers stood rigid with averted eyes. They showed all the signs of men infuriated but unable to show as much before a superior. They had turned their eyes elsewhere to give their officer a tiny amount of privacy in his embarrassment.

Ramiro's insides curled in sympathy before remembering these men were the enemy. Yet, it was hard not to view this Rasdid as a man of honor, obviously commanding his men's respect but also treating Aveston with fairness. As Ramiro had traded for supplies, the people of the city had all told him that once Rasdid took control of the army, most of the harassment of the civilian population had stopped. He wouldn't say the Northerners were kindly under Rasdid, but the brutality and rapes had ended. That didn't excuse them or make the hate any less, but it helped him remember the Northerners were humans and not beasts—and this man, so willing to let them in to try to stop Dal, perhaps even more human than the others.

Teresa nudged him, and Ramiro noticed the rest of the garden. Just behind the soldiers and the priests, the plants had been stripped away, a bench overturned and moved, and a heavy carpet of red laid on the gravel. A single table and chair sat upon it and the table had been piled high with Diviners—the bone-white ones—as if in anticipation.

Teresa inclined her head toward the table. He

caught her eye. "Wait," he mouthed to her. They could do nothing with so many soldiers in the garden. Luckily such scenes couldn't last long. Screaming at your subordinates was a tiring business.

Then to his surprise, Rasdid spoke in their language.

"And my men? You will kill them as well."

The priest on the right let his lip curl. From their voices Ramiro had concluded they were male. "The army is safe. The undeserving pass to . . . *nig via*. It be Dal's will. Some die. Be glad it's not you."

"Just the men *I* send into the city or to your ritual."

"You obey or we see your family is named Disgraced, and *you* sent to the ritual."

"Some must pass to the *nig via* to keep this *via* for others," the first priest said. "You *priat*. You understand honor. If not, you die and we find another."

"You may be ready to kill your priests, but I don't care to give my men." Rasdid spat into the gravel. "Without me, you lose the army again."

The priests bristled at this threat, bent backs going straight. The men behind them stirred uneasily, though they obviously understood nothing being said. The priests pulled Diviners from their belts, and one slid forward to hold the white rod under Rasdid's chin.

The two priests reverted back to their language, and two of the soldiers pulled out swords, while a third and fourth man grabbed Rasdid and stretched out his arm. Rasdid did not resist, and his men kept looking at each other in the way of people unsure of whether to act. The ones with swords drawn let them droop toward the ground. The soldiers holding Rasdid did so without conviction.

The priest spoke again and five of the soldiers knelt on the ground. Their faces were stricken with fear before their bowed heads hid their expressions. The men holding Rasdid left him to hold one of these soldiers instead—a fresh victim. Tension ran like lightning through the room. For the space of an instant, Ramiro believed the soldiers would resist and turn on the priests, then the priests spoke again in harsh voices and defiance fled. A sword was raised over the first victim to lop off his hand at the wrist. Ramiro held his breath—

"I comply," Rasdid said. "Stop. I comply." He said more that Ramiro couldn't understand, but the priests appeared satisfied. The soldiers with swords sheathed them and the kneeling men got to their feet.

"Resistance," Teresa hissed in his ear.

If this had been resistance, it had failed. Ramiro waited as the priests talked some more while the soldiers listened with their faces blank and unresponsive. Then Rasdid said something and they all turned and double-marched from the garden, leaving the priests.

Ramiro tensed. They wouldn't get a better chance.

He pointed at the table of Diviners, then at Teresa, and she replied with a nod. He moved from the columns, pulling free his sword and letting it ring from the sheath. It wasn't in him to attack a man from behind without warning, especially not an elderly one. When the priests turned toward him, he stepped away from the columns to draw their eyes from Teresa and moved as if circling for the doorway. They reminded him of dried-up old lizards who had sat in the sun too long, but even old lizards could react surprisingly fast and with a septic bite.

They moved with him to keep between him and the door, putting their backs to Teresa. Each held his Diviner outward in arms almost as thin as his weapon, and Ramiro saw they each wore a red Diviner as well at his waist. Mottled and frail, they couldn't match Ramiro's strength or speed, but when they could kill with a touch, they didn't have to.

"You're planning quite a party for the city," Ramiro said. "I'm here to stop it."

Lips pulled back from yellowed teeth. "You'll fail."

"Maybe. Or maybe you will. Shall we find out?"

The first charged at a surprising pace, and Ramiro met his Diviner with the flat of his blade. An electric shock rode up his sword into his hand. Unlike his first encounter with this weapon, though, he was expecting it. Before he lost feeling, he twisted the sword and thrust upward, tearing the Diviner out of the priest's grip and sending it tumbling away. His hand went numb a second later. The sword dropped from fingers that wouldn't grip. He caught the sword hilt in his other hand and kicked out. His foot hit the priest's unprotected chest, flinging the Northerner backward into a bush and out of the fight.

The other priest was already swinging at him. Ramiro struggled to regain his balance while diving away from the Diviner. His right arm had gone numb to the elbow and hung useless. A calculated sacrifice to even the odds, though he didn't dare attempt it again and lose the use of both arms. He avoided the first strike, but the priests had had years of training also. Somehow, he didn't think priests got to this age in the Children of Dal without being ruthless and effective at killing.

Ramiro jumped back yet again. This Northerner didn't take big swings, but short ones that didn't overbalance the priest, and it enabled him to strike often and keep coming. The short swings meant Ramiro couldn't run in under them. Ramiro was kept too off balance to use his sword. He danced out of the way again and again and gave ground, while all the priest had to do was press ahead.

He prepared to give ground yet again when the priest jabbed instead of swinging overhand. Reflexes took over and Ramiro's left arm shot out to deflect, catching the blow just above the elbow. The Diviner landed against the armor in a thunk of metal. The priest smiled in victory, waiting for Ramiro to topple.

The skin of Ramiro's arm prickled underneath the mirror-like armor, similar to the effect of having stinging nettles rubbed there, but nothing else happened.

No agony. No paralysis.

No death.

When he'd been hit before in his other armor the Diviner had been debilitating—like being struck by lightning—though not deadly. This time Ramiro hardly even felt the magic.

The old priest's eyes widened in surprise. He recovered and swung again. Ramiro caught that blow on his forearm, shrugging off the mild nettle sting and taking a step forward. The priest aimed for his head, but Ramiro stopped that strike with his arm, too.

Before the priest could attack again, Ramiro said, "You lose. Look behind you."

Teresa had thrown oil from the lanterns all over the table. The priest had been so busy he hadn't even noticed the light dimming. Now she plucked another lantern from the wall, flinging it at the table of Diviners, where it burst in a spray of oil and flame. The table caught fire in a flair of heat and was engulfed in an instant. The pile of Diviners smoked and turned brown.

The priest wailed in a cry of mortal grief and struck out with his Diviner again. The weapon pinged off Ramiro's hip. He cuffed the old man in the head with his sword hilt and the priest folded to the ground, going silent.

"I didn't want to do that." It went against all his

upbringing to harm the elderly, even one trying to kill him. However, the Northerner would live, and Ramiro had to silence the noise before it brought more of them. They had made enough noise as it was.

And soon there was more as whistles and cracks came from the fire as the table collapsed, catching the carpet on fire. The chair followed the carpet's example. Sparks flew upward. Smoke was sucked out of the opening in the roof. Ramiro tossed the Diviner of the unconscious elderly priest onto the pile, feeling satisfaction as it browned like the others.

Teresa tossed the other priest's Diviner into the bonfire and came to stand next to him as they watched. There must have been hundreds of the Northern weapons on the pile. All the Diviners the Northerners hoped to turn red to repel Dal. Hopefully, this left them as vulnerable as the rest of Aveston and would prevent a massacre.

The flames licked around the Diviners, but Ramiro waited in vain for the weapons to turn to ash. Already the wood of the table fell in on itself as it was consumed. Though the Diviners turned a brownish yellow, they looked otherwise unharmed. Was the fire not hot enough?

Teresa wore a frown. "I read that ivory can take weeks to burn, but I didn't think these were ivory. What should we do?"

Ramiro glanced at the doorway, but it remained empty. The smell of smoke would bring their enemies soon enough. He braved the heat to step to the pile and strike the closest of the Diviners with his sword. The Diviner on top cracked. He struck again and it crumbled into fragments like a piece of pottery, along with the weapon just below it. Two destroyed, but it was an inefficient process. Getting all the rest would take much time.

"Back to the fog," he ordered. He could just see the patch of fog waiting for them behind the columns. He gripped her shoulder. "You get out of here, and I'll stay and finish this." She pulled away and dropped to seize the red Diviner from the priest at their feet.

"I can't. We need this for Telo."

She couldn't take anything of Dal through the fog. "Go ahead and go, cousin," he told her before swinging his sword at the glowing Diviners. The task had to be done before the fire died. And there was the problem of letting his sword get so hot so that the metal shattered. He'd have to pause between to let it cool regularly. "Leave the red one. I'll bring that when I'm finished here. Get clear."

"You'll never get out alone." She glanced at the door to the nave. It would be the quicker route, but filled with the Northern priests. "I'm staying. We're doing this together, remember?"

He didn't have time to argue. She'd made her decision. He fell into a rhythm: break apart some Diviners, strike again, let the sword cool, and start over. Sweat built up on his skin. The smoke stung his lungs. His muscles ached and his movements slowed as he tired. He tried to move faster, urgency and despair beating at him. Teresa tried using the red Diviner to break up the others, but it didn't have enough weight behind it and wasn't sharp. She soon gave up. Only a third of the pile had been reduced and the flames were dying. The task would be harder when the Diviners cooled.

Teresa shouted. He looked up at a sword coming at him. A great curved blade of the Northerners; the weapon was wider than his hand. He flinched. The sword smashed down beside him breaking up four or five Diviners with one blow.

Rasdid smiled at him. "I will help." He gestured at the doorway, where a dozen men stood guard. "They will watch. We will stop this killing."

Ramiro nodded. Resistance hadn't died after all. "Thanks." No more words were needed as he went back to work. Help had come and they weren't done yet.

CHAPTER 34

The door to the nave opened and two priests rushed in, shouting what sounded like curses. They focused on the fire, failing to see Rasdid's men step out from either side of the door to cut them down and then hack apart their Diviners. Teresa slammed the door shut as they finished the task.

"No blood," Ramiro shouted before remembering they couldn't understand. It must have been a universal fear, for Rasdid was shouting as well, and the men began scraping pea gravel over the blood stains. Teresa pulled off her poncho with one hand and flung it over the first body. Several of Radid's men added their cloaks. All the while Ramiro kept up his hacking of the Diviners. But time was running out, and there were still Diviners to be destroyed.

Rasdid shouted and gestured and three of his

people hesitated, then ran over to help. With five swords breaking up the weapons, the last dozens shattered quickly. Teresa stomped among the outer-most cooling ashes, using her boots to ensure they hadn't missed any. Ramiro straightened slowly and knuckled his sore back, breathing heavy.

"Thanks," he said again.

Rasdid leaned on his sword with sweat stream-ing down his neck. His odd green eyes carried a weight—a man who knew very well he'd just com-mitted treason and signed his death warrant. "I re-member you. I let you through gate. You make way to stop priests. Do you find way to stop Dal, too?"

"Not yet."

Rasdid nodded. Disappointment there and gone in an instant on his face, replaced swiftly by the expres-sion of a man with work to do.

"Ramiro." Ramiro pointed to his chest.

"Rasdid." The Northerner put his open hand on his chest against his heart. "Honored."

Ramiro copied the gesture. "Honored as well." He looked to the corner of the room, but the fog had gone—as he'd expected when help arrived from an-other source.

He looked at Teresa. "Stay behind me. We're going out the quickest way." She'd acquired two more of the red healing staffs and clutched them to her chest with the first. "I'll get you as far as I'm able. Maybe we can take out more of their weapons on the way."

"Weapons? Diviners are not weapons," Rasdid said. "What the word? Ah—*truth*. Diviners are judgers of truth. Decide the worth of a man."

Ramiro shivered and touched mind and heart. It wasn't right.

"The Darkness doesn't get to judge me. I deny it that right. I get to decide. My worth is decided by me and not some force of evil and destruction." He touched his heart again and then his spleen as anger began to build. "Nobody is perfect. I'm no saint. I've made plenty of mistakes. But the truth of my soul is between me and the Light. No one else."

He sheathed his sword and started for the doors to the nave, letting the righteous anger carry him and block out all else.

One of Rasdid's soldiers threw open the door. Ramiro entered the nave surround by a cloud of smoke. It went rushing past him, allowing the light of dozens of candles to strike the armor and reflect back in a blazing glow. The Northern priests filling the sanctuary gawked. Then someone shouted and they rushed at him.

He was already striding forward to meet the first with an elbow into the man's diaphragm, doubling him over. Ramiro took the Diviner out of the first priest's limp hand and used it to finish off the second and third. Then too many to stop reached him. Their Diviners pinged off his armor, not even leaving the sting of a nettle slash anymore.

A fresh courage filled him. He backhanded a woman with no time for regret and punched another priest. He lobbed an elbow again and felt it crunch a throat. Adrenaline roared through his system. He threw the Diviner in his fist like a spear. It took down another. Teresa squawked at his back and he let none through to reach her. Hammering one after another.

Rasdid and his men flowed into the fight. Their swords cut into the priests. When one of their men went down to a Diviner, another stepped smoothly into his place. They gave Ramiro enough space to pick and choose, enough time to act on offense and not just react.

More priests came pouring from the sanctuary and the choir wings, leaving their bedding and seats at the pews. They focused on him with a single-minded intensity, ignoring Rasdid and his men as secondary unless engaged by them. The Northerners had training in combat, but it was a finesse sort of style. He could tell they weren't used to real resistance, and he simply overpowered them with brute force, using the strength of his armor to bludgeon them as often as possible. A knee to the groin. An armored boot to the shin. An elbow to the back of the neck. A blow to the ear.

He swept all aside and left a trail of wounded behind him. Slowly drawing nearer to the gaping front doors and escape. They pressed against him like a wave and he parted them, thrusting them aside. Unstoppable. Until a Diviner came for his head. Reflexes took over, and he reached out and seized it in his bare hand.

Time slowed down.

The moss green eye of the Northerner filled with elation. Ramiro's teeth set in a snarl. His muscles began to lock. Pain blazed.

"I . . . deny . . . you!"

He stood steadfast. The Darkness had no right to judge him or anyone. *No right.* If he died to a human, so be it. He refused to let evil decide whether he lived or died.

The pain fled.

The surprise he felt was punctuated when the Diviner burst apart in his hand. Splinters flew to tear into the Northern priests surrounding him. None touched him.

Ramiro used both hands to seize two more Diviners. They burst in a spray of white fragments. The priests shouted, drawing back. He lunged forward to grab two more. Destroying all the Diviners within his reach. Pushing ever forward toward the doors and escape.

A priest at the back of the mob turned and ran. Then another. With shouts they were all fleeing, leaving him panting and alone except for a wide-eyed Teresa at his back and eight soldiers. A trail of white splinters, mixed with a few bodies, led back toward the sanctuary.

"What are you?" Rasdid held back, trepidation on his face. "No one survives the priests."

"Saint," Teresa said, touching mind, heart, spleen, and liver. "He's a saint. We just witnessed the proof."

Ramiro shook his head as he emerged onto the portico of Her Beauty and took a lungful of fresh air. Daylight had come while they were engaged inside. The clouds had thickened, turning black, and as he raised his face, the first raindrop hit his cheek.

"The rains," Teresa said. "Another sign, maybe."

He pretended not to hear. Let them believe what they wanted. He was no saint. He'd done what had to be done—took just another step on the journey. That was all. It meant nothing. Certainly not that he was favored above anyone else.

"Just a man," he whispered.

"Covet not the miracle," Teresa quoted. "It brings death."

A group of boys ran by, shouting, "The army! The army has come!" They veered away from Her Beauty when Rasdid and his men joined Ramiro on the portico.

"What army?" he asked, but the children had fled. It was not just children who ran the streets. Adults hustled past Her Beauty with their heads down and bundles in their arms. Some carried infants or pulled small toddlers along in their hurry. Too many adults to count.

A gust of wind touched his face. It sprang from a new direction.

"Something's happening."

CHAPTER 35

I don't want to die. I don't want to die.

Julian's feet took him forward among the rest anyway. Panic oozed from his bones, like the thousands of others walking toward Aveston. It threatened to swamp him. He wanted to live. To witness grandchildren. To grow old. To see more sunrises. Instinct screamed at him to bolt. Despite the strength of that drive, the reasoning part of him prevailed. The very fact that thousands of others held together, all with like purpose, all depending on each other, kept him going forward to die.

It couldn't ease the sick dread in his heart, though.

Every part of him from feet to brow was soaked in sweat. His heart beat like a drum. His muscles hurt from clenching them.

I don't want to die.

That was the truth. But there was another truth:

He just wanted something else more.

Life. For others.

Julian felt the touch of the Santa Ildaria medallion against his skin and turned his face to the sky to catch the rain and add another treasure for his inner landscape. He'd missed the sound and the feel of rain over the long dry season and welcomed its return with joy. His trove of treasures he'd collected over the last days overflowed. So much to cherish.

In another good sign, it looked like the wind would take the rain toward Crueses and the thirsty crops when it finished here. Ahead, Aveston loomed in the distance, as it had that day he'd brought a real army here. This army, without a chance of winning, went forward just as freely as that other had. They'd left the wagons behind to walk the last stretch on foot. Many among them held hands. Beatriz walked at his right shoulder and Fronilde, the daughter of his heart, on his left. He smiled.

His muscles loosened. His heartbeat gradually settled to a normal rhythm.

It was a good day to die. He could do this.

The rain began to come down harder, going from dots in the dust to dampening the ground. Soon every cactus in the desert would be crowned with new life as flowers bloomed from every prickly branch, and birds and all the desert animals would start a new generation. Life would continue. He'd leave this world to ensure the prosperity of the next generation as well.

From his position at the front of the line, he could see that they'd been noticed. Tiny figures in black and gold like bees watched before Aveston's walls. It looked as if the whole Northern army had turned out. He could even see figures in white among them—the priests. Now how to draw them away from the walls? Because all this would be for naught if they couldn't lure the army out to die with them.

"Shouldn't they have reacted by now?" Beatriz asked, echoing his thoughts.

Julian set his jaw. His wife was right, of course. If the Northern army was coming after them, it would have done so by now. "They have reacted. They're hunkering down." The Northerners feared their god—this Leviathan—even more that his people did. They would not be attacked. They'd have to go to the Northerners instead, and that would threaten the innocent people inside of Aveston.

They'd put the retired military members at the front with their weapons, hoping the sight would fool the Northerners into believing they were a real army. Now they might have to make use of their steel to prod the Northerners into attacking.

And if that didn't work—if the Northerners still wouldn't fight them—they might have to draw their own blood to bring the monster and give it what it desired.

Julian started as a group of horses sprinted between him and the city, heading toward the encamped army. Figures clung to the animal's backs. Lumpy figures who rode about as gracefully as sacks of grain. Old women? He peered closer. One horse veered in his direction. The girl atop the dapple gray had long blond hair.

"Claire?" Beatriz said.

It was indeed the girl. And the stallion she rode . . . Salvador's horse?

"Valentía?" Fronilde said. The girl's voice was thin with shock.

"Witches!" a voice shouted from the crowd. The people around Julian began to stir with anxious muttering. They stopped moving forward. Faces pulled into worried frowns. Someone stooped to pick up a stone. A mythical foe on top of the horror they already came to meet might be too much.

"Hold! Hold!" Beatriz yelled above cries of, "Witches." "These are friends."

Julian's heartbeat picked up again, but this time with sudden hope.

Claire spotted faces she recognized in the front row of the strange army of old people in colorful uniforms. Desert people from Ramiro's home. Some carried swords. Had they come to fight? It seemed madness. Entirely improbable that they could hope to prevail against a real army of Northerners such as she saw camped outside this city that Suero called Aveston.

She scanned around eagerly, but saw no sign of Ramiro in the crowd.

She urged Valentía in their direction. She had to warn them.

This was no place for Ramiro's parents or Fronilde. When the Elders reached the Northerner army, all hell would break loose.

Beatriz was waving to her, and Valentía obediently stopped before them. "Where is Ramiro?" Claire shouted.

"Inside the city, we believe," Beatriz said. "Safe, I hope." Beatriz stepped forward to touch Claire's leg, squeezing in greeting. "He's missed you. I've had the banns read. No more of this talk of delay. A wedding, for my sake. Don't leave again until you're my daughter, am I understood?"

Claire found herself babbling at the unexpected order. Her face grew hot as the people around listened with interest, including Ramiro's intimidating father and Fronilde. "Yes . . . I mean—er. I'll try. I accept. What? The answer is yes. I'll see to it."

Beatriz sniffed. "Good. See that you do. And you tell that boy that I love him. Both his parents do. Give him that message."

Claire frowned, but before she could ask why Beatriz didn't tell him herself, his father spoke, "We need the army to come out here to us. Can you and your friends arrange that?"

Claire tossed back her hair. "I think we can manage. But . . . you'll be slaughtered. Clear out and let us handle this."

"There are too many," Beatriz said. "Just send the army this way and then get into the city. We have a plan. Understand? Don't come back out here. Go, find Ramiro. Hurry. Go."

Valentía picked up on her confusion and danced under her. "I—"

"Go," Julian said in a voice that held too much authority. "This is our part to play."

Claire grabbed for Valentía's mane to keep from falling. The stallion reacted more to the voice of his former master's father, taking off before she could put her heels into his flanks or set herself. Wind blew the raindrops into her face hard enough to sting. The world blurred around them as Valentía ran, hurrying to catch up to the Elders as they approached the Northern army. Snatches of their Song came to her ears.

Claire opened her mouth and added her voice to the Song. They'd already practiced and knew just what to use. Shunning the Death Song, she Sang of illusion, projecting her desired image into the minds of the army. Instead of less than a dozen Women of the Song headed for an army thousands and thousands strong, illusion showed the men hundreds of witches riding for them.

She'd been able to decimate the Northern army before with panic and send them running, and she'd been alone then. Now, there were eight Women of the Song. With eight, they could break the Northerners for good. Split them into small groups and take them out one by one afterward with the help of the desert people. That Beatriz's group desired the same thing and had placed themselves in their path still worried her, but there was nothing she could do to protect them now. She had to trust Beatriz also had a plan.

Soldiers began to stir, uneasily. Feet shifted. Swords came out.

A second later, Claire used her new trick to feed emotion into her Song. Ahead of her she felt the Elders do the same. Into the illusion, she pushed bone-cold fear and panic—the sort she'd felt that day so long ago when she'd first stampeded the Northern army.

The rain dampened their magic as Jorga had warned, forcing them to ride dangerously close to within a stone's throw. They trusted in their illusion, though, and continued on. Claire followed at the rear of the other women, projecting her voice with all the power and strength she could force in it. A line of priests in white holding the red Diviners called to their people to hold firm. An arrow flew. Then others. Most hit nothing, but one caught Violet or her horse.

The Elder and her mount went down headfirst, plowing into the ground in a flurry of cartwheeling legs and arms, and sending up a cloud of rain-dampened dust.

Claire's Song faltered, but she corrected and Sang all the louder, projecting more fear, more terror, even adding in confusion here and there.

"Now!" Jorga shouted.

Now Claire added bloodlust and the desire for revenge to their Song. The rain tried to hinder the power, but they were too close now. Screams of rage came from the soldiers. One seized a white-robed priest, punching and sending her crashing to the ground, then ripping away the priest's Diviner. As Claire had rightly guessed, it was the priests the Northerners truly hated. The desire for revenge pushed them to attack their own kind. Others turned on more of the Northern priests, overpowering them and snatching Diviners. They engulfed and rushed past the dissolving line of priests. Fleeing toward the desert and away from the city.

The Elders split left and right before the oncoming army.

"Hurry, Valentía!" Claire screamed, changing her Song with lightning speed to Speak on the Wind. "Ramiro," she Sang to the low-hanging clouds. Throwing a new emotion: joy. Letting him know that she was here, had come to find him, pushing that outward as well. She resumed the illusion Song almost instantly.

The stallion put on a fresh burst of speed, finding the reserve from somewhere to get them out of the way. He pounded for the relative safety and clear space around the gates of Aveston.

The Northerners continued outward, refusing to heed the orders of the few remaining priests. Right toward the army of oldsters and women Beatriz and Julian had brought.

CHAPTER 36

"**F**ather Telo," Teresa said. "I have to get to him with this." She hefted the red Diviner in her arms. Two more had been hastily stuck into her sling. "The friars will have him at the Water Gate you told me about." She hoped they hadn't been caught within the gate when the rain started. That would have been incredibly dangerous, as the gate was a dry gully, only filled during the wet season. The desert floor was rock-hard after the dry season. Water would turn into a roaring flood until the ground softened.

Ramiro turned from facing into the wind to find her. "And I have to get to the front gates. Did you hear it? Claire is here."

She blinked at him. "Claire? Here? How do you know?"

"I heard her. Felt her calling for me. From the direction of the front gates."

Normally she would have felt concern for his certainty. She had heard nothing. Felt nothing. How could he possibly know Claire was here? But after what she'd witnessed inside Her Beauty, it didn't feel like her place to question anything Ramiro said ever again. Or at least for this day, she amended. She'd allow nobody to squelch her healthy skepticism—it made her what she was—but too much of the miraculous had already happened. Why shouldn't he hear Claire?

Rasdid and what remained of his soldiers stood staring. "I must get to the gates, too," Rasdid said. "My men there will need me if an army has come."

Teresa took a deep breath against the fear tingling in her spine. Ramiro was safety for her—emotionally and physically. Their belief in each other helped balance her. Not only was he able to turn aside the Northern weapons, his sword could keep her safe from other dangers, like the townspeople turning into a mob compelled by their own fear. Hell, the sheer sight of him standing tall and straight in shining armor, head held high, would send most people with violent intentions the other way. Though nearly the same height as Rasdid, somehow the armor made Ramiro seem a head taller. Saint or not, he looked like a god-blessed hero from myth.

She had much less faith in her own abilities to

stay safe or handle situations without him. But they each had a role to play, and now all she could do was swallow and say what had to be said. "Then we part here, cousin. I'll find Father Telo. You find Claire. We'll meet at the front gates. Then we'll find a way to stop this Dal." Holding the red Diviners, it should be harmless to say that name, though the soldiers with them still flinched, checking the sky.

Concern shone from Ramiro's eye. "I don't—"

"I do. This is the time to part. I feel it."

He nodded. "Meet at the gates. Got it. If you see Sancha, send her to me." He crushed her to him in a hug that smashed her face against his breastplate, showing her a reflection of her squished features. She squeezed back, though unsure if he could feel it through all the metal.

When he released her, she held out a Diviner. "You should take this."

He shook his head, drawing his hand back. "I don't want to touch it. I'm not sure what would happen."

Probably it would splinter like all the others he touched, she knew.

"I would take one," Rasdid said, "if you are willing to share. But one hand on it at a time, eh."

"Gladly." She set the staff onto the cobblestones under their feet and let him pick it up.

"Cousin. Saints be with you," Ramiro said. Then he was gone, Rasdid and the other soldiers bustling along in his wake, like the weaker vessels they were.

People parted around the soldiers to give them space, then they were swallowed by the crowds.

"Saints be with you," she whispered to his back. "And God be with anyone who gets in his way." The man had fallen hard for the little witch girl and no doubt about it. Not much would be allowed to slow him down on his quest to find Claire. Teresa wished them well with all her heart.

Then her heart gave a great shudder at being completely alone. Standing still among the rushing of the townsfolk. One rock in a flood. The thought reminded her of the Water Gate. She only knew it was at the back of the city. How hard could it be to find? She pulled another red Diviner from her sling, then trotted off, weaving through people rushing God knew where.

Everyone and their mother seemed to be out of their houses and roaming the streets looking for trouble or salvation. People began to loot from stores, especially focused on taking any food they found. They threw stones and other items at any Northerners they encountered. The red Diviner in her hand drew too many looks and Teresa hid it inside her sling with the other. Twice young men in ragged clothes tried to rob her, but she ran the other direction and they moved on to richer prey, apparently deciding she had nothing worth pursuing.

With little idea of the layout of the city, Teresa was soon lost in the narrow streets. Nobody she tried to stop to ask for directions would pay her any heed, pushing past her as if she wasn't there.

The only landmark she could locate were the towers of Her Beauty, which she used to orient her to the rear of the city, but the Water Gate remained a mystery to her.

"Along the wall. It's a gate, dummy. It's got to be by a wall." But finding the wall around the city eluded her, too. As she walked, the rain intensified, slicking her clothing to her body and cooling her off, but adding to her irritation. The rains had to come now? She needed her poncho back. Unfortunately, her covering, which had been through so much with her, lay over bodies in Her Beauty.

Teresa frowned. The street she'd wandering into proved strangely empty. It gave her an eerie feeling. She turned another corner and walked smack-dab into a Northern priestess. That explained where all the people went. The woman had her weapon in her hand and Teresa just missed running straight into it and killing herself.

They both backed up a step out of pure instinct and the priestess's eye dropped to her sling, where the red Diviners peeked out of the end. Her eyes widened.

"Give those me!" the priestess snarled in a broken attempt at their language. Young, she would have been attractive except for the snarl on her face. Her white robe emphasized breast and hip in a way that should have been distracting in any other situation, the cloth made almost sheer by the rain. It was as alluring as the fact that she advanced with her white Diviner held before her was horrifying, and Teresa retreated until her back hit a stack of crates packed against the porch of a tavern.

"Give them me or die!"

An embarrassing squeak emerged from Teresa's throat as she clutched the red Diviners that could save Father Telo to her chest. Randomly, she appreciated that a Northerner would, of course, know the word for die. Anything with violence. It pained her, but there was no choice, even though not only would she lose the power to heal her friend, she'd have no protection from Dal. But handing them over was better than being dead.

She reached into her sling to remove the staffs, when a man in a leather vest with arms like a blacksmith crept up behind the priestess, his finger to his lips. Before Teresa could gasp, he seized the priestess by the skull and gave a great twist with his meaty arms. Teresa closed her eyes and heard a sharp pop.

When she opened them, the man was dropping the body to the ground and holding aloft her white Diviner. His arms strained again, the muscles growing more and more taut, then there was another sharp pop and the white Diviner broke in two. Teresa's mouth dropped open. She thought she heard a cheer and looked behind the man, but there was no one to have made such a noise.

"Are you hale and whole, little sister?" he asked Teresa. The rain had slicked his short hair to his head and drops gleamed in his beard and on his black skin. Attached to the back of his vest was a short cloak that fell to his waist. Hoodless, it offered scant protection from the rain and looked rather ridiculous.

"Uh. I think so." Something urged her not to ask questions. Teresa patted her sling to make sure the Diviners were safe, keeping her eyes from the body at her feet. Ramiro promised they would find help when they needed it. How right he'd been.

"Why are you burdened with those?" He pointed to her Diviners.

A chill went down her arms. The man was huge. He'd crushed the priestess like a toy. "I need them. I can't give them to you." She clutched the Diviners close again, starting to babble. "They're for a friar. Someone who knows about the Northerners and can help us. I need to find the Water Gate. He'll be there. Can you help me?"

The blacksmith man's face split into a grin. "You were not born in this city then?"

"No," she admitted. "I've visited Aveston, but I guess I don't know enough about it." As part of her studies, she had been several times, but only to see the main features of the city and its churches.

"Then I will take you," he said in a booming voice. "This city houses all my descendants. I know its every part. Follow me."

Teresa eyed his retreating back for several seconds in bemused puzzlement—*don't ask questions*—and then scrambled after him.

CHAPTER 37

Ramiro hastened through Cathedral Square, trying to keep half an eye on the enemy at his back who might have become a friend. He wanted to trust Rasdid and his men, but to do so blindly was foolish. He might have clicked with them as fellow soldiers, but they'd turned their allegiance once. Who was to say they couldn't again?

He directed one eye at his back and one on his surroundings.

The friars had done their work of alerting the population of Aveston. Half the *ciudad-estado* might have already been evacuated, but now the occupants of the second half ran through the city looking for a way out.

And that's exactly what he was looking for—not just for himself, but also before the mostly peaceful riot turned bloody and attracted Dal. Was it ironic that he'd stopped the Northerners from starting a massacre, only to perhaps cause it himself with his warning? He couldn't stop from scanning the sky for signs of the angry god or sniffing the air for the first putrid smell. He had to prevent that from happening, and opening the gates seemed the likeliest way to redirect everyone.

"No trouble. I can order gates open—if I'm still leader," Rasdid added ominously. "We must hurry, in case priests find another man to take my place."

"The priests won't start anything now, will they? With their Diviners destroyed, they have no reason to."

"The priests." Rasdid brought his fists together at the knuckles, pushing them against one another, the red Diviner held awkwardly. "They're like this. They don't like being . . ."—he sought for the word—"said. No. Told. Told how to be. They have a plan, a strategy, and they stubborn. They keep that strategy no matter what changes."

"What strategy?"

"Kill this city anyway."

Ramiro jerked to a stop, his limbs weak with horror. "Kill the city anyway? For no gain? Out of stubbornness? My god. They would do that?"

"Ah. Yes. They are priests. That is how they are. Ordoño, he had much trouble with them."

"How did he handle them?"

"He killed priests who don't listen. Why do you

think the Children of Dal liked a stranger from another land so much? Go!" Rasdid waved in the direction of the gate and they started running again. "We don't like priests. *Nobody* likes priests. So when a priest said no to Ordoño, they died suddenly. Poison. Knife in their sleep. Santabe. You know her? She's Ordoño's knife."

"I know her," Ramiro huffed as he ran, struggling to keep up with the unarmored Northerners and grateful his new armor was light. He still made an ungodly amount of noise, but that was probably an advantage right now, as people scattered from their path. The Northern woman was in the city somewhere, doing who knew what. It wouldn't be anything good.

He gestured at the red staff Rasdid carried. "She said those can rebuff Dal. Is that true? I've seen they can heal."

"Yes. Heal. And they can bring some back from death, too—if used quick. Rebuff? What does that mean?"

"Keep off. Keep away."

Rasdid slowed. "She said this to you? That does not sound like Santabe. She's too much . . ." The scowls of all the soldiers told Ramiro exactly how they felt about her.

Ramiro put his fists together as Rasdid had and pushed them against one another. "We convinced her."

"Ah." Rasdid spat. "Good. Yes. What she said is

true: Everyone around a living Diviner for eight cubits is safe from Dal."

"Cubit?" Ramiro stopped again and Rasdid and the others followed suit.

A crowd of people blocked the road ahead, standing shoulder to shoulder with their backs turned in Ramiro's direction, struggling to push forward. The mob trying to reach the closed gates.

"Eight cubits," Rasdid said, pointing at the crowd. "From us to them."

Ramiro judged the distance to be about twelve to fifteen feet, which meant the red Diviners didn't provide a very big sphere of protection. At least that much of what Santabe had said was true.

One of the soldiers with them spoke in his language and half drew his sword. Rasdid replied, grabbing the soldier's hand and ramming the blade back home, then turning to Ramiro.

"These are your people. You can get us through, yes? Without blood."

"No blood," Ramiro echoed. If the Northerner priests wanted a place to start a massacre, they'd stumbled upon it.

One step at a time.

He walked up to the edge of the crowd. The people were chanting "open the gate" and trying to push forward with nowhere to go, jammed in thickly, like a large family in a short pew. Ramiro tapped on the last few. "Let me through. We will open the gate." A calm came over him and the words emerged without shout or bluster, but with complete conviction. It was the conviction that finally reached them. He had to say the phrase three times before recognition dawned on their faces and they stopped turning away. First one than others squeezed to the side enough to let him slide through. Rasdid and his men followed.

Over and over, he spoke the words in a voice of calm. "Let me through. We will open the gates." Men and women eyed his face or his shining armor and managed to draw aside enough to expose a space. The farther their progress, the faster people moved. Whispers radiated ahead of them and to all sides.

"They will open the gate."

Anticipation sparked thought the mob. Hands reached out to touch his armor, unsettling Ramiro with the hope and near worship on their faces. People stepped aside before Ramiro even reached them, leaving a clear pathway. The chanting died as he neared the front line. Men with belligerent stances stood down, stepping back from whatever they confronted.

"They will open the gate."

Ramiro got his first glance at what they faced. Rasdid said something in his language that sounded very like swearing. A line of Northern priests two or three deep stood before the gate, and behind them was over a score of enemy soldiers with their weapons drawn.

The priests were all young, white Diviners clenched

in outstretched hands and held toward the mob. Their faces had gone dead pale like fish bellies. A sure sign of people about to lose control and do something totally stupid. They carried no red Diviners. Their ears held no jewelry to mark any rank. The youngest and the most inexperienced of their kind—the ones picked to die—they would also be the most easy to spook.

Desperation shone on the faces of the men at the front of the mob. They'd heard the friars' warning of what would happen inside the city. They had seen the ripped-open bodies of the armies murdered by Dal just days ago as proof. The people had nothing to lose.

They'd walked right into the middle of a shit storm.

"We will die here today, yes?" Rasdid whispered.

Not if I can help it. Not with a chance to see Claire so close at hand.

He had to defuse the situation. Ramiro raised his voice, at the same time keeping it calm and even. "Stand down. Do nothing rash. Wait. We will get the gate open. You will get out of this." His words were repeated back to those who couldn't hear, and to his amazement, the crowd rippled, but waited as he had asked.

To Rasdid, he said, "Tell the priests they are being used. Set up to die. Treated as trash. Explain it to them."

Rasdid wore a fixed smile that must have involved

grinding his teeth. "I think they already understand that. They are, how do you say, fanatics. That was the word Ordoño called them. My men will listen. These . . . I know not."

"But are they fanatics who are ready to die?"

"We shall see."

Rasdid began speaking to them and the world held its breath on whether a city would live or die.

CHAPTER 38

Claire let out a whoop and Valentía pricked his ears back at her. They'd done it! Sent an army scampering in full retreat without using the Death Song, calling an evil god, or killing anyone, though she had seen Suero stab a few Northerners in the back. Just the sort of fighting she expected from him, and after they warned him about bloodshed, too. The village man followed close to Eulalie, like grains of wild rice stuck together when overcooked, as if he thought physical size meant strength in the magic. Claire could have told him Muriel was perhaps the strongest among them. Modesty would keep her from mentioning her own name. Plus, she didn't want that greasy man always at her shoulder.

She put Suero out of her head to focus on the area around her. Danger hadn't gone just because most of the army headed toward Beatriz and Julian. The Elders must be a lure for a real army hidden somehow. That had to be why Beatriz stood her ground in the path of the Northerners. Claire prayed whatever Beatriz planned was as successful as her part had proven.

Her part.

Did "Destroyer" still apply to her when they'd found a peaceful means of achieving their aims? Maybe she could finally shake that name for good.

Meanwhile, the rain turned into a downpour, slicking her hair to her head and giving a new smell to the desert while washing away the last of the magic in the air. Ahead, the gates of the city loomed before her, shut fast. Close enough to reveal details. She wasn't sure if the magic of the Song could penetrate and influence whoever was on the other side to open them, especially in the rain. Jorga and the others would surely know, but none were close enough to ask.

She prepared to slide off Valentía when he stopped at the gate, but first turned her head to check for Violet, hoping to see some movement. Eulalie was arguing with Suero. Farther off, Rachael and Anna were at the spot where Violet had gone down. Rachael had her hands over her face and her shoulders heaved while the other Woman of the Song had an arm around her.

"Oh no," Claire said around a knot forming in her throat. The joy went out of her heart.

Valentía curved in a sharp arch, and Claire grabbed at his mane to steady herself. Claire wiped rainwater from her eyes to make sure she was seeing right. The gates of Aveston receded behind them. "What? Wait! That's the wrong way," she shouted. "Ramiro!" The stallion completed his change of direction and thundered back the way they had come.

Straight at the fleeing Northern army who had just reached the gathering of elderly desert people.

The other horses had turned with Valentía as the leader of their herd, carrying Muriel, Jorga, Rachael, Susan, and Eulalie along with them.

"Wrong way. Take me back!" Claire shouted again, but Valentía thundered on, racing like the wind.

For the first time, she saw clearly what had happened to the Northerners. The soldiers had overwhelmed their priests, tearing them apart and taking the Diviners, except for one priest who still resisted. Pockets of soldiers fought before the wall and in the field around the city, struggling with each other over the red staffs. Valentía took her past one such group, where a half dozen soldiers wrestled and punched on the ground. One man on the bottom was biting and pulling hair, a leg in his mouth. Claire shifted her eyes away as the victor struggled to his feet only to be tackled by another and taken down again.

Elsewhere a red Diviner turned white as two men grabbed it at the same time. A third stepped on their prone bodies to scramble away with the prize.

The rest of the Northern army had gone equally berserk, driven by the emotions the Women of the Song had put in their magic. Some simply ran, pushing their fellows, hitting the gathering of the desert people, and shoving and elbowing their way through as the desert people—for some improbable reason—grabbed and tried to hold them. Others turned violent, striking at anyone in reach whether that be their own kind or the fragile elderly of the desert people. The ones in front fought back, but not for long.

Blood splattered against Claire's face, washed away by the pouring rain as Valentía was forced to slow his headlong pace by the press of people. Claire slid from his back, stumbling as her feet hit the ground. Hands reached out to steady her and she looked up into Beatriz and Julian's faces. Valentía trotted off, disappearing back in the crowd.

"What? What happened?" she sputtered.

"It comes," Fronilde said.

A putrid smell hit Claire's nose. Someone screamed. A force of will, full of malice and evil, beat down upon her. It drove people to their knees.

"No. No. No," Claire gasped. This wasn't supposed to happen. Not now.

She could protect people from Dal, but not in the rain. She watched in horrified fascination as a slice opened down her forearm and blood welled to the surface, not even feeling the pain in her shock. Beside her Fronilde prayed aloud, not for her own safety, but to be with Salvador again and for the protection of her parents.

Julian held Beatriz in his arms. "Now and forever," he said and they kissed with the rain streaming over them.

Something cut Claire again, tearing across her hip.

"No!" Claire shouted. It had taken ages to convince the Elders her plan would work. That they could frighten off the Northern army. She'd promised if anything went wrong they could use the magic of illusion to hide them from Dal. They and others would be safe.

It was the desert. It wasn't supposed to rain.

She was supposed to see Ramiro again. More people screamed. Beatriz sobbed. Claire wouldn't let this happen.

She put all her force and will into the words of the illusion, pushing the Song out with fierce determination. The downpour washed away her magic the moment it left her mouth. She couldn't even protect herself.

Dal's hate beat down around her and upon her, crushing her beneath it.

Teresa wiped rain from her face and trotted at the heels of her guardian, who moved even quicker than Ramiro. Unlike Ramiro, he never turned to check that she kept pace or to make sure he didn't lose her. In a way, she appreciated his faith in her, and yet she also wished he'd look back *once*. She broke into a run as his ridiculous cloak disappeared around a corner. Perhaps the shortness of the cloak was due to his profession—if he was a blacksmith. She could see why a shorter cloak would be safer around a forge, though wouldn't the fire keep him warm? She made a mental note to investigate if this was a fad of Aveston, if she ever had the time.

"Our destination is just onward," he told her without turning.

Her guide seemed to take main thoroughfares and not back alleys, and yet it was as if the city had become deserted. What was before a bustle of humanity in the streets had become dead and abandoned.

She managed to get abreast of him to get a good glimpse of rainwater running down his dark forehead and rolling into his eyes. He gave no sign of irritation and didn't even blink. She dropped her sprint back into a quick trot and let him pull ahead of her again. Her curiosity burned.

Maybe just one question.

"Do you have a name?" she asked. The man seemed perfectly friendly and she found it odd he hadn't offered. The practice in Aveston was for a woman to only introduce herself if any male company went first. He hadn't. For Aveston, her question would be thought bold, but he only flashed her a white grin in his dark face, looking at her for the first time since they'd left the Northern priestess.

"Martin."

"Teresa. Can I ask you something else? If you have kin here, Martin, how is it that you haven't evacuated yet?" Most of the able-bodied citizens with any wealth had gone days ago. Especially if they had families. All that were left were the very poor or the sick, and the stubborn. He could be one of the latter.

"My fate is tied to this piece of land. I cannot leave it."

Teresa nodded. One of the stubborn then. She might have done the same if she'd been in Colina Hermosa during the siege—stayed at the university . . . and been burned to death when the city was consumed.

"We are here," he said and stopped.

No gate or wall announced that they'd gotten anywhere, but the buildings fell back to leave a vast open space that dropped off gradually onto lower levels or terraces. Her eye fell on a saguaro and then more of the majestic cacti than she could count and she knew exactly where they were.

"*Parque de Recuerdos*. Of course. I've been here. The Water Gate is here?" The remembrance park was one of the unique features of the city.

"In the back—"

"Along the wall," she said at the same time. "Of course." It made perfect sense now. She should have known it would be here. Colina Hermosa had been built on a sloping plateau; the spring and summer rains drained away naturally. Aveston, however, had been constructed in sort of a bowl. Storm sewers had to be installed at its inception or the city would flood and die. The sewers connected to the natural dry gullies in the area, like the one described to Ramiro by the friars as the Water Gate.

Parque de Recuerdos had been a result of that early work on the city. It was the place given over for constructing the millions of bricks that made up the sewers and roads, and for carving the stones that became the buildings of Aveston—all the work needed to create a new city had been done here. And then the work had been completed and the area wasn't needed anymore. Instead of filling it with homes or markets, someone had planted a saguaro in remembrance of a loved one and then another. A tradition was born.

Saguaros in every stage of life spread out before her eyes: juveniles that were yet tiny stubs just beginning to grow; middle-aged versions at a hundred years old, with only an arm or two at twenty feet tall; and the towering, aged wonders of nearly fifty feet with many arms that had been alive for centuries. All stages mixed together, for when one of the towering giants lost their life and the skeleton rotted away, the spot would be dedicated to a new cactus—a new soul being remembered. Each as unique in shape as every human.

Despite the rain, birds fluttered from one to another, and Teresa heard the rustle of rodents in the hard-packed dirt. Smaller pincushion cacti grew under their larger cousins, but no other types of plants. It was a place, not exactly holy, but with the same sanctity as a cemetery, a place for hushed reflection or grief or simply a place of fresh air. The rain had brought the smell of green, growing life. A reminder of continuance. She breathed the smell in gratefully and let it wash away all the death she'd seen lately.

Teresa turned to thank her guide and found him already gone—as if he'd vanished.

Don't ask questions.

She couldn't blame him for not saying good-bye. With the city under so much turmoil, he had to return to his kin as quickly as he could.

She moved forward and immediately understood why the friars had told Ramiro this was a difficult path. The cacti hadn't been planted in any sort of order or rows. Dead saguaros or lost limbs often blocked the spaces between cacti, requiring back-tracking or stepping over if she was lucky. One must avoid falling into daydreams and keep aware to avoid the spines, and the trail between them took her first one way, then another. The ground was rough and natural, easy to turn an ankle on loose stone, made more treacherous by the rain.

The edge of the first terrace gave her a look down, showing three more levels to pass through before the city wall. In the distance a group of people had gathered. Teresa wiped the rain away to see better, her heart filling with hope. The friars. It had to be them. Here and there throughout the remembrance park other individuals and groups picked their way toward the Water Gate as well. Others looking for a way to escape and desperate enough to hope this would work.

Teresa wound her way down and down, past the towering giants. She spotted Sancha before she reached the three dozen or so people packed in a tight circle. The head friar, with bushy black-and-gray eyebrows, came to meet her as people made way for her. Sancha greeted her with a shake of her head as she lay an anxious hand on Father Telo's brow. His fever had grown in strength. No doubt made worse by being out in the rain.

"He is not good, my child," the head friar said. "We were just trying to decide whether to stay here or go back into the city. Maybe to seek the front gate."

He gestured and another friar swung open a narrow door in the wall, narrow enough to only allow one person to pass at a time. She heard the rush of water before she saw it. The Water Gate. Teresa guessed the men of Aveston would have kept it guarded, but the Northerners might not have found this gate or considered it important enough.

Stone steps led down, and water swirled around the third step and away through the gully, no longer dry but now a raging torrent. Teresa had been hearing the sound, dulled by the wall, for some time and hadn't recognized it.

"There will be no way out here for hours, if not days," the friar added.

Teresa nodded dumbly. She had guessed as much, but seeing it brought its own disappointment. "First things first, Father. Can someone help me get Father Telo down?" She stowed the red Diviner in her sling with the other and tugged at the ropes holding Father Telo on Sancha. A friar took the bridle and two more appeared on either side of her. They released the ropes and eased Father Telo to the wet ground.

"Everyone stay well back." They looked at her with puzzled expressions but obeyed. Teresa set one Diviner on the ground and got a firm grasp on the other. The memory of Ramiro and Santabe locked together by a red Diviner and screaming in agony flashed through her vision. She bit her lip, brow tightening. She'd never been good with pain.

She tried thinking of her actions as a scholarly pursuit she could pen a paper about for posterity, but that didn't loosen the icy knot in her guts.

"Oh hells. Saints be with me. You'd better be grateful for this," she told Father Telo and then touched the other end of the Diviner to his flesh. Her eyes rolled into her head in shock as every nerve in her body exploded at once, tearing at her with a million knives.

Too.

Much.

The world went black.

She woke to terror too strong to allow her to move. If she moved, the pain would come back. Then hands did the job for her, lifting her. She blinked. The excruciating torment didn't resume.

"Wha . . . What—" Hands patted her back as she vomited. Yellow bile landed on her trousers. The sight snapped her back to herself. She wiped at her mouth with embarrassment. The hands left her back and she trembled and almost fell over, then the hands were there again to ensure she didn't fall on her face. So weak. Her muscles felt ropy and pulled out like cooked pasta, unable to support her. Her head even lolled on her neck.

Father Telo sat across from her under his own power, but not looking much stronger than she felt.

"The fever is gone," the head friar said. "How is that possible?"

Teresa plucked weakly at her sling. The arm trapped inside no longer ached. "Can someone get this off?" More friars obliged, and she flexed and bent her now healed arm, clearing her throat. The power from the healing might come from the Diviner, but the energy had come from her body. At least it didn't hurt to talk and her tongue still worked. "Magic. The Northern kind. Not pleasant."

"So it appears," the friar said. A smile drew his lips upward, looking odd with his bushy eyebrows. They were made for sternness, Teresa thought idly.

"Teresa," Father Telo said. "Where am I? I feel weak as a kitten. What has happened?"

Teresa tried to laugh and instead found herself crying with relief. It had worked. The hands holding her patted again, a comforting sensation. "A lot. I'll tell you while we find Ramiro."

"I don't think you are in any shape to find anyone, my child," the friar said with sympathy. "You both must rest."

Teresa tried to stand, but her legs gave a twitch and refused. She had a new appreciation for how Santabe had managed to run after the experience. The woman was ten times stronger than Teresa would ever be—or ten times more desperate. *Probably both.* Sancha pushed forward and snuffed at her sleeve and nudged her shoulder. "I have an idea. Get those ropes ready again. Ramiro said to send his horse to him. He didn't say Sancha couldn't have passengers."

In no time at all, the friars had her fixed to the saddle with Father Telo before her and ropes holding them both in place. Already she felt a little stronger, her head more secure on her neck and her spine able to bear her weight and keep her upright.

Father Telo flexed his left arm, the one missing a hand. "Even the ghost echoes of pain are gone." He laughed in his deep voice and the sound chased away the gloom, though the rain had begun to come down harder. Teresa's hand responded when she directed it to wipe the downpour from her eyes. Better and better.

The head friar stood at her knee. "The city is dangerous, my child. Not all who heard our message have heeded our call for peace. Law and order is gone.

Teresa spotted a thin rectangle of fog between two saguaros, holding its shape despite the deluge. Sancha had turned to point her nose directly at it. "We won't be in the city, Father. Not really." At his frown, she added, "Help is there for us when we need it. Thank you for that, Father."

She pointed to the two Diviners on the ground, lying in a muddy puddle. "The white is a weapon. Burn it and smash it when you get a chance. The red will keep you and everyone with you protected. Keep it close." She gave them some quick instructions on how to handle the Diviners safely.

There, she'd made sure some good people wouldn't perish to Dal's wrath.

"Find Ramiro."

Sancha started forward and the cool of the fog swallowed them.

CHAPTER 39

Sometimes, Ramiro decided, minutes of holding your breath could seem to stretch to hours. The mob from Aveston shifted uneasily behind them as Rasdid spoke to his people. Ramiro wondered how many of Aveston and how many of the Northerners held their breath as well. More alike in this moment than different. Surely, they didn't want to die either.

Enough proof of that came before Rasdid had said many sentences: The Northern soldiers put away their weapons. Their bodies still displayed the wariness of men on the edge, but they listened to their general and showed they wanted to avoid bloodshed. A few of them even edged toward the great capstan wheel, a rotating cylinder fitted with metal push bars, which would open the tonnage of the gates. The soldiers heard reason; it was the priests as always who caused the problem. One or two lowered their weapons at Rasdid's speech, looking troubled. The other two score held their places before the gates—white Diviners held high.

Ramiro didn't need to understand their words to read their faces. Disbelief. Anger. Distrust. They could never believe a general over what their superiors had told them, even when the truth of how they were being using stared them in the face. They couldn't accept being pawns to start a massacre of an entire city. Or perhaps they just didn't care. Happy enough to sacrifice themselves for their god.

The rain came down harder, turning into a downpour. Ramiro had to squint to shield his eyes against the drops and keep his vision. One of the priests began speaking back, arguing. Rasdid's shoulders slumped.

Ramiro read defeat in that. So did the mob. The first stone flew. The cries of open the gate resumed. "No bloodshed!" Ramiro shouted to remind them. "Wait!"

He might as well have been shouting to the wind. More rocks flew. The mob pressed forward, pushing him with them. The priests surged to meet them. Diviners reached out and men dropped. An arrow took a priest in the throat.

Some of Rasdid's men used the commotion to turn for the capstan wheel.

Ramiro seized one Diviner and it burst in a spray of splinters, but he couldn't stop forty. More citizens died. A priest got too close and the mob grabbed him, crushing him under dozens of angry fists.

Rasdid was seized and went down, judged unfairly as part of the price of his failure to stop the priests. Ramiro struggled to get to him, but was squeezed out by the press of people. The red Diviner went flying into the far part of the crowd, thrown by someone.

"No!" Ramiro yelled, only to be ignored. Holy hell. Would the Diviner work to stave off Dal with no one holding it? He didn't have time to think about it long. As if in answer the foul smell of death and rot carried on the wind. "Oh God."

An angry force of hate and malice pressed down over the surging crowd, driving all to their knees, then their bellies with its strength. Ramiro lay on the soggy ground, tangled with a dozen others as everywhere people screamed or sobbed according to their natures. Men and women vainly put their arms over their heads or tucked their faces under something to escape the malevolence—to no avail. Ramiro had been here before, there was no escape.

Claire.

He'd been so close. She must be just outside the gates. Arriving with the rain, like a breath of fresh air. Now for this to happen.

He cowered on wet cobbles, screams of terror ringing in his ears, waiting for the first strike to come and carve into flesh. But it didn't fall. Dal was obviously absorbed elsewhere. Close but not here—yet.

Reducing them to mindless thralls until the monster could take their blood.

By the saints, he'd refused to be a worm before, he could do so again. His own anger warmed his belly. If they weren't under direct attack, he could resist. Never would he go down without a fight or lie here like a lamb waiting for the slaughter. He'd made a promise to these people to open the gate. The capstan wheel called to him. If he could only get the gate open, maybe some could escape. Maybe he could get to Claire.

The hate from Dal was stronger this time. It said all life would fail. The darkness was waiting for all mankind.

"No," Ramiro ground out through gritted teeth. He tightened his arms and willed his body to respond, but his muscles trembled and failed when he attempted to stand. The best he could manage was to reach hands and knees. A woman stopped her mindless sobbing long enough to look at him. "Get up," he urged her. She shook her head and looked away, wailing as the fear took her again.

It took every ounce of determination to keep going. He inched toward the capstan, his armor clinking against the stones. The wheel stood above him as a guide like Her Beauty had once, seeming as high and distant as the great cathedral. He put one hand in front of the other and dragged his legs to follow. Pushing feebly against the waves of hate.

A Northern soldier saw him, one of the few with eyes open, and slithered after on his belly, reaching out to grab Ramiro's ankle. He had neither the energy nor the desire to shake the man off. To do so would be to lose his concentration and break his will. One hand in front of the other. He pulled them both along.

Someone else joined their creeping march. Ramiro couldn't spare them a glance. One hand in front of the other. He passed Rasdid with his head tucked in his knees, hands clamped over his ears, lost in his own demons.

The metal bars of the capstan loomed over him. So impossibly high.

All life dies. All life should die.

"No! I made a promise." A pledge to the people here and to Claire. He stretched up an arm, hooking his fingers around the bar, clinging as to the edge of a cliff. To lose his grip now would indeed send him tumbling down a dark abyss. He pulled with every ounce of his strength, fighting against the malice. Somehow, he got his other hand there, and managed to get his head even with the bar. Pulling his own weight. Chest high. He slumped over the bar, just hanging on the strong metal and panting as if he'd run from Colina Hermosa to Aveston.

It seemed ages before he could set his feet and push with his hands locked on the metal. The bar went nowhere. The capstan was meant to be moved by six men, not one. The links of the great chains running from the wheel to the gates were as big as a loaf of bread. The chain much too heavy to move without the capstan and impossible for one man.

"Come on!" he screamed to the Northern soldier who had hitched a ride. The man had hair almost as fair as Claire's.

Claire.

Her image gave him the strength to yell to the man again.

"Come on!" The soldier stirred. Inch by inch, the soldier rose, fighting, tears streaming down his face, until, he too, hung from a capstan bar. Together they set their feet and pushed. Muscles corded with effort. It came easier this time with two to fight as if having a task balanced the will of the Leviathan. Their feet slipped and caught on the rain-soaked cobbles. The wheel grated as it moved, but it didn't turn even a half click with all their straining.

The soldier slumped again, almost falling. Ramiro caught him, almost falling himself as he struggled to support them both. He managed to get the other man over the second bar, so they both could dangle weakly from the metal, suffering under the mental assault.

"Help! We need help opening the gates!" He looked for the third crawler, but whoever they'd been they hadn't made it this far.

By the saints. I can't do it.

Dal called at him to give up. To lie back down in the dirt from whence he came.

"Help." The words were weaker this time. The whimper of a beaten man with no one to hear, though his fingers tightened on the bar, bleeding from a thousand scrapes. Heart straining, he pushed against the capstan, alone this time. The Northern soldier's eyes had rolled back in his head. "I promised," he whispered.

"I'll help," a voice boomed.

A third figure joined them at the capstan. A man in a blacksmith vest that left his arms bare, wearing a short cape. Thousands of raindrops glistened on his dark skin as he set his hands on a third bar. "Push."

The Northern soldier revived and grasped his own bar. Ramiro ignored the heavy rain that blinded his eyes and heaved. The capstan moved. The chain to the gates tightened and then clicked home on the wheel. They walked in a circle, slowly at first, then gaining speed. More and more of the chain spun onto the wheel and the gates began to shudder. They cracked. They gapped.

The capstan clicked as the chain filled it, and the gates spread open to bare the sky.

They stopped moving, and Ramiro hung on his bar too astonished to do more than gasp. The Northern soldier, crying tears of joy, dropped from the wheel and crawled toward the gate.

Promise kept," the third man said. "I used to have armor like that."

Ramiro blinked stupidly in the rain as the black-smith seemed to disappear into a wall of fog. More slowly, Ramiro pulled his hands from the bar, feeling as if they'd become frozen to the metal. The hate beat down, but he refused to bow to the darkness again.

Staggering with rubbery knees, he stumbled to the gate. All help ended here. From now on, he was on his own. He had to find Claire was his only thought as he tottered outside Aveston into a killing zone.

Father Telo clung to Sancha and looked around him in wonder. The place where dreamers came. *Dreamers.* The rarest of the rare chosen of God. More uncommon than prophets or saints and almost never dwelt upon in detail in any scriptures. Yet, here he was, getting to be where dreamers went to see through God's eyes. A holy place. A most exclusive shrine that no pilgrim could find. For a humble friar to be invited here. He gawked around like a starving street boy suddenly granted access to a buffet.

It looked like Aveston, yet not.

The city of his youth passed in a fog-shrouded blur—a literal blur. Sancha galloped and everything became indistinct and piled atop one another, strangely multiplied, as if instead of one image of an inn, he saw a hundred inns all at the same time and all imposed behind and atop every other structure around them. His own hands on Sancha's mane fractured into dozens of hands on dozens of manes. He could make no sense of it.

"By all that's holy. Fascinating."

"I'm going to be sick," Teresa moaned at his back. "It wasn't like this last time."

"You moved slower, I'd guess." The weird effect hadn't started until Sancha got in real motion and begun to gallop. Telo took in a deep breath of air without a hint of contaminate. No smoke. No pollens. No sewage or cooking scents. Just pure air. The trembling and weakness of his limbs caused by the drain of his healing had gradually ceased since they'd got here.

He'd hardly given his healing a second thought; not with so much else to consider and events moving so fast. Though he'd been apparently severely ill, judging by Teresa's joy at his recovery. He patted Teresa's hand tucked around his waist. She, too, gripped stronger as if this place fortified them or maybe just weeded out any detrimental influences.

Teresa had caught him up on everything she thought was pertinent: red Diviners could heal and hold off Dal, Santabe's escape, the fog was part of the dream world Ramiro entered and allowed them safe travel, and they needed to reach Ramiro at the gates so they could find a way to help. It all seemed small potatoes compared to being here.

"There's no rain. Why would that be?" Telo marveled and received a grunt for an answer. He touched his robe with his stub and found the wool quite dry, though they'd only been in the fog a few minutes. He shook his head and took in everything around him, unsure when or how it would end.

With a jolt apparently. He stretched out his stub to catch a tendril of fog, and the mist vanished. Not just that strand, but all of the fog. Rain lashed at his face. Sancha screamed and crashed to her knees. Telo found himself rolling across cobblestones, luckily, thrown clear. Teresa screeched and came down atop him, driving the air from his lungs. The ropes still bound them together.

He set up woozily, already getting drenched in the downpour to find Teresa rubbing her head and the mare standing nearby with blood dripping from torn hide on her front legs. Both glowed with a white luminesce halo around their bodies. Telo looked down at himself and saw the same glow. He swiped at the halo and his hand passed right through.

"What in God's name."

Sancha made a mournful sound.

"Peace," Telo said, putting aside the odd phenomenon to push the ropes aside and hold up both arms as he went to Sancha. "Peace, creature." All animals were God's creation, but Telo had never had much dealing with any of them. His own two feet had been good enough. His experience with horses was limited.

"This looks bad."

Teresa pushed him out of the way to see. Sancha trembled; despite her odd glow, the flesh around her knees hung in ribbons. She held her left hoof off the ground while her eyes rolled and showed their whites.

"Oh!" Teresa moaned. "This is terrible! All my fault! Poor Sancha! Ramiro will kill me. What should we do? What happened?"

"We were thrown back into our world." Telo looked around, uneasily. "I think." All the fog had disappeared unless it was part of the halos around them. They'd reached Cathedral Square. Her Beauty stood just behind them, soaring to the heavens, though hard to distinguish due to the gloomy skies. The wind picked up, chilling against Telo's wet body, and all around the square people lay prostrate on the ground despite the pounding rain, weeping and sniveling, arms locked over their heads.

Dal.

Then why didn't they feel the Leviathan's presence? Telo had a suspicion it had to do with the glow around their bodies.

"You said the Diviners and the fog pushed against each other like opposite forces. I think we just ran into our opposite." Meeting Leviathan's power had apparently cast them out of the fog. Maybe destroying that realm. Or maybe just forcing them out. Telo looked at the people suffering from the Leviathan's evil and decided the fog indeed still protected them through the halo in some way and spared them.

Teresa had buried her face in Sancha's side. She mumbled something that sounded like "no, no, no." Blood appeared on the mare's legs faster than the rain could wash it away.

"Poor creature." Telo reached out to Sancha, trying to calm her, laying an arm around Teresa in the process. He felt useless. He knew not what to do to treat the mare. Had no such training, though he had a feeling no medical knowledge could repair this injury. He had nothing but prayer. Yet no neat, well-taught formula rose to his lips. Instead, there was just a plea from the heart. "Lord, this animal gave aid when we needed it. Give her your comfort now. In your eyes there are no least creatures under the sky, but all beings have worth from small to large, created in your image. Send healing to all in need," he added, thinking of all in turmoil around them.

The mare sank to the ground, her neck and her legs outstretched, with a sound between a whicker and a groan. If she wasn't standing, that meant the extent of the injury was worse than he feared.

Telo drew back. Guilt and grief built in his heart. He pulled at Teresa. "We'll have to leave the horse. We should get to the gate. It's not far." Sancha shouldn't be left in this pain, but he had no means to help her—if she could be helped. "We can fetch Ramiro." The boy would do the task immediately. His horse couldn't be left to this suffering.

Teresa turned on him and pushed him away.

Telo staggered back three steps. "What—" A knife flashed past his ear. Santabe emerged from the pouring rain, a maniacal grin on her face.

"This time you die," she said.

CHAPTER 40

Santabe's backswing caught Telo under the armpit. The knife ripped across his flesh, leaving a line of fire under his arm and another pattern of blood splatter on her white robe. "Always you return"—she swung on him with each sentence, inflicting smaller wounds and backing him away—"again and again. Sticking your nose in. Coming back to meddle. You. You destroyed the Diviners! This was your work."

"He wasn't there." Teresa stood at his shoulder. "I was. I helped burn them. Threw the oil on them myself."

Santabe screamed and ran at them, forcing them to flee before her. In one hand she held the knife and in the other a white Diviner. A red one was thrust through the belt at her waist. "Do you know how rare they are?"

"Much rarer now," Telo said and instantly regretted it. Gone was any chance of reaching the soul he'd witnessed deep inside Santabe: the woman who missed the love of her family and wondered at the marvels of the world. That woman with a spark of reason was replaced with a shrieking maniac.

"You will pay!" She thrust at them over and over with the knife. They became pinned against the base of a statue at the steps of Her Beauty. Telo glanced up to identify the effigy of Santiago, holding his staff and book.

Telo looked for an opening to strike back at the woman but she gave him none, working away at them with her knife. Teresa screamed as she dodged a second too late and the knife cut across her shoulder and down toward her heart. She fell. Telo tried to jump on Santabe, but she spun with such quickness, anticipating his move and managing to hold them both off. She spilled out a stream of what sounded like oaths in her language as the rain poured over them and she held him trapped against the statue with Teresa at their feet.

"Teresa, friend. Are you all right?" Telo pleaded, but Teresa didn't respond. The white halo around her from the fog that allowed him to find her in the gloom had gone out. His wounds throbbed with a fierce sting, sending blood to pool with the rainwater around his sandals.

Santabe held the knife up and a slow smile spread

over her face. "You meddled for the last time." She kicked at Teresa, watching him carefully.

Telo frowned, attempting to organize his scattered mind. Something didn't add up. The white Diviner could finish them in seconds. Even with the knife, Santabe slashed instead of stabbing. *Another pattern of blood on her robe?* Santabe had been killing before she encountered them. Why was she here in Cathedral Square and not stopping Ramiro at the gates?

It all clicked home.

Telo managed to sneak a glance past Santabe's shoulder and beyond Sancha's prone form. People lay torn and broken. Writhing under Dal's evil influence, they never would have seen Santabe coming. "You. You stabbed them while they lay helpless under Dal's spell. You murdered them in cold blood. You still want Dal to destroy this city. You are trying to bring him here. You are sick. Insane."

Santabe threw back her head and laughed, leaving herself exposed. Telo twitched to run forward and tackle her with the idea of beating her brains out. His feet stayed frozen to the stone, though.

Here, in the square of the greatest temple of God in his birth city, before the very feet of the saint of tolerance and forbearance, where the kind Father Ansuro had lived to serve and taught him to give over hateful ways, how could he murder? After being invited into a holy place for dreamers, how could he choose violence? How could he respond to evil with evil?

Inwardly, he asked Teresa for her forgiveness at what he was about to do.

"Turn away from your purpose before it's too late," he urged Santabe. "You can still change. Turn away from hate."

Her head snapped down and he saw that she'd been ready for him all along. But she had not expected this. Pity she could not tolerate. Her nose flared. Murder stared from her eyes. Her grip on the knife switched to a stabbing position.

"God always forgives," Telo said. "You can be the person you were meant to be. Turn aside."

"And be like you? Weak. A coward. Never. If you won't fight me. Return to another life and try again." She drew back her arm. Despite himself, Telo flinched, but managed to speak.

"Then I pray for your soul. God have pity on you."

A giant form appeared behind them out of the gloomy rain. Sancha seized the back of Santabe's robe in her teeth. Though standing on only three legs, the mare flicked her muscled neck and spun Santabe around. The knife rose and fell as Santabe stabbed at the mare.

Telo rushed forward to intervene and was brushed aside.

As Sancha shook Santabe, the knife fell from the priestess' hand along with the white Diviner. Sancha brayed with effort and threw Santabe toward the steps of Her Beauty.

A great blast of wind shoved Telo backward. Banners on the market stalls cracked with the force of the gust, tearing lose. A sudden, sharp coldness surging against Telo and brought tears to his eyes. The wind intensified.

A sharp crack rang out above them. Telo looked to the heavens where the clouds flew across the sky like kites. The statue of Santiago rose over them, canting over. It parted from the base of its pedestal and fell. Telo dodged, stooping to drag Teresa with him, and Sancha limped after them. A boom from the ton of stone hitting the ground shook the square as the statue landed squarely on Santabe.

"By all that's holy." Telo sank to the ground and gathered Teresa to his chest. His arms and legs shook at the near miss. The foot of the statue was inches from their heads. The wind burst over them again, making Telo squint from its blast.

Teresa opened her eyes. Her hair blew around her face as if alive. "Is it over? I thought if I lay quiet, I could do more good than trying to get up. At least I'd be out of the way. But Sancha. The statue. All that wind. I didn't expect that. How?"

"You're all right?" Telo had to shout to be heard over the wind. The rain continued to wash over him, though the clouds began to break up.

"Well, not all right. It bloody hurts. But I'm not dying."

Sancha collapsed. One minute the mare stood, the

next she slid to the ground, air expelling from her lungs in a great gust. A half dozen stab wounds covered her chest. The halo surrounding her from the fog dimmed.

"Oh!" Teresa scrambled forward to stand over Sancha's head, then embrace the horse. "Oh! Ramiro told her to protect us, and she did. She did. Though so badly hurt." Tears fell over Teresa's cheeks to be washed away by the rain and dried by her swirling hair. "This is our fault. If we'd handled Santabe properly in the first place. We have to do something. Save her."

"The red." Telo dragged himself to the statue, pulling himself over the form of Santiago.

He prepared for a gruesome sight, calling for Teresa to stay back, but words died in his throat. No body lay pinned under the statue. Santabe was gone, except for a splotch of blood and her belt caught on Santiago's staff. He searched but found no figure limping away. The priestess was gone as if he'd dreamed her.

"Can you find it?" Teresa asked.

"Yes. Stay there." Still in the belt, he found what they needed, stooping to retrieve the red Diviner. Miraculously, the staff was whole and undamaged. More worrying, Santabe had found the willpower to escape Dal's wrath without the protection of the staff. Teresa didn't need to know their enemy remained at large, with hate still in her heart. Not yet at any rate. He hurried back to her.

"If we use this now, we have no protection against

the Leviathan. It likely will be trading one sort of death for another." Telo eyed the diminishing glow around his body. The fog wore off and that would leave them exposed to Dal. His hate would extinguish them. They didn't know if the magic could heal horses. It might be useless effort and a waste of the magic.

"Do it," Teresa said, echoing his own wishes.

Telo stretched out the Diviner and Teresa gripped his wrist so they could do this together. "I pray this works. A hero is a hero, no matter whether human or not. God be with us." He touched the Diviner to dapple-gray hide. Electric jolts sent them all to the ground in one puddle of pain.

Weakness overpowered.

The influence of Dal pushed down upon them, rendering Telo unable to move. It tried to crush the spark of life in his chest. His will began to shrivel. He grasped at memories of kindness, deeds of decency, and hung on with all he had left.

Claire thrashed under more attacks from Dal. A slice started near her ear and traveled toward her neck. She clapped a hand over the area, and the slice continued to cross the thin skin of her hand. Julian was screaming defiance beside her. She couldn't stand or speak. Could barely move. Hate and putrid disgust washed over her from Dal. Hatred of all life. Disgust at the beauty of the infinite being contaminated by vulgar, grasping life. So messy. So impure. So destructive.

It tried to force everything of beauty and hope from her heart to be replaced with despair—killing her spirit before it killed her body.

A single blade of grass shot upward in front of her nose, so close that her brain saw the grass as two images. She focused on it. So green. Persisting here in the desert where only the spiny survived. A single bit of green life. Valiantly defying the odds. Refusing to wither.

She drank in the green reminder of life—too small to capture Dal's attention—but needed more. More reminders of the good.

She flopped onto her back, forcing her hands deep into the loose soil. The wetness of the sand soothed the slice across her hand. Raindrops striking her face made her blink. The clouds above caught her attention. Not simple iron gray as they seemed, but swirls of white and all sorts of grays. An infinite variety of shades. Beautiful. Full of life-giving rain.

Beside her Julian tried to cover Beatriz to protect her, while she did the same for him. Their hands entwined. A love that couldn't be divided.

Tears of unalloyed determination flooded Claire's eyes.

Agony came from her hip as another cut started, but this time Claire smiled. Death came in the end, but nonetheless even now beauty lived and love flourished. This was not the end. When she died, others would fight. Joy and thankfulness flooded her heart. Gratitude for memories of her mother, of Bromisto and Errol. Appreciation of all the beauty and kindness in the world. Thankfulness for having met Ramiro and felt love.

From her back, with no technique, she Sang. Not in words, but in sound and feeling. An outpouring of pure emotions of her delight in life to share with everyone around her and give them hope. Her joy grew. The rain might wash away the magic, but it couldn't stop the sound. She heard Beatriz add her own song, clumsy and off tune. Then Julian and Fronilde sang in their own way. A last act of defiance. Others added their voices. And their songs held a different kind of magic. Not of power, manipulation, and control of others, but of hope and love.

Not real magic, but the ordinary, everyday gift of music to uplift and comfort.

The hate lightened as if Dal pulled back. She felt its puzzlement. Then it withdrew entirely, taking its hatred and leaving only the stink of rotting meat. Someone stepped over her.

Claire lost the song of joy. She sat up.

Black and yellow. A Northern soldier with a red Diviner cradled to his chest stood next to her. His hair was plastered to his head by the rain. He inched his way forward, past groaning bodies. All around him people stirred and looked around. Outside of a perfect circle of ten feet around him in each direction, people still writhed on the ground. Claire watched blood bloom from their hips down to their thighs as Dal worked its evil.

Inside that invisible circle that included her, it was as if Dal didn't exist.

What was happening? She was in a center of peace. Dal could not reach her and it had nothing to do with her Song. This man was resisting Dal. Pushing the demon back. How?

"The staff," Julian said. "Get the staff."

Northern magic. *Of course.* Claire knew the red Diviners could give life to the dead. It apparently had another use—a use much like her illusion Song— repelling Dal.

Out of nowhere great gusts of wind swept over the field of bodies. It drove Claire's hair into her eyes and pushed the clouds, sending them flying across the sky. It struck the Northern soldier with the Diviner, sending his arms flailing for balance. A fresh gust pushed him over. When Claire tried to get to her feet, the wind forced her back down. It sent the already-rising Julian into a tumble.

The soldier inched forward, taking the protection with him, and Claire felt Dal's glee as the monster crept back on its prey, and its anger as other victims were ripped away. She tried to go after the man with the Diviner even as Julian struggled to do the same. Her limbs responded as if buried in quicksand. Too sluggish. Too slow. Dal had already taken its toll on her physically. Fear exhausted as surely as physical exertion.

She managed to brush her hair from her eyes at the expense of smearing mud and blood on her face, and somehow get to her feet only to trip on Fronilde and go back down.

Her body was still too confused for fine movement. Her mind, however, had grown clear. Clear enough to realize with a spring of hope that the rain had slowed to intermittent drops. The gusts of wind had sent the clouds elsewhere. Even now, the wind continued strong, while shafts of sunlight made their way through openings in the thinning clouds.

No rain.

The Song. Her magic would work again.

Malice. Hate. The desire to remove all life beat against her. Smothering.

Not today. Today she would live. Her magic would see to that.

Confidence grew inside her. A certainty she could prevail. After all, she'd fooled Dal before. She Sang of an empty field. With each note she added more details down to the little pincushion cacti and a single blade of grass among the stones, piling the illusion higher and spreading it farther.

An empty field. No life. Nothing to crush.

Dal receded again. She gasped with relief.

Despite her success, her will flickered and wavered.

Her body and mind was so tired, even if her heart wanted to fight on. She force-fed more strength into the Song anyway, drawing it from somewhere, though her knees folded. The illusion spread farther, making a bigger circle than the soldier with the Diviner had, but not by much. Not near enough to save all.

Then Jorga joined her Song. From yards away came the familiar raspy voice of her grandmother to add to the magic and create her own circle. From the opposite direction, Eulalie Sang with them, and Muriel added her considerable power.

The horses. The horses had carried them apart, separating the Women of the Song. If they had remained together in a clump, their magic would have been limited. Somehow Valentía had known to divide the Women of the Song and spread them out. Now it saved them.

Their circles of protection linked together and expanded to cover more souls. Rachael found them from farther away and another voice came from a different direction. Their range widened to cover more.

All around, people sat up as Dal's hate was pushed away. Not nearly far enough to cover everyone in the field—their magic couldn't reach to the outside acres of the killing zone, and there, people died as they were ripped apart by inches. Claire tried to press more energy into her magic, but had no more to give.

She could barely maintain her voice. Soon her Song would fade and allow Dal to take all.

Then the last clouds broke apart and the hot sun reappeared. The heat hit the puddles of water lying on rock or running from clothing and turned it to water vapor. The air began to fill with a thin skin of moisture as patches of fog rose with an eerie beauty. Her magic clung to the water in the air and spread more easily. Without any extra effort their protective cloak widened to include all.

If she hadn't been Singing she would have collapsed. Beatriz and Julian hugged, clinging together as Julian kissed his wife's face.

The sight heartened her, yet Claire felt only more worry on how much longer she could hold the Song. Already she used the magic much longer than she'd ever extended it before. And she couldn't stop, for Dal hadn't gone.

She sensed it not high above, but somewhere in the air exactly at the center of their circle. The demon growing more and more angry, knowing trickery robbed it of its prey, but not what sort of deception. Claire searched back along the strands of music to find each Singer in the stirring crowd: Jorga, Eulalie, Muriel, Rachael, Susan, and Anna, by Violet's body. Easy enough to spot with the naked eyes as the Elders were some of the few on their feet.

But not the only ones.

Near each Elder, including Claire, was a Northern soldier with a red Diviner. Almost as if they'd been paired. In between each pairing were other soldiers with red Diviners, forming a perfect oval around the center of the field, created by a strange happenstance. And at the heart of that oval, about ten feet off the ground, pulsed a monstrous . . . thing.

It wriggled as if trapped. A great oblong blob that floated in the air, looking somewhat like a grossly engorged caterpillar. Without clothing, fur, hair, or feathers it appeared naked, though without features. No limbs. No head. No wings or other means of keeping it aloft. Just a great pulsating, formless body with flesh that appeared spongy, like a cake that hadn't been baked long enough. Almost colorless, it matched the hue of the boiling tallow she used to make soap, though veins of blackness crisscrossed its form, cutting into the flesh like wire.

Dal.

Gooseflesh covered Claire's skin. All across Dal, spots about the size of a coin and the color of the blackest night opened and closed, then vanished. Appearing and disappearing at random as if summoned.

Eyes.

Sometimes a handful of eyes. Sometimes several dozens of them popped into existence at once. Lasting just a few seconds at a time. They moved and tracked as if searching.

Searching for them. For the source of the magic tricking Dal.

A scream of rage split the silence and everyone twisted to look. There, near Eulalie, a man broke into a run. He carried a sword and wore rusted bits of armor. He bolted at Dal hovering over the field.

Suero.

"You took my son!" Suero bellowed, followed by oaths so black they scorched Claire's ears. Somehow she maintained the Song and watched in wonder as the greasy little man charged at Dal, heedless of the people he stepped upon in the process. Dozens of the black eye spots opened on Dal, trying to track. Finding nothing because of their illusion.

Suero had to leap when he reached Dal. His sword cut into the monster. Hope blossomed in Claire's chest. *If only this killed the demon . . .*

There was a blast like a thunderclap over her head. She lost the Song as she grasped at her ears. Sound disappeared, swallowed by a high-pitched ringing. Dimly, she was aware of Suero flying through the air to crash into people lying not far from her.

The hilt of his sword was still clasped in his hand, but the blade had turned to a puddle of silver metal, melted. The pieces of armor on his body had melted as well. Hair and clothing had been burned away. And Suero . . . what was left of him resembled a man-shaped cinder. Burned into charcoal. Not an inch of flesh remained. Dead.

Great Goddess.

Claire sank to her knees as Dal's weight pressed on her again. Magic couldn't harm it. Weapons rebounded. It was over.

We can't kill it. We can't even touch it.

CHAPTER 41

An arm snaked around Claire's waist and lifted her to her feet. She shivered as a scent better known to her than her own—and more anticipated—enveloped her. "I knew you could master your magic," his voice said in her ear. His beard caught in her hair as she turned in his arms to bury her face in Ramiro's neck. "And you brought other Women of the Song."

He was solid. Real. Not her imagination. Here at last.

A little piece of her world swung back into balance, becoming whole again.

Even as she put her arms around him, she grasped for the Song and began Singing again, continuing the illusion of an empty field.

Julian and Beatriz had Ramiro's other arm, while Fronilde clung to them. Claire couldn't tell Ramiro how much she missed him, as his parents did—couldn't even kiss him while working her magic—but she showed him with the glowing look upon her face and the force of her hug.

The sun shone off his armor in a reflective blaze, blinding her and presenting an image of herself as she quickly checked to be sure he was unharmed, before focusing on his face. It looked older, graver, but she supposed hers did the same.

He wrested his arm from his parents to touch her face. "Claire, will you marry me?" His face reddened, though his eyes remained steady, locked on hers. "I know I should have asked long ago, and I know it's not part of your tradition . . . but I'm asking you now."

Her Song died as she lost the words. She found herself nodding like a simpleton.

"We can make new traditions," he said. "Is that a yes?"

"Yes."

As he kissed her, Beatriz sniffed. "About time."

Time.

Dal.

Claire pulled away from lips she never wanted to leave to take up the Song again. She barely had the magic in place again when a surge of malice from Dal swung across her, striking like a hammer against an anvil to pound her flat, and vanished as quickly as it came.

Like a probe, she felt it track away across the

crowded field. Voices cried out in fear, allowing her to trace its path as it blundered this way and that.

Ramiro's arms on her tightened as if he'd never let her go.

Julian gasped and others did the same. "It's looking for us," Julian said needlessly.

If Claire could have answered, she would have told them the illusion the Women of the Song used to hide them couldn't last forever. Dal was a god. They did nothing to stop Dal, only fooled the god into withdrawing on its own. It'd see through them eventually, even before they dropped from exhaustion, it seemed.

One of the Northern soldiers holding a red Diviner cried out and then suddenly split in half from top to bottom as Dal found him. Claire tried to block the horrific sight by ducking behind Ramiro's shoulder, but it remained etched in her brain.

Dal would discover them.

One by one, it would remove all the obstacles holding it. The soldiers with the Diviners. Muriel. Eulalie. Jorga. Rachael. Susan. Anna. Her.

Her throat tried to tighten and choke off the Song. She clenched her fists and refused to let it, making herself look at where the man had fallen and watching the others with Diviners for their fall. Ramiro made soothing sounds into her ear. An elderly desert person with a bald head had seized the Diviner as it toppled from the dead man's hand. Blood splatter covered him, but he stood on creaky knees to hold the Diviner outstretched toward the sluggish mass of Dal.

Other Northern soldiers with Diviners in the circle surrounding Dal tried to run, but the press of bodies slowed their progress to practically nonexistent—that coupled with the sluggish effect Dal produced on all of them slackened their progress. As if feeling their doom approach, several threw away their Diviners, only for the desert people to take them up and assume their place.

"Protect them," Beatriz shouted. Heads turned in her direction at the command in her voice. "We came here to sacrifice ourselves! The time is now! Protect them!" Beatriz made her way through the field to the closest Northern soldier and drew him into an embrace, using her body as a shield against Dal. "Protect them! Give others a chance to defeat the monster!" Julian hurried over to join his wife, adding his body, with Fronilde and some servants Claire recognized right behind him.

All across the field, men and women stood and put their bodies between Dal and the people willingly—or unwillingly—protecting them. Embracing their enemies—the ones who had burned their cities and murdered their kin—like long-lost friends. They formed a living shield of twenty or thirty deep, offering themselves to save foes.

Beatriz emerged from the mass of people swallowing Julian to march back to Claire. "And our allies from the swamp! Protect them as well!" It happened before Beatriz had even started to speak. People rose from the ground to layer themselves around Claire. Gingerly at first as if afraid to make contact and then perhaps taking heart from the sight of Ramiro still embracing her, they moved closer to hold her with smiles and words of encouragement. Several cried as they babbled their appreciation.

The flood of people locking her away first terrified and then soothed as Claire tightened under their touch and gradually made herself relax. Strength reentered her limbs. The Song flowed smoother again. Her parched throat felt rejuvenated with their gratitude.

Cries of pain shattered the silence outside the huddle surrounding her. She couldn't see over their heads to know what was happening. It didn't matter. She concentrated on her Song and only her Song, keeping all these people safe.

Until the arm she needed most pulled away. Ramiro retreated. People gave him room as he drew his sword. "You know what I have to do."

Claire shook her head, unable to protest in any other way. Inside she was screaming. She pointed in the direction of Suero's burnt body. Ramiro had to have seen what happened to the village man when he confronted Dal with a weapon. She put pleading into her eyes, knowing it would do no good.

Dal couldn't be stopped by hiding from it.

"I love you."

Tears rolled down Claire's cheeks. She felt more torn in half than that soldier.

"I'll find a weakness."

He wouldn't. Intuition told her Dal had no weakness. It would never stop until they were all dead.

The crowd parted to let Ramiro out. He gave her hand one last squeeze and was gone. She'd never see him again. And all she'd done was Sing at him.

Her technique for proper breathing was shattered. The words ran out.

They couldn't hide. They couldn't fight.

There had to be something else.

If only she'd never called Dal in the first place. If only it had stayed elsewhere—asleep.

Asleep.

The words to her Goodnight Song popped into her head. Maybe she could lull Dal to sleep or back to wherever it had come from.

"*Rest.*

"*Close your eyes.*

"*All is well.*

"*All is safe.*

"*Task is done.*

"*Fight is won.*

"*Sleep.*"

Claire threw all her will into the Song and directed the magic at the great pale mass hanging in the sky. It was the only thing she could still see above the people pressing around her. She had no idea if the Song would work or not. A Song needed to be tailored to the mind it was aimed toward. There was no way to estimate what was in Dal's mind—or if it had one. She had to guess.

She thrust through the crowd to run after Ramiro. They let her go. Some even dropping into slumber before her eyes, lulled by her new Song. Someone handed her a water skin. She drank greedily before tossing it aside and resuming her Song.

Was it her imagination or were there less of the coin-sized spots she thought were eyes appearing on Dal's surface? She tried to count even as she chased Ramiro. Twenty-three eyes? No. Less? Sixteen? They opened and closed, moving to a new location on the blob too fast to keep track, and she couldn't see the top of its body.

"Close your eyes.

"Return to the task another day.

"Rest.

"It will wait.

"Sleep."

She picked up her pace, dodging over people and sometimes having to step upon them.

Damn Ramiro and his long legs. Did he have to be in such a hurry? She couldn't catch up. Why wouldn't he wait for her? Her heart felt like it would explode out of her chest.

The Elders had taken up the slack when she switched Songs. They used their power to cover her area, but already the clouds of water vapor in the air thinned. The moisture on her face dried out and was disbursed by the sun, spreading over wider distances, and its amplifying effect on their magic went with it. The people would be exposed again.

She slowed as she stood almost directly under Dal. His body cast a wide shadow on the ground, and she hesitated to step within its darkness. All caught within it were already dead, torn apart. The Song had never reached here to hide them, or rather—its help had been too late. Something told her this was as far as she could go.

Ramiro picked his way forward within that shadow, his sword raised cautiously. His face was clenched as if he struggled against something—Dal's force, she knew instantly. Instinct said she would lose the Song if she fell prey to Dal. She must help Ramiro from here.

The coin-sized black spots that were eyes moved sluggishly now as her Song poured forth. Only a handful opened and closed, and they did so more slowly than before. Whatever weakness Ramiro sought, her Song gave him the opportunity to find a flaw in Dal.

He stopped just below one of the great branching ropes of black that she had decided were veins or arteries. This close, she could make out how the veins cut into the putrid flesh as if cinched tight and how the flesh between the veins roiled, never quite still.

Ramiro set the point of his sword against the thick vein, and Claire braced for the thunderclap. It didn't come. Most of the eyes had vanished. None seemed to be aimed at them. Ramiro gave a twist and severed the vein.

Black fluid poured out. Where it hit the ground, smoke rose like acid. Ramiro had jumped out of the way. Now he wiped his sword. As he dropped the smoking cloth, Claire saw the tip had been notched, dissolved away. He moved to another vein.

> "Rest.
>
> "Sleep.
>
> "Task will wait."

Another vein went, costing the entire point of Ramiro's sword. More veins crisscrossed its surface, so many, branching like rivers. And the fluid from the first showed no signs of slacking in its flow. A god, not mortal. Could such a thing even bleed out?

Ramiro put up his sword to attack a third vein. Three new eyes briefly opened and Dal flinched like a goat chasing off flies. The two punctured veins sealed and ceased draining. Ramiro was thrown free to strike the earth with a grinding crunch. His head bounced—hard.

Claire shrieked and lost the Song. Lost all semblance of poise and ran into Dal's shadow. A putrid scent of decay and recent death made her retch. The force of Dal, full of revulsion and cruelty, crashed into her, throwing her to the ground.

Die, it ordered over and over. Like a Death Song it invaded her mind and willed her to cease living.

She reached for the words to her magic and couldn't find them. Not even the Death Song or the Hornet Tune. There was only Dal in her head. No strength. No hope. No chance.

One thing pushed back: love. It cried to her.

Die.

"No." Tears streamed down her face as she lay among the viscera of its earlier victims. "Not when he needs me." She wouldn't die until she could do so with Ramiro. They had been in this together since the beginning, since the time he'd called her witch and she'd called him murderer. How that had changed. They'd summoned Dal together and brought him to this earth. The least they could do was die together. She couldn't rise, so she slithered among the dead, dragging herself ever closer.

Dal's eyes had reappeared to watch her as a child might watch an insect struggle in a web. Calm unconcern touched with a tiny thread of curiosity. It watched her struggle, knowing it could end her in an instant. She passed Ramiro's sword, melted as Suero's had been. Touched his worn and scuffed boot, and dragged herself up the length of his body.

In Dal's shadow, his armor no longer shone like the sun. Instead it reflected her face back from a dozen angles, acting like a mirror. Her skin was pinched and drawn, ghostly pale in the half-light. Her eyes too huge. The image of a panicked child. All she felt was relief that the armor had held and not melted as Suero's had, leaving Ramiro intact.

But not moving.

She could see his beard and his unburnt skin, still too far away to reach. He could have been asleep—or dead. Dal pressed down on her, but sobbing, she pulled herself farther to reach Ramiro's face and fumbled for a pulse on his bare neck. A faint throb met her fingers—faint but there.

In his head must be the same urge to die that Dal put into her own. And nothing to counter that.

Or is there . . .

A new Song came to her, born of pain, rough and uncouth. Jorga would have laughed at her attempt. Her voice sounded like a blue jay's caw, all jagged and harsh. The horrible depression that was Dal tried to smother the sound, but she forced out her croak of a tune:

"Love won't die.

"I'm here.

> "*Don't leave me alone.*
>
> "*So much yet to do.*
>
> "*Love so new.*
>
> "*Stay.*"

"Stay," she gasped, choked by tears, as she gripped the edge of Ramiro's breastplate, wishing so much metal wasn't keeping them apart. "Stay."

Dal narrowed the distance between them. One moment floating high overhead, the next only inches away. The closeness of its putrid flesh choking more words. Her Song must have drawn the monster now that she was out of the protection of the Elders' illusion. Claire tried to pull Ramiro away, to drag him, but he was much too heavy in armor, and she didn't have the strength to even move herself. She closed her eyes and gripped Ramiro's breastplate until her knuckles whitened and her fingers hurt.

"Get it over with," she sobbed. "Just do it." At least they would die together.

When nothing happened, she looked up. The putrid flesh still hung inches away. She could see a pulse beating in the black veins. Dozens of the coin-shaped eyes had appeared. More. Hundreds. Almost blotting out the pale, tallow-colored flesh.

They tracked together as one eye, moving from above her head and down her torso, to stop in the middle. She clutched at Ramiro.

Great Goddess let it end.

Part of her would rather just die then take this torment anymore. Another part knew the longer Dal stared at them, the longer it wasn't killing others.

Dal's eyes clustered tighter together, gathering right above her chest. No. Not her chest. Ramiro's.

The ones on the edges winked out. They focused downward without eyelid or lashes. Just black holes that went down, down, down like the dark water of a deep well. Empty. With no soul. Nothing in them registered as humanity.

A vast darkness.

Too alien. Too cruel. She focused on Ramiro.

The armor reflected the eyes back at her from every perspective. Dal twitched as the demon had when Ramiro touched it.

A slicing cut appeared across its putrid flesh, standing out strangely red among the paleness. Where the slice cut across black vein, fluid dripped.

Another wound appeared on Dal, and another, and still its eyes gazed at them. Fueled by hatred. A deep hatred of life. Chunks of its flesh began to rain down with the black fluid. Whole pieces as big as goats fell with plops like wet jelly.

Claire gasped, heart in her throat. There was no other sound but the flow of Dal's lifeblood as the demon tore itself apart. There could be no other explanation.

There was a hiss like a sigh as Dal's form tore in two. The two halves fell and left Claire staring at open sky.

For a while there was silence. Silence and sunshine and no explanations.

"Great Goddess," she finally croaked. "It . . . . it destroyed itself."

She'd done nothing. Ramiro's sword work had been a mere annoyance.

Ramiro didn't answer. His head lolled to the side and blood came from the ear she could see. She fumbled again for a pulse and found nothing.

CHAPTER 42

Ramiro jerked awake to Sancha nibbling his hair, and not gently. She pulled, and he sat up, rubbing at his scalp. Valentía stood next to his mare. The stallion's upper lip raised in a horse equivalent of laughter. Sancha reached for his hair again and he palmed her off.

"I'm awake, if that's what you want . . ." His words trailed off as he realized he sat in an empty field, surrounded by banks of gray fog. The world of dreams.

"What . . ."

"Happened?" A rich voice finished for him. The man with black skin who had helped him at the capstan bars to open Aveston's gate nudged Sancha and Valentía aside. "You may go back, my friends. Thanks for your help."

Sancha and Valentía vanished from the dream.

"Wha . . . what?" Ramiro sputtered. "Where?"

"I thought things would be easier for you if you woke to familiar faces," the man said. "I asked them to come. They are descendants of my own steed, and have served you well. This realm is for saints and their servants."

Saints? Ramiro cleared his throat, stumbling to find words. "Who are you?"

"Martin."

Ramiro took in the thick arms and the short cloak attached to the blacksmith vest. Threads hung lose from the end as if the material had been severed. Divided. Shared with a peasant. An electric shock ran through Ramiro, jolting him all the way awake. "*San* Martin? The soldier saint. My patron? I mean I always imagined you as watching over me. I don't mean to claim you are my patron. I mean, maybe you are. You are here, right? Or maybe I'm wrong. I don't want to presume. Um." His hand reached for his medallion to help calm his babbling and found it missing again. "An honor, sir. If I may ask, where's the other I usually see here? The one who looks like my brother, but isn't."

"That was my brother. You would call him the founder of cities. He isn't here. He rests now that the task is done." San Martin knelt down to casually lay one arm across his knees.

"Founder of ci—Santiago? I spoke with *Santiago?*" The most holy of saints. The world of fog spun as

Ramiro felt dizzy. "Wait. The task is over? Claire!" Shock turned to alarm.

"The Earth Child is well. Be at ease. This piece of Leviathan is destroyed and will trouble humankind no more. It attacked all it sees, determined to destroy all life. Yet it also lives, in its own way. So it turned on itself. You found and used the armor as we hoped, with help from the Earth Children."

"You mean Claire?"

San Martin smiled in a flash of white teeth. "Yes, that one, dreamer. She may not pray to us, but she is of us all the same. She completed a piece of the task, as did others—as you did. Some brought Dal to the spot. Another primed your enemy to work with you. And the Earth Child made Dal see."

"She's alive?"

"And in the world. She waits for you. Do you hear her?" A window opened in the fog, showing Claire sobbing over a body. A body in armor. He didn't need to see a face.

"I'm dead!" Then in a whisper, "I'm dead." The window closed.

"Aye, dreamer. Yet your miracles were real." A wooden dinner tray suddenly appeared next to Ramiro, whole and repaired as if never broken into splinters. "We helped with some, but others were your own doing. You belong to this realm if you choose to stay."

"A saint. I'm to be a saint?"

"What is in a word? That is what my brother Santiago would say. It is just a name. You and I are more simple folk, however. More grounded. Doers, not thinkers. Prisoners of duty." San Martin shifted and came out of his abstraction. "A saint. Such you will become if you stay dead. You can work much good as one of us. Or you may choose not to at this time and your deeds will be lost to history."

"I didn't do that much, sir. You said the Leviathan killed itself. It wasn't me. Whatever I did, if anything, I had lots of help."

"Such is true of all called saints. I myself choose to stay here, but my fight was not won. I knew I could do more from here to win it, and our people did eventually become stable and fixed in our *ciudades-estado*—no longer nomads. Thus, they grew in numbers and were ready for the larger fight to come: your fight. A piece of the Leviathan is destroyed, but not all. There will be others in time. Let it be many years from now and a task for our people's descendants, though even such as we cannot see all. But the battle is won for now." He peered at Ramiro thoughtfully, smiling just a touch. "I think you've made your choice."

A longing built in Ramiro's chest. "Claire."

San Martin smiled more broadly. "I understand. All is as it should be. My brothers and sisters and I will see you again someday, dreamer. One last gift will I give." The big man touched his forehead. "Heal and be well. Wake to your world. Farewell. Your dreams are over for now.

"Do one last task for me, dreamer, when you wake. Put my armor back for the next time it's needed. Remember that command, though naught else."

Ramiro sank back to the ground, suddenly exhausted. His eyes drifted closed even as he tried to hold them open. He had so many more questions. The world of fog flickered, going, and vanished as he slid into oblivion.

"Ramiro!"

He sat up to a throbbing headache and Claire calling his name. His head spun with questions. San Martin? Fog? Words about saints? A kitchen tray? Answers lingered on the tip of his tongue. It all vanished as Claire threw her arms around him and kissed him.

Tensed muscles relaxed as he drew her closer, just happy to be alive and here with Claire.

CHAPTER 43

Two Weeks Later

Julian made another circuit around the meeting tent and the stifling air caught inside it to enjoy the desert transformed into a paradise. Though requested to be at the meeting, he had left early. Beatriz did not need him to prop her up any longer. She would still want his advice on occasion, but not today. Today he was free to breathe the air.

The rains over the last sevendays had done their magic and created a lush scene of color. Pinks, reds, yellows, and blues bathed the once arid desert. Wildflowers had used the moisture to thrust up between flowering prickly pear, and the other cacti put on their yearly display. Only the scar where the Northerners had cut down the foliage marred the scene and those acres would soon regenerate.

The sound of hammers and chisels came from the old quarry as people once again mined stone, for the rebuilding of Colina Hermosa. Metal on stone rang out like a music to Julian's ears. The rebuilding had begun already. The citizens reclaimed what was theirs and cleared away debris. And with the treaty of allies signed with the Women of the Song, there would be wood for building this time, harvested selectively from their swamp. The hulk of Colina Hermosa not far from this tent would rise again—full of white stucco buildings gleaming in the sun—better than before.

The meeting tent had been spaced a distance from the rest of the camp for privacy. Over there, children ran through the camp, getting underfoot in their play and stealing food from everyone. No one snapped at them or scolded.

Every day more of their people came from Suseph, eager to remake their homes and reclaim their *ciudad-estado*. The elderly, the ill, and the orphaned among them went about their tasks with a brightness of pride in their eyes. They had faced down the monster. Had put themselves in its path as a sacrifice to save others and survived. Not only survived but prevailed. They had discovered they were of use from that day two sevendays ago, not inoperable castoffs, and they would bear that with them for the rest of their lives.

Julian drew in a deep breath and felt no tightness in his chest as had bothered him for sevenday after sevenday. Though watching the destruction of Dal with his own eyes hadn't brought him ease. Only when it became clear the Northerners had no intention of further pursuing the war had Julian found true respite.

"A new day," he said to the guards outside the tent even though it was late afternoon.

"Yes, sir," they said promptly.

"A busy day," Diego said as he exited the tent behind Julian with the other *concejales*. "Much to do." Julian offered his hand, but his old friend laughed and clapped him in a hug.

Julian knew that for an understatement as he hugged back. *Much* didn't begin to cover the number of tasks that would weigh on everyone's shoulders to rebuild Colina Hermosa, but the councilmen wore smiles to match his own. Faces full of wrinkles and topped by gray hair beamed like children. Everyone willingly shouldered the labor after their unexpected victory. Willing hands made light work, as Beatriz had said inside the tent before he exited.

The *concejales* said their good-byes hurriedly, eager to be about some important organizing before the wedding, and scurried off with promises to talk at the reception that night.

Teresa and Fronilde emerged next from the tent with Teresa's head down over pages of writing. "These are very good notes," Teresa told Fronilde. "You have the eye of a historian."

Fronilde's cheeks pinked at the praise. "I was just wanted to be useful and thought someone should record something. It's nothing."

"Have you considered university? I think you would enjoy it there, and I'm on the committee to re-build." Teresa held up the papers. "I would put in a good word for your admittance."

Fronilde's head dropped. "I always planned to be a wife."

"Can't a woman do both?" Teresa snapped with spirit. "Look at the *Lady Alcalde*." She handed back the papers. "*Alcalde* Beatriz has put much on me. I go first to the swamp villages to speak to the people and return Suero's body, and then to the Women of the Song as ambassador, plus I'm on several committees. The *Lady Alcalde* supplied me with soldiers for protec-tion, but what I really need is an assistant. Someone who can keep fair notes, manage my schedule, and allow me to bounce ideas off them. What do you say? I would appreciate the help, and I think I can manage a fair salary."

"Me?" Fronilde stuttered in surprised. "Let me think about it and speak to my parents."

"Congratulations, Madame Ambassador," Julian said as their conversation ended. "I'm happy for your promotion." Beatriz had named Teresa as the first head of a newly created diplomatic corps for Colina Hermosa. The first such office the city had ever had. And about time, too.

It had solved another thorny problem. Beatriz had named Ramiro in charge of the soldiers assigned to protect their new diplomats. Captain Gonzalo no longer had to decide whether rules could be bent to allow Ramiro back in a *pelotón*. Julian's son would still be a soldier, just assigned to another task.

"I thank you, sir," Teresa said, her cheeks rounding. Her eyes gleamed. "I look forward to it. I can't wait to learn more about the Women of the Song and the Children of Dal as well as other cultures out there. It's so exciting."

"You'll be a great success, I'm sure of that. I will see you at the wedding."

"We wouldn't miss it."

The two moved off, but Julian saw Fronilde's decision was already made by the spark of interest in the girl's eye. The most life he'd seen from his almost-daughter since the death of Salvador. A smaller worry lifted off Julian's back. Whether Beatriz had arranged that or it had been all Teresa's idea, he couldn't have been happier.

Father Telo moved over to join him as the ladies departed. "Shall I call you Father or Ambassador?" Julian asked. Father Telo had been the second member added to their diplomatic core.

"Father, please, my son. I'm first and foremost a priest, though a simple one."

"Rather more than that," Julian said. "Half of the people in that tent lean on you."

"Then I'm happy. To support others is all our Lord could ask of me, and all I want in return. I'm glad just to be normal. One doesn't need to be a saint to do good."

Father Telo hastily turned the subject. They had all become skittish of the words *saint* or *miracles*, having seen too many things that couldn't be explained. Julian was happy enough to leave them unexplained. He didn't want to delve into what had happened, and even Teresa and Father Telo only spoke of the subject with hesitation, almost as if speaking about the miraculous healings or the sudden arrival of the freak windstorm that drove off the rain just in time for the magic to work would tarnish their memories of the events. Some questions were better left unanswered.

"And of course to officiate at this wedding." Father Telo winked. "I believe that, in the Lady Beatriz's eye, that is my most important task."

"Beyond doubt. Beatriz has put her heart into the planning. She would have no one but you. Nor would Ramiro."

"I'm happy to be in such demand. Then afterward it's off to Aveston for me."

"Much luck to you. God be with you." Julian had no worries on that score. The priest was more than equal to coordinating with the *alcalde* of Aveston, and his more secret mission of scoring rebuilding supplies for Colina Hermosa. Julian would miss the man's company while he was gone. He and Father Telo had become surprisingly close friends in a short time, even good-naturedly arguing theology. They'd squeezed in a few games of *acorraloar* and found themselves evenly matched. But Julian would have plenty to keep him busy until the good friar returned.

Beatriz and the gaggle of Elders of the Women of the Song exited the tent last, all deep in talk about the wedding as Beatriz explained some of the traditions one more time. For a people who didn't engage in marriage, they had a deep interest in the subject.

Beatriz, in her deep black clothing of lace and flutters, made an odd contrast to the circle of Elders in their simple homespun, but the ladies had undeniably hit it off. Women of personality and force recognized the like in others and an instant respect had been born.

"Julian." Beatriz gave a curtsey to Eulalie and Jorga, then skipped up to him as carefree as the girl of his memories. "We are off to examine the chapel. It must be just right for tonight. Can you . . ." She waved her hand vaguely.

Beatriz had decreed Claire and Ramiro must be married within Colina Hermosa and no one dared to stand against her demand, so a space had been cleared just inside the gate and decorated with flowers and candles. She had named the space a chapel and a chapel it was. Those who had lost loved ones made daily visits and found solace there. The bishop could be found napping there day or night with a flock of other priests. Julian had stood and contemplated the bittersweet beauty of the spot juxtaposed against the burned-out hulk often. Renewal after destruction had become a theme in his life.

"See to Rasdid and the army?" he suggested with a raised eyebrow. Officially witnessing the departure of the Northern army was the reason the meeting had broken up. Unofficially, everyone knew the real motive was the wedding.

"Yes, please. Would you give their general my apologies?"

For answer he kissed her cheek, and received a firm squeeze from one of her cold hands. "Hi-ya, my *capitán*."

Beatriz slapped his chest with her fan. "Very funny. You know I only trust you to do it right."

He knew. He also knew that Beatriz didn't enjoy having anything to do with the Northerners. Otherwise, she'd not had delegated this task to him. She'd still call them barbarians if it didn't set a poor example. In her heart of hearts, she held them responsible for their son's death. He wasn't sure he felt all that differently. Salvador would never have died at the hands of the witch if the Northern army hadn't come.

Still, nothing could replace the people killed or the cities burned, but old men knew it was better to be talking to your enemy than fighting them.

Beatriz knew it, too—deep in her heart. She'd sign a treaty gladly, when it came time. But first the Northerners needed to put their house in order, or so

Rasdid claimed. He lacked the authority to sign anything for his people, so a treaty would wait.

The Northerners had spent the last two sevendays ordering their supply lines and withdrawing from Aveston. Julian believed that time had also involved bringing their priests to heel. Secretly, Rasdid had been more than happy to aid in the fruitless search for Santabe—the woman had vanished without a trace.

With the death of Dal, much had changed, including the desire of the majority of the army. Now their wishes involved returning home to check on their families, instead of subjugating the *ciudades-estado*.

And the death of Dal had also taken the magic from the Diviners, rendering the formidable weapons nothing more than ordinary sticks of horn or bone. Whether for those reasons or some other, a change of command had taken place, with the priests now under Rasdid and the army. The military gave the orders—for the time being, that is.

It was enough, and the first order was a return to their country. Rasdid had signed a paper on the cessation of hostilities and promised to send representatives within a year to talk of treaties. Julian found it hard to believe a treaty would actually happen. Once the Northerners got back to their homeland, who knew who would be in charge? They were still the Children of Dal after all—raised on killing like mother's milk.

But that was a worry for another day. For now he only had to see them off. Then he, too, could turn his thoughts to the wedding.

Yet . . . his family could not all be here.

Salvador.

The ache that could not be banished made itself known to him. For his son and all the people lost in this senseless war. Scores had died in the last battle, when Dal had torn itself apart. With so much death—so much death that had come with seemingly no effort—he still couldn't believe the evil was over. The jelly-like body of the monster had decayed and vanished in less than a day, leaving no evidence it had ever been. And worrying Julian that somehow he'd been mistaken in their success.

Beatriz must have seen the shadow cross his face, for she leaned against his shoulder, holding tight to his hand, reminding him to live for those who were gone—as she would. Tears swam in her eyes.

"Now and forever," he said. Live they would. Live fully today, and look with hope to the future. But they would also remember the past. Everything changed, whether for good or ill. Today, however, was about going forward. He squeezed Beatriz's hand in return, remembering their own wedding morning and the jitters he'd felt. How his parents and friends had helped steady him then.

He frowned. "Where is Ramiro?"

"He'll be here. He had some business to attend, he said." Beatriz's brow darkened. "If he's not here soon, I will find a switch. Beard or no, I'm still his mother."

A short ride away in Aveston, Ramiro led Claire down the steps into the larger room of the crypt, one hand in hers and the other holding a lantern. "Watch your head," he said as they reached the threshold. Claire looked up at the ceiling a good foot above *his* head and narrowed her eyes at him.

"Watch your step?" he tried again.

She dropped his hand.

Great job, dummy. Not even inside and she already knew how nervous he felt. He plucked at his new uniform, unused to the bolder color of navy blue and gray for the diplomatic corps. His mother considered his change a promotion. He knew it for what it was: a compromise. Captain Gonzalo couldn't take him back in a *pelotón*, so they had given him charge of watching over Teresa and Father Telo in the diplomatic service, another branch of the military just invented. Not what he'd hoped, but not what he'd feared either. It was a change he could accept.

He looked forward to new adventures with Teresa.

He straightened his shoulders. He'd make the diplomatic corps such a success that people would beg to become a part of it. Elite. After what else he'd been through, that should be easy.

"This is the catacomb where you've been spending so much time?" Claire spun slowly to see every aspect, from the tombs pushed against the dank walls to the small pile of possessions they'd left, and the pulley system he'd attached to the ceiling. "Which pillar?"

"That one over there." He pointed under the pulleys. "It hasn't been that much time, and a lot happened to me here. I wanted you to see it." It had taken nearly a sevenday to repair and re-raise the pillar with the armor replaced inside. Most of the work had been done with his own hands, but he'd hired a few street boys to help and then bribed them further with places as squires in his corps so they wouldn't come back and tear the pillar down to sell the armor. He still couldn't say exactly why he felt such a need to do the work, only that restoring things as they were gave him peace of mind.

For a moment a feeling of danger slid over his skin, elusive, like the whine of a mosquito in his ear. *Leviathan.* Something tried to claw its way into his mind.

He shrugged as the feeling vanished. Dal was gone. He'd had no dreams since its destruction. The Northern army had stepped down. There was nothing to fear—almost.

There had been a shadow over Claire since the destruction of Dal, something she tried to hide, but even in his preoccupation with replacing the armor he had seen it, though she'd concealed it from her grandmother and the other Elders. He could think of only one thing that could be causing the slight dim in her enthusiasm—the wedding. He'd brought her here to discover if his guess was right.

"My brother is in a tomb such as this—newer of course—put there right before Colina Hermosa fell. It will give my mother great happiness when she can see it again. Do you know what I mean?" There, he'd laid the heart of the matter before her, holding his breath to see if she understood. He had to make sure his uniform wouldn't be the only successful compromise. Two sevendays of trying to bring up the subject as the wedding preparations progressed while she'd grown more silent and he'd never found the right words. This was as close as he'd come to speaking about what might be troubling her—too afraid to hear her response.

She wandered about the dark room, moving in and out of the lantern light. To his eyes, she was a beam of sunshine. From the top of her golden head to her small feet hidden inside her sturdy boots. A tender soul with a tough exterior that he could only admire. A beacon of hope, his north star. His heart beat too fast as he waited.

She turned to face him. "When the Women of the Song die, they are burned, you know. Outside under the blue sky and in the fresh air. Like my mother. Like Errol and Bromisto." Her face fell for a moment. "But . . . But I can see the comfort of having a place to go always to be with the people you miss."

"Tending the tomb will give my mother comfort."

"My people often plant gardens or a tree where our loved ones are set free. As you said, for comfort. It's not so different." She turned to face the pillar. "I suppose one could even be burned outside and the ashes stored in a place such as this."

Something inside Ramiro eased. Claire understood. But the point of bringing her here wasn't really about burial or cremation or even showing her where he'd been. "A compromise." He had to force the next words out. "I know a wedding isn't really of your culture."

She was at his side in a moment, lying her hand on his chest. "But it is of yours. It means a lot to your family. And the Elders . . . well, they can accept it or they can get along without me. My grandmother understands. And I"—she ducked her head—"I want that permanence, too—after what we've been through." Her head came back up. Blue eyes finding his brown. "I want everyone to know you belong to me."

"Isn't that the other way around?" he teased, then grew sober. He covered her hand with his. "It won't be easy."

"Who said I like easy?" Claire's eyes snapped suddenly with determination. "We are like that pillar. Our families are the ceiling and the floor, and we are the bridge between them. We'll live in both places, half the time here and the other half in the swamp. It won't be easy. We may have to knock some heads."

The edict his parents sent out formally thanking the Women of the Song would help. Enough people from different *ciudades-estado* had been there to see the Women of Song hold back Dal. As far as those people knew it had been their magic alone that had defeated the monster before it could kill them. Gratitude ran high toward the women formerly called witches. Claire and he would receive the benefit of that wave.

His smile echoed hers. "I could be persuaded to knock some heads once in a while."

"I thought you could. Now, are you done having doubts?"

"I wasn't having doubts. I wanted to make sure you weren't."

"And I think we are late to our own wedding," she said. "Very late. After all the work your mother put into it. Not to mention Father Telo waiting to perform the ceremony. Should we go?"

He wanted to agree, but if the wedding wasn't causing the change in her then what was? "Not just yet. Something has been bothering you. Was it something I did? Something someone said?"

She tried to shrug him off and retreat, denial on her lips, but he held on to her. "No wedding until you share whatever this is with me."

"I . . . it's nothing. Almost nothing. Not worth a worry. There was hearing your fate from Captain Gonzalo. That's what mattered. And you're happy with the new position taking care of Teresa, aren't you?"

"Happy enough. But that's not what's bothering you. Out with it." He gave her the no-nonsense glare he used on Beatriz, and she looked away. Her arms tightened on his ribs, squeezing harder with each second as if her grip on him kept her alive.

Time drew out and he thought she'd refuse him. "It's the magic," she choked out. "I managed not to kill with the Song the last time I used it, but I have before. It's dark. And that makes me dark." She released him with one arm, long enough to scrub at tears on her face.

He nuzzled her hair, holding her tight. "You're not dark. Just the opposite. You don't have to use your magic anymore if you don't want to."

Now her words came out in a rush. "I don't think that will work. Your mother has all these plans for me. The Elders do as well. And I'm not sure it's what I want, but what else can I do? I've no other skills to offer your people. I don't think they need me to make soap. And I don't want the Song to be that way anymore. Beatriz already suggested I work with you at protecting Teresa and Father Telo, as a type of soldier with magic, but that isn't what I want."

"Then what do you want?" he asked softly.

Her tear-stained face came up to meet his eyes. "If the Song can put bad things in people's heads—to harm themselves—couldn't it put good? People feeling sad or lonely. Couldn't it cheer them—at least temporarily?"

He blinked at her, startled. She rushed on before he could recover. "That's what I want to do now. Use the Song to help people, instead of deceive and manipulate them." She snuggled close to him, hiding again, and he couldn't help but smile.

"And you thought my mother would say no to this idea?"

"The Elders will."

"I doubt that. A new use for your magic. I think they'll be thrilled."

"What do you think? I wouldn't be working with you, exactly."

"I think it suits you perfectly. Why didn't you tell me sooner?"

"The idea only came to me a few days ago, and I was waiting until after the wedding. I just didn't want to have to be scared of using the Song anymore. I don't want the magic to be an evil thing—like Dal."

"It's not. I'll support whatever you want to do—if you want to stop with the magic or find another use for it. I'm here while you figure it out and after. Forever and always," he said, echoing his parents' pledge to each other.

The face she showed him now was radiant. "I like that. Forever and always. Can we hurry past the wedding and get to the forever part?"

They might be two cultures, but they had much in common—like getting this day over. And getting to tonight.

"I'm afraid I can't do that. It would kill my mother. Or she would kill me. But we can hurry and get through it together."

Outside in Aveston, the fresh air still smelled like flowers and felt like *carnaval*. Even after two seven-days people hadn't stopped randomly hugging each other in the streets or handing out mugs and glasses of commemorative liquor to each other. Fading blossoms in the streets were continually replaced with fresh. Ramiro could hear distant screams of children playing, loud as if to make up for all their recent silence. Banners thanking the saints still hung from windows. Though many of the people hadn't returned yet, Aveston couldn't get enough of celebrating the pullback of the Northern army.

The joy was contagious. A beaming smile covered Claire's face as Valentía and Sancha came to greet them. The stallion had hesitated over Teresa or Claire but had ultimately adopted Claire as his own. Like the people, the *caballos de guerra* would recover their numbers also. Perhaps Sancha would have her first colt this time next year.

Despite their lateness, Claire wouldn't mount her horse until she had a few more kisses, and he was only too happy to oblige. She untangled her fingers from his hair to caress his beard. "About this."

He opened his eyes, breathing still a little ragged. "What about it?"

"Another compromise?"

"I'm not sure I like the sound of that." He drew her closer. "What were you thinking?"

"Never change it."

He grinned. "That I can do."

ACKNOWLEDGMENTS

I think every fantasy writer since *The Lord of the Rings* dreams of the trilogy. Being given the chance to complete one has been a daunting and humbling experience. I really didn't want to mess this up. I hope each book is better than the one before, and thanks to David Pomerico for giving me a chance to bring these characters to the end of their journey. May you love them for their faults as much as their perfections. David, thanks for letting me add yet another point of view character and giving me a pass on the rising word count.

I must put in a word for my agent, Marisa Corvisiero, for having my back and rising to the occasion.

Thanks are due also to my critique partner, Carla Rehse, for keeping me on the straight and narrow, and to Laura Heffernan for the unfailing support of a fellow writer. You both got me to the end. To all those who tweeted their enjoyment of these books my direction, your appreciation kept me going through the rough patches.

But the recognition for this book goes especially to my family. We had a year that tries men's souls. I admire the strength of my mother, Mary Henry, and my sister, Tracy King. You've always been the model for characters like Beatriz and Claire. In addition, my kids continue to put up with a mom who sits at the keyboard for hours at a time. This time it was the kids giving the parent space.

And finally, to my husband, who is my Julian, I say, "now and forever."

ABOUT THE AUTHOR

MICHELLE HAUCK lives in the bustling metropolis of northern Indiana with her family. Besides working with special needs children by day, she writes all sorts of fantasy, giving her imagination free range. A bookworm, she passes up the darker vices in favor of chocolate and looks for any excuse to reward herself. She is the author of the YA epic fantasy, *Kindar's Cure*, as well as the short story "Frost and Fog," which is included in the anthology *Summer's Double Edge*.

Find her on twitter under @Michelle4Laughs or her blog Michelle4Laughs: It's in the details www.michelle4laughs.blogspot.com.

Discover great authors, exclusive offers, and more at hc.com.